I0567027

THREE WEEKS

UNTIL
TOMORROW

A novel

by
Rodger Christopherson

All rights reserved

Copyright © 2008 by

Rodger Christopherson

Other books by the author
A Little Bit of Anarchy
Out of the Fire Mist
Monkey in a Tree
Beverly Hills Women
After the President Disappeared
Illusions
Beyond Science & Religion – non fiction
Health - non fiction
Origins & Meaning- How science and religion failed
humanity - non fiction
Circles in the Sand -- Poetry

intercept777@centurylink.net

ONE

It was now eighteen minutes after midnight.

In the side yard of a home on the north side of the street, teen aged Tami was doing her best to free herself from the clutches of her new boyfriend and neither of them noticed the big black Lincoln Town Car moving slowly down the opposite side of the street with the lights out.

Inside the Lincoln two rough looking men rode together in silence, intent on their mission. The passenger, Sid, fondled a canister shaped object in his hands and squinted out the window as they idled past house after house. The address numbers on the curbing were scuffed, faded an unreadable but Louis, the driver, seemed to know where he was going and when he got to the right point, put on the brakes and stopped. No brakes lights came on, either. They had been disconnected earlier.

"Did you wipe your prints off that thing?" he asked his partner.

"I may be dumb, Louis. But I'm not stupid. I have gloves on for christ's sake."

"All right, go. Get it done."

Sid looked over at him in the darkness and said nothing.

"What?" Louis grumbled after a minute.

"Are you sure this is the right house?"

"See the Jacaranda tree in the yard?"

"That's a Jacaranda? I never knew that. What's all that purple stuff on the grass?"

"Flowers, you idiot. They drop their flowers."

"Yeah. That's really pretty. Looks like a carpet underneath it."

"Well, goody for you. Now get out and get your ass moving. We don't have all night."

Sid grumbled and opened his door. Again no dome light came on as he stepped out onto the street. With a quick look up and down he moved onto the lawn and headed quietly towards

3

the large window on the left side of the house. Must be the bedroom, he thought. No glass to break, either. The window was open and the breeze was ruffling the curtains against the screen.

"Stupid people," he mumbled half outloud, thinking back to the days of the night stalker, one of the city's most prolific serial killers, and caught himself. Moving closer, he slid his left hand into his pocket and removed his small folding knife. Opening the blade with the help of his teeth, he slit the screen as gently and quietly as he could and paused a moment to listen. Then he reached through the hole in the screen, tossed the fire bomb into the room and turned and ran.

Much as she hated to admit it, Tami was beginning to react when her boyfriend rubbed her breast. She moaned. Encouraged, he reached around behind her to see if he could unhook her bra. But he was too late. The sudden screech of tires from the wildly accelerating car in the street caused Tami to jerk upright and bang his lip with her chin. Then there was the rattling boom of an explosion as the entire front room of the house diagonally across the street went up in flames. Momentarily paralyzed, they could only stare. Finally, by the time they had stumbled to their feet and Tami had straightened up her clothes, the sound of sirens was growing in the distance.

<u>TWO</u>

The house Vince Sands lived in dated back more than seventy years. A large frame building typical of the Hancock Park area. Another high end area full of old, mature trees and well manicured shrubs, some of which encompassed the perimeter of the over sized yard and ran along the circular driveway. Two large stories tall, genuine wood siding, it wasn't all that far away from the residence of the Australian Ambassador to the United States, and other prestigious individuals.

Inside the house the phone was ringing. It was just a few minutes after the fire bomb went through the window some ten miles away. Vince Sands was sitting behind the desk in his study dressed in an expensive silk robe smoking a cigarette. Slim, dark, middle aged, he was an obnoxious pretense of a man who worked at being suave. He snuffed out his cigarette in the ashtray and

4

picked up the phone after a quick check of the caller ID.

He listened for a second and hung up without responding.

THREE

Sam Corbin was angry, shocked, frustrated and extremely frightened. What had happened to Jennie while he was working late? She said she would be staying home tonight. Going to bed early. But then that call from the police. My god. She was in the emergency room! What possibly could have happened to put her there? And so far, nothing. Just a confrontation with the person behind the window over insurance information and his ability to pay. Pay for what, for christ's sake? What was wrong? Where the hell was the doctor?

A well built man about forty with intense blue eyes and a strong face, Sam scanned the waiting room. A dirty looking boy with a blood stained towel around his head sat crying on one of the vinyl covered chairs as the bedraggled mother tried to comfort him. A young man with a very pregnant girlfriend sat across the room along with a couple of victims of a street fight, an auto accident injury and other tragedies of the night. Down at the end he spotted a uniformed officer standing near the wall, talking to a nondescript individual who couldn't have been anything other than a plain clothes cop. They were looking his way. The suited cop nodded to the uniformed cop and they started towards him as an orderly came out of a side room carrying two bottles of whole blood and headed down the hall towards the double doors of the treatment area.

"Mr. Corbin?" the one in the suit asked.

"What happened?" Sam asked, bypassing any formality. "Why are the police involved?"

"We'll get to that in a moment. I'm Detective Ashby, Robbery Homicide Division and this is Sargent Wells. My partner will be joining us soon. In the meantime please tell us where you were this evening. Say about an hour ago."

Sam's eyes burned with anger as Ashby took a step backwards. He wasn't in the mood for getting his nose bashed. So he waited. Then he took the time to explain what little he knew thus far.

Sam was shocked.

"The front window? You mean the front bedroom window?"

Ashby nodded in confirmation.

"Jesus Christ," Sam said. It was almost a whisper. He moved to the closest chair and sat down. Head in his hands, he fought for control.

Ashby left him alone for the moment when his detective partner came into the room. They moved back and talked together quietly, the uniformed cop keeping his eyes on Corbin. Ashby's partner stated that he had run Corbin through all the searches. There was nothing. Absolutely clean. So far, none of it made any sense.

Then Corbin was back on his feet. Where the hell was the damned doctor, he was demanding of the receptionist isolated behind the window with a sliding glass panel. He swore. Then he pounced on Ashby.

"Who the hell did this thing?" he demanded.

"Who do you think might have done it?"

"Blow up my house? Try to kill my wife? My God!"

"Somebody did."

"But why her?"

"That's why I need to ask the questions."

"You must have some idea."

"What about your business? You're what? Some kind of hi-tech guy? Computers?"

"Not computers," Corbin replied, not offering anything more.

"But you own your own company. Do I have that part right."

"You do."

"Okay. So... Any union problems? Pissed off competitors, someone you fired, do you gamble? Christ, I don't know? Did she have a boyfriend, did she gamble, did you borrow money from a loan shark? You have to help me here."

"Nothing, dammit. None of that shit. Never."

"Any personal enemies? Did you have an affair?"

"Damn you. We didn't have that kind of marriage."

"How do you know?"

"Goddamn you. Don't even go there."

"Just part of the routine. Know anyone who drives a dark

colored Lincoln?"

Corbin stared hard at Ashby a moment before he answered. "Not that I can think of."

"What about drugs? Ever buy or sell drugs?"

"What do you think?" Sam asked and glared back even harder. But before Ashby could follow up with more questions the emergency room doors opened and a young doctor in surgical greens approached, his mask hanging loosely around his neck. He looked at the small group of men, deciding Sam was the one he wanted.

"Mr Corbin?"

"Yes. I'm Corbin."

"Mr. Corbin.....she was, ahh... very badly burned.... We did everything we could but she.... well.... I'm sorry, sir. I'm very sorry.

FOUR

Three days later a forty one foot, double cabin, twin diesel Sea Ray Express Cruiser with a flying bridge anchored half mile off shore on the leeward side of Anacapa, the smallest of California's Channel Islands approximately twelve miles out from the mainland. The sea was dead flat and glassy smooth, reflecting the intense indigo of the clear sky. Occasionally a blue shark swam around the boat, popped an eye ball above the surface and checked things out, looking for a meal. Fisherman often gutted their catch and tossed the remains overboard. They also dumped out dead anchovies from the bait tank from time to time. Maybe even some baby squid. And at the end of the day everything else not used went in the water also, bologna sandwiches included. In the meantime it was good to hang around. Sometimes a tasty cod could be ripped right off the hook as it was being reeled in. But not this boat. They weren't fishing.

They weren't exactly partying either, although one of the males aboard was doing his best to fuck his brains out while the opportunity lasted. The woman was luscious and wherever she came from, she wasn't costing him a dime. Rudy saw to that. Rudy was the host and the owner of the boat and even though it had not been confirmed as yet, he knew he already had a deal. He also knew that this guy wasn't going to confirm it, either, until he

7

was completely done indulging himself. Dumb ass. Afraid Rudy would up anchor and head for shore the minute he committed himself. Well, maybe he was right. So, let him have his fun. As for his own woman, they had a different kind of a relationship.

The two couples, all in bathing suits, were on the aft deck drinking champagne. Rudy and Margaret, Estivez and the red headed body-for-hire named Candy. Rudy was mid fifties, gray hair and course featured, doing his best. Estivez was from South America. Rudy's empire was growing and Estivez had a nice, high grade product he needed much larger quantities of. Rudy sat in a large deck chair, the Latin and the redhead were side by side on a small couch facing him across a small deck table loaded with hors de overes. Margaret was on her feet, a deep blue towel around her satin shoulders that contrasted beautifully with the black sheen of her hair. Rudy looked up at her and scratched his head. After two of the most intense years of his life Rudy was still confounded by this younger woman.

There were three empty bottles on the small table, an opened one in the ice bucket and two more in the ice chest off to the side. Margaret removed the Dom Perigon from the bucket, wrapped it in a hand towel and moved to Estivez.

"A little more?" she quizzed with a smile, looking at his empty glass.

"Please," he answered with an accent.

She filled his glass, then Candy's, Rudy's and her own.

"Bravo," Estivez said, raised his glass and gulped it dry

Candy took a drink as his hand moved down her back. She giggled and whispered in his ear. He took her glass away and set it down, then rose and pulled her up. With a smiling glance at Rudy he guided her towards the front cabin with his hand on her swaying hip.

"Do you believe that?" Rudy said. "That's the fifth time today?"

"Sixth. Jeeez, Rudy. How does that make you feel? Another guy doing your old girlfriend?"

"What do I care? You have a lot more class than she does."

"Obviously. I wouldn't do a sleazeball like him if you bought me a new Rolls Royce," Margaret said with a bite.

"That's what I said. You have class."

"And you think that rubs off on you? Why couldn't you have had the decency to bring someone else?"

"Because she's damned good at what she does. And if she wants to help out for a few bucks, what the hell."

"Yeah, guess you should know. What the hell. Just so she doesn't fuck him to death before we get things wrapped up."

"There you go again. Always making with the *we* stuff?"

"Well. Isn't that what we're doing out here? You said so yourself. We need him."

"Like hell. *Weee,* don't need him. I said, I need him. Me, dammit. I'm the guy. You're here to help. Or am I wrong about something?"

"You thick headed bastard. I would have thought that after all the help I've given you, you might begin to see me as a junior partner. And speaking of Candy babe, where were you last night? Is that why you're so tired today?"

"I'm not tired, dammit. Why don't you shut up and let me take care of what needs taking care of."

"Well, if you're not tired why don't you take me below and give me something to brighten my day."

"Because I'm still mad as hell, goddammit, and I couldn't get it up if I tried."

"Come on, Rudy! Good grief. Now what?"

"You keep sticking your head farther and farther in the tent and that makes me nervous. This is a mean, vicious way to make a living. It's a man's business. Every guy I ever knew who let his woman have a voice in his business always came to a bad end."

"More macho bullshit, and you know it," Margaret threw back at him. If Candy was curvy and luscious, Margaret was as equally endowed but strikingly far more attractive. No vapid demeanor like Candy, either, who would lay down and spread her legs on command. There was someone at home inside Margaret's head and that someone was exceedingly intelligent and full of drive. It showed in her intense dark eyes.

Rudy watched her as she spoke to him, always unable to look away.

"Just forget it," he continued angrily. "I've got enough damned things to worry about as it is. Especially lately. How did I let that happen anyway?"

"God, Rudy. Calm down. What are you talking about?"

"Everything. Even today. Here we are out in the damned boat, out in the ocean, without a skipper or a crew."

"And the usual contingent of tits and ass and drunken mafioso friends you always drag along. Stop trying to impress everybody. You wanted to do business with this guy. Let him enjoy himself without the audience. Besides, we.. you... need to keep this deal as private as possible."

"Yeah, well," he grumbled. "What if a storm comes up or something?"

"So it does. I can handle the boat as well as that ex brother in law of yours. And pour drinks better than any of those other bimbos you're so fond of."

"Yeah, that's part of the trouble. You do everything too damned well. Next you'll be telling me you know how to fly a plane."

"Not yet, but I'm thinking about it. What's the hell's wrong with that?"

"What's wrong with it is that you're always trying to change the way I do things. And sometimes that kinda scares me because I already give you too much freedom."

"Crap, Rudy. You are the most ruthless son-of-a-bitch I ever met and I'm the best piece of ass you ever had so why can't we just leave it at that? All I'm doing is trying to help you clean up some of the problems you keep bitching about."

"Yeah, well we don't need fire bombs through the wrong front window of some truck driver's house. And I sure as hell don't need you colluding with Vince behind my back."

"Colluding?"

"Colluding, collusion. I know what it means. And where the hell did he find those blottos he sent out to that house?"

"Okay. They made a mistake. What's the big deal?"

"A mistake? Not half as big as the one Vince made."

"Jeez, Rudy. Let it go. And it wasn't a truck driver. Some no count hi-tech guy. So what? It still served the purpose."

"Like hell. Some guy's wife is dead. But not the right guy's wife. And the right guy isn't dead, either. Just gone."

"What's wrong with gone? The message is out and gone is gone. Nobody else is going to step out of line."

"Better not, by god. But I wanted him dead. And you didn't consult with me first. I'm the boss. Goddammit. Me. Not you. I make the decisions. I run things. And I don't need another lieutenant. Or a, a, junior partner like you called it. When are you going to get that straight?"

"Okay, Rudy. I hear you. You win. But just remember, big man. Who took care of that narco cop, Vanalden, you couldn't seem to get off your ass?"

Rudy grumbled again. But not quite so loud this time.

"So? That was clever and you got friends that came in handy but I'm still pissed about having my toes stepped on."

"So I'm not a passive person. Jeez, I thought you liked bright women."

"Okay. But one more insubordinate act and that cunt downstairs might just become your replacement after all. I don't care how many brain cells you got or how many other guys have fucked her. At least I can keep her under control," Rudy lashed out, knowing the whole time that it was a hollow threat. He was hooked. She had him by the balls and he couldn't get free. Jesus.

So, here he was, sloshing around in the damned ocean with some slob from South America who was banging the hell out of his old girlfriend, doing what he had to do to cut a better deal. Privacy, my ass, he said to himself. Since when? He still didn't like being out on the ocean without a skipper. Not one bit, no matter how handy Margaret was up on the bridge. She might be capable in a storm but what if an engine conked out? And no matter how she disagreed, a couple of other girls along to pour the drinks and lighten things up would still be nice. Give the guy some choices. Help carry him ashore if he over did it. What was with Margaret, anyway? How many deals had he made with his people around? No one ever talked. Hell, they wouldn't dare.

But he still had to hand it to her. Through everything that had happened thus far in front of the supplier, Margaret had behaved in a most exemplary fashion. Attentive and absolutely charming. Until it was just the two of them alone together up here on the deck. Part of him wanted to take her below, all right. But another part of him knew he'd never be able to manage it until they had settled a lot of other things. Damned if it wasn't getting frustrating. He scooted his chair around and scowled.

But Margaret had never responded to his threatening words. She didn't this time, either. Instead, she filled her glass and took a long drink. Then she set it down and went over to him. Bending over, she kissed him on the forehead and shook her breasts in his face. Moving away, she picked up the champagne bottle and went to the aft railing. Making sure Rudy wasn't watching her, she removed the towel from her shoulders and dropped it down onto the swim platform below.

"Damn." she said angrily.

"What?" Rudy growled back, and turned to look.

"I dropped my towel. It's on the swim platform."

"A damned towel?" he questioned. "What the hell," he growled, as he got up and came over. Then he gave her a withering look.

"Jesus, what's with you today? A towel?" he repeated and turned away.

"I know. But I like this one. It's my favorite color."

"Then climb down and get it."

"Why? You have long arms. Can't you just reach over?"

"Jeez," he said with shake of his head. "A damned towel," he repeated.

"God dammit," she said sarcastically. "Don't be such a jerk and get it for me."

"What the hell," he grumbled, but then he bent over the rail, thinking he might be able to reach it. Anything to get her to shut up.

Margaret moved to his left as he did so. He was unaware of the nearly full bottle of champagne she held in her right hand. Her arm came up. She swung with every once of strength she had. It was like smashing a melon. Rudy collapsed, tipped over the rail and landed, still half on the swim platform, out cold, unconscious from a severe brain concussion.

Margaret set the bottle on the deck, hustled down the short ladder and eased his body over into the sea. Blood seeped through his thick hair from the wound on the back of his head. It started to spread out across the water. She reached for her murder weapon, got it, tilted up the bottle and took a long drink. Then she lowered it into the water until it filled and let it sink. Lastly she retrieved her towel, climbed the ladder and headed down to their own cabin, thinking about what she would do after the hot Columbian had blown his last wad into Candy and returned to find the empty deck. Most certainly she didn't have to worry about the body. The sharks were already fighting over the remains.

"Where's Rudy?" she would ask when she came back up. "I was taking a nap before we headed in." And when they said they didn't know she'd say, "He's probably up on the bridge checking the weather," and go looking.

FIVE

Stu Vanalden rode the elevator to the fourteenth floor of the office tower in Century City, then walked to his left down the hall until he came to the law offices of Klien, Klaus and Hampton and pushed through the ten foot tall glass doors into the reception area, a space almost large enough to hold the entire last house he had lived in. The one his ex wife ended up with. And the fact that he was there also meant that he would still be driving that twelve year old Chevy of his for who the hell knew how much longer. The attorney's retainer alone had set him back more than the car was worth way back when it was new. Even more irritating was the fact that the clothes on his attorney's back also probably cost more than Vanalden's car was presently worth in its now depreciated state, new set of tires he had just purchased included. But it was all relative, wasn't it. None of it would mean a damned thing if he went to prison. Ten to twenty for the offense. No one had to tell him that. He was a cop, dammit. Now a cop on suspension, lucky to be just an ex cop if he got a break. Damned to hell if it went the other way. A tall man who didn't quite look his forty five years. Not an exercise freak but still in very good condition. Not bad looking, either, he still got a tumble or two on a regular basis. God, that's what he'd miss the most if they put him behind bars. The sex. And the worst part was that he had been set up and he wasn't just saying that because he had been indicted.

But did his attorney believe him? He didn't think so. But he also knew what he knew and he knew it was a bum rap. He had been set up, dammit. By who wasn't exactly clear yet but he had been working on it when he wasn't running around in a fit of anger or chewing his nails worrying about where he might wind up. Jesus, damn. Well, at least his bail hadn't been revoked as yet. He was still out walking around.

He announced himself to the receptionist who put in a call, got a confirmation and started directing him into the inner reaches of the complex.

He cut her off halfway through.

"I know where it's at, thanks." he said and started out. The door he wanted was already open, his attorney of record waiting for him behind the over sized desk. The man rose and shook his hand.

"Have a seat," he said, waving to the closest chair. "Need anything? Coffee, water?"

"Nothing. I'm good for now."

"Okay. Well, let me know." There was a long pause as they looked at each other. Then it was, "So, Stu. How are you doing? Things holding up?"

What was with the first name stuff, Vanalden wondered as he only half sat on the chair. He studied the attorneys face. Nothing. Completely neutral.

"You tell me," he replied. "You called, I came. Has something changed? I hate being pessimistic but what kind of deep shit am I really in? " It was crudely put but for now, who cared. He was sure the man had heard it before.

The attorney nodded slightly as a trace of a smile appeared at the corners of his mouth and he got to his feet again and leaned over the desk as far as possible with his hand extended.

"Congratulations," his attorney said. "The DA has decided to drop the charges. For now, at least. Be in court at nine thirty tomorrow for the formalities."

Vanalden's eyes went big. Had he heard correctly? He shook his head as if to clear it, stood up and accepted the man's outstretched hand. Then they both sat back down.

"Okay. Great. Thank you. But what does the, for now, part of it mean? I'm still hanging out there, right?"

"Looks that way. It's back in the hands of Internal Affairs."

"Bastards," Vanalden muttered. "So I'm still on suspension. Is that with pay or without pay?"

"With, for now. Depending, of course."

"Bastards," Vanalden said again.

The attorney turned over a page in the file on his desk.

"Well, two gallon sized plastic bags full of pure heroin is a lot of dope no matter how you look at it. Especially when it's missing from the evidence locker. It was your surveillance that found the dealer."

"Okay. So?"

"And you were the arresting officer. So it was your arrest that put it in there. And being a narc you would know what it would be worth on the street if you could get it back out without being caught, let alone the fact that financially you're not exactly the most solvent of individuals."

"No kidding, counselor. Especially after what I paid you. But just remember this. I made the bust and there was a good fifteen minute interval in there where I could have just helped myself to at least one of those bags and never turned it in right at the beginning. So why would I risk trying to hustle it back out of evidence once it was in there?"

"Which is an additional part of the problem. The uniformed officer with you, let's see, Johnson, has also made some insinuations in that regard."

Vanalden scowled.

"Him, too, huh. So that's a place for me to start. Somebody pretty heavy has gotten to some otherwise good cops."

"What's this about a place to start? I'm not so sure I'd do that. You are on suspension."

"Yeah, and if I don't do something I damn well might be in prison before very long. Then what?"

"I don't know. But I'll stay on this for now. See what else we can do."

"Sure. Great. But once that retainer is gone you'll be doing a pro bono cause that's all I got for now. Maybe I should have helped myself to some of that priceless stuff along the way, anyway. Then I could be sitting on the beach somewhere in the South Pacific instead of dealing with all this defamation."

"Okay. But for now it's in your own best interest to try and sit tight. I'm confident we can get to the bottom of it."

"Good idea. I appreciate your help. You have no idea. But you sit tight. I never had much faith in the system. Even as a cop. Now it's nothing left to lose, as that song goes."

The attorney shook his head in disagreement.

"You're still alive. And with the kind of people you seem to be dealing with here, it might be wise to give that some thought."

"Like hell. They'll either see me in jail or in the ground." The fire in Vanalden's eyes burned. The attorney looked away.

SIX

Bud was big, strong as an ox and almost as smart. The perfect man for the job. He always explicitly followed orders and would have eagerly put himself between his boss and any adversary that came along without a blink of an eye. And until a few days ago his boss was Rudy. He had been Rudy's driver and gun carrying bodyguard for nearly five years. Driving a limo had its own touch of prestige. At least he thought so. And looking out for a guy with as many bucks and as much power as Rudy was a real boost.

But that was before Rudy fell overboard. Do you believe that? What the hell was he doing out there? He never liked the water. He must have said so a hundred times. Jeez. Too much of that bubbly stuff after too much time in the rack with that long legged woman of his. What a way to go. But now she was his boss. Wasn't that a kick? Damn. How did that happen?

Well, okay. He wasn't sure what his pals would think of him for taking orders from some babe but, so what? He still had the limo. There was a lot of satisfaction in standing outside some expensive club waiting, working the polish rag, checking out all the enhanced chicks being escorted around.

As for Margaret herself, what could he say. She had taken him aside, told him that he didn't have to worry, nothing would change and that she trusted him with her life. Could she count on him, she had asked.

"Absolutely, yes ma'am," he had assured her, proud of the way she had appealed to his manhood.

And Margaret had said. "Call me Margaret, Bud." Gee, first names, too, just like Rudy. That was good. You're the boss, ma'am. Life goes on.

So, here he was two days after Rudy inhaled all that salt water, following orders. He had just returned from the airport where he had picked up Tony Platt, the guy in charge of the San Diego part of the operation. And now, with Tony in the back, they were on the way over to get Vince Sands. Then it was back to Westwood where Margaret would be waiting. Right there on the corner of Burke and Wilshire, two thirty sharp. Same place he picked up Rudy on many occasions. No problem.

"Okay, Bud," Margaret said. "Take a left and pull up alongside the cemetery and park."

"Right," he answered with Margaret in the back of the big limo facing the two men sitting in the opposite seat. Looking out the front he could see the Federal Building on Wilshire. And there, not very far away, were all those headstones. But that's where she had told him to stop. Good grief. Feds and deads all in the same field of view. Was there a hidden message in that?

Once he had pulled in to the curb and stopped, he automatically reached for the button and raised the opaque window partitioning off the back. Then he opened the glove compartment and removed his half read copy of Hustler.

"Gentlemen," Margaret said to them in the privacy they now shared as she looked from one face to the other. "A difficult time, to be sure. Tragic. But we have little choice. When you leave here it's business as usual. No changes except that I now sit where Rudy sat. Any problems with that?"

"What?" Vince almost shouted at her. Then he almost laughed. It was inconceivable.

"You? Who the hell... " Tony followed up but ran out of words for what was one of the most ridiculous things he had ever heard of. "You're out of your fucking mind. We had no meeting or nothing. Nothing. And besides, you're just a damned.... Jesus."

Margaret sat without responding at first, staring them down with a long, hard, unyielding look. Finally the two men stopped staring back at her and looked at each other. Then she jumped in. "A damned woman, huh? Just a dumb broad? Is that it, or is there more? What else?"

"Yeah," Tony added. "That's enough by itself. And nobody takes over without our approval, no matter who, and we don't approve. And don't think we don't know what really happened to Rudy."

"And what exactly is it that you think happened to Rudy? Come on. Let's hear it. What? Can't say it? Don't want to talk? Well, you don't know a damned thing. Neither of you. And that's exactly what's wrong. Same with Rudy. I don't need your approval."

"Like hell you don't. We've been working this thing with him for eight years and we're part of the family. You're not and you never were."

"And just because you were Rudy's main source of entertainment and now you're riding around in his limo doesn't make you one of us," Tony added. "So I'm with Vince. We don't approve. In fact we aren't even going to think about it. We're going home and get the rest of the boys together and have our own meeting. Then you'd better be on the way back to Vegas, or where the hell ever it was you came from."

Margaret laughed out loud and looked at them with amusement. "Why do you think you two are the last ones I'm having this conversation with? Huh? Didn't know that, did you? So why do you suppose that is?" she said and let it sink in. "Guess you also forgot about that meeting you had with Rudy a few months back when you were bitching about me. Yes?"

Tony just shrugged and Vince looked out the window as neither of them spoke.

"So, whether or not you choose to think of me as Rudy's bimbo and you aren't able to understand how Rudy ever allowed me to get that close to him, what you had best keep in mind is that it happened, with or without your approval, so don't kid yourselves. And keep in mind that everything Rudy knew, I now know. About both of you and everything else about the business, including every dumb ass thing either one of you ever did right from the beginning. I have also come to terms with Al and Mort. And.... and, I also have Gil's blessing so if you want to go against me, have at it. Other wise, I'm it. Think of me as being on probation for the time being, if that helps, but I've got bigger and better plans than Rudy ever had and as an organization we're going to stop being bottom feeders and really start going somewhere for a change. Think it over," she said and looked at her watch. Then she lit up a cigarette, took a long drag and leaned back in her seat. "You have about five minutes," she told them.

Son-of-a-bitch, Vince said to himself. He should have seen it coming. He had seen it coming. Sooner or later he knew this woman would be trouble, but this? Holy shit. And was she telling the truth? How could Al and the rest have gone along with it? That didn't seem possible. No way! But if they had, jeez. That didn't leave him much, did it? So until he found out for certain, what could he do? With that he shrugged as an act of acquiescence and wished he had enough courage to have his own smoke in front of her under the circumstances.

Margaret nodded her approval and looked at Tony, waiting for him to speak. Tony stared out the window, refusing to meet her eyes.

"Okay, Tony. You seem to be having some difficulty with this. What's the problem?"

Tony turned his attention to his hands, then glanced up at her.

"Nothing personal, lady. But I don't like working for women. Not in this business."

Then he looked at her straight on. A hard look.

"I want out."

"You want out?"

"Yeah. I'm done."

"Done?"

"That's what I said."

"It's not too late to change your mind."

"No thanks."

Her voice was soft and cold and had an indisputable edge.

"Well, unfortunately, the chips are down, Tony. And the game stays the same."

Tony's palms were sweaty. His tie was much too tight. He felt claustrophobic. His options were obviously rather limited. What the hell was he going to do now? He sat in silence, far too frustrated and angry to risk a reply. The only thing he knew for sure was that he would damn well never go out in a boat with her aboard. Then she spoke again.

"Unless by out you mean the very southernmost tip of South America or South Africa without a severance package. Or under one of those tombstones over there."

Tony stared at his hands some more. Finally he shrugged and

sighed. Some choice that was. Then he opened his hands, palms up as a sign of resignation.

"Good," Margaret said briskly. Then she turned to Vince.

"And while we're at it you need to make some improvements in your staff."

"How so?" Vince asked.

"Christ Vince. I told you who to hit. And when. Your guys were supposed to do the rest. Anyone who can't find the right house doesn't need to be on your payroll. I don't think they need to be around when it comes time to testify, either. What about that?"

Vince wagged his head back and forth as if in agreement. This was really fucked. Wasn't she the one who had deliberately given him the wrong information? He'd swear to it. At least he thought he would. Or was he the one who was wrong? Suddenly his whole world was upside down.

"Yeah, big screwup," he finally said, taking the heat for it. "But they've been with me a long time. I'm sure they learned their lesson."

"Maybe. Maybe not. We'll let it go for now. But keep looking for that guy. The right one this time. Rudy wanted him dead. I want him dead. Find him and put some holes in him."

"Of course. Like I said, it was a serious screwup. I'll take care of it," he replied.

"That's good, Vince. I'm sure we will get along just fine. You too, Tony. Business as usual. Which reminds me. We have a deal with Estivez. Vince, you will be meeting him in Mexico City on Monday to work out the logistics. And Tony. .. Get the word out to the bigger dealers in your area. This is high grade stuff. We're also in a position to line up a few more handlers."

Then Margaret looked out the window at the cemetery and spoke again, almost as if in after thought. Soft and sweet.

"Did you know that Rudy was a veteran?" she asked. "If they ever find his body, we can have him buried right here along with the rest of those people who served their country. That way we could keep fresh flowers on his grave."

Then she tapped on the glass behind her. Bud retracted the window enough to hear.

"Lunch time," she stated.

20

Bud nodded, raised the window again and started the engine. Since she hadn't said otherwise it would be the usual place up on Sunset. Dutifully, he pulled away from the curb.

Vince said nothing. Tony loosened his tie and wiped his hands on his trousers. The last thing he was, was hungry.

SEVEN

"Goddammit, Gil. Why the hell didn't you call me?"

"Tony? Jeez, what time is it?" Gilford Hance Howard said as he looked at the small digital clock on his desk that sat beside a picture of his precious eleven year old granddaughter. "Well, guess you had your meeting. You don't sound too happy."

"That's not even the right word. How could you have done this?"

"Hold on, dammit. It's not about me. Where the hell were you and Vince last night. Haven't the two of you ever heard of answering machines or cell phones or some way of staying in touch with the rest of us? For god's sake. And don't tell me where you were cause I don't want to know. The point is you weren't here so Al, Mort and I hammered out a deal."

"With the woman?"

"Yeah. With the woman."

"Well, some deal you made. Have you lost your damned mind?"

"Not completely. What's the problem?"

"Her."

"You don't like women."

"I don't like taking orders from a woman. I especially don't want to take orders from that woman."

"Well, I expected you might have a problem with that. Which is why I wanted you here last night."

"Bad enough she's a woman. But she got rid of Rudy. Grabbing the power proves it."

"Am I giving you an argument?"

""No, but, regardless. She was just his babe. How does that make her qualified to take his place?"

"Just like you, that's what I asked myself. But I came up with a different answer."

"I don't see how. And how the hell will we ever be able to

21

trust her? We'll lose every damned thing we ever worked for."

"It was already slipping away and you know it. And if we don't play this right, we'll lose the rest of it."

"What are you saying? Rudy wasn't doing things right?"

"Was he?"

"Well, maybe not. Sometimes not. But that's the nature of the business. Up and down."

"And lately, mostly down. Why? Because Rudy was, should we say, a little out of touch in a changing social situation."

"What? Are you saying.... ? Jesus, Gil. I hope....."

"On my honor, I had nothing to do with his disappearance. It was a complete surprise. But now that it's done we need to get some perspective."

"What the hell does that mean? And what does that have to do with her?"

"That's exactly what I asked myself. Took me a while to see it, too."

"So share it with me cause I don't see nothing that's good about it."

"Well, I don't think for one second she didn't have nothing to do with Rudy's demise. But, let's face it, he knew what he was dealing with. So, may he rest in peace. But, woman or not, it took a lot of something to do that."

"Yeah, balls. She's a scary bitch. How can you ever trust someone like that?"

"Exactly. You can't. But that doesn't mean she doesn't have other attributes we might want to take advantage of."

"I don't see any unless you're thinking of banging her."

"You know better than that."

"Well, then? What am I missing?"

"What you already know but aren't letting in."

"Jesus, Gil. What might that be? That's she ruthless, overly ambitious and stay the hell out of her way?"

"That's part of it, except instead of staying out of her way, keep her pointed in the right direction. Let the competition get run over. About time, too, and you know it. Additionally, maybe she has some foresight."

"About what? Whose head to screw up by fucking them silly and then taking them out?"

"Come on, Tony. Give it a rest. We need to move on."

"Okay. My apologies. Explain it to me."

"It's a tough business. People are moving in on us. We not only need to take back some turf here, but we need to expand on it. The other thing is that if we stay in this business long enough it's eventually going to eat us all. Smart people are diversifying, accumulating some legitimacy along the way," Gil said as he looked at picture of his smiling little granddaughter. "Someday it might be nice to relax, pay my taxes and stop looking over my shoulder all the time."

"Well. I'm not ready for a rocking chair yet but I guess I can see your point."

"Good. That's progress. So if you can get over the idea that's she's a woman and take advantage of the rest of it we might get somewhere, because I can see a way where we can get her to help us do that, plus a lot of other things."

"Use her like she thinks she's using us?"

"Whatever it takes. Also ask yourself what organization in our kind of business ever had a woman as the top executive? That's pretty damned unusual, wouldn't you say? Just might keep some people from looking in our direction sometime. So I say we put some of our old bullshit ideas aside for the time being. Or don't put them aside if that bothers you, but at least see how it works out."

"Put her on probation. She said that, you know. She said she was on probation."

"Well, there you go. I didn't tell her that. She figured it out for herself so let's not underestimate her abilities."

"And if it doesn't work out?"

"Then you get to take her for a boat ride."

"Fair enough. But what about Vince?"

"Hopefully, he'll see the sense of it if he gives it a chance. Just like you're doing."

EIGHT

Shortly after Rudy's untimely death an older, gray haired man named Charley stood on the door step of his soon to be, landlady's house talking with her, looking over his glasses as he did so, his long sideburns and bushy mustache hiding a significant portion of his face. He wore baggy slacks, a shirt with an old pipe in the pocket, and loafers. He was about sixty, the doting, middle aged woman who had a furnished room to rent in her now, far too big old house decided. But hard to tell. Anyway, he certainly was polite and he talked softly. That was a good thing. The eyes were wrong, though, for her personally. A not very exciting shade of brown and he kinda kept looking off somewhere, or down at his hands. She liked blue. Her dead husband's eyes had been blue.

"You're sure it's quiet? ... I need the quiet. I'm not as young as I used to be," Charley said, as he took the pipe from his pocket, looked at it and put it back.

"I've lived here seven years since Harold died and there's never been the slightest problem in the neighborhood. Hancock Park is a good area, you know."

"Yes. That's why I came to look."

"How big did you say your dog was?" she asked. Her name was Mrs. Brown. "I really wasn't thinking of someone with a pet."

"Oh, just a little one. About this big," Charley said, indicating with his hands. "We go for lots of walks so, you know... There's never been a problem with his habits."

"We never had an animal in the house before."

"I understand. But I could give you some extra security deposit. Whatever you think would be appropriate."

Charley almost grimaced when he said it. He didn't care about the money. The room had both a private bath and a door that led out into the side yard. An interior door led into the hallway of the house but it was secured from both sides with separate dead bolts. Enough privacy for what he needed. The important thing was the location. It couldn't have been more perfect. Vince Sands house was on the next street over, backed up to this one about three houses down. The only real downside was that the woman was obviously very lonely. In addition to becoming a little tedious, she might be a bit of a snoop. And right now she was looking him over as if he might make some kind of replacement for her deceased husband. He could almost see her running through a check list in her mind.

"Well, that would be fine, Charley," she said at last. "Any

personal things you need a hand with?"

"No, just clothing. And the dog, of course. But thanks. I tend to travel pretty light these days."

"Well, okay. But if there is anything you need, let me know."

The Animal Control Shelter was half way across town. By the time Charley got there it was near closing time. With the attendant following close behind he made his way down the row of cages, stopping here and there to check. Then he came to a halt in front of one that was the temporary home of a small, mixed breed. The little animal came to the front and wagged its tail. Charley bent down.

"Guess I could make some comments about his heritage," he said to the young woman assisting him. But before she could comment, he asked the dog a question.

"Do you like to go for walks?" Then back to her, he asked, "Male or female?"

"Male."

"Does he need shots?"

"Already taken care of. That's why we have the fee. To cover the cost. All the ones put up for adoption get a complete physical and the full spectrum of shots."

"Does he have a name?"

"None that I know of."

The following evening Charley put a small tape recorder in his inside jacket pocket and pinned a tiny mike to his collar before running up the zipper. He had his old unlit pipe in his mouth and a floppy old cloth hat on his head. Then he bent down to the dog and handed him a biscuit. The dog snapped it up and licked his chin.

"Good, huh? So, what's your name, anyway? What should I call you. You're kind of a funny little rascal."

The dog wagged its tail and gave a little yip.

"Hmm. Not bad. Rascal it is. Want to go for a walk?"

Charley clipped the newly purchased leash onto the little collar and made for the door. Outside they proceeded up the street and turned at the corner. Patient and unobtrusive as possible, Charley ambled along, letting the dog take the lead. Of the several people who had to have been aware of them, some glanced at the dog but none gave him a second look. Rascal added his own scent to all the sign posts along the way. It took fifteen minutes to make it round the second corner where they now approached the house of Vince Sands. As if understanding their reason for being there, the dog made several more stops along the way.

"That's it, Rascal. Easy does it. Take your time."

Charley did his re con in quick glances, then turned toward the dog and added the information to his recorder. Well, there it was, he thought to himself as they came closer. The sons-a-bitches. And a second car. Was it Vince's?

"Black Lincoln Town Car, new, BDWT 937," Charley stated in a soft, flat voice devoid of emotion. Then he continued.

"Metallic grey BMW 310, ABX 261.

Eyes down, watching the dog as much as possible, he continued to walk on past as if totally disinterested, adding to his information.

"Two stories. About sixty feet long, at least forty deep. Front door midway. Hmm, seven windows toward the street down, six up..... Three car garage on the east end. Two cars inside. Unknown models.....What? Basement windows? Must be an old damn house. Two behind the bushes on the east end. Another two towards the west..... Lot size about three hundred wide. Maybe two hundred deep. Hard to tell. More maybe. Lots of trees and old growth shrubbery. Power pole in the far south west corner."

Inside the house that Charley was making notes about, Vince Sands was sitting in his downstairs study talking to Sid and Louis, his firebombing employees. This time he was dressed in an expensive dark business suit but Sid and Louis looked like they still had on the same clothes from days earlier. Vince lit his second cigarette since they had been there. The first butt had gone into an already overfull ashtray. Then he gave them both a hard look. His voice was harsh.

"Okay. Who was it? Which one of you screwed up?"

Sid and Louis looked at each.

"Okay. Never mind," Vince said with a wave of his hand. "Neither one of you did. But that's just between the three of us.

But if either of you ever give that up, you're gone. And I don't mean fired."

There was a long silence before he spoke again.

"But maybe you should get rid of that damned car. What the hell. Parked in my driveway. Are you out of your damned minds?"

"Jeez, Vince. Sorry. Nobody saw us. They couldn'ta," Louis replied as Sid checked his fingernails and kept his mouth shut.

Vince took a long drag off his cigarette and slowly let the smoke go as he stared at Louis. Louis hesitated before speaking again.

"It's been locked up in the Pico warehouse since the incident and there aren't any wants out for it. We..." he looked at Sid. Then, "I thought... ahhh....... right. You want us to run it down to Tijuana and sell it?"

"No. Never mind. I was going to have you to take it down to the chop shop in El Segundo. But I leave it up to you. If you're stopped, it's your ass, cause I'll be cutting you loose. Now get out of here."

"Right, boss. Come on Sid," Louis said as they both got to their feet.

Vince also stood.

"Just one thing before you leave," he said. "We are not dealing with Rudy here. Do you understand that? ...... Good. Because this lady has zero tolerance for fuckups. Doesn't matter how long we've been together. So there had better not be any. Or it will be both of your asses. All of us. Mine included."

Again, there was more silence amongst them.

"And while you're out and around, pay attention. I want to know everything you see and hear. Especially when it comes to her. Everything. And watch your backs. One of these days........ Well.... hell," he shrugged and that clarified Sid and Louis's opinion as to how their boss really felt about his new boss.

Charley was driving a nondescript old Ford Taurus he had given seven new, one hundred dollar bills for at a used car lot up in Van Nuys. A rip off, but if it didn't get him pulled over for excessive smoke out the tail pipe within the next few hundred miles, it would still be equitable. Otherwise he was in trouble. No insurance, no registration, an alias on the paperwork. And when he was done with it he would leave it in the street near a salvage yard and call a cab.

He had left his new found furry little companion behind with a bowl of dried dog food and a full dish of water and had spent the entire day traversing the city from electronics super markets, to surplus stores, to thrift shops looking for some very specific items. By late afternoon he was done. But then something else began to bother him.

He had never had a dog before and though he didn't want to admit it, he was already quite fond of the little guy. The thing had actually crawled up on the bed with him last night and snuggled in by his feet. That was kind of neat. But in his haste he had overlooked one thing. What if he was a whiner or a barker? What would his landlady think? Damn. More than anything he needed this rented room. A week, ten days. Long enough. But he needed to do it without drawing any adverse attention to himself. He cursed and grumbled at the traffic. The southbound gridlock over the Cauenga Pass on the 405 had him trapped.

Five miles, forty five minutes. East bound on the Santa Monica Freeway took another forty five. Now the problem was where to park overnight. Certainly not anywhere near to Mrs. Browns house. The evening before he had left it half a mile away in front of a crowded apartment complex. Guess it would have to do. Not enough time to look for something closer.

By the time he made it back to his room with the over sized tote bag hanging off his shoulder he was in a sweat. And there she was, around on his side of the house puttering in the flowerbed.

"Hello Charley," she said in a honied up voice. "Been out doing a little shopping?"

"Ah, yes. I, ahh.."

"How is your room? Quiet enough for you? Did you sleep okay last night?"

Jeez, Charley thought. Just what he was afraid of. Three questions in a row. He commented on her roses instead. She seemed flattered by the attention. Good enough.

"Well," he said before she could think of something else. "I'd better get some of this stuff in the refrigerator." He gestured towards his door. "Then the dog will need his walk."

She relinquished. Not a word about the dog, either, even though the opening had been presented. He hoped that was good. He stopped and listened at the door before inserting the key. Everything was quiet. He unlocked and went in. Still nothing. Then the dog slammed into him with a welcoming yip. Charley dropped his heavy load and picked him up.

"Good boy," Charley said and headed for the old refrigerator that stood in the corner.

After they had shared a salami sandwich and several chocolate chip cookies, they headed for the door. Charley peeked out. The landlady was gone.

"Okay. Let's go see who's visiting that son-of-a-bitch tonight," he said as Rascal headed down the steps, tugging at the leash.

This time Charley hurried the dog along until they reached the second corner. Then he let him have all the time he wanted. He could already tell there was a different car in Vince's driveway. A late model American car.

He started entering the description into his recorder.

"Metallic blue, full sized Buick. Looks new," he dictated. But just as he started to move closer, the front door of the house opened. A tall, slim, older man stepped out and came down the walk. Right on cue Rascal found a bush he was determined to sniff out. Charley turned and began talking, as if to the dog. But not too long. The car was still too far down the curve in the drive for the license to be visible.

"Come on, now. That's enough. Let's go."

Pulling on the leash, he got the dog moving, trying to kept his face turned away from Vince's visitor. He heard the car door shut. The engine turned over, the car began to move as the dog was now eagerly pulling him forward, straining against the leash, looking for the next canine signpost. Now Charley was too close to the far end of the circular drive where the vehicle would exit.

"Dammit Rascal. Slow down."

The car was crossing the sidewalk ready to turn into the street. Without thinking, Charley took a quick glance at the driver, then, too late, turned back to the dog. For a very brief instant they had locked eyes. Then the car was gone. Charley grumbled to himself for allowing it to happen. They moved on. An old man walking his dog. He reached up and stroked his fake mustache, adjusted the glasses he didn't need and reassured himself that even his own mother wouldn't have recognized him. But the man in the car. Who was he? There was something familiar about him. Someone whose picture he had seen somewhere? A public figure? Something. Well, he would soon know. He had at least gotten the number off the rear plate as the guy drove away.

Preoccupied, he hardly noticed the old car parked at the curb on the opposite side, a ways further down the street. There were several randomly parked cars here and there, just as on the previous night. But this one was different. He caught some movement inside. Someone hunched down behind the wheel. Pretending to keep his full concentration on the dog, he continued down to the corner. Then he crossed the street and came back up the other side.

"Early nineties Chevy Caprice," he noted. "Dark green, small dent in rear passenger side fender. ASD-276. White male. Damn."

Damn was right. Rascal was checking out the rear tire on the car. Then he lifted his leg and left his mark. Charley jerked on the leash.

"Good grief. Come on Rascal."

"Shame on you," he scolded, shaking his head in mock dismay as they went on past, not looking in the car and not looking back.

In the room again Charley gave the dog several more biscuits, playfully scruffed up his fur and told him what a good dog he was. Then he realized he really meant it. Wasn't that interesting. The dog was supposed to be just part of the disguise. He had never counted on it becoming anything more. What would he do with the good natured little thing when he had to move on? It certainly wouldn't be fair to take him back to the shelter. Maybe Mrs. Brown. Pets were supposed to be good therapy for older people living alone. He'd give it a try.

Then he emptied the tote bag full of purchases. His first priority was the lock on the door. Sure as hell the old lady would find some excuse to check him out when he wasn't there. After today, with all the equipment he had returned with, that was not acceptable. Five minutes later the new one was installed, the keys to it in his pocket.

Next he re examined an antiquated old intercom system that he had found in a thrift store way up in Canoga Park which consisted of three identical transmitter- receivers. Quite obsolete and low on fidelity, such a system still had one significant advantage. He could have used a battery operated wireless intercom, a baby monitoring device or a conventional surveillance bug but with the right scanner-receiver, they were all easily detectable to a security minded individual. To locate the unit he had purchased, one either had to find it physically, have a similar unit and be listening in, or, use an oscilloscope to analyze the power line waveform when the device was active. Most anyone who might ever have had such a device would have trashed it long ago. And who sat around with an oscilloscope hooked up to a wall receptacle looking for audio frequency traces superimposed on a 60 hertz household waveform?

There were four houses which all received their electrical power from the same transformer located on a pole in the adjacent rear yard. One of those houses was Vince Sand's and one was Mrs. Brown's, a lucky break. That meant that if he could find a way to hide a transmitter in Vince's house he could pick up what went on back in his own room with minimal risk of discovery. Which is why he knew exactly what he was looking for when he went shopping that day.

To see if his purchase was still operational he taped down the on-button and plugged one unit into the wall by the television with the sound turned up. The other two he plugged into the wall in the bathroom and shut the door. They did work but were unusually noisy and full of hum. Digging through his acquisitions again he pulled out a soldering iron and some spare components. Two fresh capacitors and a resister solved that problem. The next task was more difficult.

In addition to being able to bug both Vince's phone and his office, he also wanted to be able to send a coded signal back to one of those units at some point in the future to activate a control relay. And he wanted to do it with equipment that was basically untraceable, should things come to that. He struggled with it, adding more scrounged parts. This time the receiver circuitry from a garage door opener. Then he hard wired a voice activated recorder to the intercom unit which he would leave in his room, hoping to hell it would all work properly. He checked the time.

It was still reasonably early yet, but dark out and late enough for most people to be inside. He changed into dark pants, dark shirt and dark hat, gave the dog a cookie and apologized for leaving him behind. Hat pulled down, he walked very slowly around the block towards Vince's house. The setback from the street was at least fifty feet. As he came up to the property line he ducked in alongside the high hedge on the west end and waited. There were lights burning on the far end of the house and on the second floor. He made his way to the garage. A quick flash with a pen light showed two cars inside. The Audi belonged to Vince. The Mercedes was his wife's. They were home. Moving very slowly so as not to be noticed in the illumination from the street light mid block he slid along the garage. Once past, there were shrubs along the side of the house to hide behind.

He stopped at the first basement window. It seemed securely locked. So did the second one. Now he had to get past the front stairs. Still staying low, he went around them. More shrubs along the rest of the wall also. Another basement window. He pushed on it carefully. Hinged at the top, this one yielded a few inches. He shielded the pen light and peered in. Something was piled up against it. Old furniture and boxes. He leaned back against the wall and forced himself to relax. There was one last window up front. Clearly there had to be more, either along the sides or out back but, an experienced cat burglar he was not. Stumbling around in the dark in someone else's yard was not something he felt comfortable about.

The last front window also seemed to be locked but the pen light showed nothing obstructing it from behind. He put a foot against the frame and pushed. It yielded with a crunch. Charley grimaced and froze. After a forced silence of a few minutes he pushed it open, stuck his head in and flashed the light. Satisfied, he withdrew and worked his way further around the house until he was under the first floor window with the light on. Crawling quietly along he worked himself away from the house as far as possible and stood up. He could see bookshelves along one wall. A man's shadow appeared briefly across the window. Charley moved. He could barely see the back of a man's head. Someone sitting. Good enough. This had to be Vince's study.

"Sorry Rascal," Charley said as he pulled his legs out from under the blanket where the dog had been sleeping, bunched up against his feet. He turned on the dim light on the bedside table and checked the clock. Two seventeen am.

"Go back to sleep," he said. "This shouldn't take long."

The dog stood up on his short little legs, turned around in a circle two and a half times and settled back down. Charley dressed quickly. Dark pants again, dark shoes, hooded sweatshirt, gloves. His already well stocked small backpack was waiting. He slipped it on and was out the door in less than a minute.

Charley hid behind a tree while a car moved down the street. Then he ducked into the bushes along Vince's driveway and worked his way to the waiting basement window. He propped it open with a short stick and brushed a thick maze of cobwebs out of the way. Then he leaned over as far as possible to minimize the sound and dropped his backpack onto the floor, got down on his stomach and went feet first and backwards through the opening. He lowered the window and made a quick scan of the basement with the small penlight.

"Jesus," he mumbled.

Dust and spider webs and boxes and old furniture and who the hell knew what all. At least twenty years worth of junk. The only person who had been down here in a very long time was probably the furnace man and that shouldn't be a worry. Colder weather was still months off. He dug into his backpack and went to work.

"Well, what do you think, little guy? Is is going to work?" Charley asked Rascal after he had made it back to his room and gotten out of the dusty clothes.

"Okay, only one way to find out," he said as he picked up the prepaid cell phone he had also purchased and dialed Vince's home number. When it began to ring he could hear the sound on the intercom unit installed in his own room. He watched the recorder and verified that it turned itself on when the ringing sound was picked up. So far so good. He looked at the clock. Three thirty in the morning. That should piss the son-of-a-bitch off.

After the ninth ring he could hear footsteps in Vince's study and the snap of a light switch being turned on.

"Hello?... Hello..... Goddammit!

Charley turned his cell phone off and put it down but the intercom device that Charley had hidden in the heating duct under Vince's study continued to operate. The sound of Vince slamming down the phone and the retreat of footsteps came through clearly. Then he rewound the recorder and played it back. Everything was working as planned, including the magnetic pickup he had attached to the phone wires that ran under the floor of Vince's office. Not only would all conversations in that room be recorded, so would both sides of any phone conversation.

"Good enough," Charley said. "Move over Rascal."

"What's wrong?" Vince's wife mumbled from her own bed which she had been using almost exclusively for several years, Vince not having been in it more than twice since she had the king size replaced with two queens. A direct attack on his masculinity. Or so he thought on the day the furniture truck arrived. But after a long shared conversation with his older brother he realized it had more to do with her hormonal makeup than the stack of motel receipts he had accumulated. She simply switched off. Like overnight. Not her fault. Nature's course. A proud woman without apology.

And he? He'd never replace her. Too much upheaval. Secondly, she had never made his toes tingle to begin with. Didn't matter. She offered comfort, stability and a social authenticity he would never have been able to master on his own. Much more priceless than sex. All sex required was money. And when it was over, it was over. Just put your pants on and go home. As a result sleeping alone in his own house soon proved to be a relief. He considered himself absolved of guilt for any and all down stream dalliances and did nothing to change his habits.

At fifty six Vince was very much a man of habit. So habitual he was on the verge of obsolescence. He really didn't have an answering machine, just like Gil had said. Which was why he got out of bed to answer the phone. Thought it might be one of his people in trouble again. But, what? A wrong number? Some drinking non English speaking, dumb ass who had finally imbibed enough courage to call some chick he had met wrapping burgers at the drive through. Crap. And as for a googley computer and electronic mail, never. A cell phone in the car at Rudy's insistence was enough. But he never brought it in the house. What he liked was face to face, eyeball to eyeball. That was the way business should be conducted. And would always be with the things he had control over. Jesus.

Then he shuddered. There was still something sinister about a phone ringing at three thirty in the morning. It almost made him want to crawl in with Bernice. Sans water, he went in the bathroom and downed two aspirin instead.

Charley felt that by now he was probably just another part of the neighborhood landscape. If they noticed him at all, no seemed to pay him any particular attention. The gray hair, the glasses, the dumb pipe he chewed on and the pint sized, harmless looking little dog on the leash had earned him an automatic dismissal. But he still didn't like the exposure. The other problem was that the dog had gone from being just part of the prop, to a warm hearted little friend, to a burden. He had given up on Mrs. Brown as a candidate. Having found out that she had once been bitten, Charley didn't even broach the subject. Instead, he had his eye on a ten year old boy named Tommy from down the street. The kid had even taken the leash and walked around the entire block with them on two different occasions. Better yet, he had asked if they could walk down to his house so he could show the dog to his mother.

"Of course," Charley replied. "Should I come along?"

"If you want to."

"Well, tell you what. I think I can trust you. So, go ahead. Just be careful crossing the street."

"Wow."

"Oh, one other thing, Tommy. I have to move one of these days pretty soon. Doesn't look like I'll be able to take Rascal with me. So, if you want to ask your parents..."

"You mean you would give him to me?"

"Ask your parents. Okay? Then we'll decide."

The answer was that they would have to think about it. Understandable. And a point of parental control. But Charley knew they would concede. He'd bet on it. Two days later the dog, with collar and leash, food dish, water dispenser and a twenty five pound bag of fresh food went across the street and Charley ceased walking around the block. At the most, he would be making one last excursion to Vince's house. Depending. In the meantime he spent most of his time listening.

When he was in his room he listened to the conversations Vince had with his visitors, both those who came to the house as well as those on the phone. And when he had to be elsewhere he listened to the recorder when he returned. In between he scratched at the irritation caused by his glued on, phony mustache and hunkered over his wireless, up-linked laptop computer, hacking into the DMV files, tracking down license plate numbers and researching background info on every name he had come across. Not only was the list getting long, it had its own surprises.

He didn't know her name yet, or where she fit exactly, but when she spoke, Vince seemed to listen carefully. But was she actually important? A woman? Not in this business. But it certainly had something to say about the guy she was fronting for. Someone with more rank than Vince who didn't think much of him and was using his girlfriend as a go between just to irritate and demean. Whatever the intent, it was working. Vince's profane mutterings had broadened considerably in scope when she ended her calls. So, it was still important. She could well lead to someone of greater import. But as information came in and his mission expanded he began to realize how terribly limited his own resources were. All he had was himself. And as himself, he had his own limitations.

Judge Harry J. Adams was the owner of the big Buick. The man Charley had locked eyes with lived in front of Vince's house. He lived on Palm View Road in Cheviot Hills, not more than five blocks from the Fox Studios movie lot on Pico Boulevard. While the address was not as prestigious, residentially, it was actually a much nicer area than the flats of Beverly Hills. Gracefully curving streets, lots of old trees and landscaping, a terrain just hilly enough to lend some ambiance, large lots with impressive spreads of grass out front. There was no way Charley would ever get a bug on the phone in the Judge's private chambers down at the Federal Building. Probably wouldn't be worth the trouble, either. But at home, who knew? At least it was relatively simple. Same as with Vince, there was a land line coming in off the pole in the rear yard. Trouble was there was no way to get close enough to do any full time monitoring.

The pole itself was not that high. Maybe thirty feet to the power with the phone lines well below. The old wooden pole also had steel steps screwed into it, starting about ten feet off the ground and there was still an ancient junction box hanging up on the side that the Judge's line was tapped into. Easy enough. Another late night excursion and Charley had a very small, very short range transmitter clipped in place. Then, as he retreated from that task he hid a combined, miniature voice activated recorder and a radio frequency receiver with fresh batteries in the thick shrubbery near the sidewalk out front. It would hold at least one hundred and twenty minutes of conversation. Unless the Judge or his wife was extremely long winded, that should last for several days before he needed to retrieve it. And that brought him back to his own moment of truth. It was time to take the next step. That step required him to make one last entrance back inside Vince's basement. But that didn't make it any easier, even in the middle of the night.

It was amazingly quiet. No local traffic, no dogs barking, no overloaded air conditioners rumbling away. Cool and peaceful, whiffs of night blooming jasmine in the air. Delicate. There was no other way to describe it. What he had to accomplish was also very delicate but in a completely opposite and much more damning way.

Once done, Charley couldn't get back to sleep. He tried to read but even the adventures of Heironymous Bosch, L.A.s most prodigious fictional cop couldn't hold his attention. He stepped back outside. Dawn was near. He walked the half mile to where he had left the car, got in, found his way to Wishire Boulevard and headed west. In Santa Monica he turned right on Ocean Boulevard, went another block and swung around into one of the diagonal parking spaces on the west side of the street. Out of the car he walked south until he came to the stairway, steering clear of the homeless still asleep in the bushes and on the benches along the way, empty wine bottles, food wrappers and other assorted trash scattered about.

One hundred and sixty seven steps, if he remembered correctly. White painted wooden steps with segments and turns that followed the badly eroded adobe palisade downward to the foot bridge which crossed Pacific Coast Highway. From there a spiraled short tower of concrete that ended at the parking area, just a hundred yards to the sand. How many times had he made this trip, Charley wondered as he crossed the soft ribbon that stretched along the coast line for all those miles.

The tide was out, the fog was in. Seagulls sat along the top of the sand bank and observed as long legged terns skittered about on the water packed sand, dodging the surf, looking for breakfast. As usual, the fog bank hung tightly over the junction of sea and land, sealing visitors into a small circular world of limited visibility. Also, as usual at this early time of day, the number of human visitors was extremely limited. Sometimes a jogger or a lone individual investigating the debris left by the outgoing tide. A couple of blocks away from a megalopolis of millions where one could be completely alone. For lack of something better, it was a place to pose cosmic questions, evaluate earth bound rules and rethink definitions of morality and human misconception. It was also a time to review one's personal history, revisit old pain, re evaluate one's own past actions and either reaffirm or re consider one's private goals and plan of action.

Charley walked south towards the old Santa Monica pier, loafing along. By the time he reached it the fog had retreated offshore to beyond the breakwater and the sun was shining brightly. Instead of taking the stairs up onto the pier he went under it and continued walking the two plus miles down to the Venice boardwalk before turning around. Completing the full round trip back to his old car changed nothing, however. He still felt exactly as he had before. All he could do now was wait.

Tuesday would be the day. If Vince's life was as routine as it had appeared, Tuesday was the day his wife went to the beauty parlor, the same day Sid and Louis came by. In the morning. Mid morning, mid week. It was a good time. Most adults were at work, kids were in school, traffic in this residential area was rare. While he waited he removed his tools and equipment from his temporary abode along with most of his clothing and all his other personal items and lugged them over to his old car. Then he studied his hair, wondering how to restyle it. He put the clippers out on the bathroom counter along with a bottle of hair dye. And he would trim and reshape his add on mustache. A totally altered wardrobe already hung in the closet. With those preparations made he began a thorough cleaning of every square inch of space inside the room he didn't need to touch anymore, all the time listening to what was going on in Vince's study.

Sid and Louis arrived a little earlier than usual, just past nine thirty. Not good. What if they concluded their business and Vince sent them on their way too soon? Damn. He didn't want to have to hang around another week. The way he kept avoiding her, Mrs. Brown might already be getting suspicious. What if she did something stupid? Like somehow getting into his room when he wasn't there and seeing something she shouldn't? He always turned the sound off on the intercom when he was gone but what if the recorder came on? Would she panic and call the police? Jesus. Now he was beginning to sweat. He went to the refrigerator and dug out a soft drink. Just as he was ready to pull the tab, he heard what he knew to be the sound of the door to Vince's study open.

"I'm having lunch with Hanna after my appointment. Then I'm going shopping. See you around three," Bernice informed Vince. The sound of her voice was neither warm nor cold. Just indifferent. So was Vince's acknowledgment. But Charley was pleased.

Charley waited fifteen minutes to make sure she hadn't forgotten anything and had to return. Then he dialed Vince's number. It was picked up after the first ring.

"What?" Vince said.

"What, hell," Charley responded. "How you doing, Vince?"

"Who are you?"

"I'm the guy who woke you in the middle of the night a few days back and hung up."

It took Vince a minute to reply.

"A wise ass, huh. What the hell do you want?"

"Now that your wife is on the way to the beauty parlor, I thought we might have a little chat."

"Kiss my butt, you son-of-a-bitch," Vince said and slammed down the phone.

Charley waited two minutes before dialing again.

"Goddammit," Vince answered when he picked it up.

"Jeez, Vince. I didn't get to say goodbye."

"Good. Don't bother to call back."

"Hold it, Vince. Not me. You. And Sid and Louis. Nice to find the three of you together."

"What the hell is that supposed to mean?"

"It means that my name is......... in case you don't remember. And I'll give you about five seconds to pass the word."

"Five seconds. For what?"

"Then your house blows up, you dumb shit. There are six sticks of dynamite fastened to the floor under your study. Ready? Five, four, three, two, one and goodbye," Charley said and pushed the little button on the front of the small device wired into the intercom unit plugged into the wall socket of his room which sent a coded signal to the receiver in Vince's basement which closed a small relay which sent a small electrical charge to the little igniter caps attached to the six explosive charges.

The noise was extreme. And the way her windows rattled, Mrs. Brown would never again be able to claim that she lived in a quiet neighborhood. But the damage was controlled and precise. The building didn't even catch fire. Nor was there a great outward blast of flying debris. Instead the explosion went almost vertically upward, taking out the study floor, the floor directly above, dislodged part of the roof and tilted the walls out on that end of the house just a bit before the bulk of the destruction and three dead men all fell back into the basement. And, because of Charley's careful planning, not one piece of harmful material reached any of the adjacent property lines.

The most interesting part of it all for Charley, however, was that he had lied to Vince about the dynamite. There was no dynamite involved at all. It was the powder from four dozen easily obtained boxes of twelve gauge shotgun shells instead. Something that wasn't chemically tagged so it could be traced later. Cut the spouts off of small aluminum funnels, jam them in the bottom of 16 ounce steel soup cans and pack them full of gunpowder. Bury an electrically operated blasting cap in the middle and one had some very effective, shaped munitions charges, just like his faded old copy of Army Tech Manual, TM 31-210 said. Place them pointing upright under the floor of Vince's study and, guess what? Goodbye Vince, Sid and Louis in a carefully executed manner as shown by the way Vince's house disintegrated.

NINE

In addition to a black Lincoln Town Car, there was a fire engine, a fire department rescue truck and an ambulance parked in the long circular driveway at Vince's house. The coroner's vehicle, two black and whites and a plain Crown Victoria were parked in the street out front. Everyone was inside, down in the basement poking through the rubble except the two detectives from Parker Center Robbery and Homicide, Ashby and his partner, Benson, who had just come on the scene. They were there because of the three mangled bodies that had been discovered in the rubble under very suspicious circumstances. Dead people, no smell of natural gas, no flames, an explosion closely limited to one end of the dwelling that occurred at ten twenty in the morning.

"Well, I'll be damned," Benson said as he and Ashby stopped behind the big black auto in the driveway. "Do you think that could be it?"

Then Ashby walked around the Lincoln, looking in the windows. He opened the driver's side door, leaned in, looked under the dash and pulled back out. He scratched his head in dismay. His eyebrows went up.

"Looks like the one we've been looking for," he said. "Couple of add-on switches under there. One shuts the interior lights off."

41

"Well," Benson said as he nodded towards the house. "If the car belongs to one of those dead bodies in there,....."

"Right. Then we know who blew up the house in Santa Monica."

"Yeah, but why?"

"Good question. Let's have a look at the victims. Maybe that will tell us something,"Ashby said and they turned and headed towards the house. Amazingly, the front entrance was still intact. They started up the steps when another city owned, full sized Ford pulled in behind the row of vehicles in the drive and two men got out.

Barnes and Willett were both from narcotics. What was that all about, Ashby and Benson wondered.

"I hear there's bodies in their," Barnes said. "Have you checked them out yet?"

"Just got here ourselves," Ashby stated. "But why do I have the feeling that you already have an idea whose they are?"

"Quite possibly. And if this was no accident, then someone did the world a big favor. Should we?" he asked and waved towards the door.

Half an hour later they were all back outside discussing the case as Ashby confessed that he didn't get it.

"Why would someone like this be firebombing some poor guy's house in Santa Monica? What's the connection?"

"Looks like a stupid mistake to me," Barnes said.

"Christ, some mistake. You mean the wrong house?"

"Yeah. Something like that. The house next door was leased to a Victor Trent. It seems that Trent was trying to make a move on a guy named Rudy Stark, an old line thug who ran his own cartel of sorts. Vince here, worked for Rudy and those other two hoodlums in there worked for Vince. But instead of Trent being dead, the wrong house get's bombed and Trent disappeares. Then Rudy falls overboard out in the ocean. Next, my old team mate, Vanalden, who was accused of stealing some of Rudy's drug shipment, completely dropped out of sight after being put on leave. Then we have an ex military security surveillance guy down in El Segundo who we think was linked to Trent, he's suddenly gone too. Along with a couple of others we're not sure about just yet."

"Sounds complicated."

"It's getting that way. And this puts a whole new spin on things. So we need to go back inside and see what else we can find. Luckily, no fire so there must be something there worth looking over."

"Yeah, good luck with that. All we have to do is tell some poor man that his wife died because some dumb ass got the wrong house. How does a person handle something as senseless as that?"

"Well, maybe there will be some satisfaction in knowing that the perps also got blown up."

TEN

It was early evening when a dark haired man in a business suit came down the sidewalk that ran past Judge Adams house. No tie, shirt open at the neck, he looked down at his feet just as he came to the dense shrubbery that ran along the side of the Judge's property. He stopped and bent down, retied a shoelace, then appeared to lose his balance a bit as he stood up. Then his hand went into his jacket pocket and he continued on his way to the bus stop on the corner of Motor Avenue and Pico Boulevard where the new Charley waited for the next bus that would take him to within two blocks of his motel room in Hollywood. Here he put an earplug in his ear and listened to the tape recorder he had just recovered from the bushes in front of the Judge's house. First, there was a dial tone, then the sound of touch tone numbers being entered. Eleven short bursts. An area code and a number which he would decipher later.

"Hello."

"This is Adams. What the hell is going on? Who put the hit on Vince?"

"I told you not to call me here."

"For Christ's sake, Tony. Somebody blew up his house."

"So what? It wasn't your house."

"How the hell do I know you didn't do it without telling me. Did you?"

"Of course not, goddammit. He was on our side."

"Maybe. But you and him had issues. Just like you had issues with Rudy, along with some else. That's no secret."

"We did, but Vince and I needed each other. And that's all I'm saying."

"Well, somebody was staking out his house. He told me that."

"Yeah. That cop, Vanalden, that you helped set up. Maybe he did it. Maybe he's after your ass now. What do you think of that?"

"You have a sick sense of humor."

"I do. And Vince had lots of enemies. I bet someone rented the sports arena to have a party and celebrate."

"Dammit, Tony. Where's the humor in that?"

"Jeez, what a wimp. Now get off the line and try to keep your shit together until I get back to you. Do you think you can do that?"

There was a long silence before the sound clicked off. Charley rewound and played the dial tone sounds over three times. Sounded like a 619 area code, he said to himself. The eastern suburbs of San Diego.

ELEVEN

Victor Trent was thirty nine. Tall with dark, full hair, dark eyes, once muscular but softening, full of ego, a man of ever widening visions of his own importance had parked his silver Porsche on the turnout just south of the tunnel on Malibu Canyon Road. He shut off the engine, got out and looked at his watch. How long would she make him wait this time, he wondered. The usual twenty minutes? Less, he hoped. They hadn't seen each other in over a month and a lot had changed. Some good, some bad. The only thing that bothered him was their relationship. Everything he had ever aspired to depended on that.

It was evening, forty five minutes from darkness. He walked to the edge of the turnout and looked down. Rough country and one hell of a long drop. He walked back to the rear of his car and leaned against the fender. No traffic on the road. He hoped she would bring the big Cadillac. With this kind of privacy maybe he could get her in the back seat for a proper reunion.

Almost immediately that thought was followed by the noise of an approaching automobile coming up from the south. It slowed and pulled up, half on the road and half off, blocking his small car from behind. He swore. His hand went inside his jacket, reaching for his automatic as he moved around his own car to shield himself. It was a big Cadillac all right, but not hers. It was the limo. Rudy's limo. What the hell? Rudy was dead. He knew that. And he wasn't about to forget that someone had tried to fire bomb his own house but had made a mistake. And he knew that whoever did that had a good reason for trying to do him in. But why had Vince been hit? That didn't make any sense at all. Vince was supposed to have been Rudy's man all the way. Or was he?

Before he could analyze things further the rear door of the limo opened and Margaret stepped out. She waited a moment. He could see that she was smiling. Then she momentarily turned towards the limo and made a waving motion with her hand. The car eased back onto the blacktop and continued, heading north. Margaret began walking towards him. He relaxed, holstered his weapon and moved in her direction. Damn. Just as awesomely beautiful as always.

They stopped less than two feet away from each other and stared. He questioning, she teasingly. Helpless, he reached for her. The kiss was passionate. Then she disengaged and immediately turned serious.

"A month. Where the hell have you been?"

"Christ, Margaret, the son of a bitch tried to blow up my house. I was home that night and if they hadn't got the wrong one....."

"You think it was Rudy?"

"Who else? What I don't understand, though, is that if he was onto us.....if he even imagined that we were working together and were going to take him out.... hell, he would have done you in, too. I don't know. Maybe it was some kind of coincidence. My neighbor. Maybe he had enemies, too."

"Maybe. Guess we'll never know. Where's your wife?"

"I sent her back east."

"And where have you been all this time?"

"You sound upset."

'Very. We had an agreement. You didn't follow through."

"I was ready. Honest to god. It was set. We were waiting for opportunity."

"The *we* is you and Hines, that bodyguard you hired?"

"Yeah. Me and Hines."

"Is he still around?"

"He's down in Long Beach. You might remember the place."

"He was going to shoot Rudy? Isn't that a little crude?"

"What else? Course it doesn't matter now. Talk about coincidence and benevolent fate. I assume you were out there with him? Was he drunk? Jeez. Falling overboard. Ha. That's hilarious. I heard he was afraid of the water and couldn't swim."

Margaret gave him a hard look. "There are no coincidences, Vic. You should know that by now."

He squinted at her. "You?"

"Maybe I got tired of waiting."

"Damn, Margaret," he said, studying her closely, subconsciously taking half a step back.

"But Vince Sands too? What about him? Why would you do that?" he asked, completely puzzled.

"I didn't." She stared at him.

"Then who? Christ, Margaret. That's bad news," he said, not even a little bit convinced that she hadn't.

"Damn right. Tell me about it," she replied in a way that still didn't help all that much.

Trent was quiet, trying to unravel all the bigger implications, but he couldn't quite fathom it.

"Okay... So, who's running things with Rudy gone?" he asked instead.

She looked at him for a long moment.

"Me," she said.

"You?" He was surprised. "You? Jeez, Margaret, that's wonderful," he said, a smile growing. He wanted to hug her but she stood her ground and glared at him, a cold wall thrown up between them.

"What's wrong? I thought we had a plan. Big plans. The two of us. "

"What's wrong? You mean besides me having to do all the dirty work?"

"Yeah. If there's something more, what is it?"

"I heard that neighbor of yours, Corbin. Didn't you tell me he had a knock-out looking wife."

46

Victor acted like he didn't understand the question. Then he shrugged.

"Yeah. I guess so. So what? Damn, Margaret. You don't think... What? Come on. I know what I said but that's ridiculous."

"That's not the way I heard it."

"For god's sake. Me and her? It was me and you. All the way," he said, then he looked at her in awe. "Jesus, Margaret. Did you do that? My god."

"Maybe it was just another coincidence. Another fortunate accident."

"Goddammit, Margaret. I would never cheat on you. I wouldn't."

"What about your wife? You cheated on her. Not that I ever gave a damn," she said as she reached in her jacket pocket and removed her cell phone. She did a speed dial. It was answered immediately.

"Pick me up," she said and turned the phone off.

"Wait, dammit," Victor said. "I'm here now. We need to work this out."

"Okay," she said, looking at him in a non committal way. "Be patient. We'll work it out. Maybe that hotel on the beach up in Santa Barbara you liked so much. That might be nice. Call me tomorrow."

"Why are you in such a hurry?"

"Because I have another meeting and I'm already late."

It was almost totally dark by now and he had a hard time seeing her face clearly, not completely sure he believed her. But before he could continue the headlights from the limo illuminated them and the vehicle pulled up right behind his Porsche, almost bumper to bumper.

"All right," she said. "I need to go. Call me. Say around ten in the morning. We can have lunch first. Don't forget," she said as she stepped forward and touched him on the cheek. Then she went to the rear of the limo and got in.

Victor watched her as she did so. What the hell had he done? One kiss and that was it? She had literally dismissed him. Another meeting to go to. What the hell was that, he wondered as he began thinking about their last encounter. Passion in the car, serious sex in the motel and business last of all. Once the limo door shut he turned back around, worked his way between the two cars and opened the door to his own.

He couldn't see her through the headlight glare but he gave a wave in her direction before he got in and shut his door. Immediately he heard the roar of an oversized engine and the squeal of spinning tires as the limo, twice as powerful and three times heavier than his own vehicle, slammed into his rear bumper. Too stunned to even reach for the door handle, he went over the edge, into the deep rocky canyon below.

TWELVE

Dressed in dark jeans, tee shirt and tennies, Charley crouched behind a cluster of sage on top of a low hill and scanned the area below with his newly purchased binoculars. It was unusual to see a big, old, two story house this far out from town. A house on what had to be four or five acres, all surrounded by a combination of cement block walls and chain link fence strung together. Semi desert, the yard had a smattering of bushes scattered around, a row of eucalyptus trees lined up along the north edge and several canopied shade trees nearer the house. Under one of the trees a pair of the biggest dobermans Charley had ever seen, were laying in the shade half asleep. The same dogs that ate a full five pounds of tranquilizer laced hamburger that Charley had tossed over the fence the night before. Then he focused on the top of the telephone pole in the rear of the property, his reason for going there in the middle of the night. He could just make out the tiny antenna of his eavesdropping device. The only place it might be visible from would be the second story windows in the back of the house. But only if one was determined to find it.

Satisfied, Charley then surveyed what he could see of the road running past the property. It wasn't the best of vantage points but he could see parts of four neighboring dwellings partially hidden in the trees. Some had cars parked out front. And what was this, he wondered as he got a look at one of them. Good grief. The same car he had seen near Vince Sands house, gotten the license number of and now knew the owner's name. God! What an amateur! He put his binoculars in their case and backed away, slowly circling around to where he had left his own vehicle. Inside, he rolled down the windows, opened his ice chest, removed a salami sandwich, a root beer and settled in. The wait wasn't as long as he expected. Nor was the old car difficult to follow. It led him back to an older part of La Mesa and pulled into a motel complex that looked like it should have been razed twenty years earlier. Just down the street there were equally ancient strip malls on both sides of the street. Tucked in behind the one on the south side was a beer bar. Karaoke on Wednesdays, open mike on Thursday, live music Friday and Saturday. Hmmm, Charley thought. He'd bet on it.

At eight o'clock he returned to the area and parked down the street from the old motel. It was already getting dark. Although he had never seen him anywhere except hunched down in his car, Charley was sure he would recognize him. After all, Vanalden was a cop, or an ex cop. But no different. A cop was a cop.

Sure enough, twenty minutes later Vanalden came out of the motel complex on foot and started walking down the street towards the mini mall. Charley followed, staying way back until Vanalden entered the bar. A minute later Charley followed him inside. The place was dimly lit and still pretty dead. A long, battered, wood topped bar with high stools and a few old tables off to the side. Four customers including Vanalden, none of which looked up when he entered.

Charley sauntered down to the empty stool on Vanalden's right and pulled himself up. The bearded bartender stopped in front of him. Charley looked at the back bar.

"A draft," he said and put down a twenty. "Make it a Coors."

When his drink came, Charley took a long sip and tried to get a better look at Vanalden in the dirty mirror behind the counter but it was obscured with bottles, post-em notes, profound little signs and a most appropriate bumper sticker that was standard fare for this type of establishment. NO SNIVELLING. Great, he thought. He took another sip, set his glass down and spoke quietly.

"Well, Mr. Vanalden. Can I buy you one?" he asked.

Vanalden jerked around and stared at him.

"Who the hell are you?" he asked.

"That old piece of shit car you drive. You should be more

careful when you're spying on people."

"What are you talking about, asshole?"

"Tony Platt's house this morning. And Vince Sand's a couple of weeks ago."

Vanalden stood up, reached inside his jacket and jammed a revolver into Charley's ribs.

"This thing could make all your blood leak out in about ten seconds. Now get up and head for the back door," Vanalden said, keeping the weapon out of sight.

"What can I say," Charley replied with a shrug as he got up. "I just hope you have a permit for that thing."

Outside, Vanalden gripped Charley by the shoulder and steered him up against a parked car only partially illuminated by the low wattage bulb over the door of the building.

"Assume the position," he ordered in an angry voice.

"You're not really my type," Charley quipped.

"Shut up, goddammit. And do it," Vanalden said and pushed him.

Charley complied and remained quiet while he was patted down.

"Empty your pockets on the hood," he was told.

Again Charley complied in silence. He placed a money clip, car keys, a photo and a small tape recorder on the car.

"Cut the crap," Vanalden said as he sorted through it. "Where's your ID?"

"I bet you haven't washed your car in more than a month. I bet you can still see that place on your rear tire where my little dog pissed on it back in Hancock Park."

Vanalden jerked him around and studied Charley closely. He shook his head.

"No way. That was an old guy."

"Thank you. The disguise worked better than I thought."

"Enough, dammit. Tell me something useful before I rap your brains out," Vanalden said, raising the weapon as if to strike Charley on the head with it.

Charley held up his hand.

"May I?" he asked and pointed to the recorder.

Vanalden studied his face, then nodded. Charley picked it

up, hit the play button and held it for Vanalden to hear. The recording was a conversation between Vince Sand's and Margaret. When it ended, Charley shut it off and returned it to his pocket along with the rest of his possessions.

"What the hell are you?" he was asked. "A Fed?"

"Hardly," Charley answered. "Just private enterprise thinking about a partnership."

Vanalden backed up a step.

"What?" he said with a laugh. "Us? Why the hell would I do that?"

"Because all you know how to do is sit around in your car and jerk off."

"You got a smart mouth for someone on the wrong end of a forty five."

"So... Put it away and maybe I'll say something nice."

"Like what?"

"Well, maybe not nice. Just informative. You have a target painted on your ass."

"Says who? You?"

"No. Some of the same people who are on that tape."

Vanalden holstered his weapon.

"No doubt," he said. "And I'm sure you have a suggestion to make."

"A question. What would be a fitting reward for the people who fucked you over? The charges were dropped but you're still unemployed and seriously tainted. Next stop, warehouse security out in east L.A.. Nights. Is that what you want? "

"Does it look like it?"

"So what's your answer?"

"What happened to Vince was kind of appropriate. And if that was your dog that pissed on my tire, I have a feeling you might know what caused his house to fall apart like that."

"Perhaps. Got any beer back in that dumpy motel room you're staying in?"

Happy Acres? Holy Jesus, Charley said to himself when he first saw the sign. Why is it that some of the worst, bottom of the pit places to live have the most exotic names? Happy Acres, Oak Creek Estates, Paradise Park, Rainbow Haven. Say what you want but living ten feet away from a yard full of beer cans on one side and fifteen feet away from waist high weeds that hid who knew what on the other side was not Charley's idea of an inspirational place to dwell. But for two weeks, god help him if it was any longer, he could stand it.

The transmitter he had installed at Tony Platt's was the best he could do. There was no basement and he could see no safe way to get inside the house itself, what rooms to bug if he could, or how to monitor anything they might pick up. It was the phone line or nothing. And if Tony had a cell phone and used it for conducting business then he, Charley, was out of luck. In the meantime he would try to be happy at Happy Acres Mobil Home Park. It was the only place he could find that was within receiving range of the transmitter and the luxury of it cost him at least three times the monthly rent for the trailer space as paid for by the owner, plus the price of a room for the displaced individual at a cross town motel and enough cash supplement for more than twenty full cases of beer if the guy didn't come back and invade Charley's privacy during the short time he might be there.

Inside the eight foot wide, twenty five foot long box Charley sat listening to his tape recorder. After it had played out he got up and poured himself a cup of coffee from the large thermos. Then he placed a double layer of paper toweling down on the table and dug out his fast food roast beef sandwich. One quick look at his surroundings, however, and he put it back in the sack. Where were the yellow pages?

More out of pocket cash spent for the cleaning lady the service had sent over and Charley felt that he could at least sit down without sticking to a chair. He might even be able to get some sleep on the new blankets he had thrown over the bed. Now where was the throw away cell phone he had purchased? In the briefcase he had started carrying his equipment around in. He dug it out and dialed Vanalden.

"Did you take my advice?"

"About getting a different car? Yeah. Cost me six hundred bucks to trade my old piece of crap for an older piece of crap that only runs half as well."

"I'm surprised you value your life so highly."

"Yeah, well. Right now, what can I say?"

"Don't bother. Anything happening out there?"

"Only one visitor so far. And, yes. I got the license number. What are you doing?"

"Paying attention. Any luck on that other matter?"

"You mean the, ahh... maybe. I'm taking a run out in the desert tonight where there's some heavy duty roadwork underway. You going to be at home in case a wheel falls off this piece of shit I'm stuck with?"

"I am. I still have some homework to finish."

"Like what? Advanced calculus? Or are you working on an improved pop top for beer cans?"

"Actually I'm doing something highly creative with balsa wood and cardboard tubing."

"Yeah, right," Vanalden said and clicked off.

Charley pocketed his phone and went back to his project. Again experimental, but one hell of a lot safer than making gunpowder shaped munition charges. It kept him busy most of the night with no call from Vanalden. Hopefully, that was good news. Then he removed his shoes and socks and got five hours sleep lying on top of the blankets covering the bed. When he woke he padded down the mini hall to the bathroom on the clean towels he draped over the tattered, dirty carpet. The faucets all leaked but the cleaning lady had done a decent job of sanitizing. Bleach and cleaning fluid smells still filled the dismal, closet sized room. He took a shower and put on fresh clothing. It helped him feel a little better but not as good as a few more hours of sleep would have. It was well past noon before he called Vanalden.

"How did it go? No flat tires, I take it."

"Just a felonious offense to stay ahead of. That's Homeland Security turf these days. I hope you know that."

"So. Find something with cheese and pepperoni on it and come over. I haven't had breakfast yet. No, forget that. What kind of idiot would eat pizza for breakfast? Jeez, just bring the other stuff."

"And where would that be?"

"About four blocks west of where you're probably at."

"Was. Had a problem. Give me an address."

"If you laugh, I'll call 911."

"I'll be nice."

Charley opened the door when he heard the knock, stuck his head out and looked around. Then he looked at the sack Vanalden was carrying and nodded for him to enter.

"It's my vacation home," Charley said when he saw the wretched face Vanalden made inside. The table was still covered with fresh paper towels. Charley went to the refrigerator for two beers and told Vanalden to sit, insuring him that it was safe to do so.

"Condemned would be more appropriate," Vanalden said, then, looking anxious, held up the sack. "Will you please do something with this?" he asked.

Charley took it, peered in and put it in the refrigerator.

"Six full sticks. And some extra fuse, thank you. Now can we go somewhere down the street? Maybe a mile or two. I don't like that stuff," Vanalden stated with a nod back towards the refrigerator as he finally removed his gloves.

"Me either. But it looked fresh so it should be stable. Especially at the cooler temperature."

"What? You're not sure?"

"Never touched it before. It's heavier than I thought."

"You can't be serious. Isn't that what you used at Vince Sands' house?"

"No," Charley confided. "Gunpowder."

"Gunpowder? Cut the crap. Gunpowder."

"Well, what else? I did the best I could. That's all that was available at the time."

Vanalden shook his head in disbelief.

"You're serious, aren't you. Jesus." He stared at Charley for a good thirty seconds. "What the hell have I done?" he asked. "A fucking novice. Holy crap. So what the hell are you going to do with dynamite? Shoot it over the fence with a sling shot?"

Charley popped open his beer and took a drink. Then he sat back down and studied Vanalden's face.

"Since you're not impressed, this might be a good time for you to go your own way," he stated matter of factly.

Vanalden looked back at him. Then he shook his head back

and forth as if he couldn't make up his mind. Finally he spoke.

"Just out of curiosity, how are you going to manage it? Really?"

"If you're going to drop out, it might be best if you didn't know."

After more hesitation, Vanalden admitted that he probably no longer had a choice. Then he went on to confess that he had probably been spotted by someone leaving Tony's house when he was out there two days before. Too much coffee, he had gotten out of his car and gone behind a nearby tree but hadn't seen the other vehicle until it was too late.

Charley began laughing at him.

"What's so damned funny?"

"I already knew that. The guy's name was Jance. He called Tony right after. That's why I told you to get a differnt car."

"How the hell do you know?"

Charley reached over to the counter and played back the last piece of tape on his recorder.

"Christ," Vanalden said with embarrassment. Then, "How did you do that? His house is half a mile away."

"Radio link. I put a small transmitter on the telephone pole behind his house. Which is why I'm hanging out here in paradise valley. It's the only thing I could find within receiving distance."

Vanalden seemed surprised. He looked at Charley with growing respect, about to say something when Charley continued. He had Vanalden on the ropes now and wasn't about to quit until Vanalden completely understood who was in charge and why and if he wanted out, now was the time.

But he was in all the way, Vanalden assured Charley, what could he do to help?

"I'll think of something," Charley assured him. "Problem is, surveillance really isn't your calling. That's the second time. Vince's people made you too. Just like I did," Charley said, letting it sink in. "Want me to dig out that old tape?"

Vanalden leaned back and scratched his head. He threw his hands up and was silent.

"Now what?" he finally asked.

"I'm waiting for a call."

"Okay. Got another beer? I'll help you wait."

"In the box with the dynamite. I'm going to grab another nap."

"Where's the phone? Want me to answer it if it rings?"

"In my pocket. And it won't ring. This thing will come on," Charley said, indicating the recorder. "Wake me when it does."

"Right," Vanalden said as Charley got up and went to the back of the trailer.

Vanalden took two cans of beer out of the refrigerator and sat back down. He opened one, took a long drink and then began a survey of Charley's trailer, looking for clues, wondering what he would discover. He didn't even know the man's true identity. But he trusted him nevertheless. So far. Charley had been up front about everything else. He also thought he understood the man's motives. But blowing up people's houses? Damn. What was he getting himself into? Becoming an accessory to murder? Jesus, damn. He sat still for a moment, thinking back. So far he had done nothing but make a fool of himself in Charley's eyes and was no closer to clearing his own name than before. But Charley probably could if he had the right recordings and gave him copies. Where would he keep that kind of stuff? Certainly not here in this dump of a place.

An hour went by. It was now late afternoon. He got up and listened. Hearing nothing from the bedroom, he began looking in cupboards, opening drawers, checked the freezer. Nothing that didn't belong in the landfill, along with the entire trailer and most everything else in the entire trailer park. Then, half hidden in the corner behind the counter, a cardboard box covered with a faded dish towel. He lifted the corner and looked in. What the heck? Balsa wood, cardboard tubing, model cement. Just like Charley had told him earlier. What was this guy up to? He was about to dig further into the box when he heard a loud click. He looked around. It was the recorder coming on. And, in an instant, there was Charley.

Charley flipped a small switch on the recorder and the full sound came on. First, there was the end of a string of dial tones, then the ringing. Three rings and a male voice answered.

"Yes," was all he said.

Charley shrugged and shook his head indicating he didn't know the voice.

Then the second male voice, the one making the call. "Let me talk to her," the voice said.

"That's Tony," Charley stated.

"What is it, Tony?" the female asked with a hint of impatience.

"Well, well. Her again, whoever she might be." Charley said as they continued to listen.

The discussion went on. Tony was sending one of his people up to L.A. to pick up the pieces of Vince's operation. He also didn't trust Judge Adams and he had a few other concerns. That damn cop she had chosen to set up was now down there staking out his house.

The woman assured Tony that Judge Adams was a disposable entity, but not just yet.

"What about the cop?" Tony asked, obviously irritated. "I could have had him popped ten times by now."

"Just the kind of attention we need."

"They'd never find him where I put him."

"Be patient. The person working the problem is already in town."

"And in the meantime, what? He blows up my house too? And with me in it?"

"Go somewhere. Work on your alibi. Tonight would be good. And stay a few days."

"Does that mean he lost the tail you had on him?"

"We know where he's staying and what he's driving."

"Great. But what if he's got help?"

"Help an ex cop? Like who would be that dumb?"

"Like maybe instead of setting him up, you should have taken him out in the beginning." Tony's voice was becoming more critical.

"Just doing what Rudy wanted," she said somewhat coyly.

Tony's silence seemed to have its own implications. When he finally spoke he said, "Two more days and that's it. Then I take care of it myself." Then he hung up..

Vanalden was stunned. All he could do was stare at the recorder. Finally he sat down. Charley went to the refrigerator, took out a beer, opened it, looked at Vanalden and shook his head.

"She's the one that set me up? How the hell did she manage that?"

"I have no idea. Either as to who she is, how she did it or who she's reporting to. That's the important part. Who's her boss? But maybe we can find out. In the meantime, don't even think about it."

Vanalden looked back. "What?" he finally said. "Think about what?"

"You don't dare go back to your motel."

"Obviously. Jesus Christ, damn. So what are you saying?"

"There's only one bed in here and I'm already sharing it with a bunch of creepy, crawly, six legged friends. Sorry."

It wasn't funny nor was it meant to be. But it certainly clarified the point that Vanalden had been extremely reckless. And damned lucky. With that Charley went to the bedroom and retrieved his briefcase. Opening it, he took out his phone number decoder, hooked it up to the recorder and played the first part of the tape back. Writing down the phone number it displayed, he spoke.

"Brentwood, I'd say," he commented, looking over at Vanalden.

Still half dazed, Vanalden stared back at him.

"God," he said at last.

Charley remained quiet. He pulled a sack of potato chips out of the cupboard and sat down across from Vanalden. He opened his drink, tore the top off the sack, took a large handful of chips and pushed it over. Vanalden looked in and shook his head no.

"A woman giving Tony orders! Can you believe that? Who the hell could she be?"

"Hopefully I'll get to find out after I'm done here."

"But... You know what? I'd bet she's Rudy Stark's old girlfriend. The guy who fell overboard. Jeez. And the way she was giving Tony orders, do you think..."

"What?"

"She must have jumped from her old bed right into that of whoever is now in charge?"

"Any idea who that might be, besides the biggest bad ass on

the block?"

"Seriously?"

"Seriously, you don't have a clue and you know it. But she is definitely not your best friend."

"Yeah. No kidding," Vanalden scowled. "And what are you going to do about her?"

"Maybe nothing," Charley said contritely. "But since she seems to be talking for whoever is a step above Tony I guess I'd better find out," he continued. Then he was quiet, mulling this new development over.

"Okay. So what now? What about Tony?" Vanalden asked, too concerned about his own safety.

"That's what the dynamite is for."

"And if they don't find me first, I take the rap for that one too. Is that what you want me for?"

"Looks like it, huh?" Charley said matter of factly, watching Vanalden's reaction.

"Maybe you set me up too."

"I didn't even know who you were until I checked out your car tags when I saw you at Vince's. And from everything I recorded, they were on to you almost immediately."

Vanalden lapsed back into silence. Then he said he was getting claustrophobic. Needed to get out of there. Some coffee, maybe. Or another drink. And he knew a great place.

"And how were you going to get there?"

"Yeah, well, shit," he said, realizing they already knew what he had replaced his first vehicle with. "Good point."

"Can't leave that thing here, either. Just in case."

"What then? A cab?"

"No. Drive down to the mall, wipe your prints off it and leave it there. Then go in the grocery store and out the back. I'll pick you up in about twenty minutes."

"How you going to do that?"

"I have my own transportation."

"You never said. Where is it?"

"Parked in an alley about three blocks from here."

"This is it. Turn in here." Vanalden said to Charley as they came down the road to what appeared to be the last house on the edge of town. An older, single story structure, steps up and wooden porch out front, a glowing Coors Beer sign blinking in the window. On the door, another sign badly in need of paint that said, TINA"S. Parking was along the side and in the rear. With only four cars in the lot, Charley parked on the side and they went in.

There were about a dozen stools along the battered bar, three tables and four booths along the far wall. Three solitary drinkers sat spaced out along the bar. Charley and Vanalden went to the far end where there was a semblance of privacy and sat down to the tune of a morose country western song emanating from the juke box. A young woman came out of the back room behind the bar and spotted them. She smiled at Vanalden. One look and it was obvious to Charley why Vanalden had wanted to go there.

Medium height, great body stuffed into jeans and blouse, she removed two glasses from the cold box and drew two beers from one of the taps behind the bar. Setting the drinks down in front of them, she looked at Vanalden and smiled. He, in turn, introduced Charley as Charley. Tina put out her hand and shook his, then she and Vanalden chatted. How you doing? How's business? How late you gonna be open tonight?

The usual, she said before she left to take refills to her other customers. When she rang up their money she took half a hand full of quarters out of the till and went to the juke box where she picked several new selections.

Vanalden watched her the whole time and when she turned back around he motioned to her. Want to dance? She nodded and when they started to move, she leaned into him. He steered her towards the far corner, turned her so her back was to the bar and kissed her. She broke the contact of his lips and smiled at him. A young guy at the far end swiveled around and looked at them with an expression that said, who the hell is this guy? She never danced with me. He tipped up his glass and drained it, set it down and went out the door. After that Tina fussed around the bar, wiping it down, washing glasses, checking on the two other customers whose only intentions seemed to be to keep on drinking.

"Do they have any food in here that doesn't come in a sack?" Charley asked.

"She makes a great chili burger," Vanalden stated.

"For breakfast? Good grief."

"Breakfast? It's getting dark out."

"Yeah, and I'm starved," Charley said as he lifted his glass and called to her. When she brought two more beers he asked for a burger and an order of fries.

"Same here," Vanalden stated and when she finally returned with the food, Vanalden reached for her hand and held it. She didn't pull away and their eyes lingered on each other. Jeez, thought Charley. Something serious was going on here. Vanalden was already in enough trouble. He couldn't be walking around in a damned daze at a time like this. Then Vanalden spoke to her in a low voice.

"Why don't you call your friend. What's her name... Jane?"

"Jean," she said and looked at Charley. "I don't know. They may not like each other."

"Not for him. So I can take you back there," he said and nodded towards the back.

Tina blushed and giggled.

"Can't you wait till closing?"

"Three more hours. God no."

Tina stared at their interwoven hands and was silent for a long time. Then she went back down the bar to the phone and made a call as Vanalden glanced at Charley and shook his head.

"Don't have enough problems, huh?" Charley said.

Vanalden shrugged. "If I'm still alive in another month that woman is going to be my next wife," he said. "And if you're still alive you can be best man."

"You should be so lucky." Charley said and raised his glass, clanked it against Vanalden's and took a drink just as Tina waved her hand and signaled ten minutes to Vanalden. Ten minutes later the front door opened and a dark haired, sincere, earthy looking woman dressed in jeans and sweater walked in, holding the door for another customer who followed her in. She went around behind the bar and spoke to Tina. Tina responded and went to wait on the new customer while Jean turned and looked at Vanalden and Charley. She gave Vanalden a cool nod and turned away.

Tina popped the cap off a tall bottle of Miller's and set it in front of the new arrival, then she checked the coolers, went to the back and returned with a pack of beer cans which she put in the cold box directly behind the bar. Then she and Jean talked for several minutes. An older man came in and pulled up a stool. Another bottle. Coors this time. Five minutes later Tina went in the back room without looking at Vanalden. The juke box mechanism swung the last CD back into its home slot, retrieved the next selection and rotated it into place. A revived Emmi Lou Harris song from the seventies. When the music began Vanalden got up quietly and went down the hallway in the back that led to the restrooms. Obviously not the only place it connected to Charley thought, as forty five minutes went by before Vanalden returned with a quiet grin on his face. Ten minutes later Tina reappeared and focused her attention on the customers at the other end of the bar. Then she brought Jean down and introduced her to Charley. Jean gave Vanalden a skewed look but didn't say anything.

"Sit down," Tina told her, nodding to the stool beside Charley on the other side of the bar. "I'll get you a glass of wine."

Jean looked at her watch, then back at Tina. Tina smiled and raised her eyebrows, glanced at Vanalden then back at Jean. Jean shook her head in disbelief and sat down.

"Just one," she said.

Two more people came in the bar, a man and a woman. Tina went to wait on them as Jean, Charley and Vanalden worked on their drinks in silence. Then Jean stood up.

"Well, I have a good book to finish," she said. "Would you like to walk me home?" she asked Charley. "It's only about a block."

Her house was small and modest and they had yet to speak as they approached. Somehow the silence had seemed comfortable enough to Charley until she unlocked the front door. Then he felt that he could have done better.

"Thanks for seeing me home," she said, sounding sincere.

"My pleasure," Charley replied. "I guess I'm not very good company tonight."

"You seem preoccupied."

"Yes. I guess I am. I'm sorry. I wasn't trying to be rude."

"I know. It's okay. I'm impressed with men who aren't always trying to impress a woman. Refreshing, actually. Can I get you something before you go?" she asked as she opened the door and motioned him in.

"I'm a little tired of beer," he said inside.

Jean went to the kitchen cupboard and took out a bottle.

"Brandy," she asked.

"Sounds good," he nodded. "Are you joining me?"

She found two brandy snifters and poured them both about a third full.

"Sit down," she said as she handed him one.

He sat on one end of the couch and she sat near the middle, just far enough away to define the situation.

"Have you known Stu very long?"

"Stu?... Oh, you mean Vanalden. No. Maybe a few weeks. Strictly business. How about you?"

"A few days at the most."

"You're concerned about Tina."

"I've never seen her behave this way before. I just hope she doesn't get hurt."

"Yeah. But there's some powerful chemistry there. I don't know much about his ability to follow through but I think his intentions are honorable."

"I hope so. But, who knows. Life is short," she shrugged. "And where are you from?"

"L.A."

"Married?"

"Yes...no. Not anymore."

"What does that mean?"

"She... ah. We're separated."

"A difficult relationship?"

Charley shrugged.

"How about you?" he asked and looked at her.

"Two years ago," she said. "An auto accident."

Charley took a long sip of his brandy and was quiet a moment before asking, "You've never remarried?"

"Never met anyone I cared that much about. Would you like some more, she asked, indicating his glass.

63

"Thanks, no. I should be getting back."

She looked directly at him. "They'll never miss you."

"True enough. But I'm driving. Of course after what they just, ah....., yeah."

Jean got up, brought back the bottle and added a little to each glass.

"Why don't you stay the night?" she asked, holding his look.

God, he thought. She was a very attractive woman, full of feeling, still locked into her pain but openly sensitive to the wounded and vulnerable around her. How could he trust himself?

"I wouldn't be good for you," he told her, believing it to be the truth.

"We can just hold each other. I'd be happy with that."

It had been dark for nearly two hours when Charley and Vanalden made their way up onto the rise behind Tony's house. The quarter moon was already above the eastern horizon. It was an adequate amount of light for what Charley needed to do. He set down the black duffel bag he had been carrying, got to his knees and motioned for Vanalden to get down also. After a careful scan around the area he pulled on a pair of latex gloves, unzipped the bag and started removing a variety of items from it.

"What the hell?" Vanalden said in a loud voice when he saw what was there. "You can't be serious."

"Keep your damned voice down," Charley said harshly, "and stay still for christ's sake," he mumbled as he did another three sixty look around.

Quashed, Vanalden was quiet until Charley broke the silence.

Charley held up what appeared to be a model rocket about an inch and a half in diameter and two feet long of which there were two more.

"Two sticks of dynamite in each one," he pointed out. "Steel tipped nose cone to penetrate the window glass and lodge the thing in the wall inside until it blows. Flip out tail fins to make it go straight. Igniter and high velocity solid fuel engine in the back which will burn through once it hits its mark and light the dynamite."

Vanalden just shook his head. Are you kidding, he said to

himself. He still didn't believe it.

"Jeez, my father used to help us make those things when we were kids. Not very reliable. Or predictable. How you going to point them? Not just going to run them up the standard old steel rod, are you?"

"How about plain old pvc water pipe?"

"And put them through a window which is what, fifty yards away? Can't be done."

"Seventy five yards and says you. I've made a few refinements. And I test fired twenty three of them out in the desert with dummy loads. Put the last five through a foot square opening at a hundred yards."

"God, really? What's the secret?"

"Pay attention. I'll show you," Charley said and picked up a square wooden base with spikes protruding from the bottom which he sat on the ground and pressed firmly into the dirt. Then he picked up a three foot long piece of plastic pipe and clamped it into an adjustable metal pedestal attached to the top of the base. Next he clipped a small, four power rifle scope to the pipe. Sighting through it at the rear window of Tony's house, he tweaked the adjustable pedestal, aligning the plastic pipe guidance tube. Removing the scope, he picked up the first rocket and pointed out some additional features.

"Three little nylon bumps front and rear to keep the sides of the rocket from dragging on the launch tube. Reduces friction. And the tail fins have just a tiny bit of curve on the ends to give it some ballistic spin."

"Jeeez, just like a damned bullet."

"Yeah. My final touch. That's what makes them so accurate. So, collapse the spring loaded tail fins like this and slid it down the tube backwards....... There. Then take the two ends of the impulse signal wire and twist them onto the igniter wires sticking out the back and that one is ready," Charley said as he turned on a tiny little pen light with an additional filter over it for further dimming and made a last inspection.

"Good enough," he said. "Two more to go."

"Yeah," Vanalden said, still skeptical. "But what if you still miss? What then?"

"Look at the house. What's it made of?"

Vanalden looked but still didn't understand.

"Wood siding," Charley stated. "And the tip of the rocket is steel, remember? And very sharp. If it misses the window it will embed itself in the siding and still blow a hole in the wall.

"Hmmmmm."

Forty five minutes later they were done. Three rockets with two sticks of dynamite each, pointed at three different windows in the second floor of Tony's house, all belonging to Tony's office. Lights were on throughout the building, there were three cars in the drive and at least three people moving about inside. The electric rocket igniters were all wired together in parallel and Charley was ready with a thousand foot spool of light gauge, twisted pair, solid copper telephone wire.

Vanalden squinted at the setup in the dim light as Charley made the final connections and looped the wire firmly around a short post in the top of the last base to secure it.

"Are you just going to leave all this stuff here?" he asked. "Or are you going to drag it out with the wire? It doesn't look strong enough."

"Evidence retrieval?"

"Damn right. The less the authorities have to work with, the better off we are."

"So, let them waste their time. Everything I used is stolen, including your contribution of the dynamite. And I've gone over it all with a microscope. It's spotless. That's the idea. I want it found. And I want them to figure out how it was done."

"What? Our asses are already hanging out a mile. Jesus. What for?"

"My own, down-home, fear based kind of terrorism."

"Which is?"

"I want them to believe I can reach anybody, anywhere they go."

Vanalden considered the statement. "Guess so. You've made a believer out of me. Except for one thing."

"Really, What's that?"

"What if one of the igniters doesn't work or one of the engines is a dud?"

"Stop being so damned negative all the time. Six full sticks of dynamite is a bit of overkill, if the use of that word doesn't bother you. Even one good rocket should take care of things."

Vanalden said nothing as Charley zipped up the duffel bag and slid an arm through the carrying strap. Then he picked up the spool of wire and ran a stick through the center holes so it would unwind as he moved away.

"Okay," he said to Vanalden when he was ready. "Now get your ass out of here."

"What? Were am I going?"

"Doesn't matter. Just get out of here. You know where the car is. The keys are behind the visor. Go get Tina. Go to Vegas, get married. Don't get married. Whatever, but get your ass out of here. I'll give you half an hour to be somewhere so you have an alibi."

"But... Jesus, Charley. Or who the hell ever you are. What the hell is this?"

"You've done your part. I don't need you anymore."

"Yeah, but we're partners."

"Not anymore. I don't have anything to lose. You do, so get out of here."

"Bullshit. If you're going to take out this asshole, I'm staying, no matter what."

Charley stared at Vanalden in the dim light and shook his head. "Don't be such a dumb ass."

"So! I'm a dumb ass. I'm staying."

"Suit yourself."

"I am. Now what do I get to do that's useful?"

"Okay, dumb ass. If you insist. This amount of wire will allow me to be down behind the hill there in that clutch of brush. I need five minutes to get set up. You stay out of sight and get your butt down to the street. Hide out behind that tree you pissed on last week. When I'm ready I'll call your cell phone with mine. If everything looks okay, you call Tony on his cell phone. Do you remember the numbers?"

"I do. Then what?"

"Then tell him not to hang up on you because he doesn't have time to call 911. Tell him his house is about to blow up and he needs to get everyone outside and down the driveway if he wants to live. You should be able to see them in the drive from your position. When he tells you they are clear and you can see them, you call 911. Then you call me and get your ass out of there. I'll meet you back at the car. Everything clear?"

"Clear enough."

"What's wrong?"

"I thought you were going to do him in."

"Don't tell me you're disappointed?"

"No. I, ahh, either way. Honest. The bastard probably deserves it and..."

"And my agenda changed. Tony's only guilty by association. But the message will be just as clear. Maybe even clearer when he realizes how close he came. Maybe some of the other rats will start jumping ship," Charley said.

Then he leaned closer to Vanalden. "Unless you'd rather not make that call. Hell, we can just stand right here like a couple of dumbies and watch the whole thing if you want."

"No. Your way sounds better. Thanks. No problem," Vanalden said, obviously relieved.

"Okay, stay down, be quiet and get moving. And.... tell him you're calling for Charley."

This time Charley and Vanalden were in one of the booths along the wall at Tina's Bar and there were several empty beer bottles on the table. It was Friday evening and the place was nearly full so Tina had been unable to spend much time with them, leaving her part time waitress to bring the drinks. Still she would come by when she got the chance, bringing them more chips or just to smile at Vanalden who would squeeze her hand or try to pat her on the butt. It was clear where he would be spending the night once the bar was closed. It was also clear in the moments when she wasn't there that Vanalden had other concerns, mostly about his own future. Then he had a moment of awareness that took him outside his own corner, a question that had come to mind from time to time but that he never had a direct opportunity to ask. This time he did before it got away from him again.

"I've been meaning to ask," he said. "Actually I have a couple of questions. I mean, now that we have been through this thing with Tony together, we aren't exactly in a position to rat on each other."

"A guy will always rat on his partner if it comes to the point where his ass is on the line. Happens all the time. But I'll trust you on this one. What's the question?"

"Okay. I'm still not clear as to what brought you into this or who you really are. Not that it would be hard to find out. All I would have had to do is send one of those beer bottles you drank from to a friend who has access to fingerprint files. But I let it go. Guess I liked things just the way they were, or are."

"For now, at least. Is that what you're saying?"

"Yeah. For now. What the hell."

"And what about you? What did you ever get out of being a cop? Especially a narc. Talk about putting your ass in harm's way."

"Precisely. That's was the whole idea."

"Okay. Explain that one to me."

"Advanced calculus and differential equations were never my thing. I'm not enough of a sleaze to make a good attorney, running a business would absolutely drive me nuts. But with being a narc, I at least had one thing. I knew I was alive. Being on the street does that for you. Sure, it's a go-nowhere job but it has some excitement to it until you get to the end. And if you're lucky, maybe you don't make it to retirement. What the hell. All these dull brained people out there going through the motions, so blunted and stupefied by the time they get to forty or fifty that they don't know the difference anymore. Not me, dammit."

"Well, maybe they don't like living in fear."

"In today's world? Ha. They live in fear anyway. Every damned one of them. What if they lose their job, get seriously ill, their partner is gonna leave them, someone's going to find where they cheated on the taxes and they're going to jail, a drive by shooter is going to wipe them out, they'll never be able to save enough to retire on, they're going to do something stupid and piss God off and he'll zap them straight to hell. I mean, Jesus."

"Thoreau's lives of quiet desperation."

"No shit. Fucked up lives of quiet desperation. Ever meet anyone who didn't come from a dysfunctional family or wasn't behaving in some dysfunctional way? I haven't."

"You sound rather bitter."

"No doubt about that. My parents should have gotten some kind of award. They never did a thing in their whole lives except meaningless bullshit. And then, in the end, they get sick because they never took care of themselves so they have to make a statement and show everyone how brave they are by hanging onto nothing, dragging everyone else down with them. And the god damned doctors... Well, no point in going there. Jesus. I'm sorry. What was that all about? Damn," he said and chugalugged down his beer. Then he looked back at Charley and changed the subject.

"So, tell me," he said. "How did you ever find Vince to begin with? I had info from when I was still on the force. But I doubt if you had those connections. Or am I under estimating you? If you don't mind sharing as long as it's not too incriminating."

"Nothing incriminating about that part. I was at a crime scene last spring when I saw this Lincoln drive by with two rough looking guys in it. Pretty stupid but criminals sometimes do that. They were trying too hard not to look at what happened but still looking. Something not right about it. I even saw the rear plate on the car. It was stolen. Came off of a Ford station wagon that belonged to some old couple down in Orange County. When I asked your brothers in blue why not check out all the new Lincolns in L.A. they laughed like hell. I mean, who drives Lincolns anymore? But they said there were at least nine thousand of them less than five years old in the metropolitan area alone and who should we send the bill to when they were done checking them all out. And why? So you happened to spot a Lincoln with stolen plates on it? Lucky you, and so what? End of story."

"Okay. So you couldn't trace the car. How did you find them?"

"I asked them for a print out of all those cars and they laughed again. So I hacked into the DMV records. First I eliminated all vehicles over two years old which helped because Lincoln sales have been declining so I was down to about three. Three thousand. Then I eliminated every owner over sixty. That cut it in half again. Then I was going to do the under thirty bunch but do you know there wasn't a one in that age group? Anyway, there I was with this still impossibly long list. I damn near gave up myself," Charley said, shaking his head as he thought about it, then took a long drink of beer as Vanalden waited.

"So, for lack of anything more inspiring, I made a bunch of wild ass guesses. I removed every woman from the list and everyone with joint title, man and woman. Also all funeral homes, limo services, rentals and businesses I recognized. Now I was down to around four hundred. Then I figured, would some low life really have a car he used for that kind of business and register it in his own name? Didn't seem like it. That got me down to maybe a hundred and twenty. What kind of a business would thugs use for a front? Laundries, junk yards, trash removal, juke boxes, beer distributor, auto body shop, what? Now I was down to about thirty. That seemed manageable so I started making the rounds. I was at nineteen, I think. A small trucking company down in El Segundo. And who is driving the car but the two guys I saw in the drive by. Sid and Louis. Who just happened to be working for Vince Sands. Luck wins every time."

Vanalden pondered Charley's words. Then he caught Tina's attention and held up his empty beer bottle. When he handed her the large bill he had been trying to give her all evening she again pushed it away with a smile and patted him on the cheek. After she was gone he sat there thinking.

"Okay," he said, staring at Charley. "And a couple more things."

Charley waited.

"You really did use gun powder at Vince's? Jesus. And it did all that damage? Must have been a lot."

Charley explained how many boxes of shot gun shells he had emptied out and how he had made the shaped charges he had used as Vanalden continued to look at him wide eyed.

"Well, I hope I never piss you off," he said. "But how did you get it inside the house?"

"The damned house must have been built by some transplanted mid-westerner back in the thirties. It had a basement. So, I crawled in the basement window. Put bugs on the phone and under Vince's study. And after I got all the information I could gather I crawled back in to set the charges which I was able to detonate by remote. Nothing complicated."

Speechless, Vanalden blinked his eyes, leaned back and scratched his head.

"Jesus," he said again after a couple of minutes. "I was a narc and we walked in on some pretty bad shit from time to time that scared the literal hell out of me but you're the coolest son-of-a-bitch I ever met."

"Is that a compliment?"

"Maybe, for now."

"Well, either way. If you're motivated enough, you can accomplish almost anything. Of course, yeah. I guess you have to keep your cool doing it. Directed emotion. That's the key. Otherwise it's over the edge and you're done. Your own victim."

"So. Was Vince the big one? Is that why you didn't kill Tony? Is this the end of it for you?"

"I don't know. What about you?" Charley said, not yet willing to share his future plans.

"Well, it's been nice but I don't think I'm cut out for this kind of life. I could end up in the slammer with some of my former arrestees."

"You should have found a woman like Tina twenty years ago and gone into banking or something."

"But I didn't. So, now what?" he wanted to know. "No matter you didn't wipe out Tony, I still carry some blame because they spotted me at the scene. And at Vince's as you so clearly pointed out. And none of those people are going to forget it. Ever."

"True enough but just remember. I may have done the deed but you got yourself in trouble. All alone."

"Yeah. Stupid, rash. Like you said about cool. I was too damned pissed off to think it through. But at least I feel a little better knowing what you've done. And how you did it. That was clever."

"No. Just expeditious."

"Expeditious? Jesus, Charley. Well, maybe I should stick around. Looks like I still have a lot to learn."

"No, you did okay. But if you had some specialized electronics surveillance skills or had a bucket of money and nothing better to do, or whatever. Otherwise I don't need you and don't want you. So far as the organization goes, you've incriminated yourself. But I don't want to be responsible if it goes any further. And that's not being noble. Working alone is safer for one thing. And more flexible. I also don't visualize blowing up any more houses."

"So, what then, if you don't mind my asking?"

"Time will tell. Maybe some final outrageous, over the top act. And hopefully enough tape recordings to destroy a major west coast crime operation. "

"That woman, Margaret. I guess you have a good place to start."

Charley just shrugged and tipped up his beer bottle for a long swallow.

"Sorry," Vanalden said and finished his own beer. Then he signaled to the waitress instead of Tina. Maybe if Tina wouldn't take his money, she would.

"Well," he said after she brought the next two. "It has been interesting."

"Indeed," Charley replied. Then he nodded towards Tina. "What about her?" he asked.

Looking lost, Vanalden shook his head back and forth.

"Jesus," he said. "What a mess."

"So. What are you going to do about it?"

"Right now I don't have a clue. Except that I need to get out of her life for a while until things clear up."

"Or take her with you."

"I already asked. She won't go. Besides, where the hell would we be safe?"

"Go back to LA, get yourself reinstated and go back to work. I doubt they would murder a cop."

"You can't be serious."

"Okay, so what then?"

"I think I'll go back east till it all settles out. Maybe look up someone I used to work for back in..."

"Wait. I'd rather not know. And how are you going to get there, anyway? Walk?"

Vanalden shrugged his shoulders and again looked at Tina behind the bar, now with a very sad and distant look on his face.

"I still have some back pay coming. Except I'm not sure I want to show my face long enough to collect. But, what the hell. I'll figure it out."

"I'm sure you will," Charley said as he reached in his pocket and tossed his car keys on the table. Vanalden looked at them questioningly.

"I can't. You just spent a lot of money on it."

"You'd rather I left it outside the junkyard like we did with yours?"

"No, but...?"

"But nothing," Charley said with a dismissive wave.

Vanalden picked up the keys and turned them over in his hand.

"Jeez," he said.

Charley sat and looked at Vanalden for a moment. Then he got to his feet and held out his hand.

Vanalden looked at it a second before he realized what was happening. He took Charley's hand and they shook.

"Take care of yourself. And say goodbye to Tina for me. Oh...almost forgot. The pink slip is in the glove compartment. Or it was when we came in. Maybe you should go see before someone steals it." Charley said, then turned and walked out the door.

Vanalden was stunned at first and sat there for a good long minute. Then he took a long drink of his beer, got up and followed Charley outside. Too late, he saw a cab pulling away. He stood there another minute looking at it disappear, then he went around to the back of the dimly lit parking lot and looked at the car Charley had left him. Another older Chevy but still newer than his own original vehicle he was forced to abandon two times back. Days earlier he had thought Charley was crazy and had chided him badly. New tires, new belts and hoses, plugs, oil change and lube on that old piece of shit? Good grief. But now...? Was it just for him? Why would the man have done that? Damn.

He put a hand on the roof of the car and looked back towards the street out front, seeing the cab driving away in the night all over again. Why was he feeling so emotional, he wondered. Then he opened the passenger door and the dome light came on. He reached in and opened the glove compartment. A thick envelope lay there. He stared at it, even more confused. Then he took it out and went back inside. Alone in the booth, he pushed it around, stared at it, drummed his fingers on it and finished the half bottle of beer he had left before he picked it up and opened it. The title to the automobile was on top. Underneath was a thick pack of hundred dollar bills. He counted to fifty. Jesus. And that was only about half. He raised his eyes and looked around the barroom, wondering if anyone had been watching. Didn't seem like it but he still shoved the stack into his front pants pocket out of the way. Wiping his forehead on his sleeve, he sighed and scratched the back of his neck. Then Tina was there with another bottle of beer in her hand. She sat it down.

"You okay?" she asked with a trace of concern.

He ran his hand through his hair and over the top of his head.

"Yeah," he said. "I think so."

"Where did Charley go?"

"Back up to L.A. I would guess. Said he had another job he wanted to follow up on."

"Okay. Well, about another forty five minutes," she said as she smiled and squeezed his hand. "Just let me finish up."

God almighty, Vanalden said to himself. Somehow he felt compelled to sit her down and tell her the whole truth. She certainly deserved the honesty. But did he dare? How could he do that to her? Somehow that prospect seemed even worse than he might have felt if he hadn't made the phone call and Tony had been blown up inside his house. Then he looked at the last beer bottle Charley had drunk from and very carefully picked it up.

THIRTEEN

"You're late," the Watch Commander growled as detectives Ashby and Benson came into the squad room at Parker Center. "The Deputy Chief is going to have your asses," he snickered.

"Screw you," Ashby returned. "We just got the call."

"So why aren't you upstairs like good boys?"

"What? Didn't hear me the first time?" Ashby retorted and then made his way down to his old metal desk jammed up against the wall. Unlocking his file drawer he withdrew a rather thin folder and returned. Nodding to Benson, they left, heading for the elevator. One flight up the were told to go right in by the Chief's secretary. Inside were three men. The Chief, no scowl on his face but business as usual, was behind his desk and two men in suits and ties occupied two of the three remaining chairs in the room.

Good, Ashby thought. He didn't want to sit down anyway. Going straight to the Chief's desk, he handed over the folder he had brought along. The Chief opened it and checked the cover page inside. His eyebrow went up.

"How did you know?" he asked.

"We heard there was another house bombing down in the San Diego area."

The Chief looked at Ashby. "What? You're not going to give me any guff on this one?"

"Not a bit. No sir."

"Something wrong? Are you all stalled out on it?" he asked, thumping the folder.

"Not hardly. This fighting over turf shit just gets a little old after while, so what the hell. It's not like we have a shortage of crime in the city anymore," Ashby said. To him, some criminal getting himself blown up was already a big step in the right direction and he felt no personal ownership in trying to apprehend the perpetrator. Now if some innocent bystander had been killed like in Santa Monica, that might be different. But he wasn't about to say so.

"Okay. Well," the Chief said as he stood up and handed the file over to one of his visitors. "Introduce yourselves then and go down to the conference room. And when you're done, you two step back in here," he said to the two detectives. He didn't understand Ashby's willingness to give over a case so easily. Had he missed something?

Two hours later Stan Gibson, dressed in a light weight summer suit with tie, got off the elevator in the Westwood Federal Building. Down the hall he went into the office he had been directed too. An attractive, dark haired secretary/receptionist was typing away on her computer keyboard. She stopped and looked up. Their eyes met and held. Then, inappropriately but purposely, Gibson put out his hand.

"Hi...I'm Stan Gibson."

She rose, holding back for a second. Then she took it and they shook lightly.

"He's expecting you. I'll let me tell him you're here."

She went to the closed door behind her and knocked lightly as Stan followed her with his eyes, taking some personal notes. Long legged. Great hips in a tight skirt, nice full blouse, ohh my. After the knock she leaned in.

"Mr. Gibson is here," she said and turned back to Stan, knowing full well what he was looking at and secretly charmed.

"Please go in," she told him and lowered her eyes. Then she pulled the door shut behind him.

Jack Kremel, a man with some grey at the temples and years of experience to his credit rose from his oversized office chair behind his ordinary governmental desk.

"Stan," he said. "Good to see you. How was the flight?"

They shook hands enthusiastically.

"I'm good, Jack. Decent flight and nice reception," Stan said with a nod to the outer office.

"I thought you'd like that," Jack smiled. "But business precedes. Meet your new partner, George."

"I've heard a couple of good things about you," George said as they also shook. "I just hope they're true."

"For your sake or mine?"

"Maybe for both. And good luck. I heard she's a lesbian."

"Well, have a seat. We have a lot to talk about," Jack said as he ignored George's comment and eased back into his chair. Jack was the Special Agent in charge. George had served under him for almost three years and Stan had been pulled in on special assignment from back east where he had worked with Jack on another bombing case several years earlier.

"But before we get started, Ruth and I are expecting you for dinner tonight. We have some catching up to do. I assume you're still footloose and free."

"For the most part, yeah. But lately I've been thinking. Maybe it's time."

"Like the Sultan and bachelor story?" George put in.

Was this what he was going to be in for, Stan wondered. Some partner George was going to be. But he went along with it. "Hmmm, don't remember that one," he replied. "Must be a moral to it, huh?"

"Could be. The Sultan had fifty wives and died in bed at

ninety five. The bachelor died on the street corner at thirty five trying to pick up a woman."

Stan waited, not about to ask.

"So, the moral. It's not the sex that kills you. It's the chasing after it," George finished, getting a reserved smile from Jack and a polite chuckle from Stan.

"Anyway," Jack said after a moment., getting things back on track, knowing Stan would find a way to keep George in line by himself. "Here's the LAPD copy of the file we picked up this morning. A few interesting bits in there, especially in lieu of what happened in San Diego. But it needs a lot of follow up. That's where you two come in, for now. Don't be afraid to touch base with Detective Ashby downtown, either. Cooperation for a change."

Stan took the document, did a quick flip through it and set it on the corner of Jack's desk as Jack continued.

"As for the incident down south two nights ago, a couple of significant things. First, an immediate call to 911, probably from the bomber because the noise of the explosion is on the tape. That call got a fast response from the Fire Department no more than a mile away. When they pulled up there were four petrified people standing in the driveway. Tony Platt, the owner of the dwelling, and his wife. A goon of Tony's named Wilt Booth and guess who? A member of the state crime commission. Walt Strathern. They had been warned at the last minute and the house was empty."

"Warned? You mean warned that the house was going up? That's kind of strange," Stan said.

"Strange place for a man of Strathern's stature to be, too," George added.

"Yes, isn't it. And even more interesting are these," Jack said as he dumped out a large manila envelope containing several miniature cassette tapes.

"This morning's mail. Most are earlier recordings from what has to have been a phone tap and room bug back at Vince Sand's house here in L.A.. They have been edited but there is still enough there to show there was a link between Sands and Judge Adams on the Superior Court bench. They also link Sands to Tony Platt which further confirms our reason for taking over the case. And that one, the one with the red dot on it, that is a conversation between Tony and the commissioner. All illegally obtained but not by any authorities so they should be admissible if it comes to that. However, as you may not know yet, Judge Adams chose to end his own life a few days after Vince's house went up."

"Maybe the commissioner needs to be in protective custody so he doesn't do the same thing," Stan said.

"He will be, like it or not. Tomorrow at the latest. The investigation into his association with Platt is already underway. Problem is, without any convictions on his record, Platt is only a suspected criminal, not a proven one."

Stan took out his pen and poked around in the pile. Seven tapes, ninety minutes each. Over ten hours of listening time. Obviously his after dinner homework tonight.

"They're clean," Jack assured him. "Not a speck or a partial. Mailed from downtown L.A. last night. Nothing on the envelope either. They have also been duped so have at them," Jack said and was quiet. After a moment Stan slid the tapes back into the envelope and looked up at Jack. Obviously there was more. He nodded.

"Yeah," Jack said as he leaned back and scratched his chin. "And as usual, I saved the best part for last. First thing the morning after, the forensics people did a thorough search of the open area behind Tony's house. They found three of these," he said as he reached down and brought out one of the base plates with the improvised plastic water pipe launch tube attached to it. George hadn't seen it as yet, either, and both he and Stan leaned over to inspect it.

"Very peculiar," George said, not about to make a guess.

"Sure is," Stan agreed as he ran a finger along the plastic pipe and frowned.

"I didn't get it either until one of the lab guys figured it out. And then when they found three of these in the rubble it seems pretty clear," Jack said and also placed one of Charley's hollowed out piece of steel nose cones alongside the other items.

George and Stan both stared at the pieces for a moment and simultaneously showed their recognition.

"Couldn't be," George said with a shake of his head.

"Really?" Stan questioned.

"Exactly. Model rockets. Three windows at the back of the house, one on each side and one rear. Three guidance stands still aimed to where the windows used to be, so three rockets. The lab work says it was dynamite and the rare element tracer it was tagged with says that it was the same stuff stolen from a construction site out in the desert about a week earlier. Six sticks. The damage assessment at the scene shows an equivalence. Thus three rockets with two sticks in each."

"Astounding," Stan stated. "What the hell is this all about? Some loony, model maker kid with a grudge? But that doesn't make any sense. What was used on Sands' house? More dynamite?"

"No. Different M.O.. Gunpowder in the basement of the building. Readily available for the serious gun buff who does his own reloading. Or, if one were ambitious, I suppose they could empty out a bunch of over the counter ammunition. The serious part, however, is that whatever the source, the explosive had to have been formed into shaped charges to provide the damage pattern that resulted. Everything went straight up. That means someone with munitions experience. Maybe ex military."

"This isn't going to be easy, is it?" Stan said. "Two houses blown up, both belonging to members of the same criminal organization. So that has to be a connection, even if the M.O. was different."

"Yeah, but why kill Sands and not Tony? Why call him and tell him to get his ass outside first? Which reminds me. What about phone records of the calls to his house and 911?"

"Right. Almost forgot. An untraceable cell phone. Actually, two of them which indicates more than one individual involved. Reconstructing, phone A, if you will, the one making the call to Tony, and then 911, first received a call from a phone B, obviously nearby and off the same phone tower. Then the call from phone A to Tony. A very short time later, probably when everyone had exited the property, A called 911, then A called B and the house went up."

"So if there are two of them, maybe they each had their own separate area of expertise. A munitions guy and a rocket maker. That might make it easier. Aren't there amateur rocket societies, or something like that?" Stan asked.

"Lots of them. But they have seriously evolved. I believe someone actually shot one at the moon not long ago. And reached it."

"Jesus. And with all the open desert out here there must be hundreds of them in the area."

"Fascinating," George said. "Just when I promised my ex wife I'd drive her back to St. Louis to see her mother. Guess she'll be going alone."

"Looks like it," Jack said. "But it's the extrapolation that bothers me. Maybe some Homeland Security implications."

"How so, Chief?"

"Think about it. A poor man's surface to surface missile. Some guy could set up in the cemetery across the road some night and blow the whole top right off this building. Or one hell of a lot of other buildings, if it came to that. Like even the White House. Even worse, little rockets can evolve into bigger rockets and with a little practice someone could set the launch tube on their shoulder and fire it like a Stinger or a Sidewinder missile. But aside from that... the fact that all those tapes have edited out blank spots on them would seem to indicate..."

"More excitement to come."

"Most likely. I want you to start from the beginning. First the Sands' case, then Platt. Re canvas the neighborhoods, recheck the debris. LAPD was pretty thorough but they haven't been on it very long so there's more out there. Has to be. Find it before something really serious happens. Meantime I've already got someone in research running down anyone who might have a predisposition towards blowing up houses."

Stan had been up and down both sides of the street where the remains of Vince's house with the yellow crime scene tape around it was, and had turned the corner. The mid afternoon heat was getting to him, along with the attitudes of some of the people he had interviewed. So far nothing. Absolutely nothing. Then four more houses before he finally began knocking on old Mrs. Brown's door.

"Who is it?" a woman's voice asked from behind the closed door.

Noticing the viewing lens in the door Stan held his badge up in front of it.

"FBI. Just a few questions if I might."

He waited, listening to the sound of a dead bolt, and finally the door knob being turned. At first she peeked out the partially opened door, then undid the security chain and swung it open, staying half way behind it.

Stan smiled at her. "Sorry to bother you ma'am. I'd like to ask you a few questions if you have the time."

"Oh. Well, that would be okay. Does this have anything to do with what happened behind me?"

"Yes. I'm afraid it does. The neighbor up the block said you sometimes rent out a room in your house."

"That's not, ahh, illegal, is it? I hope I haven't done anything wrong."

"No. Not a problem as far as I know. I was just wondering if you had anyone staying there now?"

"Yes I do. I'm sorry."

"It's not for myself. How long has this person been here?

"Actually just a few days so far. A college student. He seemed like a nice boy. I hope he's..."

"No problem. I'm sure he's fine. Who occupied the room before him?"

"An older gentleman. Charley.... my, my. That's interesting, now that I think of it. I don't believe I ever knew his last name. Oh dear. But a very nice man. Paid me two months in advance and all cash. And then that thing that happened behind us... Awful, just awful. Poor man. He was so concerned about having a quiet neighborhood to live in. And that horrible explosion just a week and a half after he moved in. He left the same day. Didn't ask for any money back either, and I thought that was strange. I was home but he just left a note on the door along with the key and disappeared."

"Do you know where he went?"

"No. Like I said, he didn't even say goodbye."

"Could you describe him for me?"

"Well, sure. He was about six feet. My Harold was six feet so I know that. Kind of a muscular man for his age, which must have been about the same as mine. Sixty seven, except he seemed awfully spry. Kinda handsome, too, except for that big mustache.

He wore glasses, also, but he was always looking over the top of them. And he had brown eyes. Not very pretty but intense when he was looking at me. I'd never forget those. Hmmm," she ended, the memory obviously still clear in her mind.

"Any unusual habits that you might have noticed?"

"I thought he was too quiet. Always wanted to be alone. Always walking his little dog around the block, especially in the evening. And then he stayed in his room but would never let me in to clean or anything. Even changed the lock."

"Did he leave anything behind?"

"Now isn't that strange? No he didn't. Not even a scrap of paper. And everything absolutely immaculate. I think he even washed the walls. But you know, he had the cutest little dog. And the other day I thought I saw the little boy down the street walking it around. Well, maybe not, but it sure looked the same."

Five minutes later Stan was down the street talking to Tommy's mother in their living room.

"What did you think of him?"

"He seemed like a gentle person. He was very concerned about finding a good home for the dog. And he was always very nice to Tommy."

"Did he say where he was going?"

"Up north. Montana, I think. Some business to attend to and he couldn't take the dog with him."

"Did you see any other strangers in the neighborhood during the same time period?"

"No. But then we don't pay that much attention. We don't even know most of our neighbors. Isn't that strange how everyone ignores each other?"

"Is there anything he might have handled when he was here?"

"Well, I've washed the dog dishes a dozen times. The dog food he brought over is also all gone. Just the dog's collar and leash."

"Where are they?"

"In the kitchen," she said and Stan followed as she went to get them.

Before she could pick them up he said, "Here, let me."

83

He then took a plastic baggy out of his jacket pocket and carefully put in the two items. It was probably a worthless lead, but, just in case.

FOURTEEN

The elegant Beverly Hills restaurant interior was designed such that the dining area was visible through glass panels and potted plants from the bar where Joe Carroll sat at the curved end. He was well dressed in slacks, dinner jacket and open necked shirt. He had intense blue eyes, a hint of greying hair and a well trimmed beard and mustache. When he turned his head slightly he could see through the leaves of the philodendrons into the dining area. He had been watching Margaret Ryan where she sat in a booth with a dapper looking older man, an attorney with a disreputable Century City firm. Margaret had an intimidating beauty about her that Joe could sense even from the distance he was at. They were sipping cocktails and having what seemed to be a serious discussion. It had begun with a sheet of paper Douds had passed to her.

"That makes it official. Rudy is now legally dead. And that was not easy to come by without a body. Furthermore, since he had no family to contest things, that makes all of his assets, your assets," Douds said with a bit of a smirk, like he should be receiving some special approval. Not only for what he had done but also for not remarking about how she might have managed to get Rudy to allow her to place her signature along side his on all those other pieces of paper that gave her joint title to everything. "So... Good for you. Looks like you are in excellent shape financially," he said as he looked at her, hoping for some sign of appreciation. For some reason he had decided he liked this young woman half his age. Nothing sexual, nothing fatherly. It was the enigma she presented to him and the concern he had come to have for her after Rudy had so conveniently disappeared. He had been dealing with mobsters almost from the day he passed his bar exam and he thought he had seen it all and there wasn't a damned one of them he wouldn't have secretly liked to see in prison. But her..... no. No in spite of the fact that he knew she had to be responsible for Rudy's demise and who knew what else. Plus the

84

fact that he knew if he ever crossed her or she saw him as expendable, she'd have him tossed in the dumpster in a heartbeat. Somehow it didn't matter. It just didn't. Somehow he still wanted her to survive and prosper. And he would help her with that if she would give him half a chance.

Margaret looked at the document and nodded affirmatively. Then she looked back at Douds. Interesting, she thought. He had done it so very expeditiously. Like everything else since she had taken over. What was that all about? Did Douds have some hidden agenda all his own? Caution was the key here, just like with everything else.

"Right. Good for me," she said somewhat sardonically. "Now we can get on with it. What's your opinion on that?"

"Don't go with a corporation. It may give the, ah, company the strongest look of legitimacy on the surface but it opens you up to too much scrutiny, both public and governmental. I would suggest a private holding company. How wide are you going to spread things?"

"We just picked up another trucking company and a warehouse. But I want to give things a totally new look. Laundromats, gas stations, some MacDonald's or Burger King franchises, a good night club or two. Any kind of cash flow machine."

"You have good foresight. Rudy never agreed with legitimate acquisitions, other than this restaurant"

Now what was he doing, Margaret wondered. Was this honesty or flattery?

"Well, he had to do something to impress his friends," she purposely responded, watching him. "Along with the muscle."

"I tried to warn him about that."

"That you did. But it made him feel important, so what the hell."

"The 'what the hell' is that he should have listened to you more."

Oh, oh, Margaret thought. This is going too far. Damn right Rudy should have listened to her more. He might still be alive if he had but Douds was beginning to overstep his ground a bit with all the flattery.

Margaret leaned back, took a sip of her drink and waited.

Then she looked at him in a quietly demanding way.

"So. What do you really think happened out there?"

Douds took his time before replying, but instead of saying anything he threw his hands outward and shrugged, now determined to play it safe.

"Okay. Never mind. The bottom line is you don't know for sure either way. Neither does anyone else so let's just agree here and now that that is the way we are going to leave it and move on. We still have a lot to do."

"I.... fully agree," he nodded and waited..

"Right. Jesus, what a mess. And here is what I need some help with. You knew Rudy far longer than I ever did. So what the hell did he do to offend whoever went after Vince? Or was it something Vince did on his own? And how does that fit in with Tony? What the hell is going on? And if you are going to do any more speculation, don't. I did not do those things. If I had, I would have let Vince live and blown up Tony. Tony's the one who seems to be having a tough time readjusting to the new chain of command."

Well, she was right about that, Douds agreed silently.

"Strange happenings," he said, instead. "And like you said, none of it makes sense. But I've only served as legal counsel so there had to be things Rudy never shared. Rightfully so. Still, he had his own way of doing business," Douds said with a shrug. "Or someone new in town is trying to establish themselves. I don't know. Sometimes he gave me the impression he was getting tired of it. You know. The exposure. Did he ever mention that to you?"

"Going everywhere with a bodyguard stuck to him like a Siamese twin? All the time."

"So maybe that's it."

"What?"

"He wanted out and he thought of some slick way to do it. You said you were down below taking a nap when he disappeared. So maybe he had a helper and he snuck off the boat without telling you."

"Why would he do that?"

"So you wouldn't have to lie for him."

Margaret almost laughed in his face. What bullshit. A great

story, nonetheless. Why not go with it.

"You're right," she nodded. "Rudy was always trying to protect me. Maybe he felt I'd be safer if I didn't know. But he loved boobs and warm weather. So whatever beach he's on, it's topless."

Douds shook his head in return, as if they had now agreed on some secret cover story for Rudy's disappearance. Then he leaned closer.

"So who's working on the Vince and Tony thing besides the cops?"

"Since I still don't know who I can trust, nobody inside. But we've had enough of this old mafia style, street level mentality. Much as I loved the guy, throwing a firebomb through someone's window like Rudy did was pretty damned crude. So is all the rest of it and we have to get past that. That's why I'm looking for a good private investigator. And then we'll turn it all over to the authorities.

Douds gave her a close look and nodded, knowing full well what would happen once she learned the truth. Sticking by her was going to be tough, no doubt about that.

God, what he wouldn't have given to over hear that conversation, Joe Carroll thought as he watched. Now the look on Margaret's face was stern again, and as she talked she made sharp, slicing motions with the edge of her open hand that hit the table. Douds was nodding, reluctantly, it seemed. But from the distance it was hard to tell for sure. Then, obviously finished, she took a long drink from her tall glass, set it down and got to her feet, heading in the direction of the restrooms. Joe immediately got up also and went in the same direction, pacing himself so that he would deliberately bump into her when their paths crossed. He did it well. It seemed totally unintentional.

"Oh, gee. Excuse me. I'm very sorry," he said to her, his hand on her arm. "Are you all right?" he asked, looking directly at her. "My apologies."

She backed up a step, gave him a quick study and went on her way without looking back as Joe returned to the bar. Ten minutes later he talked to the cocktail waitress who took two fresh drinks over to Margaret's booth. The waitress spoke to

Margaret and pointed to Joe at the bar. When she looked his way he raised his glass and nodded. She stared back at him without expression but gave the waitress permission to leave the drinks and turned back to talk to Douds. Douds made one last attempt at an endearing statement.

"I just hope Rudy's old enemies don't drive you away because I think working for you will be a lot less risky. And the longer it is before the outside learns who is in charge, the better for both of us."

FIFTEEN

George was standing next to the open door of Jack's office as Stan approached and watched as Stan stopped at Joyce's desk and whispered in her ear. She smiled naughtily. Then Stan joined George and they went in and sat down. George leaned over and spoke to Stan.

"Just remember that old story about the tomcat crossing the railroad tracks."

"I'm not even going to ask," Stan replied. "Please."

"Good. Well, you see this cat was crossing the tracks and not paying attention. Just then a train came by and cut the tip off his tail. It made the cat so mad he started cussing and wailing around and before he knew it another train came along and cut off his head."

"Jeez, George. Spare me. Jack..."

"Go ahead, George. Get it over with," Jack said.

"Okay, so the moral of this story is, don't lose your head over a little piece of tail," George finished and laughed at his own joke as he motioned out the door.

Stan looked at Jack, but Jack just shrugged and was quiet. After a moment he looked at the two of them.

"Okay. What have you got?"

Thankful, Stan pushed a small, charred looking box across the desk towards Jack. Jack picked it up and gave him an inquisitive look.

"It was in the rubble of Vince's basement. That has to be the source of all those phone call tape recordings."

"A transmitter?"

"Of a sort. But it's technology is from twenty five years

ago," Stan said, and went on to explain.

"And this little thing was up on top of the pole behind Tony's house," George added and placed another small device with a tiny antenna sticking out of it on Jack's desk also. There must be more tapes. I wonder why we never received any."

"Something we are not supposed to have yet," Jack said.

"Yeah, like the name of the next asshole to get scratched off the pad," George came back.

Thoughtfully, Jack leaned back in his chair but didn't respond to George's comment. "Anything else?" he asked instead.

"There was an old man named Charley who rented a room on the street directly behind Sand's house. He seems to have spent most of his time either walking his dog around the block on a route that would take him past Vince's house or locked up in his room. And he disappeared the day of the bombing."

Jack considered the implications of that and asked, "Leave anything behind?"

"Just the dog, the dog's collar and a leash. All anyone remembers is an old man with longish hair and a bushy mustache. We weren't able to come up with anyone of similar description in San Diego."

Jack picked up the transmitter from Vince's basement.

"Right," Stan said. "Charley probably had the other end of this thing in his room. Seems both houses worked off the same power pole, so it's possible."

"I don't know," Jack said as he studied the transmitter some more. "One old man working alone? Or one younger man disguised as an old man, working alone? Doesn't seem possible. But go ahead. What does your suspect list look like?"

"We have five or six. With some odd inter connections between a few of them, none of which make any sense. But regardless," George said as he dug out his little notebook and opened it.

"First, an ex cop. Stu Vanalden. A narc accused of misappropriating copious amounts of cocaine from the evidence locker. The DA finally dropped the charges for lack of evidence but he's still on suspension pending an in- process, Internal Affairs investigation and he's been out of touch for several weeks. An independent thinker, if you will, job wise, with an ex wife

89

who says he could be very reactionary. Her words, not mine. He is also about the same height, weight and build as the Charley character."

"What does his problem have to do with the rest of it?"

"He was squad leader for the group that made the drug bust which put the stuff in the locker to begin with. The size of the take was more than big enough to make it worth the risk of stealing it back. He claims it was a set up because he was getting to be too good at what he did collaring dealers."

George paused for a moment to see if Jack had more questions. But Jack just leaned back in his chair and nodded.

"Second, one Jimmy Hudson with an extensive list of petty misbehavior on his record, the most serious being aggravated assault with a year in county jail. Jimmy's brother was a distributor for Vince Sands who supposedly was holding back on the take. Jimmy's brother's corpse was found in the Mullholland dump a few months back. Jimmy is a hothead who made some obscene threats about revenge. He dropped out of sight shortly after they found his brother's body but is claimed to be still alive."

"Third, Victor Trent. Married to the sister of a Chicago mobster now serving ten to twenty in the Illinois State penitentiary. The word is that he was making moves on Rudy Stark's operation. He also had an associate and driver named Gus Hines who had some ownership in a surveillance company down by LAX. Both of them have also dropped out of sight."

"Lastly, for now, a man named Sam Corbin. Doesn't fit the profile at all but he is tangentially connected. Corbin is the one whose house was fire bombed over in Santa Monica not long ago."

"The one who lost his wife?"

"Right."

"I thought the name sounded familiar. What's the connection?"

"Well, of all people, Victor Trent leased the house next door to the Corbin's about six months ago. LAPD says maybe the firebomb went through the wrong window."

"Corbin seeking revenge for his wife? Does he have a record?"

"Just one traffic stop three years ago. Warning ticket only. Never in the service. Never worked on a road gang or in a mine. College man, happily married till the event, no children, did a start up company a few years back and still has it. Medical stuff, I think. Nothing to do with munitions or rockets."

"So why is he on the list? He's obviously not capable of such a thing."

"Just trying to be complete."

"Well, okay," Jack said sceptically. "Anything else?"

"Rumor has it that the married Mr. Trent was also shagging Rudy Stark's live-in girl friend. What's her name?" George asked and looked at Stan.

"Margaret Ryan."

"Right. And Ms. Ryan was on board the boat when Rudy supposedly went over the side, along with another woman named Candy and some dude from South America we've never been able to talk to."

"So. Let me guess. Candy was a hooker who was there to entertain the visitor. Why?"

"A suspected supplier. DEA had him on a watch list."

"No one else on board? Body guards, crew?"

"None. Backup witnesses at the marina where the boat was kept stated they only saw the four of them head out together."

"So. Who have you overlooked?" Jack asked.

"Probably lots of people, but we're still checking. The thing that doesn't fit any of it is those tape recordings we got in the mail."

"That is one strange aspect of this case, isn't it?"

"Yeah, and with the one exception of this guy Corbin's wife, every one else that's been made dead is a total scumbag, so what the hell. Maybe we shouldn't bother looking at any of it until they've thinned the ranks some more so we have fewer suspects. Laws can fuck up a good thing sometimes," George stated sardonically, and he meant it.

"The big question, however, is why?" George continued. "Is it a singular issue or are there multiple unrelated things all coming down together? Is it revenge, takeover, deception or takedown? Or, is it something else from out in left field we haven't considered yet. I hate to ask but I think we could use some help."

"You'll get it soon enough. And you're right. Find the why, find the perpetrators."

Another week went by without significance. Summer had arrived, mean and viscous in the outlying valleys. It was 113 in Chatsworth and almost as hot in east L.A.. Stan and George were beat from chasing leads that went nowhere. Things had plateaued out. Then, on the ninth day, they got a call. Come back into the office.

What for? They always started out from there every morning and it was now four in the afternoon. The time of day when it was totally impossible to get anywhere inside the city beyond walking distance in less than an hour? Maybe two. And they were way the hell out in Thousand Oaks lamenting about another dead end. What happened?

Jack's secretary, Joyce, didn't know except that the boss wanted to see them ASAP.

"Need coffee?" Jack asked when they arrived. "You'll have to get your own," he told them since he had sent the secretary home over an hour before.

They declined and sat down, wondering what was so important. Stan in particular. George's little story with a moral was right on. Contrary to all good sense, he had lost his head over a little piece of tail. All it had taken was one. One became two, and two became three and somewhere in there they both stopped counting. Passion's rumbling train. Sex turned into making love. Never enough, no end in sight. Making love turned into being in love. Totally stunned, he spent more time obsessing about Joyce than he did thinking about the case. Would he ever recover? He'd better. There were some bad people out there. The other problem was, it wasn't a secret anymore. No one had said anything specific. Nor had he admitted anything. But now that the case had stalled out, George's little innuendos were an integral part of the daily agenda. As for Jack, who knew what he thought? Except for a raised eyebrow and a minor frown now and then, he had left it alone. And as for himself, maybe if he wasn't so compelled to do all those intimate little things that gave it away when he was around her. Maybe if she wasn't either. Maybe if he married the girl. First time in his life he had ever considered such a thing. But if it kept on going like this....Jesus.

In the meantime he had been visualizing Joyce standing there with the door open, waiting for him. Oh, god, his gut ached. What had Jack called them in for? Elbows on his knees, Stan rested his chin on his hands and waited, not sure he wanted to hear what came next.

"Okay, I can see it's been a long day for you two so let's get to it. Anything to report?" Jack asked.

"Not really. No. Nothing," they replied, and waited.

"And what do I have that's so damned urgent? Well, first you can cross Victor Trent off the suspect list. A Ventura County Sheriff's Deputy found him in his car this morning. Over the edge and down in a steep ravine off Malibu Canyon Road. The prelim is inconclusive but it looks like he died in the crash. The decomp also indicates that he's been there a while. An inspection of the roadway where he went over showed some deeply burned in tire tracks on the shoulder with a track width much wider than the man's Porsche. "

"So it wasn't an accident. He was pushed over the edge."

"Yeah," said George. "So whose victim was he? The bomber's, or someone else? This is getting messy."

"Which brings us to the next item of interest. The IRS has a new payroll deduction for that cop, Detective Vanalden. A carpentry shop back in Love Point, Maryland, on the eastern side of Chesapeake Bay, no less. Does that make any sense?"

"Only if he's completely innocent and willing to work below his qualification level."

"Or he's done doing what he was doing and is trying to leave it behind by being completely stupid about it."

"Or someone borrowed his identity. But how and why?"

"Which is where you come in, Stan. We need to find out. Clear him or lock him up."

"Oh shit," Stan said.

"You guessed it. You got the short straw. Tonight's red eye into Dulles. The DC office is sending an agent out to keep him under surveillance until you arrive. They'll have an arrest warrant waiting. Lock him down till we check his alibies."

93

An old building in a row of other old buildings just two blocks from the shoreline. Inside, everything necessary to build a set of kitchen cabinets, replicate an antique chest of drawers or build a boat. Mr. Croft, an elderly man with glasses hanging off his nose who's been around as long as the weather and is just as cantankerous, was hand sanding the top of a wooden table when he was interrupted by an FBI agent, a lean looking man in a suit.

"Mr. Croft?"

Croft kept on sanding for another thirty seconds. Then he ran his fingers over the area he had been working on and at last looked up, not saying anything.

"I'm special agent Walberg, FBI," the agent said and flashed his ID at Croft.

"Well, bless me," Croft said as he looked at him, thinking that Walberg seemed awfully young to have such a title. Not that he was impressed, either. He had always had a certain disdain for law enforcement. "What's your problem?"

Walberg stalled out for a moment. Then he scratched his head and began.

"Federal records show that you have a man on the payroll named Vanalden. Is that correct?"

"I do. Why do you care?"

"How long has he been employed by you?"

"Has he done something wrong?"

"Not that we know of. We are just trying to locate him. He may have been a witness to something."

"Like what?"

"I'm not permitted to say at this time."

"Then why should I tell you anything? At this time, that is."

"Okay, look. Let's start over. I just need to know where he's at and if the man you hired is really Mr. Vanalden."

"You're kind of an antagonistic individual, aren't you. But I'm going to do you a favor and answer that question because I have known Stu, Mr. Vanalden, to you. I've known him since he was a boy. How's that for confirmation?"

"Good enough. How long has he been here working for you?"

"A couple of weeks, plus or minus. How did you know he

was here?"

"You filed an employee withholding for him. That seems a little unusual under the circumstances. Why not just pay him cash?"

"And give people like you some more reasons to bother me? I told him that was the only way I'd take him on."

"So, how did he happen to wind up here, working for you?"

"What's wrong with that? He could do a lot worse."

"That's not the way I meant it. Just tell me why he picked you?"

"If you want to know, don't be so grumpy. You haven't got enough seniority. "

"Right. Again, my apologies," Walberg said and then shut up, finally realizing that would be his best tactic.

The old man took another swipe at the table with his sanding block, then began.

"I knew his father from way back. Hadn't seen the kid in years. Then he showed up and asked for work. Part time to start. Something was bothering him. I could see that right off. But it weren't any of my business as long as he could be useful. The payroll part seemed to bother him the most but he finally accepted. And if you're wondering where he's at this time of day, he's fishing."

"Fishing?"

"Works mornings. Out in the bay most every afternoon. Loves to fish. Why, I don't know. It's so damned boring."

"Does he have his own boat?"

"What for? They have rentals at the dock. Local folks get a discount. Keep your eyes open. It's on the left when you get to Front Street."

Walberg had been standing on the boat dock for the greater part of an hour, looking out into the bay. The object of his interest was a small outboard sitting at anchor not more than a quarter mile off shore. He could make out a man and a fishing pole. Barely. But he knew it was the right boat because the rental agency owner said so.

Impatiently, he began pacing back and forth, glancing out over the water every time he came back around. A sail boat was heading out on a southward tack. Below it, and farther down the bay, a big power boat came into view. An open runabout, still a good distance away. Walberg stopped and watched, then he started pacing again. The next time he looked up the power boat was much closer to Vanalden, seemingly on a direct course and moving fast. Two figures were visible. The driver and one standing. At the last minute the boat's speed was reduced drastically and it came alongside Vanalden's boat on the landward side, hiding it from Walberg's view, momentum carrying it slowly past. Then, just as quickly as the speed had been cut, it went full throttle. The big boat's nose came up sharply as it accelerated, then dropped again as it reached planing speed and moved quickly off to the northeast and out into the open part of the bay.

Walberg was no longer pacing. He was squinting, trying to see through the glare of late afternoon sunlight reflecting off the choppy water. What had happened? He could no longer see Vanalden in his boat. He scanned the crowd of tourists on the dock, flashed his ID and helped himself to a pair of binoculars. Vanalden's boat appeared to be empty. In a state of near panic he handed back the binoculars, ran to where the rental boats were tied up, jumped into the nearest one, started the motor and headed out.

Full speed until the last second, Walberg cut the engine, came alongside Vanalden's boat and grabbed the gunwale. Vanalden was lying in the bottom. There was a massive, bleeding hole in his stomach. Blood and foam were coming from the corner of his mouth. He tried to say something but it was indistinguishable. Then he coughed and went unconscious. But Walberg was too inexperienced as yet to realize there was no hope.

"Sorry about that," Walberg said to Stan at six twenty the next morning as they came down the ramp. "By the time rescue arrived and the recon helicopter showed to begin a search, you were already on the plane."

"Tell me about it. The call came twenty minutes after take off."

"Well, at least you have time for breakfast. As long as we eat in the terminal. We have you on the seven forty five back to

LAX."

"Yeah, what the hell. Four hours sleep on the way here. Four more on the way back. Can't complain about that," Stan grumbled. "But this time I'm bringing my own sandwiches on board."

Over eggs, ham, toast and coffee, Stan explained why Vanalden had been wanted. Then he made the statement that it would be nice to talk to at least some of the people on the suspect list before they all wound up dead.

"Vanalden is number seven on the body count," he said as a trace of emotion crept into his voice that he hoped didn't show. What next?

Sam Corbin could easily have afforded a Rolls Royce but he drove a Cadillac Coupe de Ville instead. It had been purchased new but was now six years old. He had never looked at it as any kind of status symbol and never maintained it as though it might have been. It got a wash job about once a year and had never been waxed, detailed or fussed over. The primary reason for buying was that it was big, solid and comfortable. The secondary one was that it was made in America but that aspect had nothing to do with patriotism. It was in keeping with his policy of keeping America green, money wise, running against the tide of outflowing dollars. But nothing to obsess about. And when the car did get a bath, he did it himself. Just like mowing his own lawn and making his own home repairs which, unlike the auto, always received prompt attention. And in spite of never having been inside a health club, he was in excellent condition. None of that slope shouldered, artificial gorilla look from pumping iron or working against some machine made resistance, but the real thing. And he was often scandalized to hear that some of the people he knew actually paid some kid who couldn't get a better job to act as a personal trainer for them. Dumb and dumber.

The other thing that he never did was to return to his home in Santa Monica after it had been burned. He sent a friend in to recover a list of personal items, then donated everything salvageable to a thrift store operated by a homeless shelter. The house was renovated by a contractor and sold privately to avoid the morbidly curious, netting nearly twice what he had paid for it a dozen years earlier. His other major asset was his debt free business with its twenty seven employees, the major control of which had been turned over to his Operations Manager. But it too was on the block with negotiations underway with an eastern firm. At first the demands on his time had been good therapy, forcing him to focus his attention onto something other than the tragic death of his wife. In the beginning many well intentioned people had told him to get away, go somewhere to take his mind off of what had happened. Alone? And where the hell would that be? And do what? Go fishing? God dammit. But as the weeks went by he stayed away from his company for greater, varying lengths of time.

But still, too many memories, too much pain that hadn't gone away. And every time he went out to a party or to a social function he spent his time looking for her in the crowd. She had been too much a part of his life. She couldn't really be gone. She had to be out there, somewhere. But every time he thought he saw her across the room or on the street he was always crushed when he got closer and when he went home to his newly leased apartment, he was always lonelier than he had been before he left. And that was not nearly half as bad as it might have been if he had to return to his old home where she had always been such a bright, fulfilling presence. God almighty!

It was late on a Thursday evening and against his better judgment Sam had gone to a large, predominately singles house party in down Palos Verde at someone's semi mansion and was returning home fighting his resultant disappointment and depression. Not light, but considerably diminished from normal daytime density, traffic was flowing smoothly along at the normal ten miles an hour over the speed limit with Sam in the middle lane, keeping up, north bound on the 405 Freeway. By the time he reached El Segundo Boulevard he was becoming concerned. Two miles back a new white Ford LTD had rolled up along side of him in the fast lane and hung there for a few seconds before dropping back several car lengths where it stayed mostly in the middle lane behind him. Once it moved over into the fast lane behind three other cars, then it moved back to the adjacent lane and slowed as other vehicles passed it. From what Sam could tell in his side mirror, there was no front license plate. At first he dismissed it as a case of mistaken identity on the part of the other car's occupants and felt some relief when the vehicle dropped further behind and finally disappeared. There had been two men in the car, the passenger being the one he could see best, and that individual did not have a very friendly face. But so what. LA was full of mean looking people.

Another mile and Sam's thoughts had started to drift. But as he was coming up to the underpass beneath the runways at LAX he noticed the quick flash of white in his mirror. The same car, pulling out from behind a truck, overtaking him rapidly. Once alongside it slowed to match his speed and he jumped over into the slow lane. Without hesitation, it moved over also, still right beside him. The passenger side window was down and the second he was in the underpass tunnel with the solid concrete wall to his far side, the passenger's gun bearing arm came up. But as assassins they had erred badly. If they had followed through the first time, he might have been frozen in surprise and unable to respond. But not this time. This time he reacted with a hard stomp on the brakes that took them on past far enough for him to see three muzzle blasts across the hood of his car. By the time the other driver had time to respond to his tactic Sam had his foot off the brake and back on the accelerator and jumped lanes, now less than two feet behind. Here he slammed down the gas pedal, connected bumpers with a crash, gave the wheel a sharp twist to the left, slammed back on the brake and pulled on around the Ford as the driver over corrected, skidded left, then right, banged against the wall and left a fifty foot long shower of sparks behind as concrete ripped gashes in the sheet metal before the driver recovered and gained control.

Sam watched in his own rear view mirror, sure that no other vehicles had been involved. Then he sped away knowing that there had been no license plate on the rear of the Ford, either. He got off the freeway at Wilshire, took side streets up through the UCLA area and clear up to Sunset. Satisfied that no one was following he made his way over to the circular tower of the Holiday Inn on the west side of the 405 and spent an almost sleepless night.

In the morning he cautiously circled his own apartment building several times before parking and entering. Inside, he first checked with the doorman to see if anyone had been around asking for him. With no for an answer he took the stairs up four floors to his unit and quietly let himself in. The lock looked untampered with and everything seemed intact and in place as best he remembered. Yesterday he had gone straight from his office to the party. Maybe they had picked him up there and tailed him down. Then back again, trying to make it look like a late night, road rage shooting.

Sam walked around his apartment. Never liked the damned place anyway, he told himself. Thank god it was furnished. Everything else would fit in the car. But before he started carrying he called Lieutenant Ashby of LAPD, the first cop he had encountered after the fire bomb and the cop he had called and hounded periodically for progress. Not recently, however. The last time had been over a month ago.

"I didn't call you to bitch," Sam told him. "Just thought you should know what happened last night," he said.

"Like what?"

"Somebody shot at me on the freeway."

"Road rage?"

"Definitely not."

"How can you be so sure?" Ashby asked and Sam told him the story.

"Did you call 911?"

"Seriously? The car was still moving. You think they waited around to be interrogated?"

"No, but hang on. Let me check something," Ashby said and Sam could hear the sound of fingers on a computer keyboard.

"All right, looks like no one else called it in either. Did you get a license number?"

"No. There weren't any plates on the car."

"Okay, well, I'm not sure if I can help you here. I'll hand it over traffic control."

"But what if it's related."

"To what? You mean the bombing of your house?"

"Why not? Someone obviously tried to kill me then. Maybe they are still after me."

Ashby was silent for a moment before replying. "I see your point," he said. "But we closed the case on that after the bombers were killed in the Hancock Park house. There was evidence at the scene which left no doubt that they were responsible. But if something else is going on, you will have to talk to the FBI."

"The FBI? Why?"

"They now have jurisdiction," Ashby said without explanation. "Give me your phone number. I'm sure they will want to talk to you."

An hour later Corbin got a call from George Dixon. After introducing himself, Dixon asked Corbin to repeat his story. After he listened to it George summarized. The car description, no license plates, the face of the shooter. "And," he said. "It happened in the tunnel?"

"In the tunnel. The car has to have some serious scrapes on the passenger side."

"I get that but how many shots? Do you remember?"

"Jesus. At least three. Maybe more. What difference does it make?"

"None, except we can send someone down to see if we can find the slugs. Or what's left of them."

"Good idea. Then you'll know I wasn't making this up."

"Did I say that?"

"No, but who knows what you might be thinking. Maybe you think I blew up my own house. Or had it done."

"Not at all. But you would have had motive to have blown up the Hancock Park house."

"Damned right. The sons-a-bitches. Is that what you think?"

"No. I don't think you're the type and as near as we can determine, you didn't have the capability either."

"What does that mean?"

"The background training and expertise."

"So, you've checked me out?"

"Of course. Thoroughly."

"But maybe someone else doesn't know that."

"Or they are making sure they cover all the bases. After all, three houses have been blown up besides yours."

"Three? My god. Sounds like a war."

"That may well be the case but it's all I can tell you for now."

"Well, hell. Now what?"

"Now you come down to the federal building and look at some mug shots. Then maybe you should be in protective custody."

"Why would I want to do that?"

"Well, for one reason they have also already killed another individual."

"Holy jeez. Who? I didn't hear anything on the news."

"An L.A. detective. It happened back east."

"That's not good."

"No, it's not. And it looks like you're on the list too. Do you get that?"

"I see what you mean," Corbin said after a long silence. "But I think I'll try it my way first."

"What way is that?"

"I'm moving. All my personal stuff is in my car. And don't try to reach me at my business. I won't be there, either."

"Leaving town?"

"Yeah. But not the area. I was looking at a place out in Moorpark. Maybe I'll go do that."

"Well, your choice. I'm not sure it's right but.."

"But it's my life."

"Yeah. But get down here and look through the photo files. And don't wait too long."

"Just in case."

"You got it. And in the meantime keep your head down," George said. "Maybe drive a different automobile for a while, too. And stay in touch. I mean that. Much as I sympathize with your situation, you need to be available."

"I already sent someone down to see if they can retrieve any of those slugs. Just in case they might be intact enough to run through the system. Even if they're not, it will still verify Corbin's story if we find something," George said in his meeting with his boss and his partner, Stan, after he finished relating the account of what Corbin had told him earlier.

"Could he have made the whole thing up?"

"Of course. But I can't see what he would have to gain from

it."

"He said three shots were fired?"

"Three or more. And he was guessing a large caliber weapon."

"Okay. Let me know as soon as you hear from the tech at the scene. If he finds slugs or even fresh chips in the concrete consistent with that kind of impact, then we need to discuss this some more," Jack said. "And get the man down here before something really happens to him."

The first thing the next day Corbin appeared unannounced at the federal building but was immediately shown to Dixon's office after the receptionist called upstairs.

"Well," Corbin said without introducing himself or being asked to have a seat. "Do you believe me now?"

George looked him over carefully before responding. "Have a seat. Want some coffee?" he asked, motioning to his own untouched paper cup full on his desk, just out of the machine.

"No. I'd rather know what you found out," Corbin said and sat down.

"Well, since I didn't know you were coming, I hope you don't mind if I finish mine first."

"Not at all. Go ahead."

George took a sip from his cup, made a face, reached in his desk drawer for some sugar packets, added two, gave his coffee a stir with his pen and slugged down the entire cup.

"Bah," he said and threw the cup in his waste basket.

"All right, then," he said as he opened the new folder on his desk. "Let's get to it."

"Hmm. Well, look at that. They found several fragments and one partial slug that may have traceable markings," he stated. "It's in the lab. Maybe it will lead somewhere. And, looks like you were right. Big gun. A forty five. Would have taken your whole head off if it had connected."

Wide eyed, Corbin just stared at him.

"Just thought you'd like to know what you're dealing with," George said. "Did you find a place to stay?"

"I did. I took the place out in Moorpark," he said and handed over a slip of paper he had written the address on.

"Is it a security building?" George asked.

"Only in appearance. Keeps the salesmen and amateurs out but essentially worthless otherwise."

"I'm glad you understand those kind of things."

"But I did use my right name on the rental agreement and for the utilities.

"What? Are you crazy?"

"No. I don't really intend to stay there. I just needed a place to park my Cadillac."

"Yeah, right. And you're thinking we might have the man power to stake the place out. Is that it?"

Corbin shrugged. "I guess that would be entirely up to you. But I made sure the security camera in the lobby is functional if that helps. I also gave the manager your phone number as my emergency contact."

"Well, good for you, trying to be clever and paying a lot of rent for nothing. Your job is to stay out of it and let us do our job our way," George said, looking like he wanted to slap Corbin.

"You're probably right. My apologies. Except, god dammit. Getting shot at is enough to piss anybody off. Maybe I'll get a permit so next time I can shoot back."

"And get yourself killed for sure. Do you hear me?"

"I do."

"Okay. Now tell me where you really going to be staying? That's what I need to know."

"Looks like it will be motels and hotels for a while."

"Now you're being sensible. Out of state would be even better."

"I'll give it some thought," Corbin stated as he stared at George.

"Good. Now let's go down stairs and look through some mug shots."

After George tagged his partner, they went into Jack's office.

"Corbin has rented an apartment in a multi story building out in Moorpark," George began and told them the rest of it. The ruse of the automobile out front, the security camera, Corbin's motive for doing it.

Jack leaned back in his chair, listening.

"What about the photo file? Did he recognize anyone?" he asked when George was done.

"Not exactly. There was one, sort of, but not right so I left him him with the artist."

"And what do you think about the rest of it?"

"What? Trying to bait us into doing a stake out. I think he over stepped a big one."

"True enough, but still."

"But still it's not a bad idea, actually," Stan put in.

"I think it could work," Jack said. "Depending how badly they want the guy. That's the key. How long do you think it would take someone to track him down?"

"If they're serious, maybe a week."

"So," Jack said as he looked at them questioning.

"There's nothing worse than a damned stakeout," George said and looked at his partner. "But..."

Stan made a face and looked at George as if to say, why not.

"Okay," Jack said, approving the idea. "Everything else is stalled out. So, wait till the end of the week and let's see what comes up. Oh, yes. Before you go. Tell me about Corbin."

"What about him?" George asked.

"What was your impression of the man. Do you think he could in any way be responsible, or have a hand in what's going on?"

"Do I think he's capable of blowing up a bunch of gangsters? Extremely doubtful. And I doubt that he would have access to the kind of people who would be willing to do that for him. But I think the idea of it pleases him immensely. He is still carrying a lot of anger around over the death of his wife and he's be happy as hell if someone comes looking and we take them down.

"Sorry about that, partner," George said in the office several days later. They were going to run out to Moorpark again. Do another mid afternoon to somewhere into the evening surveillance. "I bet you had other plans."

Yes he did, Stan said to himself. George knew it, too. But, no acknowledgment on that. He was too tired for game playing excuses.

"Must have had ten cups of coffee today," he said instead,

and got up, heading towards the men's room. Some privacy so he could call Joyce and tell her he might be late coming over that night.

It was a six story structure perched on the edge of a hillside, facing north towards Oak Ridge and Big Mountain. With George at the wheel of the government owned vehicle, Stan and George came up the long curving driveway and pulled into a space at the far end of the outside parking area, situated so both the front entrance to the building and the driveway were visible from the same location. George ran all four windows down to the bottom before he shut off the engine.

"Well, shit," he said. "What's this, day five?"

"Don't remember, except it's my day in the lobby."

"Well, shit," George said again, as he opened his door and got out. He slipped out of his suit jacket and tossed it into the back seat. Then he loosened his tie and got back in.

"I think it's time to tell Jack that we need to give this up," Stan said.

"And do what? Nothing else is working."

"Maybe we could use the key to Corbin's apartment. Watch the tube, take a nap, leave a note on the door for the bad guys to wake us up if they happen to drop by." Stan said. "Or better yet, leave our phone numbers inside and go home so they can give us a call. Leave some beer for them while they wait for us to return."

"What if they call when you're humping Joyce," George quipped. "And you're not home?"

"Says who, wise ass?"

"Don't look at me. My breath doesn't smell like pussy."

"Screw you, George. She's a very nice lady."

"Is that why she won't even sit down when you're around cause her pants get so wet she's afraid she'll stain the back of her dress?"

"Jesus, George. What a... Enjoy your bright, sunny afternoon," Stan said instead as he got out of the car, accentuating his comment with couple of raps on the roof of the vehicle and walked away.

Two hours later George lit up his fifth cigarette and grumbled to himself. Damned stakeouts would be the end of him yet. Ordinarily he would drag on one cigarette until it was only half gone and then toss it. But sitting hour after hour, he sucked them down to a tiny stub. So what the hell. He was practicing conservation. Twice as much poison for the same amount of money.

He rolled his head around, limbering up his neck, took his last puff and flipped the butt out the window. Then he started to lean back. A moment later he picked up the binoculars and took a close look. Then he got on his communicator and hit the talk button.

"Hey lover. Still awake?"

"Talk to me."

"Car in the drive. It's not any of the regulars I recognize."

"I'm listening."

"Okay, I can see a blue sticker on the rear view mirror so it's a rental. Two dudes in suits. One grey, one dark blue. Couple of heavies, I think. Might be the competition."

"Anyone you recognize?"

"No, but they've parked. All right, now they're out of the car and obviously packing iron. So, on your toes."

Stan got up from his chair off to the side of the lobby and went to the only other person there. A middle aged lady reading the morning paper. He bent over and spoke to her. She nodded her head in refusal. He showed her his ID and pointed to the office manager's closed door, telling her to get in there and stay. She got up and went towards it, looking back angrily. That accomplished, Stan moved to the elevators as George's voice came through again.

"Speak to me."

"I'm heading upstairs. I'll be down the hall from Corbin's and out of touch."

"Stay loose. This may be the real thing. I'll tail them in," George said as he waited for the two men to get inside before he got out of the car. Then he took an indirect path that led him alongside the building until he could peek through the lobby window. Maybe thirty, forty seconds, he guessed. No more. Nobody in sight, he entered. Cautiously scanning everywhere, he went to the manager's office and tapped on the door. The day man peered out, looking frightened.

"I felt compelled to tell them Mr. Corbin's apartment number. Six o four. They looked pretty mean."

"I know the number. Did they both get on the elevator?"

"Yes. I think so," he said, looking in that direction.

While they could see the area in front of the two elevators from where they were, they could not see the floor lights above the doors and did not know that the number five came on over elevator one long enough for the door to open and close, then the sixth floor light came on and stayed lit.

"Call that emergency number I gave you," George instructed the man. "Now. And tell whoever answers to get more people out here immediately," he said, already half way to elevator two, waiting at the lobby floor.

On the sixth floor, Stan was waiting around the corner from the elevators with Corbin's apartment in the opposite direction down the other hall. The stairwell was behind him about twenty yards. He made sure his hand held radio was off so as not to give him away, stuffed it in his side pocket and unholstered his shoulder carried weapon. Keeping it out of sight inside his jacket, he stepped out quietly after he heard the elevator doors open and then close. He was surprised to see only one man.

The grey suited one was at Corbin's door, knocking lightly. Stan looked around for the other one. Too late. Grey suit noticed him and was turning, reaching inside his own jacket as he did so. Stan had both hands on his own gun now, aiming at grey suit. Grey suit stopped with his hands extended out to the side as Stan kept him covered and moved closer.

"That's the idea. Keep your hands out. Now turn to the wall and spread."

The man obeyed silently. Stan patted him down and removed a thirty eight revolver from a shoulder holster. He checked the safety and dropped it into his own jacket pocket.

"Okay, big man. Where's your partner?"

"Right here," came an angry voice almost directly behind him.

Surprised and shocked, Stan started to turn his head. Where the hell was George, he wondered, instantaneously realizing the

108

trouble he was in. Keeping his gun on grey suit, he looked around. But, before he could make out his accoster, blue suit fired.

Oh, God, Joyce, his last living thought. Then, in dying reflex, his finger pulled the trigger on his own weapon. That slug in turn, took out a section of grey suit's spine just above the waist.

The two shots, different in sound, greeted George as his elevator door came open. Down low, running, he turned the corner and made a rapid appraisal. Two men, neither moving, down on the hallway floor with Blue suit standing and turning towards him with gun raised. George fired three shots in rapid succession. The first two thumped home in blue suit's chest, turning him and taking him down. The third lodged itself heart high in Corbin's door.

Outside, pulled up close to the front door, were two ambulances. These were flanked with two black and whites and a three unmarked cars. Four uniformed cops and a local detective were inside, checking out the scene. Jack, George and two other agents were outside along with ambulance attendants. George had handed over his nine millimeter to Jack but now he was in pain and on the verge of collapse. He couldn't sit, he couldn't stand still. Furiously, he paced back and forth, just happening to pass behind one of the ambulances as blue suit was being loaded in.

"Take it easy, man," one of the attendants said to the other. "What's the hurry? He's going to be DOA anyway."

With the words barely out of the man's mouth, George had him by the shirt and slammed him up against the side of the ambulance.

"You dumb son-of-a-bitch," he shouted. "If he is, it had damn well better not be your fault. Get your ass moving before we need to call another one," he said as he spun him around and pushed him back towards the stretcher.

"God dammit, we need him alive."

Jack was too late. Before he could intervene blue suit was inside and the doors were shut, with one attendant in the back hanging onto the IV bottle. George was there also, leaning over the casualty, shouting at him, trying to get him to talk. Engine, lights and siren all came on together and the emergency vehicle roared away. Once the sound level was down Jack spoke to the two new agents who had followed him there.

"Round the clock on this place. Front and back just in case."

Then he stopped. Oh my god! Who was going to tell Joyce. Holy jesus.

It was Thursday. Sam Corbin sat at one of the window tables in Dora's Cafe where he could see down the road and up the hill to the apartment complex a third of a mile away where he had rented that sixth floor unit. An apartment he hadn't even spent a single night in. And this was the first time he had been near the place since then, driven by some unexplainable curiosity.

He had missed all the sirens going to the place, the first ambulance on the way back to the hospital and the departure of two police cars. It was only after he had sat down and placed his order that he noticed the black and white and an unmarked, white, possibly police vehicle up near the lobby entrance. Then, emerging from behind the trees along the drive, an ambulance, followed by another unmarked car, heading down to the street below. Elsewhere in the parking area, a half dozen random makes of automobiles here and there, including a blue, four door sedan with no one in it.

Dora's special hamburger with fries came and his coffee cup was refilled. He ate slowly at first, sampling the fries, wondering about the ambulance and police vehicles but largely unconcerned. There were older people living there. That would explain the ambulance. But not necessarily the other official vehicles. He stopped eating, dropped enough cash on the table to cover the bill and the tip and left. Outside, he walked the short block back towards his car, parked in the lot by the mini mall that also served a number of other businesses. When he got close he went into the convenience store and bought a pack of gum. Before coming out he scanned the parking area for anything unusual. Anyone sitting in a car, anyone suspiciously hanging out, a pretended window shopper, whatever. There was nothing of note. He went to his car, unlocked it and got in. Taking his cell phone out of his pocket, he dialed a number. It rang at least fifteen times before it was picked up.

"Clearview Apartments. This is Mr. Roberts."

"Yes, Mr. Roberts. Sam Corbin. Hopefully you remember me."

"I.. Mr. Corbin. Oh my god."

"What's wrong? Tell me what happened? What are the police and ambulances there for?"

"I, ahh, yes, sir. Why don't I let you talk to the officer here? Just a moment," Roberts said and put Sam on hold.

Sam hung up. After waiting for a full five minutes, he dialed again. This time the phone was answered immediately.

"Clearview Apartments."

It was the manager again.

"Okay, Mr. Roberts. This is Corbin and don't do that to me again. Do you understand?" Sam said in a harsh growl.

"Ahh, yes sir. How can I help you?"

"Answer my damned question. What happened?"

"Yes, ahh, there was a problem outside your, ahh, up on six. Two men were shot. One of them was an agent. I think he's the one who didn't... ahhh," Roberts said and then a new voice came on the phone. "Is this Mr. Corbin?"

Sam closed his phone, started the engine and drove off. Two minutes later he was on the 118 Freeway, heading east. Roberts had said an agent. Not an officer or a policeman. An agent meant a fed. FBI? They must have staked out his place after all. Something he had purposely made it easy for them to do. But someone was dead as a result. That was not a good feeling. He turned on the car radio, hoping to catch a news break.

SIXTEEN

Joe Carroll, looking especially well groomed, cruised down a tree lined street in Brentwood for the second time in less than twenty minutes. This time he stopped before he got to one particular house about half a block away and waited. It wasn't long. A limo backed out of the driveway into the street. Margaret was in the back. When it moved forward, Joe followed at a safe distance. Fifteen minutes later it pulled to the curb on Wilshire Boulevard in front of Nieman Marcus. The rear curbside door opened and Margaret got out, heading towards the front entrance of the store. Joe went on past, took a left at the second street and went into the multi level parking structure half a block up.

111

Leaving his car, he walked rapidly back towards Wilshire.

The store was just too damned big.

The reason he couldn't find her the first time through was because she was inside a dressing room in the women's clothing department. She had taken two selections in with her to try on. She first hung them up and started to slip out of her jacket when she saw herself in the mirror and stopped. Mostly she stared at her face, studying it. The eyes, the chin and cheeks, the set of her mouth. Then suddenly she felt confused, couldn't reach the underlying conflict her image evoked and it frightened her. Not overwhelmingly, but just enough for her to pull her jacket back on, turn, unlock the door and leave the area.

It took Joe nearly twenty minutes to spot her. By now she was coming from the cosmetic department carrying a cord handled, white paper sack with the store's name and logo printed on it in gold. The trouble was, he was on the floor above. Luckily, however, she was headed for the up escalator. He got on the down side. Then, when they were about to pass each other, he blurted out.

"Well, hello," he said with a big smile, catching her attention. "How are you?"

Margaret looked at him but didn't respond, at first not sure where she had met him. In spite of that, Joe turned around and started walking quickly back up the moving escalator against the traffic, continuing to talk to her in a seemingly genuine voice although she still refused an open acknowledgment

"What a nice coincidence. I thought I might never see you again."

At this, she turned her head and stared at him. He studied the look. While her female side might be interested, the business side was coldly curious and wary but he kept up with her until the top. When they get off their opposing escalators he gently took her by the arm and steered her out of the way.

"Are you alone?" he asked. "I don't see your companion."

Then, "Oh, oh. That was dumb. I'm sorry. Maybe you're married," he stated and looked at her left hand. It was devoid of jewelry. Trying to appear relieved, he said, "I couldn't tell the other night when we bumped into each other but..... well," and he quit talking while still maintaining eye contact.

"And of course you aren't married either, are you? And you're not trying to hustle me, either. Am I right, Mr....?

"Carroll. Joe Carroll. And no, I'm not. Not married. But, damn right. I am trying to...

no, that's not right. I don't want to hustle or hassle you. But I am interested. I hope that's, ahh. Never mind. How about a drink instead? Maybe dinner? A walk on the beach?"

"No, Mr. Carroll. I don't even know you."

"I don't know you either but that didn't stop me from asking. Can I at least have your name?"

Curious now, she stared at him. "Margaret," she said at last.

"So. Dinner then. What time should I pick you up?"

"I am not a pickup, Mr. Carroll. Thanks anyway."

"I didn't mean it that way. Can we start over?"

"Perhaps some other time. Maybe we'll run into each other again."

"Tomorrow night then? I'll meet you somewhere."

"I don't think you heard me."

Joe purposely took a short step back.

"I apologize. Sorry. I'm new in town and I just thought it might be nice. You're... very attractive, and, well, maybe some other time. That would be okay," he said, still looking into her eyes.

Breaking eye contact, she did a quick scan of him, up and down, and back. up to his eyes. After a long pause, she finally said, "Well.... actually Tuesday might work. I can meet you around eight. Does the Lermitage suit you?"

"Excellent."

"Do you know where it's at?"

"No, but I'll find it...... Tuesday then," he said with a smile and a nod and turned around just in time to see her companion from the restaurant, Attorney Douds, approaching them. But, pretending not to notice him, Joe promptly got on the down escalator.

"Who was that?" Douds asked in a concerned voice.

"He said his name was Joe Carroll."

"What did he want?"

"Dinner."

"Don't tell me you accepted?"

"Maybe. I'll see."

"But you have absolutely no idea who he might really be."

"And I haven't been laid since before Rudy went over the side, either," she said sarcastically.

Douds looked at her sideways and shook his head. "But ..... it could be dangerous. Don't you realize that?"

Margaret shrugged.

"And what if he's a cop? We don't know everything that goes on in that department. Or worse, a damned fed?"

"Now that would be a challenge," she replied. "On the other hand, what if he's just some guy who wants to make out? And a damned good looking one. I'd hate to pass that up."

"Christ, Margaret. Do you always have to play it so close to the edge?"Douds said. Much as he cared for her there were times when she sorely tested him.

"That was another of Rudy's problems. Always so damned boring. And look what that got him."

"Jesus, woman. I'm glad all we got going is attorney-client."

"Don't you wish. And what are you doing here, anyway? Following me around?"

"I couldn't get my damned secretary to come down and pick out a gift for my wife's birthday so I had to do it myself. And what does that, don't you wish, mean?"

"As an analogy, and since Rudy isn't here to object, I'd say you also had a seat on the board of directors."

Douds knew it was a meaningless thing but the figurative gesture of it secretly pleased him. So much so that it stalled his thinking momentarily.

"Okay....." he finally said. "Well, then. In that capacity I'm asking you to watch your ass. Or at least watch where you peddle it, if that's not being too crass. Are you listening?"

"I always listen," her eyes flashed. "Especially where my ass is involved. But you have to admit. A little diversion sometimes makes for an interesting game." she said with a daring look.

After two off days, George walked into Jack's office. There

was a new girl sitting at Joyce's desk, typing rapidly. Older and plain looking, she looked up as he came in.

"You must be George," she said. "I'm Joanne."

'Hello," he responded, both surprised and not surprised to see a new face there. One he recognized as being from the secretarial pool. A temp. It took him a moment before he could ask if Jack was in his office.

"I believe he is expecting you."

"Thanks. Nice meeting you," he replied and went towards the open door to Jack's inner office. Once inside he shut it behind him and sat down.

"Is she going to be okay?" he asked, referring to Joyce now that Stan was gone from her life.

"It's going to be difficult for her. She said Stan had asked her to marry him as soon as this case was cleared."

"Oh, jeeeeez." George replied in surprise, now more glum than ever. "He never said a word.."

"I know," Jack said quietly and went silent.

"Goddammit," George said with anger and frustration as he got up and went to the side window in the office and looked out. Joyce was such a total sweetheart of a woman and in spite of the way he had razzed Stan, he had always still felt very protective of her. So had Jack. And now this. What could either one of them do about that? He had never felt so helpless in his life.

Jack remained silent, lost in his own repetitive agony. Before his promotion and move to California, Jack had spent as many hours on the street and on stakeouts with Stan as George had. Maybe more. They, too, had been partners and friends. The man had been in his house on many occasions over the years, as had George. His wife liked them both and she was hurting badly also.

He also had the additional burden of having been the man in charge. Whoever winds up in harm's way, it could always be argued that their boss put them there. But it was a bad argument. Any time anyone put on a badge there was a risk. But when someone lost their life in such a needless fashion and you were close to that someone.... And, god almighty, what about Joyce? Fate had played such a horrible trick on her at such a young age. What about that? Something else to think about. And George. What must he be feeling? All those hours together with Stan.

Most of them good, he hoped. They seemed to have had an easy time of it, lots of banter back and forth. George a little over the edge at times about the relationship with Joyce, but well intentioned and Stan taking it with a smile. And now the open question that would probably always haunt George. Had he somehow failed Stan as a partner? Failed to back him up properly?

"Do you need some more time off?" Jack asked after a moment.

George whipped around. "And do what?" he almost shouted in his frustration. Then, as if coming out of a trance, he shook his head and looked at Jack.

"Jeeez. I'm sorry," he apologized and then sat back down.

Instead of a reply, Jack opened his door and leaned out to ask Joanne if she wouldn't mind bring them some coffee. "One black, one with sugar." Then they waited in silence.

After a few sips George asked, "Is he still alive?" referring to the man he had put the two slugs into, his head down, staring into his coffee cup as he said it.

"Barely. And not talking. But we know who they are."

With that, George looked up.

"Guns for hire out of Las Vegas. The Guzman brothers. Dan and Will. Will is the survivor. And... they were definitely in Maryland, on the Chesapeake. The one who ... the other one. He's the one who rented the big power boat from a place up near Baltimore."

"What about the ammo?"

"Not the same weapon as in Maryland but the one... the one you killed had a forty five and there is a partial match to the freeway slugs."

"Which proves what? There was a real connection between Vanalden and Corbin? Or Vanalden and whoever blew up Vince Sands house? Or all three of them? Or just an imaginary one? Not that it matters anymore. But if someone was that serious about shooting Corbin, then maybe we should be taking another look at him, regardless."

"Except we've already done that. Up, down and sideways. There's nothing more."

"Okay. But then the other question is, how did they get a line on Vanalden so quickly? I don't like the implications of that one."

Neither had an answer and they sat quietly for a moment.

"So, let's hope our son-of-a-bitch in custody lives long enough for us to find out who hired him. Then maybe we can get some idea as to who is trying to do what to whom," George said, breaking the silence.

"Which reminds me," he continued. "I was talking with Detective Barnes, LAPD narcotics. One of his informants told him there was a rumor back then that Rudy's girlfriend, the Ryan woman, was banging that guy Trent who was trying to muscle in on Rudy. How's that for hanky panky?"

"But also Corbin's neighbor. Which would indicate that the firebomb must have been meant for him instead of Corbin, as ordered by Rudy."

"Maybe. But Rudy was already dead before Trent's car was pushed over the edge of Malibu Canyon. How does that work?"

"Whoever took over still considered him a threat."

"Which is what it always comes back to. Who took over?"

"We'd better find out. The body count is rising faster than the tide comes in. Do you know who Marvin Douds is?"

"The Century City attorney that represented Rudy Stark before he fell off his boat. Why?"

"His name was on Stan's summary sheet of the recordings I gave him to review."

"Yeah, I think he was one of the people Vanalden was investigating when he got in trouble. Is it possible Douds picked up the pieces and is trying to clean house?"

"I don't know but I think it would be out of character for an attorney. They seem to prefer hanging onto coat tails rather than being out front."

"Well, you're probably right. Is your computer on?"

"Help yourself."

George came around Jack's desk as Jack gave up his chair. George pulled up an unsolved case search file, then started typing as Jack watched over his shoulder.

"Well, now. That's interesting," Jack said as he looked at the monitor.

"I'd almost forgotten. Nat Mouceri, Douds' senior law

partner, was nabbed by two gunmen right in front his house. What... five years ago."

Jack looked at the dates in the file. "That explains why I didn't remember him. I was back east working a serial killer case with, ah..... But, look at that. Douds was suspected of complicity. That's interesting."

"Except he was very conveniently having diner at Chasin's with Rudy Stark when it happened. They were each other's alibi."

"Well, okay. Let's take another look at Douds."

Even though it was no longer in the best of locations, Douds still lived in the same condo where he and his wife had spent the last fourteen years. There were four, two story buildings in the complex with six units per building, such that each unit had both a first and second floor. Living room, kitchen, spare bedroom and bath down, master bedroom suite with double bath and walk in closets up. It was the following Tuesday and Douds was alone in his living room, talking on the phone.

"Next week? Is that the best you can do? ..... I don't like it..... All right, all right. I guess I'll have to live with it. I know they're trying to subpoena our records but no judge will ever sign off.... They don't have enough. But they do have a cop sitting out front in a car. Followed me home from the office today.... What? ..... No, I'm not complaining. He can stay as long as he likes. After what happened to Vince and Tony I'd even let him sleep on the couch. Right... I will," he ended and hung up. Then he reached for the tall glass of bourbon on the coffee table.

At the same time Joe Carroll was seated at a prime table in the Lermitage restaurant, waiting. He had been there promptly at eight. It was now twenty minutes later. Had he been stood up? He finished his vodka tonic, looked at his watch again and was about to get up when she appeared. Stunningly dressed, she waited while the maitre de pulled out her chair, then sat down. The waiter was at their side before they could even speak. Joe looked at her, questioning.

"Wine," he asked.

She nodded. Having already looked at the wine list and making a guess, Joe ordered a bottle. He looked at her and smiled, raising an eyebrow as he did so. She gave him a touch of smile back, took a sip from her water glass, sat her over sized purse on the table and dug around in it, then placed it on the floor by her feet. By that time the wine had arrived. The waiter opened the bottle and poured a trace amount in Sam's glass. Instead of taking a sip, he held up the glass, looked at it and took a brief sniff. He nodded at the waiter. When both glasses were poured, he raised his to Margaret.

"To happy coincidence."

"And to presumptuousness," she said in turn as she raised hers.

They both drank.

He told her that he was glad to see her, not too sure he hadn't been stood up but happy that he hadn't been. She complimented him on his patience.

"Thank you," he replied. "And don't worry. I'm not going to ask you what do you do when you're not shopping or dining out?"

"And why is that, Mr. Carroll? Is that right? You said your name was Carroll. Joe Carroll."

"You remembered. Good. But please.. Joe, Especially since I only know your first name."

"Ryan. Margaret Ryan. But if you call me Marge, the date is over."

"No doubt. And I'm not going to tell you that you are beautiful, either, because you already know that so... "

"So then what? You told me before that you weren't trying to hassle me or hustle me but you were interested. What does that mean? And why should I indulge a man who doesn't want to hustle me, as a woman, I mean? What else could you possibly be interested in if you don't know anything else about me? Or do you?"

"Not yet. But do I have ulterior motives? Damn right. But am I going to try and flatter my way into your bedroom? I don't think so. But would I like to get you there? My first impression says, damn right. But maybe after I get to know you a little better, assuming that even happens, well, who knows. And I'm sure the same goes for you which is why, if I am right, then I'd like to hustle you. "

"Are you saying that you think there is more to sex, than

119

sex? Never mind. Don't answer that. You said you were new in town. If that wasn't a line to get me to feel sorry for you so I would go out with you, where are you from and how long have you been in L.A.?"

"Cleveland originally. But I've been out of the country for several years. Europe mostly, chasing deals for an English company. Made some good money but it cost me my marriage," he said, wondering how many lies he would be able to tell and keep them all straight.

"Do you have children?"

"No. That's my one regret."

"Regret? I should think you would be happy."

"You don't like kids?"

"Pregnant and barefoot would be way too restrictive for me," she said in a way that didn't seem quite right but all he could do was let it go.

"Well, there is that side to it, isn't there?" he said in reply.

"So let's not go there," she stated somewhat curtly. "Tell me what do you do when you're not bumping into strange women instead."

"I'm in search of a new business venture, career challenge or whatever. Something with money attached to it. That's why I'm in L.A.. If I'm going to take some risks, I might as well do it here," he said, wondering how that came off.

"That's what life is all about, isn't it? Taking risks. Without that, there's nothing," she stated, looking directly at him. She didn't particularly like the mustache but the rest certainly measured up. She also had a difficult time breaking eye contact. Such serious intensity. What was behind all that? For the time being that was her big question.

Holding her look, he answered. "Yes. I'd rather chase something with dedicated pursuit and come up short than settle for a glass half full. And you, dear lady, are certainly a glass far more than half full," he said and raised his wine glass.

"So. I am going to be pursued after all," she stated.

"More than likely."

She responded by holding up her glass also. "Well, I hope you find it worth the chase."

They both sipped their wine.

"Hungry?" he asked.

"Very," she replied, and Joe signaled the waiter, thinking, well, so far so good. But would he ever be able to find out the true level of her involvement in that monstrous organization? Was she in any way a part of what had drawn him into the picture? So far that seemed unlikely. But she could be the thread that led him to the one he wanted. And if not? Well... either way, ...damn... he went on, unable to keep his eyes off her.

"And so...." he asked her. "What does Margaret Ryan do when she's not shopping or dining out?... An intriguing question, but none of my business. But if I had to guess, let's see... Your daddy was probably very rich. You married early, it didn't work and now you devote a major portion of your time to charity... No? Well, you own a very large ranch in Wyoming but you can't stand the smell of horses so you spend all your time in L.A.. Or... as a last possibility, you're a lady airline pilot."

Margaret actually laughed, surprising Joe.

"Well, that's a relief."

"Really? What?"

"You'd never make it as a psychic."

"Just as well. Knowing too much about a person right up front might take all the fun out of it."

"Undoubtedly. But actually, I lead a rather boring life. Occasionally I get involved with properties that have commercial value."

"That doesn't sound completely boring. Do you have an office somewhere?"

"I do. It's called The Trident Company. But you won't find it in the phone book or the yellow pages. Referrals only. And with a good attorney and a good banker, the rest is relatively easy."

"You make it sound so simple," he replied, convincingly impressed. If he didn't have evidence to the contrary, he would have believed every word.

"It is," she responded with ongoing sincerity.

"But why so modest? You are obviously a strong woman in your own right."

"Some men are intimidated by strong women."

"And I'm sure you could be very intimidating at times."

"Does that bother you?"

"To the contrary. I like women who have a clear sense of who they are and what they want. In the long run, they are much easier to deal with."

"Really? And why is that?"

"Because they are more distinctive. You either like them or you don't and that's that. Life is too short to be playing games with wimpy people. Is that too harsh?" Joe asked.

"Not at all. I find it well put."

Later, she thanked him in a formal way and refused to give him her phone number. She did take his, however. His cell phone. And promised to call. What she didn't know was that he didn't need her phone number. He already had it. And he knew her home address and at least half of the places she went during the day. One was the office she admitted having. A place where she spent varying amounts of time, from minutes to very long hours. No business name on the door, however. Not even a number. Just an expensive suite in the office tower adjacent to that of her attorney, Douds. Unfortunately, with twenty five other palatial offices on her floor alone and hundreds of others located in those two, and other surrounding buildings, all connected by underground parking facilities, it would have been impossible for a single individual to monitor who visited her office, no matter how many surreptitious disguises they came up with. As for getting inside the office itself without her knowledge. Impossible. Neither she nor Douds so much as used the services of a commercial janitorial company. But, now, having finally met her in person, there should be other alternatives. Assuming that she would call him.

Six days later she honored her promise. Nine o'clock at night. Did he want to meet her at the same place? She was already there. Of course he did. But that was as far as he went. Nothing stupid like trying to steal a kiss good night afterward, or a plea to see her again. In her own good time, that was the tactic, letting her think she was the one in control. Wait and let her come to him. Difficult and time consuming, but as he saw it, the only way to get beyond her suspicions.

Then another week went by before it happened again. Earlier

this time. And before she climbed in the back of the limo when it was over she actually extended her hand. Which he took, of course, and held it a little longer than necessary. And after she was gone he got in his own car and once again made sure he was not the one being followed.

"Shostakovitch," Margaret said on the phone.

"Okay," Joe said after a brief pause. "Sounds good. Where?"

"At the Hollywood Bowl. Tonight. I have the tickets and a picnic box from Mauri's Deli. Come early so we can stake out a shady place to eat before the concert. Bring a blanket and the champagne."

"Right."

This time Joe was confused. Here was this chicly dressed, stunningly aloof woman sitting on a blanket drinking hundred dollar a bottle champagne from a plastic cup and manhandling a monster turkey sandwich. Beautiful and conflicting. Inimitable and enigmatic, separating herself by a projected wall of defiance that kept most of the world at a distance with nothing reflected back except a summary rejection of most things around her. Under any other set of circumstances Joe would have taken a brief, treasured look and passed on by, feeling better for having done so. But here he was and what the hell were they doing at a concert? He had no idea. Then, when it was time to find their seats, she actually took him by the hand and held it the entire way.

Nor were their seats in one of the private boxes up front as he had somewhat expected, but almost dead center, several rows back. There was no moon, either, but when dusk had passed and darkness came, it was still an awesome night, full of orchestral passion filling the sky with the sounds of strings and horns and drums and soaring overture. Then the evening temperature began falling as Joe took the blanket and spread it over their shoulders and across their front and legs. Sitting on her right, he put his arm around her shoulders and she leaned into him, her head against his. He put his other hand around her waist in front and pulled her close, feeling the softness of her breast weighing down on it. Then, under the blanket, she unbuttoned all the buttons down the front of her blouse and snuggled closer as he put his hand inside. There was no bra and far more softness than just a handful.

For another hour and a half there were no words, no attempts at kissing, no further groping. Just two people alone among a few thousand, isolated in their own moment, eyes closed, leaning together, feeling each other's warmth, surrounded by the music. And when it was over they sat there still, waiting for the crowd to disperse, gathering stares, unconcerned.

There was more than wordless magic in her bedroom too. Passion on a plane that surpassed even that of the full orchestra earlier on. At four in the morning, Joe, exhausted, fell asleep, only to be awakened half an hour later. Margaret, wrapped in a portion of the sheet, was sitting up with the night light on, smoking a cigarette. He had never seen her do that before. She had shaken him lightly. Now she spoke.

"It's time for you to leave," she said matter of factly.

Well, what the hell, Joe said to himself, at first a bit offended, then not overly surprised. The game had changed again. Okay. He got dressed, bent and kissed her on the forehead and went out the door without a word. Then, when he reached his car and dug in his pocket for the keys, he found a slip of paper with a phone number on it. Wasn't that great? Yes. But what wasn't great was the fact that he had finally been inside her house and never had a chance to look around. Did she have an office there, too? A computer? Where were all the phones located? Was the number she had given him a land line or a cell phone? Probably a land line from the prefix. But unless he knew where it was installed, there was no way to tap in. Still, he was reasonably confident that there would be a next time. There were some things a truly excited woman could not fake. It was also pleasing to see that this tough lady had at least one fear. Real emotional involvement. Fair enough. If he just left her alone the worst thing that would happen would be that she would surely fuck his brains out. If he didn't have hers first. And if he had enough strength left while that was going on, it might be interesting to see how much stress Attorney Melvin Douds could handle. And how that would domino over onto her.

To the FBI, Douds was the most boring man alive. Office, home. Office, home. Office, home. One night out to dinner with the wife, home by nine. Always in the window, the TV screen flickering away until nine thirty sharp. Then it was lights out downstairs, second floor lights on for no more than ten or fifteen minutes, then darkness. No chance for a search warrant. Nothing good enough to get authorization for something on the phone line, either. Home or office. Nothing in their full background check they didn't already know. Jack pulled back on the surveillance after five days.

Without such legal restraints, however, Joe Carroll could approach things differently. The first thing he did was to spy on Douds' two neighbors, the ones whose condos butted up on either side. The older couple on Douds' left were ideal. Living as they were with a false sense of security that probably came from being sandwiched between other people's dwellings, there was no security system. The same for Douds. Also, there were no kids and no pets. Serious recreational gamblers, they were free to spend a three day weekend each month in Las Vegas. More information that was easy to come by. They also hung out in the nearby bar and loved to talk about their out of town adventures and would be off to Nevada the following weekend. Time enough to be ready to get inside their dwelling when they were gone.

The rest of Joe's homework took him to the city building and planning department, a redundant exercise which simply confirmed his suppositions. Developers saved a dollar any way they could. One way was to minimize architectural fees. Forget creativity. Use the same floor plan for every condo in the complex. Just reverse it for every other unit in the building. That way bathrooms ended up adjacent to neighbors' bathrooms, kitchens to kitchens and closets adjacent to closets. It also saved on wiring and plumbing costs. There were no real fire or heavy security walls between older units either. This made the number of tools Joe required very minimal. Extra pairs of latex gloves, plastic bags to cover his shoes and a tightly knit ski mask to avoid leaving trace evidence behind. A tiny little pen light for illumination, a small chisel to scrape out the glaziers putty from around one of the panes in the rear kitchen window. A small suction cup to keep it from falling and breaking while he reached through and undid the lock and deadbolt from inside. More putty to reinstall it before he went to work, to avoid suspicion while he was inside. Then, two short deck screws, a small phillips screwdriver, a box cutter, a miniature bolt cutter, a small magnet on a string and a sandwich sized baggie with a solution soaked cloth inside for completion.

Upstairs, per the plan, there was a large walk in closet off the master bedroom that was supposed to butt up against the same, but reversed closet on Marvin Douds' side of the separating common wall. He picked the man's side of the closet, removed enough of the clothes from the rod to give himself working room and threw them on the floor outside.

The small magnet allowed him to located the vertical rows of nails which held the drywall to the studs. The box cutter allowed him to cut through the relatively soft drywall, making a removable panel between the studs. The two screws driven half way in gave him small handles to manipulate it with when he pulled it free. Joe guessed an elapsed time of twenty minutes to get that far, primarily because of the need for quiet. Then, some horizontal cuts across the fiberglass insulation blanket inside and it was removed. In the middle, a minimal security screen of number ten wire mesh. It looked substantial enough but the wire was not hardened steel. It did not snap when it was cut but parted easily with the bolt cutters. After that, another layer of insulation and then the final layer of drywall inside Douds' closet. The only problem was the fine, chalk like, dust generated from cutting into the drywall. There was only fourteen and a half inches of free space between the studs . He wished he had brought some masking tape to put over the exposed raw edges to keep it from getting on his clothes.

Douds must have had at least a dozen suits, all of the same cut and style. All were pinstripes, either charcoal grey or medium grey. And about twenty white shirts, laundry fresh, on hangers. Joe pushed them gently aside and, with a quick blink of his light, determined that the closet door was shut. So far, so good. Then, his first glitch when he tried to ease the door open. It made a small squeak He froze and listened through the narrow opening. He thought he could hear someone snoring lightly but he waited anyway. Then he retreated back out, went to the bathroom of the violated condo owner and found some hand lotion which he rubbed into the closet hinges. He gave the door a short but quick move. Nothing. He did it again. And again.

When it was open far enough he got down on his hands and knees and stuck his head into the room and looked, his eyes now well dark adapted. There was a dim, luminescent night light glow coming from the bathroom down at the opposite end of the over sized bedroom. Against the wall away from him, a queen sized bed. Squinting, he could barely make out the two separate body mounds. Both large, the biggest one on the right side of the bed, the place where the man, the dominant partner, would normally sleep. Thank god for the thick carpet.

Slowly, slowly, he crept around till he was along the far side of the bed. He had guessed right. It was the location of the snoring. He got up on his knees, careful not to touch the bed itself, and peered over the edge. Dammit Douds was almost to the middle, crowding his wife. But he was on his back, that was the important thing. Joe was about to open the plastic back he carried when he had a bad thought. He got up a little higher and squinted carefully. Jesus. Douds' wife was bigger than he was. She was the one sleeping on the right side of the bed and she snored. Poor bastard, he almost chuckled. And then, just before he had completely sunken back out of view, she turned on her side, facing him. She also stopped snoring. Almost ready to make a run for it, he dropped down and froze.

Resisting the urge to give it up, he waited and listened. Once sure that her breathing was regular again, he withdrew and cautiously crept around to the opposite side. The rest was easy. Douds was on his left side, placing himself and Joe almost face to face. Joe held the liquid soaked cloth under Douds pointed nose and counted to thirty. Although tempted, he didn't want to kill the man. Not yet, anyway. Instead, if the home brewed chemical concoction worked properly, Douds would be completely unconscious for about three hours. Then he would wake up feeling worse than he had ever felt in his life.

Maybe he should give the wife a small whiff too, just to make sure she didn't wake up until after he was gone, Joe thought, but dismissed it as he backed away from the bed, careful to replace his potentially lethal weapon back in the plastic bag. Reaching out to steady himself, he put his hand on top of the nightstand next to the bed and felt something familiar. It was a ring of keys. And next to it was a thick, heavy wallet. He pocketed the wallet.

Back inside the closet again, Joe chose to pull the door shut behind him just in case he made any noise getting back through the wall. He gave it a trial jerk. No squeak. He pulled it the rest of the way, turning the knob to retract the latch before the final closing. Holding it tightly shut he released the knob but didn't feel the latch engage. Damn. The door was misaligned just enough to have the latch hang up on the striker plate. He started to turn the knob again only to hear a loud click as the latch let loose and engaged. Jesus, damn.

Then he heard a more distant, fainter click and saw light coming into the closet from the crack at the bottom of the door. Since it couldn't have been Douds', it must be his wife's bedside lamp. The silence bore down on him. Then, a sound. Maybe footsteps muffled by the carpet, and then more silence. No sound of a phone being picked up or a call being made. Finally, the flush of a toilet, and another forever moment before the light went back out. Joe took some long, deep breaths to calm himself. Then he felt around in the dark, found some unknown piece of clothing and placed it along the bottom of the closet door to block the light. Feeling reasonably safe, he turned on his small penlight and made very sure he was not leaving anything behind.

Of course he could have avoided all this right from the beginning and just gone in through Douds' own kitchen and up the stairs to the bedroom. It would have been far simpler and less risky, but that wasn't the point. It was over three months since he had blown up Vince's house and two months since Tony's house was turned into splinters. If it was just the headache, Douds might choose to keep the whole thing quiet. But with the hole in his closet wall and the neighbors' living quarters violated it would not only re-emphasize the earlier point of mob members' vulnerability but fairly well assured Joe that the police would be summoned. Maybe even the FBI.

At last, back outside with a few traces of white powdery

drywall dust on his dark clothes, he made his way from behind the neighbor's over to the outside of Douds' rear entrance and located the phone wires coming in. Reaching up, he was barely able to clip a small magnetic pickup device onto the cable and slid it up as far as he could. If no one discovered it within a day or two, he was in business. Surely Douds would call some of his people when he finally came to in the morning. Maybe even Margaret. That might be interesting. Now to hide the receiver-recorder down the alley somewhere. About to proceed, he had an after thought. Back at the neighbor's he removed the window pane once more, set it down and stepped on it, just hard enough for it to break and not make much noise. That should help get the police out there before the gamblers returned home with their impeccable alibi..

At five in the morning Douds woke with severe stomach cramps that completely doubled him up, a throbbing, unbearable headache and a feeling of total panic. He began to sweat profusely. God, he was dying. He moaned and tried to sit up, but he couldn't. He swung his arm around and hit his wife on the side of her head, bruising her ear. She put up her hands to defend herself, jerked backwards, lost her balance and fell off the bed.

"Goddammit," she said and picked herself up, leaning against the bed. Then she found the switch and turned on her bedside lamp as Douds let out another horrible moan.

"Marvin, What's wrong? Marvin! What's going on? You look terrible. Are you having a heart attack? I'd better call 911."

"No," he said loudly, waving his hand wildly. "Call the doctor. Jesus," he groaned, all doubled up and rolling back and forth. "The doctor. Call the damned doctor."

"What doctor? It's the middle of the night. Which one? You mean...?"

"Amato, god damn it. Amato."

"I think I'd better call an ambulance."

"For god's sake. Call the damned doctor."

"What if he won't come?"

"He'll come, the sonofabitch. God... oh, jesus, go!"

"I'm going. I'm going. Just let me get my robe. And don't you die on me, Marvin. Not at this point in our lives, dammit," she said as she hurried around the bed and over to the closet door. She yanked it open, found the switch, flipped on the light and headed to her side of the large room when she tripped over the shirt Joe Carroll had left across the bottom, almost falling. She kicked it out of the way, found her robe and slipped an arm in when she noticed that her husband's suits had been pushed aside. What.....?"

"Marvin" she cried as she backed out. "There's a, a, ah... There's a big hole in the wall in the back of the closet. Oh.... my....," she said, pointing to the closet, and started sobbing.

What was she blubbering about now, Douds was wondering. Jesus, how could his head hurt so damned bad. And his guts, how in hell... what hole in the wall? Was she going crazy? Somehow he managed to swing himself around, get his legs over the side of the bed and on the floor. Half crawling and with great difficulty, he made it over to the closet. Then, barely able to focus his eyes, he came to a sudden realization.

"Anna. Stop it, damn you. Call the god damned doctor. Tell him I've been poisoned. Hurry."

At ten o'clock the following morning Joe dug out the scrap of paper with the phone number on it and called Margaret from his car. A man answered.

"Hello." That was it.

He asked for Margaret.

"She's not here."

"Can you give me another number?"

"Not without her permission."

"Can I leave a message?"

"That's up to you."

Joe ended the call, crumpled up the paper and tossed it out the window. But he hadn't forgotten the number.

SEVENTEEN

Someone had tried to be an Oklahoma City copy cat but had failed badly. A twelve year old Ford Explorer which had been reported stolen two years earlier, was converted into a fuel oil and fertilizer bomb and parked in front of the superior court building in downtown L.A.. There wasn't enough volume of material to do anywhere the same kind of damage but if it had gone off during

130

the lunch hour when it had been left there, it would have still maimed and killed a large number of innocent people. Fortunately, however, it was either rigged improperly or something in the timing-igniter mechanism failed, or.... No one knew for sure, as yet.

The way it had been left there was an interesting deception also. As witnessed by the traffic cop on duty, the paint faded and dented vehicle looked barely drivable when it came down the street. As it approached the location it coughed and sputtered a few times before the driver pulled it into the curb, right in the red, no parking area. Then he cranked the engine over several times to no avail, leaving the policeman sputtering also, as he approached from behind. All the rear windows were covered with a thick layer of window tint, making it impossible to see inside. Before he made it around, the driver got out, lifted up the hood, put the steel support rod in place, stuck his head inside, jiggled a few things and backed out as anti freeze started leaking out of the lower radiator hose which a later check indicated had been pierced with a sharp instrument. At this point the driver swore loudly, kicked the bumper and walked away, refusing to heed the officer's order to stop.

A backup was called, along with a tow service. Before either arrived, however, the officer opened the passenger side vehicle door to see if there was any registration in the glove box. It was then that he noticed the extremely strong smell of diesel fuel and something worse. Looking in the back he saw a dark plastic tarp covering some kind of load that went clear to the roof. He took out his pocket knife, made a slit in the tarp, reached a hand in and felt. It was relatively soft and the combined stink of diesel and fertilizer almost choked him. Immediately, Timothy McVeigh came to mind.

By the time the bomb squad had arrived, the officer had flagged down a passing patrol car and with the help of another backup pair, had cleared the area and stopped all the street traffic a block away on both ends, shaking in his boots the whole time and staying as far away from the Explorer as he could without looking like a complete wutz.

Within minutes half the official vehicles in the city were there. Fire and Rescue, Bomb Squad, a dozen black and whites, unmarked Chevy Suburbans from Homeland Security along with gas and electric company trucks, water and sewer trucks, and a whole lot more, with all their attendant passengers huddled behind the largest of the fire engines, more than half a block away. Was it a fertilizer bomb? Damned right. But now what? What the hell did they do now besides having enough sense to stuff their ears with Kleenex and pray?

The last thing anyone wanted was for it to go off, even if there were no human casualties. The damage might run into millions, the mayor was running for re election and budgets were tight. But it was going to go off anyway, or so everyone thought. If it was a bomb, it had to. The question was, when? And that question brought more questions. As described by the officer who called it in, maybe the Explorer had really quit running right there of its own accord. Then this might not be the intended target and maybe it wasn't timed to go off just yet. On the other hand, maybe it was the target but the bomb builder only wanted to do a lot property damage and purposely let it be discovered so the area could be cleared before it detonated. Or maybe something failed. That would be the best scenario. But how to find out? What were their options? Time was going by.

"Well, we don't have any big-ass magic blanket we can throw over it to soak up all the shock," the bomb squad reported.

"But if we had some super thick, reinforced concrete slabs and some crane operators dumb enough to get that close, we could build a deflecting barrier around it that would send most of the shock upward."

"If we had a big enough, remotely controlled fork lift, we could pick it up and load it on a remotely controlled truck and try to haul it away. But what if it blew on some other street before we got to the largest open parking lot in the city, wherever that is."

"Or we could have it airlifted out with a military cargo helicopter, but again, what if it went off in transit?"

"Or we can get the ten cops together who graduated at the bottom of the last academy class and draw straws to see who gets the privilege of trying to defuse it."

The Mayor showed up, along with the Chief of Police, the

County Sheriff, half the city council, some members of the county board of supervisors and ninety nine percent of the local media. After three hours no major decisions had been made as to how to safely deal with the threat but things had settled enough so that coffee and donuts were brought in for the strategists. As three hours became five, the number of excuses began growing as to why many of them suddenly had to be somewhere else and the crowd thinned as powered generators and trailers of floodlights were brought in for later, when it was dark.

At six forty seven, when all the city's day workers were home watching the networks trying to keep the story alive, the foot soldier cop who had made the initial determination said, "Well, shit," in a very loud voice. Then he took off his badge, took out his semi automatic handgun and handed them to his captain who was beginning to insist that someone had made a mistake. With that done he turned around, left the safety of the oversized fire engine and headed towards the rear of the Explorer, which faced their way. Several people shouted at him to stop but no one was brave enough to step out and restrain him, especially since by the time anyone fully realized what he was doing, he was already half way there.

When he got there he grabbed the tailgate handle. It was unlocked. He lifted the tailgate full up. For the second time that day he took out his pocket knife and cut a huge flap out of the plastic tarp and let it drop, exposing the dark pile of saturated fertilizer. Then he turned around and ran just as fast as his over weight body and his damned feet would allow him to go.

"You crazy bastard. What the hell did you do that for?"

He patted the side of the fire engine and said, "Get the hose going. Spray some water in there, wash some of that stuff out onto the street. The more you get out and the more it's dispersed, the smaller the explosion."

Much to the disappointment of some elements of the media, the bomb did not go off. And since the act did not appear to be a threat to national security, Homeland handed it off to the FBI, care of Jack Kremel. Jack quickly assigned the case to George Dixon.

George was not doing well on the personal level, however.

His wife had left in a nasty divorce four years earlier. He didn't have a girlfriend to divert him. He didn't associate with hookers. He didn't have a hobby and he didn't play poker with the boys and he found spectator sports to be an annoying waste of time. Instead, he compensated by working. Especially since he had lost his partner, Stan Gibson. After all these weeks, Jack felt he was still in shock so he loaded him up. Anything to help get him through the crisis. Now George was in Jacks' office giving him a progress report.

"Over-confidence does it every time," he said. "There were more fingerprints than we could count. All the same individual. And he's in the system. Would you believe that?"

Jack smiled and shook his head.

"Yeah, dumb. Like the guy who robbed the bank out in Van Nuys by writing his threatening note on the back of his telephone bill and forgetting to take it back."

"Or like the one in Long Beach who lost his wallet when he ran out the door."

After they chuckled over it, Jack asked if the guy had been picked up.

"Can't find him. He's an illegal. Picked up twice and sent back twice. The last one after a year in county for car theft. Extremely abusive in court also. Called the judge a string of bad names and threatened to do what he just tried. The judge was in district court at the time and only recently made it over to superior."

"So, he's south of the border."

"More than likely. But he'll be back. Count on it. And we'll get him."

"Well, one good thing about it. It's obviously not related to the other bombings.

Next, they discussed two other cases George was working on. Sale of automatic weapons and interstate trafficking. After that it was back to old business. Jack began by digging through the scattered papers on his desk. Finding the single sheet he was looking for, he passed it over to George.

George looked at it briefly. "What's this?"

"I just got it this afternoon."

George looked at the sheet again.

"Jeez. Douds. We had him under surveillance?"

"The same."

"Somebody cut through his wall in the middle of the night and drugged him? Now that is pretty damned weird."

"Drugged him but didn't kill him."

"On purpose?"

"Hard to tell. Maybe."

"Like letting Tony Platt live. Jesus, Jack. What kind of half ass criminals are we dealing with? This is getting ridiculous. Can we stick it in the file cabinet and come back in a year?"

"Might be nice. Technically, this one belongs to LAPD but we know it's related and we need to stay involved."

"Meaning me."

"Meaning you. The probability of Douds actually providing us with anything useful is pretty small. But maybe someone left something behind. Maybe you can help find it. And while you're doing that, this time I'll order an in-depth background check on the man."

"I'd sure like to come up with sufficient cause to search his office."

"See what you can do. And count on coming over to the house Friday night. Ruth is doing her home made ravioli dish again," Jack said but didn't tell George about the recently divorced neighborhood friend of his wife's who would be inadvertently dropping by.

EIGHTEEN

At the risk of his receiver-recorder being found, Joe waited until mid day on Tuesday to pick it up. It was garbage collection day. The gas company meter reader would also be making the rounds. If he wore work clothes and a helmet and carried a small clip board, maybe he could make it look like he was inspecting power poles or something, and no one would bother.

He entered the alley from the south so he would not have to pass behind Douds' condo but as he approached the block wall where it was hidden, two men came out the back door of Douds' residence. He ducked behind a dumpster and waited, pretending to scribble on his clip board just in case someone else had seen him. A quick glance over the top convinced him that they were plain clothes cops. Jeez. Another twenty feet and he would have retrieved what he had come for and been out of there.

The cops came down the few steps and went next door where they viewed the window that had by now been replaced. Then they knocked on the door. When it was answered they talked briefly with whoever had come, then went inside.

Casually, Joe moved further up the alley. When he thought he was at the right place he felt along the top of the high wall. He cursed to himself. It was gone. No, not the right place. A little further. Closer to the next telephone pole. Better be or he was in trouble. He kept going, stopped, placed his clip board against the wall and once more pretended to write on it. Then he reached up and felt around. Found it, but damned near knocked it off the top into the yard behind. He slipped it into his pocket but just as he was ready to retrace his steps the rear door of the condo opened and the two cops started out. By now Joe was less than half a block away. Quickly, he looked up at the telephone wires, took his clip board, pretended to take a note, turned around and casually began to walk away, quite sure he was being watched. Fighting the urge to panic and run, he stopped and bent over as though tying a shoe lace. Then up again, another few feet to go and he would be out of there. Then a man's voice.

"Sir. Sir, just a minute."

Joe kept going.

"Sir," the voice much louder this time.

Joe turned the corner. Now hidden by the last building in the long row of condos, he began to run, taking off the helmet as he did so. But he didn't dare toss it or the clip board, just in case. Then he darted left between parked cars, crossed the street and made it to the next cross street. Should be okay, he had had at least a football field worth of distance before he started running. There was no one around except some woman getting into her car farther along. He slowed down and began walking casually as he also slipped out of his jacket and wrapped it around the helmet and clipboard. The bus stop was on the next corner. He checked his watch. It was going to be close. He speeded up a little, then when the lady in the car had passed, he began to run again. But like he was running for the bus and not away from something.

Joe had subleased a condo on the ninth floor in one of the towers along Ocean Boulevard in Santa Monica that had a panorama of the Pacific and a section of the beach below. He had always liked a place with a view. If he ever bought another house, that would be one of the major requirements. That and quiet. He had once lived in another high rise on Wilshire Boulevard in Beverly Hills but the noise of unrelenting traffic at that location was too overwhelming. Fresh air and open windows were impossible if a person wanted to sleep.

This place was far better. The steep palisades blocked the noise from Pacific Coast Highway below and the traffic on Ocean was tolerable. Aided by prevailing off shore breezes, the temperature was always comfortably less than in the city just a few miles east and occasionally there was a sunset that made even the worst of everyday occurrences fade away. In between there were walks on the beach to help clarify controversial issues. At the moment Joe was out on the balcony, earphones on and plugged into the recorder he had retrieved earlier. Already rewound, he hit the play button. There was the sound of a ringing phone. It was picked up on the fourth. A man's voice.

"Tony?"

"Yeah. Who's this?"

"Douds."

"Jeez. It's still the middle of the night. What happened?"

"You'll never believe it," Douds said, in an over stressed voice.

"Maybe not. You sound like you're half dead."

"Yeah, was anyway," Douds said and went through the explanation.

"God damn!"

"Exactly. Are you going to be up this way this week. We need to talk."

"Anything in particular?"

"Yeah. Any ideas on who blew up your house yet?"

"Don't I wish. But this is getting pretty damned serious."

"For sure. Thought you might like a heads up, just in case."

"Are you still sure you still trust her? You know my feelings about that one," Tony continued.

"I do. But it's just not her style. Can you bring that new guy along?"

"Vince's replacement? Sure. I'll call you back for time and place."

Well, well, Joe thought as he hit the pause button. He got up, going over it in his mind. Then he went inside, made a cup of instant coffee, came back out, sat down and picked up the headset. The second call was also initiated by Douds but since the recorder was voice activated and only came on when there was someone on the line, there was no way to tell how long between calls. Probably not much later, Joe decided. And the way it was answered could only mean that Margaret had caller ID and knew who was on the other end.

"It's Sunday, the sun isn't even up yet. What's wrong?" she asked in a harsh voice.

"Jesus Christ. Are you surprised to hear from me?"

"At this time of day, yes. Where are you calling from?"

"Home, dammit"

"Can't we get together tomorrow at the office?"

"We might. If I live that long and can get there."

"What's does that mean? You don't sound ill. You sound mad as hell."

"I am mad as hell," Douds almost screamed, his voice now raspy and hoarse.

"Goddammit. Enough. It's Sunday and it's too damned early. Give me a clue."

"Rudy, Vince and his helpers, Tony, Trent. All of it."

"What are you saying?"

"I don't know but under the circumstances maybe it's my turn. Except there were reasons for what happened to them. What the hell did I do?"

"I don't know. Is there something you haven't told me? And what the hell are you so hot about? Care to share that with me before I hang up on you?"

Douds was silent for what seemed like a long time. He was calmer when he finally spoke. "The doctor just left. Someone tried to poison me in my sleep."

"In your sleep? How could someone do that without waking you up? That doesn't make any sense."

Douds went on to explain the hole in his closet wall and his theory as to how it might have happened.

"But... My god. Are you all right?"

"No, but I'll make it," he said and went on. The doctor had had him on pure oxygen for over an hour before he left. The stomach cramps had diminished but the headache was still maddeningly painful. He wouldn't be in the office in the morning. Maybe not even for the whole week. Now if he just had some assurance that she hadn't masterminded the episode, he said to himself. Then he might be okay. If he was sure he could believe her.

Amazingly, she seemed to have read his mind.

"Dammit, Douds. It wasn't me. You know exactly where you stand and I have no intentions of changing that. When and if I do, you'll be the first to know. That's a promise."

"Does that mean that you never made any promises to .....?" he started to ask in his confusion, his mind not working too well as yet, now realizing that it was a stupid comment.

"Only one," she replied coldly, answering him anyway. "I told the bastard that if he didn't treat me right, I'd have his ass. Now go back to bed and get some rest.. I'll see you tomorrow."

The tape had two more calls on it. Both were with Douds' doctor. The first had to have been during the day. He was feeling slightly better. Good, call me again later, the doc said. And then, on the second call the doctor quizzed him extensively, said if he was feeling okay the next morning, he could resume his activities, and, make an office appointment for later in the week.

Joe shut off the recorder, stripped off the headset, leaned back in his chair and put his feet up on the railing. So. There was dissension in the ranks. He had to get back inside Margaret's house. But with her security system, that could only happen if she invited him. Which, with Douds' mishap, might take a while. Or it might not. Margaret might already be ten steps ahead of the situation. Meantime, give it a couple of days and try to find the new guy in the organization. If he hadn't heard from her by then, there were other options.

Douds viewed his physical recovery as miraculous. But his mind had been shattered. The closet wall had been repaired, an expensive intruder alarm system installed but his sense of security was forever destroyed.

So was his wife's. She seemed hysterically unable to deal with it. He had difficulty coming home at night, fearing she would no longer be there, gone off to her mother's, or her sister's and he would have to be there alone. That would really be difficult. Despite all that he had still been in his office early Tuesday morning, giving his secretary instructions to tell no one that he was there and to say that he probably wouldn't be in all week, either. Take messages and leave him alone. That's what he wanted, so he could do some serious thinking about his future. But in spite of all that, on the following day before he could even begin, Margaret walked into his office unannounced. Startled, he looked at his watch, then up at her. What now?

"I didn't tell anyone I was coming in today. How did you know I was here?"

Margaret simply shrugged. "I have someone you need to meet," she said as she turned and motioned for that someone to come in. A big, solid looking man, not a person to be messed with if you met him in an alley. But not a thug or a bully. There was a reasonable intelligence in the eyes.

"Mr. Greer. This is Mr. Douds, my attorney. Mr. Douds, Jake Greer."

With that introduction Greer stepped forward, hovered over Douds' desk and extended his hand. Douds stared up at him for a moment, then came to his feet and with uncertainty, shook hands. Then he stepped back and scratched his ear but kept silent.

"Mr. Greer is a private investigator," Margaret said. "He's the one who located Vanalden for us."

Douds took a better look at the man, then back at Margaret. His face went pale. Had this guy tapped his phone and reported some of his conversations to Margaret.? Was she their to confront him?

"He has contacts within the police department," she told him. "And some federal agencies. I thought it might be good to have him review the circumstances of your break in. See what he can find out."

Douds relaxed. "Good to meet you," he said, warming up. "Yes. Okay. Well......sure, why don't we leave it in your hands.

And let me know how I can be of help," he said, feeling better.

But then something else occurred to him. Why hadn't he heard of Greer before? An outsider snooping around. Damn right he'd like to find the bastard who violated his home and almost killed him. He'd cut his balls off. But did he want some stranger digging through his life? That might be even more dangerous. And the guy had already tracked down Vanalden. Did he know the reason behind it? Did he know how Vanalden's life ended?

"Jeez, Margaret. I hope you know what you are doing?" he said to himself. And then one final thought. Was it some of both. Part truth, part ruse? Certainly Margaret wanted to find the individual who came after him because that person might well be coming after her next. But at the same time she might also be using the situation to check out his own loyalty. Or....

But before he could analyse things any further, Greer said, "well, get back to you later Mr. Douds," and they left. As soon as they were gone, Douds sat back down and stared out of his tenth floor window for almost half an hour. Then he swung around, picked up the phone and dialed Margaret's private number. When she answered, he began expressing his concerns about Greer. He didn't get far.

Margaret assured him Greer was safe. He was an old associate of Rudy's and leave it at that. Well, it was the first Douds knew about it, but, so what and okay. If she trusted him, why not take it a step further.

"Maybe you should have him check out that guy you went out with. Carroll, right? ....Nothing personal, just a thought," he suggested, hoping that is what it sounded like.

It was at this same time that Joe Carroll was also trying to reach him. He had dialed the number of Douds' office and received the usual secretarial interrogation and was told Douds was not in the office. Maybe not till next week.

"Tell him I found his wallet and that I'd be happy to return it for a small consideration," Joe said, ignoring her comment.

"But sir. I told you he's not in today. If you leave a number I'm sure he'll call as soon as he can."

"His car is in his reserved spot down in the garage so give him the message and get him on the phone."

141

"But, sir."

"But nothing. He'll thank you for telling him."

The phone went on hold. No music. Not dead. Just silence.

"Hello. This is Douds. Who am I speaking to?"

"Maybe the guy who cut a hole in your closet wall. Do I have your attention now?"

"You son of a bitch. You tried to kill me."

"If that had been my intention we wouldn't be having this conversation."

"Okay, goddammit. Then what do you want?"

"Just the answer to two or three questions."

"Are you crazy? You did all that just to ask me some questions."

"No. I also want answers to my questions. And if I don't get the truth, I can cut another hole in your wall, or I can blow up your car or I can send a rocket through your office window someday when you are on the phone. Clear enough?"

"Yes, but.... Jesus, I'm just an attorney. And if I violate someone's confidentiality and answer the wrong question, I'm dead."

"I guess you'll have to work that out for yourself. And now that Vince Sands is no longer in the game, the first thing I want to know is who he took orders from? That shouldn't be too hard."

"Well, Rudy Stark was the man in charge. You must know that by now."

"Of course, dammit. But where was Sands in the chain of command? And who specifically gave him his orders? Who, for example, told him to send his thugs out to firebomb that house in Santa Monica last fall?"

"How do you expect me to know that. I just handled certain legal aspects for the firm he was the head of."

"Yeah. The same firm you are still a part of. So who is deciding which legal aspects you devote your attention to now that he's gone?"

"I can't tell you that. It's confidential."

"Damn right. Just like this conversation is as long as you cooperate. Now answer the question and hurry up about it or next time I pay you a visit you won't be so lucky."

"Oh, god. You're just as, as...."

"As she is. Right?"

"Ahh, well.."

"Okay. Good. And now that we agree on who we are talking about, I am probably worse. So get on with it. Tell me exactly what you do remember about that situation at the time."

"Well, I can't speak with absolute certainty but there was some talk about that whole thing. The rumor was that she... You don't mind if I don't say her name. She was fooling around with the guy next door. Trent. Trent was also infringing on some of Rudy's business interests so it was complicated. Some say Rudy ordered the hit to put an end to his competitor, some say she did it to teach Trent a lesson for messing around. Either way someone got the address wrong."

"Do you really believe it was that simple? I know Vince and his two thugs weren't very bright but were they really that stupid? So what were her's and Rudy's reactions when they found out? Did they both treat it like it was a mistake?"

"You are really getting me in deep. Whoever you are. Christ, I can't believe I'm doing this. I don't even know who I'm talking to."

"The guy who found your wallet, remember. So keep going.

"Yes, well.... dammit... My secretary just passed me a note. My "client" is on the other line. What do you want me to do?"

"Just don't put me on hold. Have your secretary tell her to wait. And I want to hear your voice. Then tell her to go out and close the door behind her."

It took but a second and Douds was back. "Let's see. Where were we? Oh yes, damn. Well, you have to keep in mind that I wasn't in on any privileged conversations."

"Bullshit. Answer the question. What was Rudy's reaction?"

After a short pause Douds responded. "I think he seemed rather surprised."

"About what?"

"The whole thing."

"The whole thing? You mean like he didn't know about it ahead of time?"

"That's just my guess, mind you. I never knew for sure."

"What about her?"

"She was different," Douds admitted and the phone went

143

dead.

Not having heard from Margaret by Wednesday, Joe checked out the below ground parking area adjacent to the elevators where her driver usually picked her up at lunch time. The man was always there with the limo at least ten minutes early. And he was there today. Joe was a good distance away, somewhat hidden by his own vehicle, ready to get in and follow her, having planned another random encounter once she got to her destination. Not only to see her again in person but to somehow get her to use her cell phone during that time and be within a certain range when she did it. He had a new piece of electronic gear in his jacket pocket.

There was a steady stream of people getting off the elevators. But at last, there she was, dressed in a snug fitting black skirt, white blouse and black jacket, her dark hair elegantly coiffured. God, he thought. If only she wasn't who she was, or at least who he thought she was turning out to be. But maybe just as well. This way he was safe. He really wasn't ready for anything else, anyway.

As he watched, her driver got out and opened the rear door but instead of getting in, she stopped and dug in her purse. Taking out her cell phone, she opened it, dialed a number and held it up to her ear. Joe jumped in surprise as his own phone rang. He ducked down, hoping it couldn't be heard from where she was.

"Hello."

"Joe?"

"Ah, yeah. Margaret?"

"Where are you at?"

"I.. was just going into the bank in Westwood" he lied. "Need something?"

"If you're free, would you like to meet for lunch."

"Hmm. Sure. That would be nice. Where are you?"

"I'm not there yet. But I know a nice place over on Sunset with an outside patio."

"Sunset? What's it called?"

"Butterfields. If you come up Doheny and take a right, go down about.... wait, let me ask my driver what street you turn on next. The parking is down below in the back."

"That's okay. I think I know the place. Probably could be there in half an hour."

"Half an hour, then," she said and hung up as Joe ducked into his car and kept his head down while they drove on past, towards the garage exit. Then he checked the digital display on his new toy and smiled. What a coincidence. Couldn't have been easier, he said to himself.

He gave her a five minute lead, then followed. By the time he had left his car with the valet and came up the sidewalk, he could see her at an outside table, back in the corner, under the shade of an immense old elm tree. He smiled at her, gave her a quick kiss on the cheek and sat down.

Joe told her she looked stunning. She thanked him. He asked her if she would like to have another night out sometime. She demurred. He told her about his new condo and said that next time she was in the area she should stop by for a drink. She quizzed him about other things, all very subtly, skillfully interweaving her questions around the rest of their conversation. In the end, however, it was clear she was looking for some tangible piece of background information that might be used to check him out.

"My mother's maiden name was Thomas," he said to her.

"What?"

"My mother. Her last name was Thomas."

"And you're telling me that because?"

"Because maybe a woman has the right to know something about the men she's having sex with," he said, lightly enough, as if it were all in fun.

"Hmmm," she returned. "Except it's man. Singular. You're it for now. But don't get too cocky about it," she said and laughed at her choice of words. "And as long as you keep in mind that what we had was sex and none of that making love BS. Who's kidding who."

"Okay. Cocky but not too cocky. And yeah, we don't have to molify it. There's honesty in just getting laid," Joe said as he got out his pen, took his still clean white napkin, wrote on it and handed it to her with a playful shrug.

"What's this supposed to be?"

"My high school English teacher's name as a personal

reference and my shirt size in case you ever want to buy me a present," he said as if it were all in fun. Then he said, "oops," took it back and wrote some numbers on it also. "Okay, that should do it. Just in case you have any reservations about my ability to buy you lunch or something."

"And the numbers are... what?"

"My checking account balance and my social security number. I'd give you my Swiss Bank account info if I knew you better," he said, hoping it was far enough over the top so that she wouldn't think it was done deliberately because he purposely did want her to check him out. Even though the social security number wasn't his, it at least belonged to the guy whose name he had assumed.

Glancing at it, she looked back at him as though trying to catch him in a lie but it was gone in an instant as he gave it a new slant.

"Well, you already know how big my dick is, so what the hell," he smiled and shrugged.

She laughed and left the napkin lying on the table as if it were unimportant. Then she made eye contact and held his gaze.

"It's been more than a week. You wouldn't mind if I checked it out again?"

"What's that?"

"Your dick, you sonofabitch. I was going to take the afternoon off and sit in the sun but sitting here looking at you, I'm getting horny as hell. There's been a lot of pressure at work recently. A good fuck might help me get my perspective back."

"Probably wouldn't hurt," he said after he had stared back at her for a few seconds. Then he dug out his cell phone and dialed a random number. "This is Joe. Yeah. I need to cancel my appointment for this afternoon if that's not too inconvenient.... Right..... Maybe tomorrow at the same time. Is that okay? Thanks," he ended, put the phone away and signaled the waitress. "Your place or mine?" he asked Margaret.

"Mine," she said and picked up the napkin. "And if you only give me half as many climaxes as last time I'll still buy you a new shirt. Maybe a blue one."

Neither of them had spoken a word in what felt like some

interminable amount of time, expended by intense bouts of heavy breathing, interlaced with short moments of recuperating, side by side inactivity. Then, after another intense bout, Margaret sat up in bed and reached into her night stand drawer for a cigarette.

"Do you always smoke after sex?" he asked.

"Only if it was any good."

"Okay. And does that mean it's also time for me to leave?"

"Is that what you want?"

"Depends."

"Did you like your piece of ass?"

"Is that how you look at it?"

"Why not? I wanted to get laid and you gave me a great fuck. So, I hope you enjoyed what you were doing."

"Damn right. Couldn't get enough."

"Well, it's nice to know you're fully functional. That's a plus."

"Meaning what?"

"You're not one of those dysfunctional males who need a prescription to get it up. Thank god. But don't get any wrong ideas. Just because you've been there on two separate occasions doesn't mean there'll be a third."

"Okay. It's your ass. If you want to share it, I'm available. But maybe I should start charging for services rendered," he said as though it was an attempt at humor. Then he looked at her mouth and wondered how she would react if he tried to kiss her intimately. Probably throw him out the window. Sex was one thing. Kissing would be an infringement. Which was just fine with him. He didn't have to play silly games about pretending to be in love with her.

"You mean you would take money for sex?"

"Would you pay me?"

"Never. Would you pay me?"

"Only by trying to make sure you were fully satisfied before I put my pants back on."

"That's good to know. And since I'm feeling fully satisfied, maybe I'll invite you back again," she said and took a long drag on her cigarette.

"Well, then I'd better go home and rest up. Just in case," he said with a smile as he found his shorts and trousers. Then he turned his back to her briefly as if he were going to get dressed but got something out of a pocket, instead, and palmed it.

"Mind if I use your bathroom first?" he said as he dropped the clothes back on the bed.

Assuming she would take advantage of the opportunity, he dawdled, giving her plenty of time to go through his pants and learn there was nothing there except his keys, a wallet with a California diver's license, two credit cards with Joe Carroll's name on them and a wad of hundred dollar bills and a few twenties. When he returned, she left for the bathroom, and while she was gone he slipped on his shorts and pants, dropped his keys on the floor, then got down and looked under the bed. Finding the phone wire running from the phone on her night stand to the wall, he slipped the phone bug he had palmed over the wire and pushed it back out of sight.

"What are you doing down there?" Margaret asked, having returned before he had been able to get completely to his feet.

"Dropped my keys," he said as he showed them to her. Then he finished dressing while she sat on the bed and watched, somewhat lost in thought.

NINETEEN

"The guy's pretty damned lucky," George was telling Jack. "At least his timing was. Ten minutes after he disappeared, I found this bug on Douds' phone line out behind his condo. The second I saw it, I knew it had a limited range. Probably just about as far as where I first saw this guy. But he had on work clothes, a helmet and was carrying a clipboard like he was inspecting the telephone poles in the alley. I knew something didn't seem right but the LAPD cop was giving me so much static about being there and then when we came back outside, it was too late. Anyway, about six feet tall. Couldn't see the face well except there was hair on it, but from the way he walked I'd say thirties or forties. No older. And no sign of anyone else around. There was some traffic in the street but I didn't hear a car drive off in a hurry. Or see one when I got around front."

"Did you canvas the area? Anyone else see him?"

"Nothing."

"What about Douds?"

"Fully recovered, scared to death, but tight as a clam. Probably has no more idea about who did it than we do."

As near as Joe could tell, Margaret's occasional need for ravishing sex was an anomaly in her life. And having followed her for weeks, he had the exclusive on that one. At least for now. Running the organization was her work, her hobby, her entertainment and recreation. The only time she was ever home was to sleep or change clothes. It seemed he had taken an unnecessary risk by putting the tap on her phone. A week went by without one call, either in or out.

Then she broke silence.

"Jake Greer," answered the recipient.

"This is Margaret."

"Right. Has something else happened?"

"No. Just wondering if you have made any progress. Have you come up with any new names?"

"Nothing specific. I have all the police case reports. And, as I'm sure you already know, the FBI was out to see Mr. Douds and his wife on that one. Other than that all I can say is that I have my best man on it."

"What about Corbin? Have you located him yet?"

"Seems to have disappeared after that incident out in Moorpark. He was living in Arizona before coming to California. We're checking that out to see if that's where he went."

"And what about Carroll? Is he who he says he is?"

"So far. In the present, at least. The social security number looks legit. How far back do you want me to go?"

"I think the police missed something. At Vince's or Tony's or Douds'. They must have. I think you should concentrate on that for now."

"Are you involved with this guy Carroll?"

"Why do you ask?"

"If I'm going to do the job you hired me for, I need to know."

"It's nothing serious."

"Has he ever been inside your house?"

"On two occasions, yes. Is that a problem?"

"It's eleven pm. Where are you calling from?"

"My home. Why?"

"Have you ever had it swept for bugs?"

"What for? I haven't used this phone in weeks. My business calls are from the office and you check that regularly."

"Every week. And so far always clean. Want me to send someone out to your house?"

"It's not a priority. But wouldn't someone have to get inside to do that? And if so, where would they hide it?"

"Unless you have underground utilities it could be on the outside as with Douds' condo where the phone wires come in. Or in the headset of the phone, the answering machine or lots of other places. Depends on the device."

"Would I recognize such a thing if I saw it?"

"Probably not, but again, it depends on where its at and how big it is."

"Well, maybe you should check. Just in case."

"I'll try and get out there before the weekend."

"Let me know. I need to be here."

"Absolutely. And I probably don't need to remind you but...."

"Thank you, but no you don't."

"Well, best to be prepared. And I still think you should make me a list. Anyone, inside or out."

"Yes. Maybe I should."

So..... Greer had to be a security guy, maybe a private detective, one with good contacts inside the police department. Something else to damn well keep in mind, Joe told himself as the tape played out. Meanwhile, it sounded like all Margaret wanted of him was for him to simply be just some guy who accidentally bumped into her at a restaurant a few months back and was keeping her happy in bed. So far, so good. Take advantage of it while it lasted. But if Greer went out to her house and found his phone bug, then what? As for getting back inside Margaret's house, the only way he was going to risk that was by direct invitation. That might be tomorrow. Or it might be two weeks from now. Or never.

But maybe there was another way to solve that problem. To find the device he had left behind, Greer would have to either crawl under Margaret's bed and physically spot it, which might be difficult because it was very small and was tucked down into the

150

thick nap of the carpet, or they would have to pick up one of the house phones, causing the dial tone to activate the sound responsive device, then scan the room with a very sensitive broadband directional receiver to pick up its transmitted signals. The key to negating the bug was in the battery.

The battery was a tiny little watch battery. Its life was severely limited. Probably three or four hours of full time use because the bug drew far more power than a watch when transmitting. The device came on every time there was any signal on the phone line. Even the ringing. Joe didn't think Margaret had caller ID, but it could have been on another phone in the house. Just in case, he would be using a new throw away cell phone. Nor was an answering machine a problem. It would only make the job more tedious. But it wasn't as difficult as he had imagined. There was no answering machine so all he had to do was wait until Margaret had left for her office in the morning, then call her home number and let the phone ring steadily for several hours. This he did on four separate occasions over the next two days. Then he drove down her street and parked out front long enough to call her number again as he waited with his own receiver. There was no return signal, meaning the battery was dead and the device was inoperative.

It would have to do until his next visit to her bedroom, when he could physically retrieve the evidence. A possibility in no way guaranteed before someone else discovered it. But, if someone else did and she confronted him he still had an out. Provided he could get her to explain what condition it had been in when found. He might then argue that the dead battery would indicate that it had been there for a long time. Longer than he had known her. Would she believe that? It was a hell of a stretch.

Somewhat relieved to find that the bug no longer seemed to be working, he started his car and was ready to pull away when, as coincidence would have it, his other cell phone rang. The one whose number he had given to Margaret.

"Hello. Joe here."

"Why haven't you called me?"

"Oh, Margaret. Hello. And I did call. Several days ago, actually. But you weren't in."

"You didn't leave a message."

"No. Your male secretary, or whoever he was, was about as cordial as a .... well. So I hung up."

She didn't respond, so he continued. "Anyway, it's nice to hear your voice," he said pleasantly. "How have you been?"

"I thought you might like to take me to dinner tomorrow night."

"I could do that. Where would you like to meet?"

"Since you know where I live, why don't you pick me up. Say about eight?"

"My pleasure. I'll see you then."

There was a new, black, full sized Chrysler parked out in the driveway of Margaret's house when he arrived. He pulled in at the curb and went to the door. One push of the bell and it was answered immediately by a man Joe quickly decided would be a real challenge in a physical confrontation. A very business like guy.

"Come on in," he said, holding the door open. "She should be here in a minute. Said help yourself to a drink if you like. Do you know where it's at?" he asked after Joe was inside and the door was closed.

"I do. But nothing for now, thanks," Joe said, wondering who the hell this guy was and what he was doing here. A body guard. Or someone about to beat the crap out of him? He looked around. No Margaret in sight and only the one guy but he wasn't about to sit down at this point. And when he turned back around he knew he was being studied. Especially his face. Turning away again he walked across the room so that he could see out through the full glass doors into the back yard and remained there until he heard her voice.

"Hi, Joe. Right on time," she said as she approached.

He smiled at her, gave her a peck on the cheek and told her how lovely she looked. Then he glanced at the man still standing in the same place as before. At this point she took his arm and led him over.

"Joe, this is Jake Greer. Mr Greer, Joe Carroll. I've been having some problems with my security system and Mr. Greer came over to take a look. But nothing serious. He'll have it fixed long before we get back."

Jesus Christ, Joe said to himself, the taped message of her conversation with this man was suddenly very clear in his mind. Greer was the private investigator. Damn her. She had set him up. This isn't about dinner. This guy was there to check him out in person. But then he smiled. He had to give her credit. The game was getting interesting.

Greer stuck out his big paw of a hand and they shook. Joe prepared himself for a bone crushing exchange but it never happened. Just like Margaret, this guy didn't need to prove anything either.

"Shall we go?" she said when they were done.

Joe opened the door and held it for her. Then he closed it behind him without looking back at Greer, keeping his concerns well hidden. First, the bug. Had it been found? And secondly, could Greer make out his real identity? How the hell would he ever find out before it was too late? That was the part that bothered him most. Unless Margaret told him, there was no way to gain access to Greer's findings or Greer's opinion of Joe. In the meantime, watch your ass, Joe Carroll.

"Something casual?" he asked once they were in his car.

"Perfect."

He drove to the Hamlet on Sunset, parked at the curb and handed the keys to the valet. Inside they found an out of the way booth in the back of the bar room and she asked him to order. Red wine and bacon cheeseburgers.

"Casual enough?" he asked after they were served.

"Perfect," she replied with a smile, taking a large bite. A very congenial smile which only added to his concerns. Margaret was behaving in a most adorable manner. Almost, but not quite too much. Was it yet another facet of her personality or another side to the deadly game he was caught up in? An open question, no clear answer in sight except that if she now knew who he really was, then she was openly taunting him and that was disappointing. Did she really think he was that stupid? He didn't think so because if she thought he was stupid and treated him that way, that would mean that she wasn't half as smart as he felt she was. No way. It couldn't be that she was just glad to see him, either. Something else had to be up. Or did it? Guess he would find out before this night was over.

153

But he was enjoying it, nevertheless, and deliberately avoided any reference to business, home security or anything else even remotely related. Instead he asked her innocent questions about the kinds of music she liked, did she ever go to the movies, did she like to travel, where had she been, what were her favorite places. Was she a tom boy as a child, or did she play with dolls? What were her religious convictions or absence thereof. Had she ever been married?

She responded with her usual repartee, a contrasting mix of candor and elusiveness that kept things lively, the marriage question being the single thing that seemed to pique her as they slowly worked their way through the meal. When it was over, she suggested a piano bar that was but a two block walk away.

"Great place for a nightcap," she said and told him the name of it.

"Never been there but sounds good."

"Great place," Joe said as they listened to some creative excursions on the piano from their place in a booth along the wall where they sat side by side facing the keyboard artist.

Margaret nodded and smiled, then subtly glanced at her watch. Minutes later a short, dark haired woman with beautiful features and interesting proportions climbed up on the grand piano, took the mike and began to sing. Joe was impressed as she went through a long repertoire of songs, American and French. He looked at Margaret. She certainly didn't look bored. He ordered another round. Then twice more he caught her subtly looking at her watch. And that raised another set of questions. Was she giving Greer a certain amount of time to check out her house. Would Greer still be there when they got back? Had he found the bug or seen through Joe's alter self? If so, would he be waiting to stuff Joe in the trunk of his own car and drive it out into the desert?

"Another date?" he asked, half joking.

She seemed surprised that he had noticed and it took a second for her to respond.

"Would you be jealous?"

"Would you want me to be?"

"Only if you're going to try and manipulate me into bed

154

tonight?" she said with a devilish smirk and put her hand on his leg.

Okay. One last roll in her big bed. And then what? Time to find out, Joe decided and signaled the waitress. They had their drink and then they left, he ready to make a last minute excuse and drop her at the curb if things didn't seem right. But as he turned the corner onto her street he could see the black car was gone from the drive and the rest of the street was largely empty. No cars in front of her house or parked close by. And none anywhere in sight that he recognized. He pulled in the drive, got out, went around and opened her door.

By the time she was up the steps, she had her keys out, quickly opened the door, stepped inside and tapped in her security code. Once the red light cleared she motioned him in. It was then that she saw the plain white envelope lying on the wet bar. She opened it, took out the single sheet of paper and read it. Without visible reaction, she tucked it and the envelope in her purse, turned to him and asked if he would like to fix them a drink. Joe complied, listening for the sounds of anyone else who might be in the house.

TWENTY

Once again Margaret went from her usual, sex was an all consuming lust mode, to her semi sullen morning after mode. But, being still alive, Joe was happy. So happy he kissed her on both cheeks and once on the mouth and told her he would be out of town for two or three weeks. He had to go to Europe to tie up some loose ends of his previous life. Then he went back to his sub leased condo and shaved off his mustache and his short beard and reviewed the changes in wardrobe he had been stockpiling. Next he walked the five blocks down the street to the bank and removed a package from a safe deposit box. Back at home he pulled on latex gloves and reinspected the contents for fingerprints, dirt, hairs or other debris and repacked the items in a sterile envelope, all the while being careful not to disturb the one clear print he knew was not his. Then a left handed, printed address and carefully applied postage and he retraced his steps down the street to the corner mailbox.

After responding to the multi level phone menu with a two, a five,a three and a six, Sam Corbin finally reached an operator.

"Federal Bureau of Investigation. How may I help you.

"George Dixon, please."

"One moment. Let me see if he's in.... Can I tell him what this is regarding?"

"Sam Corbin."

"Is that a case name?"

"No. It's my name. And I'd like to talk to him."

"Does he know who you are?"

"Hopefully."

The receptionist put Sam on hold.

"Dixon." came a man's voice after half a minute.

"Sam Corbin, George."

"Really? And to what do I owe the pleasure?"

"I thought it might be best to call in like you asked me to."

"That was way more than a month ago. Where have you been?"

"Your last words to me were to watch my back. I've been trying to do that."

"No. My last words were to call me and let me know how to get in touch with you. But you didn't do that. And if you've been watching the news you know what happened out in Moorpark."

"I did and I do," Corbin said, and paused, not about to try and express his condolences on the phone. "Just trying to keep a low profile. Sorry."

"Too bad for sorry. Why are you calling me now?"

"A progress report might be nice."

"Regarding what?"

"Who is trying to end my life?

"Want me to make something up?"

"In other words, no progress."

"I didn't say that. But if you want to discuss it, come in to my office."

Corbin delayed before responding.

"Doesn't sound like much to discuss but maybe I'll drop by in the morning," he said and hung up.

"No matter how much sympathy I might have for him, his attitude kinda offends me," George said to Jack after his conversation with Corbin.

"How so?"

"I don't know. No respect for authority. Something like that."

"Understandable, don't you think? No one is in jail for killing his wife or for shooting at him."

"I know, but I guess I'm still not completely comfortable with the idea that his house bombing was an accident."

"Well, I don't know. He couldn't possibly be involved with the rest of it. Other than his house, we know for a fact that he never had any associations with any of the other people involved at any level. Ever. That seems pretty clear."

"Yeah, but."

"Let it go, George."

"Can we put a tail on him after we meet?"

"What?"

"I think it's quite a coincidence that he just happens to call the day after we get another bunch of tape recordings in the mail. I think he's playing with us."

"That would be kind of arrogant."

"And sooner or later the cocky ones always go too far. That's what I'm waiting for. Maybe he already did. Have they run that print we found on the one cassette yet?"

"Let's find out," Jack said as picked up the phone, dialed a number and asked the person who picked it up a question.

"Hmm, really? ...... Yes, I know," Jack said and hung up. Then he looked at George.

"Was it Corbin's," George asked.

"No. So forget him. It was Vanalden."

"Vanalden? The LAPD cop? He's been dead for months. What was on the tapes."

"Three were the unedited originals for the ones we got back in the beginning with all the blank spots. The rest are recent but edited. Two have the attorney, Marvin Douds voice on them. One has a woman's voice speaking with some man, maybe an employee but lot's of gaps. They go on from there."

"So Vanalden had a partner after all, one who's still alive. I'd certainly like to give Corbin a lie detector test."

"Dammit, George. There's no evidence of any previous connection between the two. Completely different backgrounds, nothing in common and nothing in Corbin's background to indicate he is in any way capable of blowing up people's houses."

"Except a possible need for revenge. But yeah, you're probably right. It's a stretch and I'll try and get past it."

"So, unless we get something off those recordings, thus far we have nothing."

George thought it over, nodded his head back and forth as he considered it. Then his face went dark.

"But I still think the son of a bitch helped get Stan killed," he said.

"Corbin?"

"Damn right. He deliberately set the whole thing up."

Jack was somewhat shocked. They had been over it several times before but George's anger was still hanging out.... The problem was that it was George who had wanted to stake out Corbin's apartment in the first place and his guilt was still making him take responsibility for everything that had gone wrong. But Jack didn't respond to George's remark. He just sat there and gave George time, hoping he would reconsider. If not, how could he trust him to deal with any of it effectively?

"No," George said at last. "Much as I hate to admit it, I have to admit that Corbin really had nothing to do with it. Dammit! Sometimes I.... How damned long does it take before...?"

"You never do. That's the problem. All you can do is learn to live with it. And so far I think you've been doing a decent job of that."

"I don't know. Maybe. But no matter. Logic still creates a problem. I tell myself Corbin didn't pull the trigger on Stan but if he's the one who set the whole thing in motion by doing away with Sands, then he's still responsible. But that's not true either, because if someone hadn't set Corbin's house on fire then...and, and, and."

"Exactly. Might as well blame George Washington for winning the war with the British. But just remember, there's a lot more going on here than just that. Rudy's disappearance, Trent's murder. Drugs, prostitution, extortion, money laundering. Somehow, Corbin's wife was just collateral damage. We need to keep that all in perspective."

"Yeah, it's a bitch. But don't worry. I'm not going to do anything rash."

"Good enough," Jack said. "What time is he coming in?"

"First thing in the morning. But just for the hell of it, let's say he is involved."

"George, please."

"I know. Sounds like I'm obsessing but let me cover all bases and give you one last, what if. If, just for the hell of it, he was involved, he can't be a hundred percent sure we don't have some piece of evidence to link him to something. Unfortunately, my reaction is that he'd risk it, either way. And regardless, it's pretty damn clear that Corbin's being shot at on the freeway wasn't about road rage. Whoever did that has to be involved in the rest of it, whether Corbin is or not. That's what I'm hung up on. Why was Corbin shot at? Wrong house, wrong guy? A double coincidence. If nothing else, even if he's not part of it, someone obviously still thinks he is and that's what's got me hooked. So, maybe we could tail him and hope they try again."

"Yes, I see your point. Well taken, but we'd have to tell him first. And he'd have to be willing to come out of hiding. And under the circumstances we don't have the right to do that. Especially if he is someone's innocent target."

"But he already knows he's in danger. Under the circumstances we'd only be trying to protect him."

George lived alone in a small two bedroom stucco halfway up the hill, just a few blocks off Beverly Glen, with a partial view of the valley below. The un attached single car garage was around on the north side but it was still half full of his ex wife's possessions so he was forced to leave his own vehicle in the driveway when he was home. The payoff for that inconvenience was a somewhat imaginary connection to her that made him feel only slightly less lonely when he was there by himself. Maybe someday she would return. Not to collect the furniture but to stay.

House secured, George walked to his car, hit the remote to unlock it and got in. Forget the seat belt he never wore, he reached under his sport jacket and pulled his shoulder holster around to where it was more comfortable. Then he reached into the utility tray in the center console, grabbed his cell phone and was about to call the office when the passenger door opened and a man got in.

"Jesus Christ," he said as he reflexively freed his weapon before he realized who it was. He looked him over.

"Goddammit," he continued and scowled at Sam Corbin, embarrassed at how easily he had been duped.

"Take it easy, George," Corbin said. "I'm unarmed. I don't even have a sharp pencil on me."

"Is that supposed to be cute?" George asked as he took further notice. Corbin had on jeans, tennies, a colored T and a casual sport jacket. Big enough guy. Probably bigger than himself. Obviously fit. But the same as with their previous meeting, it was the eyes that got to him. Piercing blue and serious no matter what he might be saying. Then he tried to see if Corbin fit his memory of the guy in the alley behind Douds' condo that had disappeared. A guy wearing a hard hat, work clothes and carrying a clip board. Could be, but also, maybe not. The man had been too far away right from the beginning.

"No. I just don't want you shooting me," Corbin said, the door still open, his right foot still on the ground outside.

"Don't push your luck."

"With you, never."

"Then what are you doing here invading my privacy? You are supposed to be at my office."

"Okay. So I thought I might ride down the hill with you," Corbin said as he pulled his other leg in the car and shut the door.

"Like hell you will," George stated and opened his own door as if to get out. "Drive your own car."

"I got rid of it. And if you tell me to take a cab, I'm going home."

George glared at Corbin while Corbin stared back at him and shrugged. Then George got an idea. He shut his door, started the car and backed out of the driveway where he swung around and headed towards Beverly Glen.

"I'm sorry about your partner," Corbin stated a few blocks later.

"Don't even go there. He was a bright young guy with his whole life ahead of him," George once again reacted blindly in spite of all his good intentions to the contrary.

"You trying to lay the blame on me?"

"I think... never mind. Forget it, for christ's sake."

"So now I'm responsible for every son of a bitch who ever used a gun. Well, just remember this, you righteous bastard. At least he died quickly. My wife was thirty three with her whole life ahead of her and she died a very painful death after three long hours of suffering. And her life was my life. She was also two months pregnant and that life hadn't even begun yet. So don't judge me. You have no idea as to what I'm all about, or what I have or have not done, or what I am going to do from here on out."

George was shocked at the outburst as he looked at Corbin. Then he gripped the steering wheel with both hands and stared straight ahead out the windshield as he tangled with the increasing traffic on Beverly Glen and kept his silence.

"Okay," he said at last. "Let's start over."

"Depends on your attitude."

"Then what?"

"Maybe I could use some help."

"You?" George said as he turned to look at Corbin.

"Me. What's so strange about that?"

"First, tell me whatever it is that you haven't told me yet. What's your real connection to all this."

"All of what?"

"Your house getting blown up, you getting shot at on the freeway. Vince Sands, Tony Platt and Mr. Douds."

"You're the law enforcement expert. You tell me. Meanwhile, give me a break. Not only am I one of the victims, I'm on somebody's hit list for god sake."

"How about cassette tapes? Know anything about wire tapping?"

"That's enough, dammit. Stop the car and let me out."

George quit talking and didn't say a word for several blocks as he mentally admonished himself for a whole list of things.

"Okay," he said at last. "But if the reason you way laid me is to get a free breakfast, you can forget it."

"Already had mine," Corbin said in a neutral voice, quite content to leave the rest of it alone.

Two blocks before they got to Wilshire Boulevard George looked at Corbin for any signs of reaction and said, "Well, if you're not in too damned big of a hurry, how about we take a ride over to Hancock Park?"

Corbin remained passive. "Anything is better than sitting in your office," he said and that was the extent of his reaction.

George got in the left lane, put on his blinkers, caught the tail end of the green and turned left on Wilshire.

George purposely said no more. Any story he invented at this point would sound phony. Corbin remained silent also, which puzzled George a bit. The man seemed totally unconcerned. Not the behavior of a guilty person. No devious probing, no nervous chatter. Nothing.

Ten minutes later George pulled up in front of Mrs. Brown's house. When he had shut off the engine and pocketed the keys, Corbin looked around at the houses along the street as if seeing them for the first time.

"How long you going to be?" he asked.

"Just a few minutes," George responded.

"Okay. Want me to wait in the car or can I get out and walk around?"

"Want to tag along?"

Corbin didn't say anything but opened his door and got out. He waited until George came around the car.

"Where to?" he asked, as George pointed to the house directly in front of them and started up the walk to the front door. While George stood on the steps and knocked, Corbin looked at the over burdened flower beds along the front of the house. When the door was answered he bent down, fondled some of the roses and sniffed them deeply. After looking first at George, Mrs. Brown looked at Corbin. He stood back up and smiled at her.

"Mrs. Brown?" George said as he flashed his ID at her. "I'm agent George Dixon. You may remember my partner was here a while back and talked to you about a man who rented a room from you," George continued, keeping a sharp eye on Corbin while he did so.

"Why yes. Of course. A really nice young man. And is this your partner?"

"No ma'am. He's not. He's...," George started to say something but Sam cut him off by stepping up.

"Mr. Corbin," he said. "And you are. ...? Did I hear Mrs?"

"Mrs. Brown. But I'm widowed."

"Well, I certainly like your roses. Mine were always such a disappointment."

"Well, thank you," she said and put out her hand. Sam shook it heartily and looked her straight in the eye the whole time. Then he backed up a step as he smiled at her again.

"And how can I help you gentlemen?" she asked as she glanced from one to the other.

"I was just wondering if there has been anything else you might have thought of in the meantime about that tenant you had back then. The one Stan talked to you about."

"Oh, him. Charley. The older man. No. Nothing that I can think of. Just always wondered why he gave up his extra rent and security deposit. That was a bit strange. Never sent me a letter or anything or I would have given most of it back. Well, maybe he still will one of these days."

"That is a bit odd, all right. And he was only here for what, two weeks, I believe you said."

"No, not that long. Kind of a strange fellow though. Much too quiet. And I don't think he liked my flowers, either. Just as well, now that I think of it."

"Why is that, ma'am?"

"Well, this may sound silly from someone as old as me but at first I thought he might be someone I could take an interest in. You know. On a personal level. But then after he was gone I realized he wasn't for me. Not only did he not seem to like my flowers, he had those kind of insipid brown eyes. Not very attractive, and he would seldom ever look right at me, if you know what I mean. My husband Bill, now he had blue eyes. Sparkly ones like your partner here. Sometimes I wish I weren't quite so old. Oh, well. Nothing to complain about. I had a very dear relationship with him before he passed on. A lot of good years."

"Okay, sure. That's good, Mrs. Brown. Sorry to have bothered you. But if if this Charley should ever get in touch with you I would appreciate it if you would give me a call," George said as he handed her one of his cards.

"So, what was that all about?" Corbin asked George as they were back on Wishire heading west. "Didn't seem all that urgent to me."

"No. Just something I told my boss I'd follow up on. And today all my status reports are due. That's why I need to know when, where and how you met Vanalden."

"Vanalden? That cop you told me about who got himself killed? Didn't we get that straight the last time?"

Jesus, George thought. What the hell was he doing? Why was he trying to interrogate the guy when driving? And why didn't he just leave it alone like he should have? But he couldn't so he responded instead.

"We got nothing straight. All I did was to tell you he was a guy with a revenge motive just like you, who got himself killed. I never asked if you knew him?"

"No, but I'm getting the impression you did your best to check it out?"

George didn't answer so Corbin came back with another question.

"So, what's the point? What else?"

"You're a pretty smart guy. Ever bug anyone's phone?"

"We covered that one, too."

"Where were you on the night of July 17th?"

"Jeez. I don't know. Probably home. What day of the week was it?"

"All right. Forget it. Just tell me if there is anything you care to discuss now that you've been shot at and tracked down at that apartment of yours?"

"That's why I'm here."

"Really? Something else happen also?"

"No. I decided it's time to kill myself, instead."

George's head spun around and he stared at Sam until an approaching car honked at him. He turned back just in time to jerk the wheel over and avoid an accident.

"Cut the crap," he said.

"Just figuratively speaking. I'd like to disappear in a more realistic manner."

"Seems like you've already done a good job of that."

"Not good enough. I've moved twice in the last month, just got another car but I swear someone is still following me. I'm tired of it."

"And you're still saying you don't know what this is all about?"

"No. But I'm beginning to believe your story. Someone thinks I'm involved and they are determined to eliminate me, right or wrong."

"That's it? Nothing else?"

"No, but until I find out, or you find out, or LAPD finds out what's really going on, I'm going to try and make an exit that will convince people to stop looking. You're the only one who will know the truth. Not that you really give a damn. All I was hoping is that you might authenticate it some way, if it ever came to that. Unofficially, at least."

"Sounds rather extreme. Why not just leave town until this is over? Leave the country if you have to."

"Because it may never be over. Not based on any progress I've seen so far."

"So you're going to stick around and help us solve the case by going underground?"

"Who knows. Maybe I'll get lucky."

"Bullshit. What you are telling me is that you are involved. And probably have been right from the beginning. And if that really is the case, if you don't wind up dead, you'll wind up in prison. Probably for life."

"Bullshit, is right. I've lived in this ungodly, disgustingly overcrowded city most of my life and I happen to like it here in spite of all the negatives and I'll be damned if someone is going to force me out."

"And you want me to believe you're that stupid? Sorry. I don't buy it one bit."

"Well, I'll tell you one thing. I'm not about to let myself be used as live bait again. That's for damned sure. Other than that, I'm just telling you how I've decided to handle it without trying to convince you of anything."

"So? Why bother? Why not just do it?"

"Because as soon as the story hits the paper, you'll know

anyway. And if my pursuers really think I'm dead, they'll relax and move on. Maybe then if you are doing your job, you'll get a break."

George didn't respond. But he was a little angry. And frustrated. Mrs. Brown had totally failed to identify Corbin as possibly being the Charley character and he, George, was getting nothing but what appeared to be side stepping misdirection from Corbin about everything else which renewed his earlier suspicions. Additionally, unless he could somehow get the man back to the office, he had lost any chance of having him followed.

Neither man spoke for several blocks. Then George asked his question, the intent being to keep Corbin distracted, keep driving towards the Federal Building and somehow get him inside.

"All right. Tell me how," he said.

"What? My plan? Well, the best, most convincing scenario would be for me to get shot by someone like you in a mock gun battle. But I'm not even going to ask. So... That leaves having an accident."

"Like a car accident? You'd need a body to pull that one off. And I don't know how you'd get your hands on one without committing some other kind of a crime."

"I could always go down to the morgue and claim a John Doe as one of my kin. But then what? That whole approach gets far too complicated and too much chance of screw up."

"So you're telling me the what but not the how. Is that it?"

"Hopefully, you'll read it in the paper."

"Okay. But why let me in on your little secret ahead of time. Why not just do it?"

"It's a backup measure," Corbin said as he reached into his jacket pocket and removed a folded piece of paper and a small photo.

"The photo is from my driver's license. Not very good, but good enough. The paper contains a very short personal bio and description of my demise with some blanks that I'll fill in before I put it in the mail to the newspaper. But just in case they decide not to publish it my only request is that you make sure the story shows up anyway."

"In the Times? That might not be easy."

"No. Just the Beverly Hills Courier."

George looked over at Corbin and raised his eyebrows.

"What? That rag?"

"I know. But they're always short on news and they'll never check the facts. Plus, some of the right people still read it."

"In other words you already know that the person or persons you're trying to scam do read this particular paper. That tells me they must live on the west side of town."

"Along with half a million other people."

"Crap. Well, come on up to the office with me and meet my boss. Maybe he'll have some other questions you can help with."

"No. I think we're done we're done for now. Just pull over and let me out."

"I'd prefer that you come in with me and do this in a more formal manner."

"Well, it's not going to happen. So either pull over or I jump out at the next signal light."

George grumbled, put on the blinkers and swung in to the curb. When he was stopped, Corbin got out and walked quickly away, purposely leaving the car door open behind him.

"Dammit," George said as he put the car in park and slid over far enough to pull it shut.

TWENTY ONE

"I just don't know," George was telling Jack back in the office. "He still aggravates the hell out of me."

"Obviously."

"Doesn't help anything from his standpoint, either. I started out thinking he had to be involved in the Sands' bombing. Somehow. But absolutely no reaction when we went over to Mrs. Brown's. And she was adamant even though the guy who rented the room from her had to be involved, what with disappearing the same day the bomb went off and leaving the place more sterilized than an operating room. And he also denied everything else. As for his reasons for wanting to disappear... who knows. I'm not that convinced. A normal person would just get out of town. So, I just don't know. Not a damned thing to go on."

"And we can't even tail him."

"Yeah. That was pretty slick, showing up at my house like

that. Now we don't even know what kind of car he might be driving. If any. Which leaves us nowhere. What about his request?"

Jack shook his head and shrugged.

George heard it on the news coming down the hill the next morning on the way in to his office. A house in Alhambra had been partially blown off its foundation three hours earlier. The explosion had been so violent that it had damaged the nearest adjacent home. Two people were dead and one injured. He called in, told Jack where he was headed, then made a U turn back to Mulholland, took Mulholland east to the Hollywood Freeway, south to the 10 and east to Atlantic Boulevard.

He showed his ID to the uniformed officer at the street blockade and proceeded but still had to park more than half a block away. Walking towards the scene he saw a single fire engine that had remained behind, three black and whites and several unmarked, full sized Fords and Chevys.

One end of the house which had exploded was completely flattened. Roof blown off, walls blown outward onto the yard, all badly burned. The wall of the neighboring house was also seriously charred but the fire had been extinguished before it had affected the rest of the structure. There were still traces of steam coming from both buildings. In the back yard a small crane swung a piece of the roof from the first house up and around to where it was dropped on the grass. George went to the officer out front and made his inquiry. The cop pointed to a middle aged man in a grey jump suit standing in the rubble. Then he made a call on his radio. The man in the jump suit looked their way and responded.

"He'll be here in a second."George was told.

They introduced themselves and shook hands. Grey jump suit was Tod Wilson, head of the Bomb squad.

George told him why he was there.

Wilson laughed and shook his head in amusement as George waited. Then Wilson scratched his neck.

"Sorry," he said. "Nothing sinister about this one that I can see. Just tragic. Stupidly tragic. Unbelievably, stupid tragic."

George continued to wait.

"Let me show you something," Wilson said and motioned.

George followed him around to the end of the house. Wilson pointed at the scorched gas meter suspended on its two pipes coming out of the ground. Then he tapped the cylindrical mechanism located in the piping.

"Here's my best guess," Wilson said. "Pressure regulator. Looks like the regulator had a catastrophic failure. It suddenly caused the gas pressure inside the house to rise drastically, so much so that it blew out all the pilot lights. Two on the kitchen stove, one on the furnace, the hot water heater and the gas clothes dryer. It was early morning, barely light out and the house was full of gas. Should have stunk like hell but for some people, well... And here I'm speculating."

"Two people live in the house, two guys living together and the bedroom was down there on the far end so maybe they didn't smell it right away. Anyway, I'm guessing the first one gets up and heads towards the kitchen, smells the gas and calls to the other one. That one gets up, no clothes on either, except this guy has a habit. He needs a cigarette first thing, so he grabs one, along with his lighter and starts out and by the time he's at the bedroom door he flicks the lighter and blooie," Tod said as he watched George's face. But before George could express his opinion, Wilson continued.

"I know. Sounds loony, but here's the thing. The first guy was in the kitchen, the second by the bedroom door. But honest to god, the second guy still had the cigarette in his mouth and was still hanging onto one of those cheap butane lighters. Fortunately the fire was largely restricted to this end of the house where the meter and appliances are and the fire station is just a few blocks away. The amazing thing is that neither the meter and regulator ruptured or this could have been a real disaster. And, thanks to the guy in this adjacent house," Tod nodded. "He said he was up and out in his own garage when this place exploded. He took one look, grabbed a big crescent wrench and ran over here and shut the gas valve off. Pretty damned unusual. How many people even know where it's at or how to do that? Put the poor bastard in the hospital with some third degree burns but he probably saved most of his own house in the process, along with the lives of these other two idiots."

169

"Pretty wild," George said. "You don't think it could have been intentional? Somebody tampered with things on purpose?"

"Anything is possible, but we'll know for sure once we get the regulator down to the lab. If it failed, that's the best scenario."

"Well, I'm glad I quit smoking," George said.

"Yeah. Me too."

TWENTY TWO

Somehow, it seemed appropriate. It might even make the story more believable because it would appear to be such an odd coincidence. At least to some people. Or hit some kind of note. If Rudy Stark had disappeared in the ocean, why not himself?

Sam Corbin drove up the coast to check out boat tours and boat rentals and spent the night in an Oxnard motel. He used credit cards in his own name for the room, for meals and for the rental boat. Then he used cash to buy another used vehicle and paid a kid twenty bucks to take it over to the tour boat company parking area at the far end of the Marina.

Up at six the following morning, Sam had breakfast and then found his way through the heavy fog to the marina in his regular automobile and parked in front of the boat rental agency. He was almost surprised to see the open sign in the window, the red neon light cutting through the haze from fifty feet away. He got out of the car. It was exceptionally quiet. Fog seemed to do that, muffling sounds, distorting perception. There were three other vehicles in the parking lot that he could see, the distant sound of the fog horn down at the far end of the jetty coming through. Lonely, eerie, fitting and perfect, he thought, for a man's last day on earth as excitement quietly drummed at him.

Before going into the rental office he walked out on the pier and up and down all the side stems.

"How about the one in slip seventeen?" he asked when he was inside at the counter.

The attendant looked at his log book.

"We can do that. I'll need your driver's license and a credit card."

Sam handed over the items as the man took his pad of forms and began writing.

"How long before it starts to lift?" Sam asked, referring to the fog.

The guy looked up and grimaced.

"This one is pretty thick. Nine o'clock or so. Before it lifts enough to take the boat out. I'll just finish this up. Then you can come back in a couple of hours. Unless you want to cancel?"

"No, no. Go ahead. I'll just wait around."

"You're from L.A.. Every been in the water up here before?"

"Yeah. I had a forty two foot Hatteras that I had to give up when the old lady walked out. But, yeah. Many times," Sam lied. Enough to end the inquiry.

"What kind of coverage do you want for the insurance? Deductible or full?"

"Hundred percent."

"Who's going out with you?"

"Just me."

The man put down his pen, turned around and walked to the back where he picked up a bright orange life preserver, came back and put it on the counter.

"Oookayyyy, let's see," he said as he went back over the form. "That should do it."

"Oh, wait a minute. Can you add a bucket of bait to that?"

"Anchovies or squid? People seem to be doing better with the squid lately."

"All right, go with that."

"Anything else? Have your own rod and reel I suppose."

"I do. Nothing else that I can think of."

"All right. Sign here on the bottom.... Good. Here's your license and credit card. The tank is full. We'll fill it when you get back and add that cost to the bill. There's a live water bait tank with pump in the back. You need to return the boat before dark, which will be about eight thirty."

"How big is the fuel tank? How much range?"

"Thirty five gallons. You'd have to cruise all day to use it up."

"Okay. Where's the key?"

The attendant looked at him skeptically.

"I just want to load up and check it out. Last week the one I rented from your competitor across the way had a sticky choke

171

that wouldn't close. Don't know how they got it running but after I got out to the island and it sat for a couple of hours it wouldn't start. Had to stuff my shirt in the air intake to get going. Good thing the wind wasn't coming up and I knew something about engines. I'll never go back there again," Sam related his fictitious story. Enough for the guy to remember him clearly, he decided, as the man went to a pegboard wall rack and removed a set of keys.

"Thanks," Sam said as they were handed over. "Let me get my bait can."

The twenty three foot, all aluminum, deep V, open run-about in slip seventeen was driven by a hundred horse Johnson outboard. Enough power to get the light weight hull up to about forty knots. More than enough for what he had in mind. Slip seventeen also happened to be near the end of the farthest pier from the office and out of sight from the employee counter inside. The first thing Sam did was to go on board and start the engine to lend authenticity to his earlier concern. A few revs in case anyone was listening, then he let it idle before he shut it down. Nice and quiet. Then he went to his car, got out his bait bucket and had it filled. That out of the way, he made two more trips before everything was on the boat. After that he went back inside the office and asked if there was someplace close where he could get a donut. Another chance to reinforce his presence there.

Half a block down, he was told. He left, went out the door, around the building and back to the pier where he got on the boat, undid the lines, started up and eased on out into the channel. The fog hadn't thinned. He quietly started the engine, and idled along, hugging the southern bank, barely able to see. The fog horn was blaring as he finally reached the end of the channel and turned south. Once he felt confident that he had passed the end of the outlying breakwater he headed farther out to sea. There was no wind, the water was flat, the fog holding. He put the engine in neutral, dug in one of his waterproof bags and took out his hand held GPS and a map. He picked a southwest heading and leaned on the throttle, a dangerous thing with the visibility so low. The twelve mile wide channel was a shipping lane with ocean going vessels in it. The big guys had radar. All he had was eyes and ears and an on board compass. But he needed the cover and felt the need to hurry.

Half way out he slammed into the wake of something big but the deep hull took it well and he recovered quickly. Forty five minutes later he checked the GPS and slowed. Right on the mark, he was passing just short of the great stone arch at the south eastern end of Anacapa Island. The fog had lifted some this far out from the mainland and he was able to identify it through the soup. He loosened his life jacket, unzipped his windbreaker and forced himself to relax. The air temperature was only in the sixties but he had been sweating heavily from the tension and the strain of staring into nothing, worrying about colliding with someone else, always with an eye on the compass, worrying about being off the mark. No wonder people got lost. The forward motion in the drifting fog produced an over riding feeling of moving in a circle, a compulsive need to change course that had to be completely suppressed, placing full trust in the compass. He took some deep breaths, dug a root beer out of his bag and drank half in one swallow. Then he brought the boat around to the north west and picked up some speed. Time to finish it up.

Ten minutes later he re checked the GPS. He was a quarter mile off shore on the south side of the island, just below the pelican sanctuary. He stopped, put the engine in neutral and opened his heaviest bag of gear. Inside was a small, inflatable, one man dingy, a foot pump and a two piece plastic paddle. He pumped up the tiny craft, tied a rope on it and put it over the side. The other end of the rope he tied around his waist. He removed his life jacket and dropped it in the bottom of the runabout. Then he put his wallet and windbreaker in the waterproof bag. He kept his jeans and sneakers on, along with his tight fitting, light weight sweatshirt and pulled on a snug pair of thin leather gloves. The rocks would be sharp.

Tying the steering wheel in place would be a dead giveaway, so he couldn't do that. But there were dock side floats on board. He was able to wedge one in on each side of the big engine to keep it going straight. The impact should dislodge them so it wouldn't looked rigged. That completed, he looked around, going down his mental check list. Was he ready? Had he forgotten anything? The fog was thinning and there were occasional clear patches. He caught a brief glimpse of the rocky cliffside of the island, but then it was gone. With the help of the canoe paddle that was on the boat he went aft and lined it up on a collision course with the rocky shoreline. Then he climbed up on the rail, cleared the line to the dingy, shoved the boat throttle almost all the way down and dove overboard.

Jesus. The water was shockingly cold. Couldn't be more than sixty five degrees. Where the hell was the wet suit he had considered wearing under his clothes. Fifteen minutes of this and he'd be dead from hypothermia. He pulled in the line and rolled quickly into the dingy. If he paddled like a mad man he'd warm up and dry out. He dug at the water with the paddle, all the while listening.

The runabout had quickly disappeared into the fog bank but he could hear the engine humming, growing quieter with the distance but still sharply audible. He started counting. The quarter mile the power boat had to travel would take about a minute. He had twice that far to go in the dingy to a protected place further west along the rocky coast but at the speed he was going that might take half an hour. There was no keel on this little blob of a thing and he was all over the place trying to find a rhythm with the double ended, kayak type paddle and by the time he settled into one the compass told him he was headed farther out to sea. Coming about and still counting, he could still hear the big engine doing its job. It had to be within a football field length of the rocky shoreline by now. Then suddenly he sensed a change in pitch, like it was working harder. Dammit, he swore. The kelp bed. He should have checked the damned kelp bed. He didn't remember it running this far east along this part of the island. He thought the bottom would be much too steep and far too deep in the that area. Now what?

Would it appear plausible that some guy out fishing might get hung up in the kelp and somehow fall over board? Or that the guy might be dumb enough to try and swim to shore after the engine stalled out? Maybe? Most boating accidents were caused by stupidity. But if they found the floats wedged in between the engine and the transom...... He turned the dingy, heading back towards the sound, cursing to himself.

But the engine didn't stall out. It kept grinding away. Maybe, he kept hoping. Maybe if it didn't suck too much vegetation into the cooling water inlet and overheat. Maybe. He kept paddling, harder now. Then, just as suddenly as the engine had slowed, the rpms ran back up. If the propeller hadn't fallen off it had to have made it through and broken free. But was it still on course? What if it came full around? What if went completely astray and slammed into some other poor bastard? What if it even ran over him? Dumb shit, he said to himself. Some headline that would make. Man run over by his own boat. Nothing could be stupider than that, Christ. This was not good. Son of a bitch.

No... The sound still seemed to be going away from him. And then it happened. The boat must have hit the rocks head on. The crash was loud and distinct, even as far away as he was from it. And the engine went crazy. The shock must have thrown the throttle into full ahead and the engine must have come up out of the water. Unmufflered, it began to scream. A dreadful scream that seemed to go on forever. Then, out of cooling water, it overheated, froze up and came apart with a terrible noise. A terrible noise followed by an even far louder explosion. The gas tank must have ruptured. The flash from the explosion was so bright he saw the red, orange and yellow clear through the fog even from where he was at.

Well, hallelujah. A dramatic end to Sam Corbin, the man who cheated someone else out of assassinating him. The man who must have been thrown out into the water and whose body had floated away. But damn, again. There was a light chop on the water. The wind was coming up. Not only was it getting harder to paddle his ridiculous little craft, the fog was lifting. He checked his compass. If there was anyone awake up on top of the island above those four hundred foot cliffs, they had to have heard the explosion. If there was anyone out there in the fog fishing with their engine off, even several miles away, they had to have heard it. If there was anyone just trolling slowly along within a couple of miles or more, they had to have heard it also. Time to get moving.

Ten minutes later he turned in towards shore, still expending larges amounts of energy. His clothes were almost completely dried. He was skirting the kelp bed, looking for a pathway through. Then he swore. The sound of diesel engines. Another powerboat was out there. A big one and not far away, running at a pretty good clip. The fog had thinned and was turning patchy. He couldn't see them yet but if they had radar, more than likely for something that sounded so big, then they could see him. He shuttled into the kelp bed, staying as low as possible but if they were alert it wouldn't be enough. He withdrew the fish knife from its sheath on his belt and punctured the air chambers of the dingy, letting it sink around him. Luckily it didn't completely submerge. With his legs drawn up the plastic fabric wrapped itself around him, keeping his body dry, his head and arms above water level. What strands of kelp he could reach, he pulled up close around him.

The big boat slowed radically. It was very close now, obviously in neutral, drifting, the engine noise down low enough so that he could hear voices. And then, there it was, maybe a few hundred feet away through the diminishing haze.

"It was right there, off to starboard," a man's voice said. "Then it disappeared off the scope."

"Maybe it was a sea lion."

"Too big for that."

"Well, I don't see anything."

"Yeah, but something sure as hell ran up on the rocks back there. Might have been a survivor. Should we hang around here just in case?"

"I think we had best go back and see what happened. Maybe there's something we can do till the Coast Guard gets here."

At least a forty footer, Sam decided. Big flying bridge up top. One guy at the controls, one guy on the forward deck. It began backing away to stay out of the kelp, then came around and went back east, down the island towards the wreckage on the rocks. They hadn't found him, thank god. How would he have ever explained it? Worse, he wouldn't be lost at sea. What then? But Jesus. He was still two hundred yards from shore and he had to get there while there was still some cover. The only way he could do that was by swimming. By giving up the protection of the thick plastic of the dingy and swimming, hoping to hell he didn't succumb to the cold. Then there really would be a dead body. That should make Margaret happy. Or would it? What the hell did he know? Sometimes he was almost sure he understood her. Most of the time he didn't. Especially when it came to what was driving her. Not yet. But if he lived through this one, he sure as christ was going to find out.

Shivering violently, hiding behind a large slab of stone, salt in his mouth and stinging from the scrapes caused by the sharp rocks he had been forced to climb over, Sam pulled off his soaked sweatshirt and fumbled with the closure on his waterproof pack. At last, with a change of clothing and sunlight bleeding through the dispersing fog, he stopped shaking. His divers watch was still working. He had four hours before he needed to be up top. And he was well hidden. Time enough for Hershey bars, bottled water and a short nap. The shear rocky cliff behind him would be another tough challenge.

No one seemed to notice when he dropped into the rear of the line after the rest of the group had made their way up the grueling flight of stairs from the boat dock to the top of the small island. Just another old putz in his sleazy print shirt with the palm trees on it, sunglasses, doofus, old man's hat and sneakers. Not even the tour guide. She was already bored with the crowd, having been forced to ride across the channel with them to this jutting piece of rock, now a National Park and place of interest due to pelicans, sea lions and peculiar plant life. But Sam had bought a ticket just in case. And his name was Charley in case anyone asked. But no one did, so he obediently followed them around and stood in the back when they stopped to hear the guide recite some seemingly important piece of knowledge. The sun was out now and it was getting warm. Enough to make him extremely uncomfortable. He had tried rinsing some of the salt off his skin in the men's room sink but his torso and legs were still unwashed. Please let this be over soon, he said to himself. But out loud he carried on.

Well, isn't that interesting, he mumbled a couple of times, fitting right in. Actually, some of it was quite interesting but there didn't seem to be a single person amongst them that would still be remembering any of it by the time they reached the mainland again. And who knew about tour guides. Maybe they just made the whole thing up. Pure fiction. Who would know the difference? Probably none of them and just as well. None of them would remember him longer than ten seconds after they disembarked either, although there was some chatter about a boat which had crashed into the shoreline earlier in the day. Someone even asked the standby park ranger about it but he only shrugged and said it was under investigation. Then, finally, by four in the afternoon, he was behind the wheel of his latest automobile heading south down the Coast Highway, back towards Santa Monica, ready to be Joe Carroll again, in the next scene of his ongoing drama.

Well, there it was in black and white, sounding very factual. He was officially dead. The Beverly Hills Courier said so.

'The body of Sam Corbin was recovered from the ocean late Tuesday afternoon after his boat crashed on the rocks off Anacapa Island near Oxnard, California. Corbin's wife, Jean, was killed in a mysterious fire bombing of their Santa Monica home a year ago. They had been married nine years. The crime was never solved. Etc, etc...'

Even though he had composed it himself, he was still surprised at how shocked he felt from seeing it in the newspaper. He particularly liked the part about the body being recovered. Pure fiction. But as he had told George, this was one paper that would never take the time to check the facts.

The part about his wife, however, wrenched his heart just as badly as it had when he originally wrote it. Jean. Dear, beautiful Jean. God, how he missed her. Every hour of every day. Every day of every week. Always. And it wasn't over. Probably never would be. Probably, hell. Not even after he did what still needed doing. But it might help. It had to or he was doomed forever.

Sam had also purposely called Margaret while he was up on the island waiting for the tour group, to let her know that he, Joe Carroll, was back in Los Angeles. And when could they have dinner? He was relieved that she didn't say that evening. But at least she had heard from him on the day on which Corbin was supposed to have died. And with that he went to bed and slept ten hours straight.

Margaret was secretly pleased to learn that Joe had returned but she was damned if she would ever admit it. Not to him, not to any other man, either. What was the point. They were all the same in the end. Weak, needy, demanding. Just like the father she had spent so many years trying to forget. The inept, wimpy, wife beating failure of a bastard, drinking his way through his existence. Was he dead yet? She hoped so. And her ex husband, the rich, accusatory, condemning son-of-a-bitch and all the tragic memories surrounding the only one which never seemed to go away. Then there were the men from Beverly Hills and west L.A.! They came on full of bluff and bluster, doing their macho best to put another notch on their belts. Some of them, she had found out, were even taking bets as to who would get the first piece of her. But she let them take her to dinner and out to dance and sent them home with their balls aching and laughed when they came begging for more. And that was as far as it went.

As for Victor Trent, he had been real. For a while. Married, but so what. He understood what she needed. But in the end he failed too. He was going to help her take care of Rudy and they were going to run things together. But he waffled. And then he had let it slip that he was hot after his neighbor's wife. That the women was interested and he was going to get some of her. Sam Corbin's wife. And she, Margaret, had found out about it. At first she wasn't sure she believed it. The woman didn't seem the type but that wouldn't have stopped Victor. He was already married and cheating on his wife with Margaret. That part was real. A wife was one thing, but if he cheated on his girlfriend, her, after all the crap he'd told her, well, shame on him. There was also the more important fact that he said he could get rid of Rudy for her. But the bastard kept stalling and stalling and she had to do it herself. So, screw him. He got what he deserved.

And then there was Joe Carroll. What the hell was that all about? And how the hell had she wound up letting him into her bed? Not once, but twice, then again, and again. Why? Just because he had always fucked her like it was the best piece of ass he'd ever had and couldn't get enough. Or because he wasn't calling her the next day and falling all over her begging for more like the rest always did. On purpose or otherwise, he waited, damn him, until she couldn't stand it anymore and then he took her apart and gave her so damned many climaxes she thought she'd go crazy. Then she would wake up angry and confused. How does a woman deal with a son of a bitch like that?

She never thought she'd miss him, either. Not that much. But the two weeks he was gone turned out to be a long time. If she wasn't so damned proud and so damned scared she would have had him come over to her office and make him do her right on her desk with the drapes open so the people in the next office tower could look in and watch her getting humped. Jesus. She had to get it under control. Make him wait until tomorrow night at least. But none of this wasting time going out to dinner stuff. Just champagne and sex. Sex and champagne.

And that was when it occurred to her. There was a lot going on with the business. More problems than usual, lots of stress, no sex since Joe. There was a long holiday weekend coming up next month. Mexico might be nice. They could be alone. No interruptions. She'd make him do her so many times he couldn't walk. Then she'd tease him and make him beg for more. And when he finally woke up and realized he couldn't live without her, she would dump him and find some bastard she wouldn't be so needy over. A good screw once in a while but not so great she couldn't keep her mind on the more important stuff. Like staying alive.

But what if the son of a bitch turned out to be a cop in disguise? Or someone else even more perilous? What if indeed, it was Sam Corbin turning things around, personally coming after her like she had sent people after him just in case he also went by the name of Charley? What then? What was she doing, putting out to some bastard who was going to drive her crazy before he... what? And what was wrong with Jake Greer? Why hadn't he found out yet, one way or the other? She picked up the phone, dialed his number and almost swore at him when she asked for a progress report.

"I was just about to call you," he said to her.

"Are you just making that up because I called first or do you really have something?"

"Sam Corbin is dead."

180

"What?"

"I just picked up a copy of the Courier. The guy is dead."

"Jesus. Are you sure?"

Greer read her the short article.

"Well, that's the end of that," she said, clearly remembering Joe's earlier call.

"Looks like it."

"But..."

"Yeah. But. You still don't know for sure that he was the right one to begin with."

"Or if he had a partner who is still around."

"That's right. You don't."

"God dammit"

"Well, it's still one less to worry about. Now you can concentrate on other things."

"Stay with it, " she told him and hung up, thinking, yes, one more loose end cleaned up. But was that the end of it? Finally? There was no way to tell. But Joe was still alive and well, the arrogant bastard, getting her all turned on and confused. So to hell with Douds' and Greer's precautionary attitudes. She'd go to Mexico with him anyway. Maybe she could use their alone time to her advantage. And if worse came to worse.....

TWENTY THREE

"Goddammit," George said when he got the call. This one had to be for real. A big, rambling, five bedroom house on a steep incline in Woodland Hills, half of which was now scattered down the slope as of eleven o'clock on a Tuesday morning, the same time Vince Sands' house had been blown up. The property owner was listed as Jesse Talmato, a man with a record as a drug dealer who had served three years in the pen. He had been back on the street for over a year and was suspected of not only picking up where he had left off before he had been arrested but trying to expand his territory. Instead of immediately rushing out to the scene, however, George remained in his office and went through all the computer files on the ex con. Then, mid afternoon, he called the bomb squad leader and asked if he could come by, hoping things had been sorted through enough to determine where the FBI fitted in and how they might help.

"No fire?" George questioned as he looked at the debris shower.

"Luckily for us," Tod Wilson said. "Makes the job a lot easier."

"What have you got so far?"

"The explosive was in the master bedroom which stuck out on the east side of the house there. It was C4. Probably stolen from the military back during the Iraq war. And who was in the military at that time? Jesse Talmato, ex con whose wife divorced him when he was in prison. And who ended up with the house? She did. And who let the guy who ratted on her husband move into the house? She did. And who ended up dead along with lover boy? She did."

"Just the two of them?"

"Yeah."

"In the bedroom at eleven in the morning?"

"In bed at eleven in the morning."

"Don't tell me the charge was under the bed?"

"Why not? Seems appropriate under the circumstances."

"Meaning what? Really?"

"Really. And from best we can tell, she was in the superior position."

TWENTY FOUR

"I found it in London," Joe said as he handed her the gift wrapped box from one of the most expensive jewelry shops in Britain.

Margaret knew the difference between fourteen and twenty four carat gold. This necklace was expensive.

She looked at him as he smiled at her. What kind of a smile was that? He wasn't behaving like some ass who had just cheated on his wife. Nor was he acting like some love stuck lap dog. What then? Men who gave women expensive gifts always wanted something. He'd damned well better not ask her if he could move in.

She took the gold chained extravagance out of the box, draped it over her hand and toyed with it. Then she looked at him again. He nodded.

"Sure. Let me put it on for you," he said as he took the necklace, unhooked the clasp and put it around her neck.

"Looks good. Especially with that black blouse."

She remained silent the whole time and put her hand up to it when he was done.

"Sorry," he said after a long wait. "I guess you don't like my gift."

"No," she said with hesitation. "I do."

"Well at least I knew better than to try and push an engagement ring off on you," he chuckled.

"What's that supposed to mean?"

"You're a marvelous woman. Intelligent, attractive, resourceful, motivated, independent and very sexy. But any guy who would try to turn you into a housewife, a trophy wife or any other kind of wife would be a damned fool. And I am in no way trying to insult you or put you down. That's just the way I see it. So, if you want to throw me out..."

Margaret hesitated, considering how to take his remark.

"Well, just so it's not a reward for the sex," she said with a mock serious look.

"No way. I'd never try to put a price on what you've got."

"There's champagne in the refrigerator," she said as she started unbuttoning her blouse, leaving the necklace in place.

It was so obvious he almost didn't notice it. In the morning she didn't prop herself up against the headboard with a sheet around her and light a cigarette. She sat on the edge of the bed and watched him gather his clothes instead.

"Oh, jesus," he said as he stopped and looked at her.

"What?"

"I guess I'm in trouble."

"Why? What's wrong?"

"You're not smoking."

She looked at him for a second before she realized what he was saying. "It's pretty hard to smoke the whole pack at once," she replied with a coy look.

"Hmm, yeah. I hadn't considered that. Any chance you'd have time to go out for breakfast?" Dumb question, he thought. Not her. But she surprised him.

"I know a place down in Venice," she replied.

He headed for the guest bathroom to shower, wishing he hadn't asked. This was not the way he wanted things to go. Next thing he knew she would be in there with him expecting him to be soaping her all over. Sex was one thing. Kissing and showering together was a whole different level of intimacy. And breakfast? How big a hypocrite would he have to become to find out what he needed to know?

After he was dressed and she was still in her bathroom he knocked lightly on the door. "I've never seen the rest of your house," he said. "Mind if I look around?"

"No," she said after a moment. "Go ahead. I'll be ready in a minute."

He strolled around, trying to be casual about it in case she came out. It was an exceptional house. Very expensive, very well furnished, but stiff and with an uncomfortable edge to it. Not a place where you would feel comfortable kicking off your shoes and taking a nap on the couch. Nor was there a single dish or a dirty spoon in the sink, a water spot on the faucet, just their empty champagne glasses and the bottle on the Italian tiled counter top. Neither was there a book or magazine lying about or a personal item casually left somewhere, a spot of dust on the dining room table. With the exception of her own bed and bathroom, it appeared almost unlived in. And certainly not a trace of evidence indicating masculine presence anywhere that he could see. He wondered if Rudy Stark had had his own place and how they had worked out whatever living arrangements they had. All very interesting. Then, down at the end of the hall, one last room with the door closed and locked.

He went back into the living room and sat on the large sectional, tempted to put his feet up on the glass topped coffee table. But she was there almost immediately. He got back to his feet, always impressed by her appearance. Although she would probably be just as stunning, he'd bet his bank account that she didn't own a pair of jeans, designer or otherwise. Today it was a soft, buff colored silk blouse, dark skirt and jacket, the jacket unbuttoned, unable to hide the bounce that was there when she walked. No big, pointy shoes for her either. Petite feet, elegant in heels that made long legs even longer. It was a damned good

184

thing she was the enemy.

"Nice house," he said matter of factly, forcing his focus away from her. "How long have you lived here?"

"I don't know. Three years, plus or minus." It was just a reply as if it were of little importance but the way she was looking at him told him there was something else on her mind. He raised his eyebrows inquisitively. She held out her hand as she watched him intently.

Holy christ, he thought as he looked at it. He hoped he'd had his poker face on. He reached over and touched it with his finger, then looked straight into her eyes and shrugged with ignorance.

"What is it?"

"Mr. Greer says it's a pickup device for a phone."

Sam looked at it again. "Okay?" he said. "Whose house are you going to bug?"

"It was under my bed."

He made a show of surprise. "The bed? Good grief."

"Relax. It was on the phone wire."

"So?"

"Greer said it will only pick up phone conversations."

"Well, I'm glad we never had phone sex."

"Be serious, dammit. I'm mad as hell."

"Yeah, I guess I would be too. Sorry," he said, wondering if this was going to be a confrontation and how much trouble he might be in. Had she believed the bit about him dropping his keys? Probably, even though it was more than a month ago. But surely she must have gone through his pockets when he was in the shower that time. He had given her more than ample opportunity. He kept his mouth shut for a while. Then, since she hadn't said anything, he hit it face on.

"Who do you think put it there?" he asked, mentally scrambling for a story in case she blamed him. He was both surprised and not surprised at her blunt answer.

"My first reaction was that it had to be you. But then I remembered that the only time you were alone in my bedroom was when I was in the bath. But that was after I checked out all the pockets in your pants and your jacket so it couldn't have been you."

He laughed and looked at her with a smile. "You looked in

my pockets?" he questioned with a quizzical look.

"Damn right. A first time tussle is one thing but if I'm going to keep screwing some guy I like to have some assurance his intentions are honorable."

"Honorable?"

"Honorable in that he's fucking me because I turn him on instead of doing me with some ulterior motive in mind."

Joe just looked at her and decided the best thing to do might be to not say anything at all. He was right because she continued.

"I just wanted to be sure," she said. "You always hump me like you'll never get enough so I take that to be a good sign."

"Okay, thank you. So who do you think put it there? Or shouldn't I ask?"

"It's none of your business who else might have been in my bed. But my private investigator says the battery was completely dead so he thinks it's been there for quite a while."

"Okay. But you still showed it to me. Any particular reason?"

"No," she said. "I just saw it lying there and the fact that it was under the bed made me wonder. What if it picked up everything and someone was listening? That would be pretty damned distressing," she said looking at him. "And then I was trying to remember how many times you fucked me and how long and how much noise I must have made and... you know what?"

"Maybe I shouldn't ask about that either."

"That's okay. I'll just tell you anyway. I'm hungry and I could use some breakfast but I've never done it on a couch before. Or the floor, so..." she said and reached for him.

A light breeze was coming in off the ocean less than a block away as they sat in the shade of an acacia tree out on the patio of this little resturaunt down in Venice. God, what a foul game this was, Sam was thinking. So up close and personal and so utterly distracting. Last night. This morning. And now, having breakfast together. Would he ever find the answers he sought? He had to know. But time was going by. The reason for his being there was fast becoming ancient history, even to those who had been involved. Creating more havoc wasn't going to revive it or bring forth any confessions, either. All he had left was Margaret, with no clear way to get inside her office, her business files or maybe even her head. Or did he?

Then, taking him completely by surprise, she invited him to Mexico. He purposely put sugar in his coffee and stirred it before answering.

"Hmm. Business or pleasure?"

"Business. I thought we might work on our intense obsession, as you put it."

"No pillow talk?"

"Just moans and sighs."

Their food came and they began to eat. When they were done and the dishes had been taken away he leaned back, grinned at her and purposely made an oblique comment that many women might find offensive. But how else did a guy compliment a woman who would take almost every compliment as a ploy? Not that he felt he particularly wanted to compliment her. Nor did he enjoy all the sex talk, but it was a place to start.

"Speaking of moans and sighs, what I like about you most is that you never try to fake a climax."

That got her attention. "How can you be so sure?"

"You don't play those kind of games. At least I don't think you do. Either you have one or you don't, and it's real."

"If guy needs a woman to fake it, well, what would be the point? Let him go work on his technique with someone else."

"Exactly," he said as the waitress appeared and refilled their coffee cups.

"Any other hot topics?" she asked once they were alone.

"Ever done drugs?" he asked point blank.

"Are you serious," she immediately responded, almost angrily.

"Just curious. Just a question? You know. Like, did you ever smoke a joint when you were in college?"

"My parents were poor. I never went to college," she lied. Something she had become very good at. "I hope that doesn't bother you."

"Not at all. Look at you. Big house, expensive clothes, private limo with driver, office in the high rent district. Not many college grads ever get that close. Certainly not at your young age," Sam said, bothered by the fact that he had allowed the conversation to veer off on a tangent. He wanted to get her back on the subject of drugs. Not to see if she used them because he believed she was too smart for that, but to try to see where she was coming from and how she could justify the twisted business she was in.

"And how about you? How do you judge yourself?"

He hunched his shoulders and shook his head. "I drive my own car and I'm subletting a condo."

"And that doesn't bother you?"

"Should it?"

"Well, Joe. Maybe that's the big attraction. You don't give a damn. Your car is a clunk but you're not poor. Not the way you spend money. But you don't throw it around trying to impress everyone, either. And you never once tried to bullshit me by telling me you're in love with me when you're between my legs. That makes you a success in my book."

"If you're happy, I'm happy. Mexico sounds very interesting. You said in three weeks?"

"Labor Day weekend so make sure you get some rest before we go."

He didn't answer. Just watched her face and smiled.

"We've known... We met a few months ago and except for the kind of food you like and your bedroom preferences, I know very little about you. None of the real homey stuff. We talked about music, movies and things like that. But then there's politics, religion, philosophy, cosmology, human rights, law and order, crime and punishment, where do you want to be in five years or ten?"

"Too many unknowns. Who wants to think that far ahead?"

"Well, you're probably right. None of it matters all that much anyway. Just as long as you don't play golf."

"Good grief, no," she said as she went from serious to a light laugh. "And, no. I never smoked a joint, never shot up, took a hit or any of those weird things some people do. Never, ever, needed to escape from my life or mess with my mind. Well, sorry to cut this short but if we're going to Mexico, I need to get back to work."

Me, too, Joe said to himself even though he hadn't been

hanging around pool halls when he was supposed to have been out of town, either. The basic homework was all done. Going to Mexico in three weeks gave him a time frame to work against for the rest of it. He hoped she was still up to the game because, one way or another, it had to end there. He needed a new tomorrow. Three more weeks. Three weeks until tomorrow.

TWENTY FIVE

People did what they did. He was doing what he felt he needed to do. Might be best to leave it at that, Corbin said to himself. The mission he was embarked upon now was to simply do whatever it took to harass, undermine and make Margaret crazy. Get her back hard against the wall and keep doing it. Everything possible except end her life. For now, at least. That everything required research, home work, diligence and lots of time. But it had paid off and that brought him to the point where all he could do now was share information. He hoped he was making the right choice.

"Detective Barnes, please."

"One moment. I'll ring his desk."

"Barnes."

"I have some information you might be interested in."

"And who might you be?"

"You can call me Charley. Pretend that I'm one of your snitches."

"I don't like talking to people I haven't met."

"We've met. I even bought you a drink once. Maybe I'll tell you where and when someday, if this relationship works out."

"Wise ass, huh? Why should I be wasting my time with you?"

"Depends. If you're not interested in furthering your career, I can call someone else."

"Okay. And why should I put any trust in what you seem determined to tell me?"

"Check it out. That's what cops do, or used to do."

"I'll give you five minutes."

"Got a recorder in your desk? Get it out and turn it on. This should qualify as an anonymous tip so if you can't get the warrants you can still move on it."

"Just a second... this better be good. What have you got?"

"Two distributors. One in Hollywood, one in Compton. Both good sized. The one in Long Beach lives at......."

It took over fifteen minutes to put it all out there. Then Barnes began to interrogate Sam. How could he be so sure? Was he an insider? What was the source of all this information. What, what, what?

"For christ's sake, hold it, goddammit. Let me give you an example of how I put it together. On Monday you used your cell phone fourteen times during the day. The number of the phone is 301-6641. You had lunch with your partner at one forty five at Barney's on Santa Monica. Then you split up and..... On Tuesday you checked in at your office at eight thirty. Then you went on to a stake out over in Echo Park. Your were in a tan Ford Crown Vic and you were observing the residence on Hamilton Street near Walton. I could have had more but that's all the time I felt like wasting on you for now."

"Okay. So I'm impressed. But technically you are guilty of eavesdropping without a warrant. Federal offense. You admitted it on tape," Barnes said, wondering why he was reacting the way he did. If this information was correct......."

"Okay, Detective. Play it back. I told you how many times you used your phone. Not what you said on it. And if your ego blinds you that badly, then kiss my ass."

"No, no. Please. My apologies. Anything else?"

"Yeah. Both distributors will be getting their next shipments on Thursday and will have it all weighed and packaged for street sale by Friday noon," Joe went on, giving Barnes more. "So, the rest is up to you. And, PS. I have also recorded this conversation so try not to blow this one."

Good choice, Sam told himself a few days later as he called Barnes again. The detective had not only listened, he had acted in an expeditious manner. There were fifteen new faces in the city lockup. Some of them would be off the streets for years. Barnes started out by saying that he didn't care who Charley was or how he got his information, he owed him a big one.

"Just a concerned citizen," Sam said and laughed. "But that's not why I called."

"Name it."

"Have any friends who work auto theft?"

"Yeah. A couple right here in Parker Center. Want me to see if they're in?"

"No. Get your recorder out again. You can pass it on. "

"All right. Just a second here, ahh, Charley."

"Let me know when you're ready."

"Yeah. Almost. Some name. How did you pick that one?" Barnes asked. Anything that might give him a clue as to who his informant really was..

"I didn't pick a name similar to my own for my alias like most people do, if that's what you're thinking. I chose it because it's the dumbest, most innocuous, misleading name I could think of at the time. How's that?"

"Yeah, well, sorry. Dumb name, dumb question. Okay. The recorder is running."

"This one is a major chop shop. It's probably dragging in as much cash as both the drug distributors you took down. It's in El Segundo just off Century Boulevard. No auto body shop for a front on this one. A converted warehouse with access on Dover Street and a big back door out to the alley behind. Stolen vehicles disappear into the back in the evening, the goods come out the front in the daytime packed in appliance and furniture boxes. Washers and dryers, chairs, sofas and even a piano crate for the bigger pieces," Sam said and paused.

"Any idea where the stuff is going?"

"None. My resources are limited. But it's always a big three ton Ryder rental and I think it comes from over on El Segundo. Probably another side business for the same people. Anyway, the shop is a bitch for surveillance. No place to hide a stake out. And in the evening when the cars start coming in they have spotters out on Century. Look like homeless guys, but with cell phones."

"How do you know all this?"

"Let's say I spent some time being homeless myself."

"Okay, Charley. We appreciate this and I'll take care of it."

"Wait, dammit You can't just send a bunch of raiders in there. You'll screw it up. And next time I won't be so helpful."

"Oh, shit, Sorry. What else?"

"The drivers."

"Hmm. I see what you mean. Don't tell me you know who they are."

"Not a chance but that's the key. The dumb shits seem to hit the same shopping malls on a fixed schedule. Always early evening just as it's getting dark. And always the same rotation. Pico Mall on Mondays, Santa Monica on Tuesdays, and so forth. When they start into the shop they always come down Century from the east and take the right on Trask. I don't know if the drivers have cell phones or not because three blocks back they flash their lights on and off a couple of times. Then they slow way down until there are no cars behind them and wait for the spotter to wave them in. Then they make the turn."

"So, keep the protocol and we could follow them right on in," Barnes said, his mind working, already visualizing a plan of action.

"It would seem so. If you had a high end car with some troops hidden in it you might be able to drive right into the building. But I can't swear about the drivers not having cell phones."

"I think we could make that determination easy enough. Jesus. Anything else?"

The good news was that Margaret had broken two dinner dates with him since his phone calls to Barnes began. Always last minute. Always because something important had come up. No explanations, but he could tell by the voice that things were getting to her. Now for number three. That should really put her up against the wall. But not in the dumpster. None of it led directly back to her. Not that woman. Not yet. But the pressure was definitely on her. And rising.

They always returned late on Sunday afternoons when the Tijuana border crossing back into California was severely backed up. An old white Ford Super Van, appropriately battered that had 'Black Bird Plumbing' painted on the sides. It was registered to the driver, one Daniel Young, who had a legitimate business license in the City of Los Angeles. In the passenger seat was the female dispatcher from a trucking company down in Torrance,

192

Janice Murdock, posing as his girlfriend. Being towed behind the van was a medium sized, single axeled trailer. Today it was carrying two all terrain vehicles, several folding lawn chairs, a couple of ice chests, some red plastic gas cans and various other camping odds and ends. Two weeks ago it was loaded down with dirt bikes and the time before with three jet skis. Sometimes, instead of the trailer, it lugged along an old aluminum fishing boat. And sometimes Dan changed girlfriends, bringing an office worker from the waste disposal company instead.

Daniel had made the trip so many times over the last two years most of the border patrol had grown comfortable with waving him through. But not before getting him to roll down the window so they could check out his passenger, look at her Pass Card, take a good look at her as if to verify her identity. Unless it was rainy or unusually cool. If the day was warm like today the girl would most likely have on short shorts and an over stuffed tee shirt. It was still a bright spot in a hectic day of hard to make decisions about who to stop and who not to. Occasionally they would even stretch their opportunity, holding up the line behind by asking some inane question or other subterfuge in order to get a longer look.

It was all a front. Dan didn't know a crescent wrench from a pipe wrench and couldn't care less. Who wanted to unclog sinks and replace wax gaskets under toilets? Jeez. His expertise was in being a mule. One or two trips a month into Baja and he was dragging down more loot than four full time plumbers did with overtime thrown in. He also always slept in the same bed with the girls when they were down there and they actually went tearing up the landscape with the dirt bikes or ATVs, or fishing, or whatever. All legit and part of the plan. And all he had to do was leave the van unlocked on their last night out, wherever it was, and drive home with half a fortune of plastic wrapped white bricks stashed in the back of the vehicle. The plastic wrap was a super thick, impermeable, vapor proof substance that had been sanitized on the outside and smeared with old motor oil. Dog proof. So far at least. The inside of the van contained interior walls of box like shelves filed with pipe elbows, Tees, nipples, couplings, adapters, soldering equipment, plumbers tape and hundreds of odds and ends, along with assorted tools and other paraphernalia. The van had been sniffed and passed on several earlier occasions. Therefore, with it's test passing history, the madness of the backed up border and, for the last ten months, the gland stimulating presence of bountiful flesh up front in the passenger seat, the crossing barely qualified as a formality.

Dan was always polite, looked the agent in the eye, controlled his nerves and never talked more than any other, impatient, innocent American citizen anxious to get back home. Today was no different than any of the others.

Three hours later, Dan and Janice transitioned from the 405 Freeway onto the north bound 110 where he got off at Rosecrans and zig zaged through the back streets to drop Janice off at her home. Then he stayed on surface streets until he got to the cyclone fenced storage yard behind the phony plumbing company. He pulled up, got out, unlocked the gate and backed the loaded trailer into a space between two other old panel trucks. Then, leaving the engine running and the driver's door open, he got out, went around behind, unplugged the electric cable for the trailer lights, undid the safety chains from the eye bolts on the truck bumper, undid the trailer hitch and began cranking away on the trailer jack to lift the hitch off the bumper ball. He didn't notice the very slight sway of the van as the two vehicles separated but he was totally shocked when the van door shut, the engine revved and the truck roared out the gate and up the street.

Two hours later Detective Barnes in LAPD narcotics got a phone call. This time it was at home.

"Barnes, here."

"Detective Barnes. How have you been?"

"I'm trying to have a peaceful dinner. Who's this?"

"Guess you don't recognize the voice."

"Should I? Jesus. Charley?"

"Made Lieutenant yet?"

"No, but I got a commendation. I owe you a big one, who the hell ever you are."

"Well, like they say, it's a secret.. And how many commendations does it take to get promoted?"

"Depends. Anyway I could buy you a beer? Anonymous

like?"

"You don't have time for that right now."

"What? You have something else?"

"Does that mean you're interested?"

"If it's half as good as the last one, damn right."

"Good. Get your narco ass over to Rampart Division before someone else finds this thing or tows it away."

"What am I looking for?"

"A white Ford van with a plumbers sign painted on it. Make the effort to dig around in the back. The street value of the cargo would buy a house in Beverly Hills."

"Jesus!"

"Yeah. And I know you'll trace the vehicle. The owner is a major courier."

"Weed, powder or tar?"

"White stuff. And bring a four footed friend. One of the bricks has been opened and enough sprinkled around to give you probable cause to search. The dog can't miss it."

"You sure about the substance? Sounds too damned good to be true."

"Never used, so I'm not an expert. But it came in from Baja late this afternoon. And, if you make that two beers, I'll send you a picture of the guy behind the wheel. Three beers and I'll tell you how he got the stuff. But I don't know from whom."

"How about a case of champagne?"

"Sounds fair. I'll E-mail you the pics later tonight. But right now you're not more than twenty minutes away from Rampart so put your dinner in the oven and get moving."

"You know where I live? How?"

"If I can find dope dealers and smugglers I'd be a failure if I couldn't find where some cop lives."

"Right. Dumb question."

"Okay. One case of champagne. But could you at least make a call and have it locked down so some asshole doesn't steal it from the guy who stole it first and left it there. Meaning me. That is not a good part of town."

"Consider it done."

TWENTY SIX

It was a Poker Club down in Torrance, recently acquired by Margaret as part of what she now referred to as the consortium. Her word for the growing legitimate side of their business. Out front at the bar a man was doing his best to go unnoticed amongst the crowd. He was employed by the Los Angeles Police Department. A rogue cop halfway up the chain of command with information to share. For a price. Summoned by Margaret, he waited, wondering what she was after this time. Everything, it seemed, even though he knew most of her questions were just a cover to keep him from knowing what she was really after. Too bad. If he had something tangible he would have followed up on it. Set her up for a much needed, good sized bust to get back the promotion he had been passed over for. Or, should it go wrong, give him something to plea bargain with if he ever got caught selling out. They never talked on the phone, but always met at a different place. A coffee shop, a parking lot, a hotel lobby and now here. He wasn't aware that she was part of the ownership and if she didn't show in five more minutes, he was gone. A minute later the bartender came and stood facing him from behind the bar. The bartender nodded his head, indicating that he should look in a certain direction. He did, and saw Margaret headed towards an empty both at the end of the darkly lit bar room with a reserved sign on it. He watched her go on by, waited till she was seated, then went back and sat down facing her across the table.

"Another drink?" she asked, but he declined.

"Are you okay here?" she then asked.

"Yeah," he said as he looked around and then back at her dress. "You'd have a hard time wearing a wire under that."

It was a crude, obvious remark but he couldn't help himself. There was an ache in his groin when he was around her that left him wanting. And the way she disdainfully ignored his every attempt to cross the line into some small part of her personal space also left him feeling slightly embarrassed, off center and frustrated. But there was no arguing about the envelope of cash she always handed him when their meetings were over. He tried to think of that instead and not look at her anymore. This time it was already laying on the table between them.

As always she led him round and round but her face told him

nothing as he answered and it was five minutes into their session before, unbeknownst to him, they had finally gotten around to the series of incidents she was really paying him all the hard cash for.

"Every one of these things came in to the station at the last minute," he was saying. "None of it went up the normal chain of command inside the department and none of it required a warrant so there was no way I could have known about any of it until the busts were over."

"How does something like that happen."

"Informant."

"That's interesting. The same person all three times?" she asked as though it were simply a matter of curiosity.

"Looks like it. Sounds like some guy working alone. All I could get was that he calls all the stuff into Detective Barnes in narcotics as he gets it. The only clue to his identity is that he calls himself Charley."

"Charley?" she said, almost too quickly.

"Do you know who that is?" the cop asked reflexively. Wasn't that interesting, he thought as he studied her face. A face suddenly hard and unreadable again as she stared back at him.

Margaret took another drag on her cigarette, inhaled the smoke and let it out slowly.

"No," she answered with a dismissive shrug. "Just seems odd that an informant would use a name, that's all. And such a dumb one, too." she said and moved on to ask him if there were any other tips that had come in that hadn't been acted on as yet. When he said there was nothing she got up and went down the hall towards the rear of the club, leaving the envelope on the table as she walked away.

Down at the end of the hall, Bud was guarding the door to the back room. She nodded to him and went in. They were all there now, waiting for her. Mort, Gilford, Tony, Al, a man named Burk who was Vince Sands' replacement and Marvin Douds, now considered to be an integral part of the group upon Margaret's insistence. Most conveniently, they had also heard every word of Margaret's meeting with the cop, thanks to their newly installed eavesdropping system. Tony was the first to remind the group that Charley was the name used by the caller when his house was blown up. Douds also swore loudly. He still had bad dreams about the hole in his closet wall and the aftermath of physical agony that went with it. Margaret said nothing but the name gave her chills and secretly gnawed away at her more and more as time went by. The discussion went on from there.

They were an angry, frustrated, spiteful bunch, not knowing what exactly was going wrong, or why, or who to blame for what and the air was full of accusations and uncouth explicatives before it unraveled itself almost two hours later. Most surprisingly, none of them ever considered laying any of the blame off on Margaret. Most even looked to her as the one most capable of leading them out of the growing attack on their beleaguered organization. Not only did she have cops and judges on her payroll, she was even more ruthless than the best of them. Unable to agree on much of anything except to meet again on the weekend they began to disband, not enmasse, but one at a time, leaving the room and going out the back door of the club to their cars. Except for Margaret, Gil was the last to go. Then, once he was gone, she went across the hall into another room where six of the organizations' biggest dealers now waited. Three of them were out on bail, along with the man who had been running the chop shot, also out on bail. None of them were happy about being there because they were in trouble. And that was before they knew who was running the meeting.

Margaret entered the room still dressed in her raw silk, navy suit with the white blouse still buttoned to the top. A splendid looking women for them to stare at. But what was she doing here? Rudy's old girlfriend, for god's sake. Where the hell was Gil? That's who they were expecting, sitting around the table, waiting as they had been for at least half an hour, and none of them had been informed of anything different, organization wise.

Margaret looked them over, looked at the way they were seated and went to stand beside Carl, sitting at the head of the table.

"Would you please get up and go take that empty seat between Luke and Emilio," she said and pointed.

"And why would I want to do that?" he asked with a sneer.

"Because I asked you to, that's why. Now get your goddamn ass up and go do it or I'll get someone in here who will move it for you."

Carl scowled and thought it over, finally got up and moved, but he was livid.

"Thank you," Margaret said as she sat down in the vacated chair. "Now we can get down to business."

"What?" the one called Dugan said in a harsh voice. "Where's Gil? I thought he was running things."

"Sorry fellas," she said, "but he's too damned disappointed in all of you to even want to be in your company. So if it's not clear to you by now, I'm in charge here and I have some things to say that you aren't going to like so get used to it. Unless you don't want to be going home tonight."

Seeing that she now had their undivided attention Margaret stood up and began moving back and forth like an irritated cobra in front of them, attacking them with the full weight of her personality, the sound of her voice cutting clear to the bone.

"This is not a god damned board of directors meeting," she started out telling them. "This is not a fucking management committee meeting. And it sure as hell is not a company picnic. This is a fact finding inquisition and I'm the god damned pope and I want to know what the hell is going on and how come all this shit is coming down the pike and why not a single god damned one of you saw it coming. Anyone have any ideas?"

No one volunteered an answer so she went one. "Any of you ever heard of a man who calls himself Charley? Old guy. Young guy in disguise. White. Someone asking questions, someone just hanging around where they shouldn't be. Or anybody who has even mentioned that name. Get the word out. That is your number one priority for now. That and the fact that someone has been bugging phones and it isn't the cops. Yours may have the same problems. Someone will be around to check. Meanwhile, don't do anything stupid." And then she ended by lashing out at them one last time.

"First thing in the morning I want each and every one of you to get your complacent asses out of bed and out on the street. Don't even stop to have breakfast. Make the rounds of everybody under you. Shake them up, make them change their routines and security measures. And keep on doing it regularly. Review everything. Kick some ass. And then kick some more. You people are running things out there. What happened is inexcusable. It had better never happen again," she said, her voice now soft, but very precise, clear and impossible to misunderstand.

Once the room had cleared she told Bud to take his two backups and go have a drink. She would call a cab. "And, when you're out and around, see if you can pick up anything on a guy named Charley," she said and explained to him what it might be worth if he came up with up any leads.

"If I find him, ma'am, I'll drag his ass in here for you."

"Good man, Bud. But I need him alive and talking, so take it easy."

"Right, boss," he said and left.

After he was gone she locked the door, sat down behind the table and put her feet up. Charley? Who in the hell was Charley? Where in the hell had he gotten all that information. Inside information. And how, unless he were an insider. But there was no one around anymore that was that privileged. Certainly not Douds. If it had been Douds he would have come at it from an entirely different direction. Illegal bookkeeping, phony corporations, the holding company, the paper trail. Not that he didn't have the balls for such mutinous deviousness. He did. But he also knew that if Margaret went down, he would go down with her. If he even lived long enough to go to trial.

Bud knew parts of it, yes. He had driven her to meetings with some of these guys. But he hadn't known about the chop shop operation. That was new and she had never had him take her there. She had never personally been there herself. And why would he even get involved in such an extremely risky thing, even peripherally? There was no point to it.

But Bud was living with a fluffy, over the hill, ex Playboy centerfold blonde in an grand sized apartment where at least one, two or more nude pictures of her in various poses still hung on every wall. Living room, dining room, baths, bedrooms, hallways, from when they had been placed there more than fifteen years ago. A low browed, high maintenance bimbo who demanded an extreme amount of Bud's attention. And, unless Bud was one hell of an actor, he had never displayed an ounce of lingering loyalty to Rudy or displayed an ounce of regret once he was gone.

"Charley," she whispered to herself as her face turned cold. The name they had for the person who had blown up Vince's house. The same for who had destroyed Tony's. The guy they had once thought was Vanalden and then the one they had come to suspect was Sam Corbin. But Vanalden was dead. So was Corbin. Who then, goddammit? One of her own people? It wasn't possible. Except for Gil, not a one of them knew all the details about what the rest were doing, didn't want to know and wanted to keep it that way. Besides, Greer had a whole crew of guys following them all around and they had been doing so for over a month before any of these last episodes began going down. Margaret even had Gil under surveillance. Gil, who had far more to lose from what was happening than any of the rest of them, and god help her if he, or any of them ever found out. And to further cover her bet she had someone else looking over Greer's shoulder because Greer was also learning things from that exercise that she wasn't comfortable with him knowing. Not yet and maybe never. And so in addition to everything else she had done, she had also set them all up with little tests to further check their loyalty. Unfortunately, nothing seemed to be working. So who the hell was left? That was the million dollar question. And where the hell was the answer? Jesus Christ. Suddenly she felt very alone and frightened.

She dropped her feet to the floor and put out her third cigarette Then she made a phone call. Sam was halfway out the door when his house phone rang but he hadn't forgotten who he was supposed to be.

"Joe Carroll," he answered.

"Joe. I know it's last minute but are you busy?"

"Margaret! Hello. Good to hear from you. No. I was just thinking about going down the street to have some Thai food. Have you eaten yet?"

"No, but I'm hungry."

"Where are you? Want me to pick you up?"

"No. Tell me where it's at. I'll meet you there."

God damn it, Margaret said to herself as she looked across the table at Joe while they were having dinner. How nice it might be to have a partner. Not another damned mobster like the ones she had hooked up with but a real one like Joe. But what would he ever want with her if he ever found out what her life was all about? Absolutely nothing. But if she could get that mad dog, Charley, off her tail, save the organization, turn it around and go legit, well, who knows? Meanwhile, enjoy the sex. Get him to fuck her brains out. It was the only escape she had. Everything else was in jeopardy.

Holy Christ, Joe said when he took her home after they ate. She had half her clothes off before they made it to the bedroom where she attacked him with a passionate vengeance. And again before they finally went to sleep. But at four in the morning she was on top of him again, riding him with frustrated fever. Finally, she began having a monstrous, prolonged climax. He rolled her over in the middle of it and pounded her back. Got you now, you bitch, he said to himself, wondering how much longer he could keep on doing this. It wasn't getting any easier. But when it was over and they were lying together on top of the sheets, he asked her if they were still going to Mexico.

"Damned right," she said. "That's the only way we'll have time enough to find out who can out fuck who." Then, like a little child, she snuggled in close to him so that he had to put his arms around her and promptly fell fast asleep.

In the morning Joe woke with a jolt. The bedside clock said nine fourteen. He tried to extract himself from around her. She hadn't stirred once all night that he knew of and his arm was hurting. He eased it out from under her but woke her in the process. They got up. Could they have breakfast together, she asked as though she needed to have him near a little longer. And then could he drop her off at her office. All right, he said, but they needed to get going. He had a business appointment he didn't want to cancel.

Two days left, Joe said to himself, once he dropped Margaret off and returned to his high rise condo. Two days left. So what one last thing could he do to really stir her up? He made himself another cup of instant coffee and took it out on the balcony where he sat and watched a sailboat just beyond the breakwater tacking back and forth, heading out into deeper water. Nothing came to him. Worse, he found himself suddenly feeling very sad. But now was not the time. That would have to wait, he told himself as he pushed it aside, locked up, walked across the boulevard and went down to the beach for a walk. Later he went off to the sporting goods store for a couple boxes of shotgun shells and on to the electronics supermarket, then came home and went to work.

"Hey, mister. Do you have any matches?" the old man with the long hair, big mustache, glasses and ill fitting clothes said as he waved his old Dunhill pipe at Bud.

"Get lost," Bud said angrily." He had just pulled into the lot at his girlfriend's apartment and gotten out of the limo. It was dark out but the street lights were on so he saw the man fairly clearly.

"No problem," the old guy said but came closer anyway. "Just a quick light and I'm gone."

'Jesus," Bud said and dug in his pocket for his lighter. He flipped it open, snapped it and held the flame of the old man's pipe.

"Thanks Bud," the guy said.

"What? How did you know my name?"

"You're a popular guy. I thought we might go for a ride together."

"Get your ass out of here, you old shit. Before I shove your glasses up your nose."

"I don't think you'd be able to do that if I put some lead in your belly button," the man said as he jammed a gun into Bud's gut, reached under his jacket and removed Bud's thirty eight from its shoulder holster.

"Now just stand there and be still," came the next order as the man moved around the front of the car with Bud in his sights.

"Now get in," Bud was told.

He got in. So did the old man.

"Now shut the door and back on out. Be cool about it."

Bud took another look at the big forty five and did as he was told. They had only gone about three blocks before the man spoke again.

203

"Good enough," he was told. Now make a U turn and park over there, facing back towards your place.

Thinking he was being forced to drive himself somewhere and dig his own grave, Bud was both surprised and relieved. But still mad as hell about having been hijacked.

"All right. Pull into the curb, and shut off the engine. Leave the keys."

He did it.

"Now try and relax. And listen. If you listen, you live. If you don't you're dead."

Bud squinted at him in the dim light. This guy wasn't half as old as he was trying to make himself appear. And that meant he had best be careful. He made it clear that he was giving his full attention to the matter at hand.

"Good idea. Call me Charley, if you need a name. And the reason I came here was to present you with a suggested plan of action."

"A plan of action?" Bud said, his fear suddenly gone. "Are you sure that's a real gun?" he said with a light laugh.

"Better take another look," Charley said and held it up slightly higher so it was more visible in the darkness. It now had a silencer attached to it. In a quick flash of movement he raised it and blew a hole in the roof above Bud's head and moved it back to where it was again aimed at Bud's gut. The katunk of the gun was much milder than the sound of the slug going through the sheet metal.

Bud jerked back against the door and turned white.

"What do you think, Bud? Is the gun real?"

"J..ja, ja, jessuss," he responded and looked out through the windshield, hoping someone had head the sound and would call the cops. But then he realized it sounded far louder from inside the vehicle than it would have outside. He swallowed hard and kept his mouth shut as Charley started speaking again.

"And now that I've got your attention the next thing you should do is go home, pack a bag, hit the road for a while."

"Yeah. I, good idea. But why?"

"Because that would be the sensible thing to do under the circumstances."

"I can see that but what circumstances? I mean, if you don't

204

mind me asking. Jeez."

"Your boss has been having some serious problems lately. Houses getting blown up, drug shipments intercepted, all that disruption. And right about now I would say that you are somewhere near the top of the suspect list because I just put you there. Then there is that thing about you pushing a guy in a Porsche over a cliff. And last, there is still me hanging around. If that doesn't bother you, give some thought to what happens next. It should be self explanatory. So, with that in mind, step out of the car, come around and get up on the sidewalk. As soon as I drive away you can start walking back towards home," Charley stated and waved the weapon at him.

Bud eased himself out of the car as Charley slide over behind the wheel. The engine was running by the time Bud reached the sidewalk and the limo disappeared down the street. He began walking back to the apartment. He was still a block away when he heard the explosion. He started to run. Then he saw the flames. He ran faster. The sound of sirens came next. God almighty, he said to himself when he got close enough. It was very obvious that there had been a bomb under the driver's seat of the limo. But the seat was empty and there was no sight of Charley.

Where the hell was Bud? Margaret wondered. He was supposed to pick her up first thing and take her down town. Dammit, she was going to be late. She tried his cell phone but there was no answer. She called his girlfriend's apartment but there was no answer. Grumbling, she locked up the house, got in her own car and drove down to her office only to find a Sargent Miller from the bomb squad waiting for her upstairs. She invited him into her inner office and offered him coffee.

She sat behind her desk, he sat in one of the over stuffed chairs in front. She got out her cigarettes and lit up, not bothering to ask if he wanted one or cared if she smoked..

"What is it, Sargent?" she asked as she exhaled a long cloud of smoke. "Anything I can help you with?"

"I don't know. It's not very clear how your company is structured and who I should be talking to."

"Well, I'm sure we can figure it out. Has something

happened?"

"Your company, The Trident Company, has a standard sized black Cadillac limo registered to it. The license is D657ANV. Is that correct?

"Yes. We have a black Cadillac. I'm not sure of the license. What about it?" she asked. Then it connected. Sargent Miller had said he was from the bomb squad. "Are you trying to tell me that... Jesus," she said, thinking the worst. Bud had been taken out. "When did this happen?"

"Last night. Somebody did a number on the car. We're trying to find the driver. The one employed by your company. A Mr. Langer, I believe."

"What does that mean, did a number?"

"Blown up."

"Blown up? Oh my god. But... you said you were looking for Bud. He wasn't in the car?"

"Lucky for him. The charge was under the driver's seat."

"So he's alive."

"As far as we know. Just missing and wanted for questioning. Any idea where he might be?"

"No.... None. He was supposed to pick me up this morning but never showed. And that's never happened before. What about his, ahh, lady friend? He was living with a... I can never remember her name."

"Tinsley. She seems completely confused. All she could tell us was that he packed a bag and left real early this morning. Wouldn't say where he was going, or why, or how long he would be gone."

"But she talked to him after it happened. What did he say?"

"Nothing that made much sense, I guess. Lot's of swearing and... do you know anyone named Charley? At least that's the name she thinks he mentioned."

The only thing that saved her was the fact that she was drawing on her cigarette and had her hand up, half hiding her face at the time he said it. Charley. God damn. She held the cigarette there for a half second longer, then dropped it and tapped it on the ash tray before responding.

"Charley? No, not that I know of. Is it important?"

"Miss Tinsley said Langer acted like he was in shock and

mumbled something about some guy named Charley. Said Langer was barely able to sleep and was gone by the time she got up."

Margaret looked at the Sargent and raised her eyebrows.

"The thing is that when our officers went knocking on doors last night to see who the car belonged to, none of the neighbors seemed to know and no one answered the door at the Tinsley apartment. Not until this morning when she was there alone. Said she hadn't talked to anyone else. But she was extremely irate because the guy walked out on her."

Margaret chuckled.

"Okay," the officer continued. "So it was your automobile. Do you think this might have had something to do with your driver on a personal level or was it directed at your company? Or," he continued as another thought came to mind, "since he wasn't in it at the time, could your driver have had a grudge with you over something big enough to make him blow up the car just for spite?"

Margaret laughed. "Bud loved that car more than he did his girlfriend and it was his to use for anything he wanted anytime he wasn't hauling me around. Which wasn't much. And for that I'd bet he was making twice as much money as you are, Sargent."

Miller gave her a hard look and tried to ignore her last comment. "So someone was trying to scare him. Or you. What do think that might be all about?"

"I suppose it's possible. I can't speak for him but I find it hard to believe it was directed towards me."

"Well, you're probably right. The bomb was under the driver's seat and not in the back. What kind of person was he?"

"Maybe a little rough. Kinda macho, hung around bars quite a bit before he met this lady of his. But never a problem when it came to the job. To the contrary. I found him to be attentive and protective both."

"Yes," Miller nodded. "I'm sure you did," he said with a straight face. "But to blow up an automobile, over... whatever. That seems a bit extreme, don't you think? I mean, good grief. So think about it. If you think you might be in danger it would be best to discuss it. Maybe we could offer you some protection."

"What? Ride around in the back of a squad car? No thanks."

"Okay," Sargent Miller said as he got to his feet. "Thank you for your time. We'll be in touch if there's something more. The car's in the impound lot. They'll give you a call when forensics is done with it."

"Jesus, Jake. I need some answers."

"Right now I don't have any. Unless Bud blew up the limo to take the suspicion away from himself."

"I considered that but he could never have pulled it off. He just wasn't that smart. And who would have wanted him for a partner? He didn't have enough inside information, either. And there's no one left that I have allowed to know everything that's going on, business wise. Not even you."

"Especially me. Maybe that's the reason I can't find this person. I don't know enough. Or persons, which I'm beginning to think is the case. It has to be. No one individual working alone could create this much havoc."

"You know the names of everyone who is in any way remotely qualified to create any of these problems. Even the guy I'm seeing. And he's it. There hasn't been any one else in my life for over six months. He knows nothing about my business life and I damn well keep it that way."

"How often do you see him?"

"Once a week at the most. Except when he went to Europe a while back. And I've been to his place. There's nothing there. Nothing suspicious in his car. And besides, you checked him out."

"And he came up clean, as far back as I went. But, who knows."

"Yeah. And maybe Corbin really isn't dead. What about that? Did you ever check to see where the body went after he was found. And who buried him, and in what cemetery?"

"Good point. But if it's him, where is he getting all his information? Even him and your boyfriend working together. There has to be more."

"But there's not. No one knows how it all fits together. Just me, and I don't talk in my sleep."

"Okay, no comment on that last part. But what about your attorney, Douds? I know we've been over it before but don't forget, he was with Rudy right from the beginning. Are you sure he doesn't resent you enough to sabotage you? Or, better yet,

208

could he have made a deal with law enforcement to keep his own ass out of prison?"

"Well, you've been bugging his office and his phones for the last three months so what do you think? And damned right he resents me. And would he like to see me gone? Damned right to that one too, at least half of the time. And would he consider making a deal with the cops? Damned right, if he thought it would work. I'm sure he could get immunity when it comes to business. But there's other bodies buried out there and he now knows that I also know whose and where."

They continued to discuss it further. Cops arrested people based on garnered information but they didn't blow up houses and limos or cut through condo walls in the middle of the night and poison someone. They didn't wire tap without warrants either. And even if they had, some of the information couldn't have been obtained that way to begin with. Margaret had other ways of making contact. So where were they? Nowhere, it seemed.

"What about Mexico?" Greer finally asked. "Are you still going under the circumstances?"

"First thing in the morning. Maybe it will help me get my perspective back."

"Or get you killed. Is that wise?"

"It's complicated."

"Obviously. But don't bet your future on it."

"Well, maybe he's just plain Joe."

"And maybe you're crazy."

"And maybe I'm in heat."

"And if he turns out to be something other than your hotdog, what then?"

"Then I shoot the son of a bitch and it's over."

"Well, I'd still like to see him without all that hair on his face."

"Don't worry. It's on my agenda."

"Good. I'll get some more guys on things. Where are you going to be in case we come up with something before you get back?"

"Manzanillo. A resort called Las Hadas but I'd rather you called Douds and let him relay it to me. It will make him feel like he's still in the loop."

"I've heard of it. Some Bolivian tin miner built it as a private retreat, but it was made public after he died. Expensive. That the one?"

"Yes."

"Okay. Will do, but it's highly unlikely your cell phone will work down there. Do you have their regular number?"

"I'll have to look it up and call you back."

"All right. And forgive my language, but watch your ass."

Damn, Margaret thought after she hung up. Out of them all, Greer was the only one she had the slightest bit of trust in. Maybe it was because of his age. Too bad he wasn't twenty five years younger.....

TWENTY SEVEN

Perfect, Sam thought. Margaret had hardly spoken a word when he picked her up and the taxis ride to the airport was in silence. On the plane she sat and looked out the window. Occasionally she would respond with a slight smile, a nod or the barest of response. When he asked if she were feeling all right, she said she was just tired and overworked. Was everything else okay, he queried. Nothing serious, she replied. Nothing that couldn't wait until they returned.

Right, he told himself. But he still had to give her credit. She promised to be more companionable once she had a good nights' sleep and even placed her hand on top of his when she said it. He consoled her and told her he'd do his best to see that she had a good time. Damn right. Then he tilted his seat back and shut his eyes, pretending to sleep. Great, he thought. She was a mess. This highly assertive, almost overpowering woman was suddenly looking wistful, pensive, frail and somewhat defeated. But what was that? Was she biting her lip trying to keep from crying? He hadn't counted on that, didn't even think she was capable of it. Jesus, what was going on? Was he suddenly beginning to feel sorry for her? Better damned well not let that happen or he might be coming home in a box. But even with that in mind she still looked so forlorn that a part of him wanted to reach out and hug her. Should he? No! He wasn't that big of a hypocrite.

They had an upper set of rooms with a balcony that gave them a sweeping view of the bay. Once inside, Margaret began to unpack, hanging her clothes in the small closet to keep them from wrinkling. After she was done Sam asked her if she might like to take a nap.

"Are you taking one too?"

"No. I'm not tired. But please. Go ahead. I'll just go wander around the place. Maybe have a beer."

"All right. But there is one thing you can do for me."

"Name it."

"I've seen the rest of you so would you shave off your beard so I can see what you look like without it?"

"Let me think about it. But, what if you don't approve? Will you send me home early?"

"Not a chance."

"I wish you had done it sooner," Margaret told him at dinner as she looked at his face. A most handsome couple, straight out of Vogue. They were seated at a small, candle lit table outdoors on a large brick patio drinking margaritas that were served from the outdoor bar. The sky was dark, an abundance of stars filled the void, the night temperature was perfect. Three Mexican violinists played softly in the background.

"You think it's okay?" he asked as he felt his chin.

"Why did you ever do that to yourself? You're much better looking without it."

"Well, thank you. I wish I had known," he said and raised his glass to her. "But tell me. How was the nap? Are you feeling better. You look like you do."

"Oh, god. I can't believe how good it feels to get away. I didn't realize how stressed out I was getting. Maybe if we go to bed early tonight I'll get caught up. I hope that's okay."

"Of course. I could use a little extra rest myself. What about tomorrow?"

"We could rent a car and go into town in the morning. The old part, if there's any left. I always enjoy seeing things as they used to be."

"Before Americans."

"And Mexican entrepreneurial greed and corruption. But

forget that. We should still be able to have an authentic lunch, then come back here and maybe lay around the pool for awhile. By then I'm sure I'll need a good fuck."

Jesus, Sam said to himself. Did she always have to be so damned blunt? He was having enough trouble with the situation the way it was, even though he knew that the bluntness was a context she had to keep having sex in to protect herself from emotional involvement. But a little went a long way. Worse, his perspective of her was changing. At first he had seen her as a tough and invulnerable, somewhat evil person, completely deserving of whatever happened to her. And that had made the entire adventure much easier. Even the sex. It had also kept her more predictable. But now that she was feeling severely threatened and under extreme outside pressure, her flaws were quickly becoming more evident. But, if all he began to focus on was her flaws, he would lose respect for her. And, if he lost that, he was in danger of doing something stupid. Life threatening stupid because he knew she had to feel like her back was up against a wall with everything she had ever fought for at stake. Her over riding sensual beauty might help him get through this but he had better never, ever, let it sidetrack him. Even for a moment. Trouble was, at this moment he couldn't think of any suitable comeback for her remark. So he looked at her and said nothing.

"What? Not interested? That doesn't seem like you."

"It's not all about sex, in case you ever wondered. You said you were tired and stressed and I respect that so I'm just trying to be cool and give you some space."

"How come I never met anyone like you before?"

"Maybe you weren't looking."

"I wasn't looking this time. You found me, remember?"

"Ahh. So I did. Not too many regrets, I hope."

"I don't know. I just hope I don't remind you of some old girlfriend you never got enough of."

"What? Why would you say that?"

"Because you always seem to do me with such a vengeance."

Yeah, well, that was kinda what it was all about, wasn't it, he acknowledged to himself, because under the circumstances he damned well wasn't making love to her at all. It was, in fact, an almost act of vengeance where other forces were driving him, somehow trying to screw her into submission. Or oblivion. But what if he didn't have all these suspicions about her being involved in his wife's death? What would it be like then? And if she did turn out to be completely innocent ....?

"What do you expect? You always act like you want to be humped until you can hardly walk," he replied instead.

"Well, maybe you're right. And I like the feeling that when we're done I know damned well I have been laid. Keeps me looking forward to the next time."

He looked at her and shook his head in amazement.

"What? Do I shock you?"

"No kidding."

"Ha. Without the beard I can actually see you blushing. Jeez, Joe. Maybe I'd better stop."

"Don't tell me there's more?"

'No. I just hope you think I'm a great piece of ass. That's all."

"Holy Christ," Sam said, looking around. "Where's the damned waiter when you need one?"

They had their salad, got up and danced to the music, finished dinner, danced again and went back to their suite.

Even though it was Saturday and a holiday weekend, George Dixon was back in the federal building tower. He slept at home. Sometimes he even had breakfast or dinner there, but without a woman in his life, a hobby or other extracurricular activity, his job was it. Yeah, there was that neighbor woman Jack's wife had tried to fix him up with but he wasn't interested. Maybe if she hadn't reminded him of his ex wife somehow... So here he was, back at the office. But in these off hours he only worked on an active case if it was extremely interesting. Otherwise he spent his time on the more notorious unsolved ones that still plagued him. The one he scratched his head the most over was the mystery that seemed to revolve around Sam Corbin. The house bombings, the tape recordings, Corbin's faked disappearance. Where was he now? What was he doing? And, most recently, did he have anything to do with that recent car bombing of the limo and the missing driver?

Not wanting to butt into LAPD jurisdiction and create an unnecessary flap, he started with the limo and learned the same thing the city police had. It was owned by the Trident Company. And Trident used to be Rudy Stark. And Vince Sands, Tony Platt and Marvin Douds all seemed to be tied to Trident. But who was running Trident now that Rudy was dead? For some reason he had never checked. Did Rudy have any heirs, insurance or personal bank accounts? George was putting it all together for himself when Jack happened to come in.

"Hey, George. How you doing? No point in telling you it's Saturday, I guess."

"What. Again?" George replied good naturedly. "I'm going to have to requisition a calender. What are you doing here?"

"Ruth is at her mother's for the weekend so I thought I'd pick up a couple of files to look at in my spare time. Can't find anyone to play tennis with anymore."

"Well, beating on this keyboard is about all I have the stamina for."

"What are you working on?"

George told him.

"Come up with anything new?"

"Nothing overwhelming. But kind of interesting in a peripheral way."

"What have you got?"

"Well, check this out."

Jack pulled up a chair and sat down as George started down the list.

"Rudy had a half million in insurance. The beneficiary was Margaret Ryan, his old girlfriend. His personal bank account was also joint with the same woman. That alone seems very odd for a hoodlum like him. Additionally, Ryan is now on the record as chief operating officer. That's a big damned, almost impossible step. Particularly for a woman in a mobster's world. Factor in the coincidence that she was on board the boat when Rudy was lost at sea with his insurance already in effect and her name on the bank account, plus her name now painted on the front door of the company and we have one hell of a success story."

"Plenty of motive for first degree murder."

"Damned right."

"What about the boat?"

"Still registered as company property."

"Which means we'd never find any evidence of foul play on it or she would have disposed of it long ago. And business as usual for the company."

"But with some changes. It was formerly listed as an import-export until she took over. Nervy bastards. Import drugs, export cash. But now it's called a holding company."

"Holding what?"

"Hard to tell exactly. There are so many levels of built in isolation between everything the company is suspected of being involved in that it's impossible to link it all together. But there have also been several recent acquisitions of established small businesses. All seemingly legitimate. But who the hell is she kidding?"

"Money laundering at its nearly impossible to prove best. Smart lady."

"Overly ambitious, smart lady, playing in the big leagues. But she sure screwed something up. Now she seems to have some fire breathing dragons following her around. Already singed a few feathers. I'm believing that those two big drug distributors that got busted were hers. And the chop shop down by the airport. Add Vince Sands and Tony Platt to the mix, and one newly bombed out limo and she has to be getting nervous."

"It's almost like someone's playing Russian roulette with the gun always pointed at her."

"And going round and round in my head are all those tape recordings we got. And when everything stops, I don't see some tring to do a takeover with all those assets being destroyed. Some competition trying to put her out of business, maybe. Otherwise it's just revenge. And somehow it all seems to have begun with Sam Corbin losing his wife. Except, if that is the case, he has to have a helper. It's not possible for one person do have done everything that's happened all by themselves. Is it?"

"I don't see how."

"So, what's it all about? If someone is that angry or just plain wants her gone, why not just take her out instead of picking away at everything around her like a sniper in a tree? I can't figure it out."

'But we will, sooner or later." Jack said. "And you right about one thing. It pretty much eliminates a take over. Insider or outsider. It would be pretty dumb to destroy half the bounty in the process. Plus, while it may be beginning to look like Corbin is involved from where we're at it could well be someone setting him up to deflect the investigation away from themselves, instead. That seems more likely. Could be something else in her past. Have you had a chance to do a complete background on her yet? I'd bet she has a record."

"Not yet. I've been asking around about her, though and, guess what? I've also been looking at AeroMexico and Mexicana flight manifests for the last six months to see if I recognized any names. Tony Platt was a regular until about three months ago. And guess who was on a Mexicana flight yesterday? Miss Margaret Ryan. How about that?"

"Where to?"

"Puerto Vallarta with a connector to Manzanillo."

"The same place Tony used to go?"

"No. He always went to Mexico City."

"So, what's in Manzanillo except resorts?"

"Nothing that I know of. But, yeah. She was booked with a man so I guess it could be recreational. Let's see. Where did I put that?" George said as he shuffled through his pile of notes.

"Ahh. A, Mister Joe Carroll. Guess I'd better run him through the system too."

"Well, damn. Why don't you check DMV while I call my wife and see how she's doing."

"Here's his mug shot," George said when Jack hung up the phone.

"You've seen Corbin up close. Without the beard, is there any resemblance between Carrol and Corbin?"

"I don't know. Could be. The hairline, the nose. And the eyes. Especially the eyes. Jesus, Jack. If it is Corbin, what the hell would he be doing in Mexico with her? That would be like knowingly climbing into bed with a live rattlesnake."

"I don't know but before we make any rash assumptions, can you do the run through on Carroll first. We could be wrong."

"For Corbin's sake, let's hope so. Let me close this out and then... pull this up and punch him in .... It would help if we had a social security number or a middle name but his driver's license said he was forty one so....."

They waited, both watching the monitor. George typed in some additional information and up it came. They read through it.

George leaned back in his chair. "Doesn't go back very far, does it?"

"Anything else you can access?"

"Sure. This is just what's in the public domain," George stated and hunched over the keyboard again.

"I'll do the bureau files this time," he said and did his two finger routine.

"What's my password again? Intercept, right?" he said to himself and typed it in.

"Well," he said after a couple of seconds. "Look at this."

"What is it?"

"Someone else was after the same information. Their password was Liberty 355. Wonder who that might be?"

"Anyone helping you with this?"

"If they are, they haven't told me about it."

"Sounds familiar. But with thirty seven agents here.... Anyway, what's coming up on Carroll?"

"Well, well. How about that. Seems like the real Joe Carroll died seven years ago in Cleveland at the age of thirty one."

"So. Corbin must be passing as Carroll and he's in Mexico with the speculative head of a major crime organization."

"With his butt hanging out a mile and a half."

"Yeah. And by now that someone else has to know he's not legitimate."

"Maybe not. When was this Liberty looking at the file? Does it say?"

"Last night. Nine thirty seven."

"That's a bit odd. I don't know of anything active that would have required anyone to be here that late. None of my people, anyway. Let me sit down so we can pull up some of this confidential stuff."

The first thing Jack had George do was to check the door codes for the building.

"Not a soul in the building after seven thirty except you. And

217

you left at eight twenty nine."

"They must have done it from home."

"And if that someone is not one of Corbin's friends, Corbin could be in trouble. So, let's get back to Liberty."

"How do I run him down? That must be privileged."

"I'll do it. It's in a restricted registry." Jack said as he pulled his chair closer and hit a few keys. "Okay. Now.... let's see. ..Maxwell?"

"Isn't that the guy down on third floor?"

"Yes, but he's on bank robbery. He just briefed me yesterday. Never mentioned anything regarding Joe Carroll. Has he ever talked to you?"

"Never."

"Okay. Where's your phone roster? Let's see if we can get him in here."

An hour later they were sitting across from Jim Maxwell in Jack's office. Maxwell was under the impression that he had been called in to assist on an emergency case. He was ready. But he didn't understand what George was doing there so he looked at Jack and waited. Then Jack nodded at George and George handed Maxwell a computer printout. He looked at.

"Who's Joe Carroll?" he asked with a puzzled expression.

"You're supposed to be telling us."

"I have no idea. Never heard of him."

"You're sure?"

"Of course. Yeah. I'm sure."

"Okay," George said as he reached over and drew a circle around the password entry at the top of the page.

Maxwell looked surprised and confused. He shook his head, looked at it again, then back up at Jack.

"Somebody used my password. When?"

"Last night, dammit. And how might they have done that?" George asked, taking the lead, playing the heavy for Jack.

"I don't know. I haven't..." Maxwell said and stopped in mid sentence.

"You haven't what?"

Maxwell appeared to be completely astonished as in, ohh shit, and his jaw went slack. He put his head down and was silent.

"Okay, Jim," Jack said to him. "Let's have it. What's this all about?"

"I... god. I never thought.... Jeez, I'm really sorry. He promised me he would never use it."

"Who?"

"Dammit I screwed up. I knew it was wrong but it didn't seem like such a big thing at the time. It has to be that. I was just trying to do someone a small favor. I didn't mean ..... jesus. I hope I haven't compromised anything."

"Not bureau wise. Not yet, I don't think," Jack said.

"But you might have cost some guy his life," George growled. "What's the rest of it?"

"I went to college with this guy, Jake Greer. He was my best friend. We came to the Bureau together. But he left after five years and started his own private agency. I ... god. I ran a make on a guy a while back as a personal favor, with him looking over my shoulder. He made a comment about my password so I know he saw it. I warned him about what might happen if he ever used it and he promised me that he never would. I was going to change it but... dammit We've just been so damned busy. I forgot."

"A little late for that now. Any idea who he's working for?"

"No. None. I haven't talked to him in weeks."

"Okay," Jack said. "We need to know. Call him now. Find out who his client is."

"What do I say when he asks how I discovered what he did?"

Jack shrugged and looked at George.

"Tell him the system has a built in safety feature that gets back to you at your business e-mail address with a verification update. And that you want to get back in there and delete the trail he left. Whatever. Make something up. And tell him you need to know who the client is. Period."

"Use the phone here," Jack said and motioned to his desk.

Maxwell took out his cell phone, looked up the number, put it away and dialed Greer on the land line. Luckily, he was there. Maxwell sounded nervous at first but finally told Greer thanks and hung up. Then he looked at Jack and George.

"He says it was for The Trident Company. The client's name is Ryan."

Jack and George exchanged a look.

"Did he say he had already called her with the information?"

"He said he had been instructed to relay it to her attorney."

"And what was it that he found for her?"

"That someone is using an alias of a person named Joe Carroll who died several years ago."

"Son-of-a-bitch," George growled as Jack leaned back in his chair, put his hands behind his head and was silent. When he spoke he did so without anger.

"Okay, Jim. Thank you. Now I'll need your ID and your weapon. And I'll expect to see you in my office bright and early on Tuesday, after the holiday. And... not a word to Greer. I'm going to trust you on that. And I'll deal with him after you and I have had a chance to resolve this."

"Damned fool. He could get someone killed," Jack said after Maxwell had left.

"Maybe he already has. Ryan's attorney is Douds. And if he's already called her...."

"Even if he hasn't, there's no way to prevent it. We can't pick him up and hold him till Corbin comes back. If he's coming back."

"So what can we do?"

"Technically? Nothing. Did you make any coffee when you came in?"

"Shouldn't be too scorched yet," George said as he got up and they went down the hall to the service bar.

On the way back, Jack said, "Don't know what good it would do but you should be able to find out where they're staying if Ryan and Corbin booked a place through a travel agent."

"Okay," George was saying with the phone sandwiched between his head and shoulder as he typed into the computer. "Right. Gotcha. Oops, just a second. There it is.... Thank you."

"Las Hadas," George said. Then they both looked at each other and shrugged. They now knew where the two people were staying but, so what. There's nothing they could do at this point anyway.

"Well," Jack said as he looked at his watch. "All you can do now is wait. You going to stick around?"

"Guess so. I still want to do the background on Ryan. And take another look at Corbin's history. See if he really is capable of doing some of this stuff. After that, I don't know. Any suggestions?"

"Guess you could contact the phone company. See what calls have been made to that destination number from the L.A. area. Want me to come back later?"

"No. You've got things to do. I'll give you a buzz if I hit anything important."

"Okay. Think you might try calling Corbin?"

George scratched his forehead. "I don't know. He might just deserve whatever happens to him. But I'd kinda like to know if Douds got through to her."

"Well, I'll leave it up to you. But nothing official at this point."

George spent the next hour making inquiries of the phone company and waiting for people to pull up information. He got all the listed and unlisted numbers for Greer and for Douds and learned that Greer had called Douds at home at nine that morning. Records also showed that Douds had almost immediately called the Las Hadas number. But the time duration of the call was too short for him to have talked to anyone. Then he had called three more times, each time an hour after the proceeding one, also each for one minute, the minimum amount of time logged for any call. Corbin and Ryan were obviously not in their room and Douds did not want to leave a message. That also told George that if he wanted to meddle in Corbin's affairs, it wouldn't do him much good to call, either. Unless he left his name with no message. There was little chance Ryan would know who he was and it might be enough to let Corbin know something was up. Or, or, or... and, but. If Corbin had been the perpetrator of all those events then it might be Miss Ryan who was in big trouble, instead. What about that? Best thing might be just to leave the whole damned thing alone for now.

With that he got up from his desk. He was hungry. Guess he'd walk over to the village and get something to eat while he gave it some thought.

Sitting at home reviewing his own options, Marvin Douds was also giving it a lot of thought. How many damned times had he warned her about getting so involved with someone she knew so little about. Four, five? And always some smart ass answer back. Even if the guy had been legit, where did she expect such a relationship could ever go. Nowhere, probably, and didn't care as long as the guy's stamina held out. An animal. At one point even Rudy had questioned his own sanity to Douds during a weak moment, implying he's never make it to fifty the way she was on him all the time. Well, she didn't screw him to death but who the hell was she kidding, thinking he didn't know damned well that if she hadn't somehow put Rudy into the ocean all by herself, she had at least been the major conspirator. But, if only he had some, just in case, proof hidden away in a safe place along with some of the other stuff he'd collected since she came along. There wasn't a soul on the face of the earth that wasn't expendable in her eyes. Even him, chief council and advisor. And when the day came when she felt he knew too much .....

When all was said and done, however, the best course of action for him might be to plead ignorance about Joe Carroll being an interloper and say nothing. Let the man take her out, hope to hell that was the end of it and start over. Stake out the top job for himself. He was certainly in the best position to handle it. And so who was Carroll, anyway? He had to be Corbin. At least according to Greer because having traced backwards, Corbin's accidental death had to have been faked. No body actually located, no death cert. on the record. But why would Corbin have gone to Mexico with Margaret? That seemed so totally unnecessary if all he was after was revenge. But on the other hand, if Margaret didn't come back, that might be a blessing. Maybe the best thing to do would be not to call her and warn her. But if he didn't and she still came back, how could he keep Greer from telling her the truth...?

Douds continued on, thinking his way through the whole thing. That took him back to Sam Corbin alias Joe Carroll. And was Corbin also the mysterious old man named Charley who kept popping up everywhere something bad happened? Was that possible? And then something else connected. It made him so suddenly angry he got up, went to his wet bar and poured himself a double scotch. It was only two thirty in the afternoon.

Christ. He'd better calm down before he had a heart attack. Christ, Corbin had to have been the guy who came through the closet wall and poisoned him in the middle of the night. Christ. Jesus-fucking-Christ. He walked round and round the room, thankful that his wife had gone to the store, not realizing how long ago that had been until he heard the door open and her silly little, youuu whooooo, I'm home. Can you help me with the groceries?

He slugged down the scotch, put the empty glass back up on the shelf unrinsed and went into the kitchen.

"Marvin. What's wrong?" she said when he was still more than ten feet away.

"Wrong? Wrong with what?" he grumbled as he came closer, irritated all over again by her use of his first name and the question. Why did his wife always insist on calling him that at all the wrong times, putting that funny little twist of her's on it. Like now, when he needed it the least.

"You seem upset," she said as he got nearer, even though he had done his best to hide his emotion. "And what's this?" she sniffed. "Have you been drinking in the middle of the day?"

"Dammit, Anna," he said with a suppressed growl. "If a fifty six year old man can't have a drink in his own damned house when he needs one, what's the point?"

"Yes, but listen to what you just said. You said, need. Aren't you feeling well? How long has it been since your last checkup?"

"Not long enough. And how many times have I told you that studies show one or two ounces of alcohol a day are beneficial to health. Particularly for people who have stressful jobs. And I shouldn't have to remind you that just because I sit on my tush behind a desk all day that my life isn't stressful. So can we just get the damned groceries in so I can get back to what I need to get done."

"Well, just so you know I'm only looking out for you."

"How could I forget," he mumbled inaudibly under his breath as he went out to the car and grabbed as many sacks as he could carry.

When he was done he went back into the den and sat down. He would never think of trying to help put things away. That was her turf and when she was satisfied, she followed him in, dug out her knitting and sat down in the big chair by the fireplace like her presence would somehow help. What the hell was she making this time? Another stocking cap? Or a super bulky sweater? When was she ever going to realize that she had been living in southern California for the last thirty years instead of North Dakota?

Two hours went by before she finally got up and asked him if he would like pork chops for dinner. Great, he said and once the kitchen noises began he went back to the study and closed the door. He had decided. He would try to reach Margaret one last time.

TWENTY EIGHT

What a damnable experience, Sam thought all over again as he peeked in at her standing before the bathroom mirror touching up her makeup. Something she needed little of and barely used. They had been in the same bed until morning many times before but always, once they were awake, they showered and dressed separately and then went their own way. Being together round the clock, bed, bath, breakfast, lunch, wandering through all the shops in the old part of town, more sex and now about to go to dinner was so overly domestic and every bit a sham. Tomorrow he would shake the truth out of her, one way or another.

It was then that the room phone rang. He wasn't surprised. She had said she might be getting some calls. He answered it as she came out of the bath. He thought it sounded like her attorney, Douds, but he passed it on to her without a word.

"Hello," she said as Sam motioned to her, question like, as to whether he should go outside. She shook her head no, emphasizing with a hand wave but he still walked out onto the balcony as a gesture of indifference.

"Yes," she continued. "I'm fine....... ," he heard her say.

Then she let out a sharp, "What," but quickly mellowed it to a soft, "Oh really. Well, that's nice."

No wasted words, Douds had gotten directly to the point on the other end of the line.

"Not only did the bastard fake his own death, he assumed the identity of a dead man. There is no other explanation. You've been partying with Corbin."

"Well, I guess I'm not totally surprised," Margaret said, trying to lighten her voice for Sam's sake, in case he was eavesdropping.

"How are you going to feel when he sticks a knife in your back? Have him bring you back. Tell him it's a family emergency. I'll have someone take care of him when you get here."

"No," she replied very calmly, as if it were a minor business problem. "That's not the way I'd like to handle it. But listen. We were just on our way to dinner. Where are you going to be for the rest of the evening?"

"I'm at home and I'm not going anywhere."

"Good. I'll call you later."

"Okay," she said to Sam in a pleasant enough voice after hanging up. "Ready to eat?"

"Anything serious?" he asked after they had been seated and the wine had been poured.

Margaret picked up her glass, took a sip and looked at him. "No. Nothing important," she said, hoping she had been able to hide her concern.

"That's good," he commented, not so sure he believed her. Hide it as she might, that phone called had changed something in her. But what? How would he find out?

"Nice," he said after a taste of the wine, wondering what to talk about so they could at least get through the meal.

"Well," he said after it was finally over and he had written their room number on the bill and signed it. "You have a call to make so why don't I go in to the bar and have a drink. I can wait for you there. Then we can have a nightcap."

"That's not necessary," she lied, relieved nevertheless. How in the hell did he do it? Always so damned cool about everything. The son of a bitch. No wonder she was so intrigued by him. And now totally frightened to death.

God damn you, Sam Corbin, she said to herself as she looked across the table at him, studying his face. What the hell am I going to do with you, you handsome bastard, now that I can't stop thinking about you more than half the time. The only man who has ever reached that far inside and made me feel so glorious in bed and so damned needy every hour they were apart. And so damned lonely. Damned if she wasn't in love with him. Damned if he didn't have her in a corner almost ready to beg. Damned if it didn't hurt far more than she would ever be able to bear. She had no choice. His destruction was her only salvation.

"See you in a bit," he said as he got up from the table.

Sam went into the lobby, heading in the direction of the bar room, but turned and went down the long hallway instead. At the end he found the small office like room with the resort's telephone switchboard. A middle aged Mexican woman sat facing the large, antiquated panel that dated from at least thirty years earlier with its many phone jack receptacles. The only modern feature was the headset she was wearing. She ignored him for a moment, speaking in Spanish to someone on the line, picked up a cord, plugged it into a receptacle, removed another and turned to look at him with a scowl. What was he doing in her office?

He asked her if she spoke English. She nodded and he showed her his room key with the number on it so she would know he was guest. Then he told her there was a phone call on their line but that they only had one phone in the room and he needed to hear the conversation. At the same time he held out a twenty dollar bill to her. She looked at it, pointed to another phone sitting on a small table in the corner of the room and took the money. Then she selected a cable from the maze and plugged it into one of the panel jacks. Sam went to the auxiliary phone and carefully picked it up. The timing was perfect.

"I can talk now," Margaret was saying.

"I hope you heard me loud and clear when I called earlier, " Douds replied. "I hope you not in denial any longer."

"I never was. I was just hoping for something else."

"Your something else is going to get you killed if you don't get out of there."

"So I leave? And then what? After all he's done, there's no way to hide."

"Which is why he has to go."

"I know that, dammit," she said very loudly. "But what if he's not in this alone? Then what?"

"We have to start somewhere?"

"I'm beginning not to like this one bit."

"What? Mess around, fall in love. That couldn't be you. Could it?"

"Cut the crap. You know better than that."

"If you say so. I've chartered a plane for tomorrow morning but it's at least five hours to get down there so be careful and leave him to me."

"You? That's ridiculous. It's not your kind of thing."

"Not until now. Now it's personal and you damn well know why."

"Yes, I remeber. But you can't just walk in here. That would be suicide."

"Don't have to. Tony knows a guy who is familiar with the area. To the north about five miles up the coast is an exclusive restaurant up on a cliff. It's isolated down at the end of the road and it's closed this time of year but he won't know that. If you can get him up there on some pretense like dinner, I can be waiting. Then we can fly back together."

Margaret took some time to consider it. Not the best of plans to be sure. And could Douds do something so ruthless? Maybe. He was still obsessed over what had seemed to be an attempt on his life. And if he botched it she'd still be there to finish it. Joe Carroll was Sam Corbin and he was making her crazy.

"What time?"

"Not earlier than five. Say, five thirty to six."

"What's it called?"

"Los Rocos."

At that point Sam eased the phone back into its cradle and went to the bar where he ordered a tall vodka tonic which he immediately drained to less than half. He was finishing it when Margaret came in.

"Ready for a drink?" he asked her.

"Sure. Whatever you're having is fine."

"Would you like a table? Or should we go back outside. I believe they're still playing music."

"Let's go outside. And make that a double round."

It was better outside with the surrounding darkness, the candle light softening what had quickly become a difficult situation. She would have had a hard time looking at him in the brighter lights of the bar room.

"Everything resolved?" he asked her.

"I hope so," she answered.

Sam almost chuckled but asked her how she would like to spend the next day. Sunday. He said he hoped she wasn't Catholic.

By then she had finished her first drink and was working on the second.

"God, no," she replied. "You don't have to take me to church, so relax."

"Isn't that amazing," he said. "How much we still don't know about each other after all this time."

"There's always lots of things left unsaid. No matter what the relationship," she replied, trying to keep her voice under control.

"I'll drink to that," he said and took another drink. Then he waved at the waitress.

"Two doubles," he said to her and was quiet until she returned a couple of minutes later. Understandably, Margaret was preoccupied.

"Anything else you want to tell me?" he asked after the next round of drinks had been served.

"What?" she said, almost with alarm.

"Well. Were you a girl scout? How old were you when you first discovered boys? Have you ever been sky diving or bungy jumping, that kind of stuff."

"Oh," she said, catching herself. God dammit, he was playing with her again. And then she smiled.

"I saw a UFO once. Honest to god. I was coming home from Vegas in the middle of the night and saw it skirting the edge of the mountains in the distance. As for boys, I'll leave the part to your imagination. And why anyone would ever want to jump out of a perfectly good airplane is beyond me. What about you? What's the riskiest thing you've ever done?"

"Hmm. Well, probably coming here with you."

What a ruthless son-of-a-bitch, she thought as she looked at him. Maybe it wouldn't be so hard to get rid of him after all. She smiled again.

"Think so? Why?"

"You'll probably fuck my brains out, make me fall in love with you, then dump me for the guitar player with the big Pancho Villa mustache and sombrero."

"Right. And ride away together on his donkey in the middle of the night and live happily ever after," she laughed in spite of herself, then asked, frowning this time. "Where did that ever come from? The, live happily ever after, part. That's just so damned stupid. Does anyone ever live happily ever after? After what? Falling in love? I think that's all backwards."

"So... You've obviously been in love before."

"Hasn't everyone? You have, I'm sure. Was it good for you?"

"'As a matter of fact, it was. While it lasted."

"What happened? Did she dump you? No. Of course not. Any woman would be a damned fool to do that."

"You sure you want to hear about it? It's pretty personal."And maybe a little cruel, he said to himself. But damn her. She needs to hear it anyway.

"Of course," she lied. "Unless it bothers you."

"I met her as a blind date. She wasn't ready when I went to pick her up so I was standing there when she came down the stairs. The only word I can think of to describe her is lovely. Then we went off to a party and I can remember dancing with her. I was nervous, she was nervous, but holding her as I tried to dance was absolutely overwhelming. Unfortunately, at the time, I was going to college and the last thing I had ever considered was getting married so it took three years before we finally did it. But, say what you want. Yes, I could have lived happily ever after with her. We were together nine years before she died," he said as he stared at Margaret for a quick second before looking away.

"But," he said and continued. "I never realized how terribly lucky I had been. Most people have never had that. Most people never even come close. Most people spend their lives in dysfunctional, emotionally starved, confused disarray, battering each other to death mentally and physically, fighting over money and power and ideological bullshit, never once realizing what is more important than what. But some people are blessed. I was blessed and I am eternally thankful. But do you know that hardly a day goes by when I don't think of it? Not a one. No offense meant to you but that's where I'm at half the time. Cut off from the world around me."

Margaret's eyes were turned down. Suddenly she was afraid to say anything, afraid to move, afraid to do anything that might in any way betray her but still prepared for the worst. That which was still unsaid and yet to come. But once again he surprised her.

"Well, my apologies," he said, sounding sincere. "Really. That's the first time since she... that I have ever vented my feelings about it so I got a little carried away. But it's unfair to dump that on someone else. Especially you. I guess I was just thinking about how we go through life bumping into each other but never really getting to know each other. Anyway, enough philosophical self indulgence, let's have another drink."

Margaret nodded and mumbled something about it being okay. Then she leaned back and lit a cigarette, trying to analyze what had just happened. Whatever it was that he was trying to do, why hadn't he finished it? She downed the rest of her third drink and started on the fourth. Sam asked her to dance. She accepted and forced herself to focus entirely on the music. When they returned to their table Sam pulled his chair around closer to hers before he sat down. He ordered another round of drinks, then placed his hand over hers, but only for a moment. They danced a second time. Then she excused herself for the restroom and when she returned she didn't notice that her glass was much fuller than when she left. She tossed it down and wanted to dance again. When they sat that time she snuggled closer, took his hand and placed it over her breast, then leaned her head against his shoulder.

Perfect, Sam thought. She was a little tipsy but still coherent. Just the way he wanted her. After a few minutes he helped her to her feet and they made their way back to their suite. Margaret slipped out of her clothes and fell across the bed. She was fast asleep before he was undressed.

"Dammit," he said to himself. He had purposely gotten her drunk to loosen her up. Answers. The singular reason he had come to Mexico with her to begin with. But what the hell was this? He had over estimated her capacity for alcohol. He lifted her feet, swung them up onto the bed and pulled the sheet over her.

Then he quietly unzipped her large handbag and looked inside at the nine millimeter semi automatic. No wonder it had seemed so damned heavy when she had been carrying it around. She must have somehow hidden it in her checked luggage to get it on the plane. Okay, he said to himself as he went around and got in the other side of the bed.

He woke several hours later. Margaret was rubbing her hand over his chest. She moved down over his stomach, up and down his thighs and back up. Then she swung herself over and straddled him. It was almost an attack. Passionate and ferocious. At last she moaned deeply and spasmed, then continued to moan before collapsing onto the bed where she backed up into him and pulled his arm around her. Never a word spoken. Sam laid there with his hand on her breast, aware of her breathing.

"Don't say a word," she told him once the sun was shining in and they were awake.

"I won't even ask how you feel. How's that?"

"Thank you. Jeez, looks like it's going to be a slow starter. Unless..." she said as she threw back the sheets and reached for him. "Unless you get the blood flowing to my brain, so the headache goes away."

"Might help," he said as he climbed on top of her, thinking this was probably it. The last time for them. Maybe she felt the same way. Even though she was on the bottom she was still as aggressive and insatiable as she had been in the middle of the night. And just as out of control when she went over the final edge.

Afterward, after showers and breakfast, she asked if he would mind if they went down to the pool to get some sun.

"Sure. It might be nice to just have a quiet, low key day for a change. Let me get my strength back in case of an emergency."

Margaret glanced at him. Another off the cuff remark that seemed more than coincidence. But how could he know? He couldn't. Still, if he was just jesting, why hadn't he followed through with another comment like he usually did? Wasn't he supposed to say something innocuous like, in case she needed to get laid again? But this time he had made the comment and immediately turned away. Jesus, she told herself. Try and keep it together. Calm down before he gets suspicious.

Margaret headed to the pool. Sam said he would be right there, then he went into the lobby of the hotel and when he came back he had a spiral notebook and a pen. She raised her eyebrows in question when he looked at her.

"Just thought I'd take notes," he said. "You say some of the naughtiest things when you get turned on. They'd work well in my detective story."

"What story? Are you serious?"

"No, but maybe it's time I started. Only some mainstream sceenplay I can crank out in a hurry. Everyone else in L.A. is writing one."

"You're teasing me again."

"No. Seriously. It's all right there. Would be terrorists, gangs, people shot in front of their own houses, drugs, corruption, bodies in the landfill. And then someone even got their limo blown up. That would make a great opening chapter. The characters could all be modeled after real people. Want to be in it?"

"I don't think so. You'd probably make me out to be a real sinister bitch."

"Hmm. No. I think I would make you into a lady detective. A super sleuth. One so overwhelmingly beautiful that the bad guys would all break down and confess the minute she got them alone in the interrogation room."

Margaret actually laughed. "What else?"

"She's also totally stacked. Like you. Jeez," he said and made an appropriate face. "But she's cool. And very selective. But when she gets turned on, watch out. She's also very complex and there's a side of her where she'd almost rather put a bullet between a bad guy's eyes than bring him in and may even be guilty of that. But in the end she goes through all this stuff and turns out to be this really human person who loses her black and white perspective of things, meets another cop with a really big shlong and they run off to Tahiti together, leaving LA to sink into the slime heap. How's that?"

She laughed again. "Shlong? Where did that come from? Never mind. What about this other cop? The one with the big... Who's the model for him? Yourself?"

"Definitely not. But while I can certainly visualize the lucky

232

bastard climbing into bed with the beautiful lady and having his brains screwed out I think he has to be a little more ah,... accepting, maybe. I mean, she has all this depth but... and here I have to deviate from you, the role model. She's gone through dozens and dozens of men, popped a criminal or two. And she's out there every day seeing the worst of everything. Out of necessity, she's pretty tough. Some of the men in her life have also been pretty rough, so she's got her guard up. And because she's a woman in a still largely man's world, she's had to make some hard decisions. But in the end, goodness prevails," he said and turned to her.

"Well, just a thought," he commented as he stuck the pen down inside the notebook spiral and tossed it on the ground. He knew it was way over done but he couldn't resist his one last chance to poke at her, no matter what the reaction or how silly it came off. To hell with it.

"Would you like some iced tea? Or a lemonade?" he asked and got to his feet.

"Nothing, thanks," she said.

"Okay," he answered. "Well, guess I'll go take a nap. Just in case," he said with a smile, not really caring which way she might take the comment. Douds was on his way to Mexico and Sam needed to think about it.

George Dixon just couldn't leave it alone. He was back in his office again early on Sunday and had already learned there had been a twelve minute phone call from Douds to Las Hadas. Then Douds had made another one. An aircraft charter service working out of Van Nuys' airport.

George called, wondering if anyone would be there. A man picked up the phone.

"What kinds of planes do you have? George asked.

"A Lear jet, a single engine Mooney and an Aero Commander twin. Old but reliable. What did you have in mind and when?"

"Just myself and probably today."

"Where are you going?"

"Puerto Vallarta."

"One way or round trip."

"Round trip."

"When would you return?"

"Depends. I only need to be there a couple of hours."

"Well, wish I had known. The Commander left two hours ago for Manzanillo which is just down the coast from there. If you need to go today it would have to be the jet. Otherwise, they're supposed to come back tonight so we could go first thing in the morning. Might save you a few dollars."

"Yeah. That might be better anyway. Let me see what I can work out. And, ah, what's the flight time to Manzanillo in the Commander?"

"Approximately five hours. But you said Puerto Vallarta. That's about forty five minutes less."

"Right. But that seems rather fast for such an old aircraft."

"I know. But the engines have been upgraded, the weight has been trimmed and we added extra tanks so we have a range of almost a thousand miles. No refueling en route."

It didn't make any sense. Why would Douds be going to Mexico? What couldn't wait two more days until she returned? There seemed to be only one answer. Plus, it wasn't just Douds. The guy at the airport had said, they? What was that? Did he mean Douds and the pilot or was someone going with Douds? If so, who and why? Nothing good, that was for sure. Finally, George put those questions aside and went back to Corbin, running him through the computer again, looking at everything. A bright guy with a bachelors degree in Physics, a masters in computer science, another in business. Never been in the service. Didn't hunt, didn't own a gun. Lots of odd jobs in college but nothing in construction or anything involving explosives. Nothing that would have been of any use in any of the chain of incidents for which he was now a prime suspect. He was middle of the road politically, never involved in demonstrations. Nothing, nothing. The same for his wife.

He moved on to Margaret Ryan. Thirty six years old, born in Iowa, an only child. Her mother was a high school dropout who threw Margaret's father out of the house for drunkenness and physical abuse when Margaret was nine. No report of abuse directed at the child. The mother worked her way up to department manager in one of Des Moines's largest retail organizations but before this happened Margaret began running away from home, the first time at fourteen. The second time at fifteen and a half where she was tracked down in Alabama living with a thirty year old man who she had married illegally. The mother had the marriage annulled but at seventeen Margaret packed up and headed to Wisconsin. There she worked as a waitress and went to night school and became a stenographer. She also got a high school diploma. Then she worked in the office of the RayOVac company in Madison for nearly two years before coming to Las Vegas. Here she married a big time attorney, had a child which died in the crib when it was two months old, divorced the attorney and ended up with nothing. From there she worked in the casinos. Waitress, bartender, black jack dealer. No indication of ever having resorted to prostitution. She was caught up in one drug bust in someone's home but was released for lack of evidence.

At this point she took the entrance exams and was allowed to enroll in the University in Vegas, the only reason being that she had scored in the top one percent of all applicants in spite of her previously impoverished scholastic history. After a first semester of B grades she moved up to a 4.0 and stayed there until she left after three years. All of her elective courses were in mathematics and philosophy. Her next address was Beverly Hills, California with no record of employment for three years. Then she showed up on the payroll of the Trident Company as a receptionist. Taxes paid, no wants or warrants, no parking tickets. And now she was suspected of running the show with no personal investigations under way that George could uncover at the moment.

It was well past noon when he finally printed out the four page summary and walked back over to the Village to have lunch at the same place as the previous day. He took his time, had three cups of coffee, chatted with his waitress as the lunch crowd dissipated, then walked around checking out shop windows, wandered into the book store, looked at the best sellers and came back out on the street. He used his cell phone to see what time it was and realized that Douds would be in Mexico by now. Then it occurred to him that Manzanillo was in a different time zone and that it was actually an hour later there. But, so what? he asked himself as he started back towards his office. It was still eating away at him when he sat back down at his desk and it was then that he realized that his attitude towards Corbin was changing. If the guy had done half the things he was suspected of and he was convicted, he would never see daylight again. A lawbreaker, a vigilante, a character out of the old west, but hardly just a wanton, insane killer. And if he had done it, blown up Vince Sands' house, it might have been considered to be justifiable homicide. Regardless, it took a lot of brains and a lot of courage to get it done and it didn't seem fair to just let the guy get blindsided. Not after all that. Get him home first, then keep him under investigation and see that he got a fair trial if they found enough evidence to go that far.

Using his cell phone, he called Las Hadas and asked if they had a concierge. They did. His name was Ricardo.

He asked Ricardo if he was familiar with the American couple who had been there since Friday afternoon.

"Certainly, sir. A most striking pair. How could I forget Miss Ryan and the man, Mr. Carroll."

"Do you happen to know if they are in their room or somewhere on the premises?"

"Premises?"

"Somewhere around the resort. In the bar, restaurant, do you have a pool? I would like to get a personal message to Mr. Carroll."

"Si. Premises. But no, they are not here. I believe they went somewhere in their rental automobile. Perhaps two hours ago."

"Okay. Thank you. But when he returns could you give him a message from me. When he is alone. I would consider it a personal favor."

"Certainly, senor. How can I help you?"

"Tell him that George Dixon tried to reach him and that I'd like to...."

"You are Mr. Dixon?"

"I am."

"Could you.. What is your phone number please?"

George gave him his cell phone number.

"Si, that is the number he gave me. And a very strange message. I hope you can understand it. He said they were going up to a restaurant named Los Rocos. I told him it was closed this time of year but he said it was of no importance. They were only going to look at the scenery. But then he told me that if he was not back by seven o'clock this evening that I was to call you. He said even if the lady returned alone. That you would know what to do."

"He said that?"

"Si. I'm very sure of it."

"Very good. And if he doesn't return will you still call me, even though we have already spoken?"

"That is what he asked me to do."

"And how much did he pay you for this request?"

"Fifty dollars. He was most generous."

"That's good, Ricardo. I am very sure he will be back. And when he returns you may tell him I called. But do it in private, like I told you. Alone. And then you may tell him that he should give you another fifty dollars because I said to."

"Si, si. Bueno, senor. But if he does not return?"

"Then you will call me and I will send you fifty dollars after you have told me what has happened."

Not wanting to alarm the man or create an unnecessary problem, George hung up. Then he called another agent at home who was just firing up his barbecue and quizzed him about law enforcement jurisdictions in Mexico. Who could he call to find out without creating a big flap down there?

"Okay, George. Where are you, at the office?"

"Yeah, well, what can I say? One of those things."

"Why don't you drop on by. I'll be throwing some sausages on the grill as soon as the fire is ready."

"Well, I appreciate that Marty, but I need to hang around here a couple more hours. Maybe next time."

There was a large sign on the highway announcing the restaurant and Sam turned off the pavement and went down the long graveled road leading towards the west. Several hundred yards down a gate blocked their way. A sign on the gate said, Cerrado. It was only ten minutes to five. Margaret was nervous and upset. In spite of her stalling, they were much too early.

"Well, so much for that. It's closed," Sam said. "Why didn't they tell you that when you asked?"

"Maybe they didn't know. After all, this is Mexico," Margaret replied.

"Well, too bad. Looks like it might be an interesting place. Maybe next time." What the hell was he even doing there, he wondered. He could have simply made some excuse and refused to go along with it, tell her he preferred to have dinner at the hotel. Or.... There were lots of other choices, too, but for some, suddenly not too clear, reason he had decided to let the whole thing play itself out here, win or lose. And now he was stuck with it. Or was he? He started to turn the car around.

"Wait," she said.

He stopped the car and looked at her.

"Let's leave the car here and walk in," she said. "The view from the cliffs is supposed to be awesome."

"Awesome?"

"Good, great, beautiful. Come on, the walk will be nice."

Sam pulled the car over to the side of the road and they got out. Margaret hung the strap of her king sized, draw string purse over her right shoulder and they started walking as Sam looked for any signs of Douds having gotten there before them. The gate wasn't locked so he dragged it open just enough for them to slip through. They went on past the restaurant building and out onto the large, open grassy area behind, that led to the edge of a rocky cliff several hundred feet above the ocean below.

"Marvelous," she said.

"Yes. It is beautiful. No doubt about that."

"Let's go over there," he said after a minute. "Not so many trees. We can see better." He took her hand lightly and casually guided her across the short grass to where a single large rock stood back a ways from the edge. One big enough for two people to hide behind. There he leaned his back against it and said, "Come here," and gently pulled her into him, his left arm around her waist as though he wanted to hold her close in a loving way. She hesitated briefly, but complied. Releasing his hold on her waist, he raised his arms and pulled her face around to where he was able to lean over her and kiss her. It was a long, hard kiss

238

which gave him time to reach into her partially closed purse with his right hand and remove the loaded weapon without her seeming to notice.

"What was that all about?" she asked when he stopped and stared at him suspiciously.

He dropped his left arm back down to her waist and encircled her as he spoke.

"Let's hope not, but for one of us that may well have been the kiss of death," he said.

Instantly, she tried to jerk away but he held her tightly.

"And forget the gun. I already have it."

Again she struggled but he put the barrel of the weapon up against her chest so she could feel the cold metal.

"God, Margaret. Sometimes you can be such an ornery bitch. I know it's not your nature but now might be a good time to try and be a little more compliant. It might also help save your life. Or isn't that important to you?"

For a second she was speechless. Then her face took on a vicious, spiteful look.

"What difference does it make? Sooner or later you're going to kill me anyway."

"Maybe. Maybe not. So far I haven't made my final decision so let's just enjoy the time we have left."

"God damn you , ..."

"Sam. Sam Corbin. But that's no secret, is it? Especially since Douds confirmed it yesterday."

"You bastard. How did you know it was Douds?"

"How do you think I knew it was Douds? I listened in at the switchboard. But what the hell. You should have already known that.

That shut her up. But not for long.

"Now what?" she asked.

"That depends on you and your attorney."

"I'm sure we can work something out."

"Not any more. Douds is already on his way. In fact he may already be here."

"How do you know that?'

"I think I just heard a car out there. He's a little early."

"I can talk to him. Make him back off."

"You should have told him to stay home when you had the chance."

"You know I didn't invite him," she said as she tried to turn around, but he held her tight.

"Right, so just don't make this any more difficult than it already is."

"Is that why you're using me as a shield?"

"No. I'm curious as to whether he would shoot you just to get at me."

"He would never do that."

"Guess we are about to find out. If that places you in jeopardy, too bad."

"I can control him, dammit. Give me a chance. Let me talk to him before it's too late."

"So we just shake hands and go have another drink together? Cut the crap, Margaret, and be quiet until this is over or I may shoot you myself. And I will shoot you if do anything stupid. I will shoot you if you do something even half stupid."

This time Margaret remained quiet as Sam scanned the trees and rocks looking for Douds. Where the hell was he? Margaret's little nine millimeter automatic didn't have much range. He needed a clear shot, close in, or it was the end of the story. Then he picked up a quick movement back in the trees.

"Turn your head to the left again," he ordered Margaret. "I'm going to kiss you on the cheek this time."

Douds moved up quickly to a large tree at the edge of the clearing as Sam pretended to nuzzle Margaret. Sam almost laughed. A blind person could have seen him. The tree wasn't quite big enough, either. Doud's jacket tail stuck out behind him on one side as he peeked around the other. But he was still a good twenty five yards away. Half of that would be a lot better. Sam waited, his head down like he might now be kissing Margaret on the shoulder, but watching and waiting. Unless Douds was going to come out blazing away, the man was out of options. But so was Sam. He didn't want Margaret dead, either. Not yet, anyway.

"Now, my dear," Sam said quietly. "Don't look straight ahead but stay turned a little. Out of the corner of your eye you will see him behind the largest tree in the foreground."

"Good, now turn your head back this way and ask yourself. Is Mr. Douds as devious and power hungry as you are? What do you think?"

"I..."

"Exactly. Now ask yourself if you want to live badly enough to do precisely what I tell you. Nothing cute, nothing brave. Marvin is not going to save your pretty ass. The only way you are going to get out of here is if you go with me. Clear?"

"I don't... I..."

"Don't bullshit yourself. Make your choice and make it quick."

"All right, dammit! You win."

"Good. Now as naturally as you can, turn around, put your arms around my neck and kiss me like you mean it. Then, leaving your hands on my shoulders, back up a small step and keep looking at me. When I say go, you move to your right just as damned fast as you can and get behind this rock. And keep your head down once you're there. I'll do the same. Easy now. Arms up. A nice long, hot kiss. Move your ass a little like it's really good. That's it. Now, which way is your right?"

"That way, god dammit Want to do it again?"

"Are you kidding?"

"What the hell. You might as well die happy. Maybe I could give you such a good one you'd die of a heart attack instead of a bullet."

"Nice thought. But I had my final piece of your ass this morning, so stop squirming. That's better. Now, take a deep breath and let it out. Good. Slowly drop your arms. Okay, go."

It was utterly anti climatic. Nothing happened. Down on his knees, Sam took a quick peek. Caught completely by surprise, Douds hadn't moved. Sam dropped down, leaned the pistol against the side of the rock to steady it, took careful aim and fired a shot into the tree right at eye level. He could see Douds jerk his head back as bark flew off. He then looked at Margaret to see if she was behaving herself. Damned if she didn't look genuinely frightened. And then Douds was down lower, took a quick look and pulled back. His gun came up along side the tree trunk, his hand shaking slightly, his nervousness keeping him from realizing that his right leg was exposed halfway to the knee.

"Give it up, Douds," Corbin shouted. "This isn't the kind of fight you can win."

Doud's answer was to fire off a round that went completely wild, tearing up the grass off to the side ten feet away. Then he screamed as Corbin's slug tore through his ankle. Then it was quiet. Sam wiped his sleeve across his brow. This had to end quickly so they could get out of there before someone became concerned about the gunfire and called the police. Getting caught with a gun in Mexico could mean half a lifetime in prison. He took a quick look at Margaret. She was leaning back against the rock, eyes closed and hands over her ears.

"That tree isn't big enough, Douds, because now your ass is sticking out. Drop the gun so I can see it and come on out," Corbin yelled. "Or the next one will hit you where it really hurts."

"No way. God damn you, Corbin. I want you dead," Douds yelled as he groped his way up on his one good leg behind the tree.

"You were lucky once, Marvin. It won't happen again. The only reason I took pity on you was because your wife is bigger than you and she snores."

With that, Douds let out an angry roar and came out into the open, screaming and cursing, hopping along badly on one foot, the gun out in front, pointed at the rock Sam and Margaret were hiding behind. Two more wild shots and three good hops and he went down, stumbling over something, flat on his face, losing his grip on the gun as he tried to save himself. Sam was on his feet immediately, feeling safe, his upper body now exposed when he simultaneously heard a muffled pop from off to his left along with the sound of a slug ricocheting off the rock right in front of him and the sharp sting of rock fragments cutting into both his cheek and his forearm. Down he went, back out of sight. Sure that she was about to pounce on him he pointed the barrel of his own weapon right in Margaret's face and told her to be quiet as blood stared to run down his cheek and neck.

"It's not fatal," he told her, "so behave yourself. No, no. Don't even think about it. And if you try to run from me, I'll shoot you in the back."

She settled back. "Now what, wise guy?" she asked, taunting

him.

"Now you are going to find out who else is out there. Unless you already know."

"Like hell I am. You're dead."

"Not yet," he said as he grabbed her by the hair, jerked her face around and put the muzzle of the gun against her ear. "If nothing else my dying reflex will splatter your brains all over this rock so you are going to call out to your unknown hero and tell them I'm fatally wounded and you are okay. Do it, goddammit. Then stand up very slowly so they can see you. Mess it up and you're dead."

Margaret hesitated. Jesus, what if Douds helper was Tony? She had never made peace with him. And what if it was Carl, or Luke, or... Then she was dead anyway.

"I'm okay. I have the gun," she shouted out anyway, thinking it was her best choice. "He's badly wounded. I'm standing up now," she ended and rose slowly as Corbin tightly held onto her left arm, ready to jerk her back down if she tried anything.

She peered over the top of the rock, looking in the direction the shot had come from. Nothing. Oh shit, she said to herself, waiting in fear, a sense of panic overtaking her. Then she saw another man step out into the open and look at her from farther back in the trees. A man holding a chrome plated nine millimeter automatic with a long silencer on it. She squinted at him. "My god," she whispered.

"Bud?" she practically shouted with glee, immediately realizing her error in identifying him. Then she looked over to where Douds had fallen down. Good, Douds had at least crawled over and recovered his own gun. He was sitting there in the grass, the weapon pointed at her, a look of complete agony on his face. Then he lowered it slowly, grimaced and almost passed out from the pain in his fractured ankle. Damn, she thought and looked back at Bud.

"Miss Margaret. Are you okay? " Bud asked and started coming towards her cautiously.

Margaret tested Corbin's grip on her arm, wanting to pull away and run, but it was too tight. Then she wondered if she should warn Bud. But no. Corbin was cornered and he damn well

243

might shoot her in the process.

"Talk to him, dammit," Sam said. "Get him over here."

"I'm okay, Bud. He's almost dead. What are we going to do with him? We have to help Douds, too. Hurry."

Jesus, Corbin thought. Bud? How did this happen? Bud had almost as big a score to settle with him as Douds. Now what, Corbin wondered. He didn't dare let go of Margaret. But unless he did he wouldn't be able to get around the rock far enough to take care of Bud, either. But, hell. He didn't want to just shoot the poor bastard.... Then he heard Bud tell Douds to hang in there. He'd get him some help after he finished off Corbin. He sounded like he was at least half way to the rock. Maybe twenty feet to go. He waited a few more seconds.

"Okay," Sam told Margaret in a quiet, cold voice as he rose up behind her. "This is it."

He came up slowly, out of sight to Bud long enough for him to get a look at Douds who was moaning in pain and trying to stop the blood with his handkerchief after having crawled part way back to the tree he had been behind, leaving his gun, now out of his immediate reach.

"Far enough, Bud," Corbin said as he stood all the way up and pointed his gun directly at Bud's chest.

Totally surprised, Bud stopped in his tracks and stared. Somewhere in the back of his mind he was still expecting to meet the man who had blown up his limo, an older man with a beard and mustache. It took him a few seconds to recover. Then he looked at Margaret. Then he looked back at Corbin and saw the fresh blood on the side of his face. He got him, all right. But how bad was it? Sure as hell wasn't fatal. And now he was hiding behind her. No way in hell would he shoot her to get to the guy, however. He loved this woman. She didn't know it and he would never have told her that, but he did, so help him lord. Working for her, escorting her around, having the role of being her protector, she had stolen him away. Helplessly, he looked at her again. What was he supposed to do now?

The look in Bud's eyes was too much. As if picking up on all that Bud was thinking, Margaret felt a wave of extreme compassion wash over and she suddenly felt lost in her ability to deal with it. Until then she had always seen him as driver and bodyguard. An employee. Expendable. But no longer. He was there because of her and no matter what, she didn't want him dead because of that.

"I'm sorry, Bud," she finally said. "I'm really sorry."

Bud watched her face closely and knew it was the truth. Whether or not the guy was seriously wounded, he certainly didn't look it, and badly as he wanted to he couldn't take the risk of hurting Margaret just to settle things with this Charley character, Corbin, or who the hell ever he really was. He slowly lowered his weapon, flipped the safety on with his thumb and dropped it on the ground.

"Kick it over this way," Corbin commanded him. "Good, now stay put. You, too," he told Margaret. "Especially you," and with that he came our from behind her and the rock to retrieve Bud's gun.

As Corbin did so Margaret turned to see what Douds was doing and another surge of hope flowed through her. Douds had stopped moaning during the confrontation between Bud and Corbin and had somehow been forgotten about. This had allowed him to retrieve his own automatic. It was now coming up, pointing itself in Corbin's direction.

Bending at the knees, reaching down for Bud's gun, Corbin noticed Doud's motion out of the corner of his eye. But, too late. Doud's starting firing. One, two, three, four, five shots in rapid, uncontrolled succession, none of which hit Corbin but one of which hit Bud squarely in the side of the head, dropping him instantly. Douds stopped shooting, shocked at what he had done and looked at Corbin still standing. Corbin who now had his weapon aimed at him. It was hopeless. If Corbin didn't shoot him he would sure as hell leave him here in Mexico to suffer the consequences of killing Bud. What kind of choice was that? Before Corbin and Margaret even realized what had happened he was dead by his own hand, brains and blood scatter pattern spread out over the grass.

Margaret gasped in horror as Corbin stopped just before putting his hand on Bud's gun. He stood up and left it there. Then he went back to the rock and grabbed Margaret by the arm.

"Come on, dammit. Time to go."

"But! Oh my god!" she replied, unable to move. A good thing because Corbin had overlooked something important. In the beginning he had fired two shots at Douds. He ran his hands around through the grass, found the two empty cartridges, pocketed them and looked for Margaret. Damned if she hadn't come to, gone around the rock and was just about to pick up Bud's gun.

"Go ahead," Sam said. "I dare you."

Margaret froze and her face went white. Almost dragging her to the edge of the cliff, he dropped her arm long enough to wipe down the gun he had taken from her earlier and threw it over the edge, keeping an eye on her as he did so, while also noticing that it fell into the water amongst the rocks far below. Then he did the same thing with the two cartridges.

"Do you want to be next?" he asked her scornfully as she backed away from the edge. Then he pulled her over to Douds, looked at the body, saw a bulge in the jacket pocket, patted it and reached inside. He pulled out Douds' cell phone, almost threw it down but put it in his own pocket instead. Then he reached back in Douds' pocket and retrieved the piece of paper he had felt in it.

"Come on," he ordered her.

But Margaret wasn't moving. She seemed frozen in place, staring. He looked where she was looking. To the north, on what had to be the adjacent property. A man stood there, a couple of football field's distance away, staring back at them. Too far away to see his features well, he was dressed in work clothes. A neighbor, a caretaker, hard to tell. Obviously, he had heard the shots. Especially all the rounds Douds had let go with his big forty five. He had to have seen some of what had gone on too.

"Let's go, dammit," Sam said and jerked her around by the arm, hoping that the man didn't have quick access to a phone, further thankful that he was on the other side of the property, away from the road and away from where their car was parked. If he hadn't seen their car and wasn't able to describe it, there was a chance.

TWENTY NINE

When Sam had rented the car he had purposely taken the oldest, most innocuous one on the lot. An under powered, beige Toyota sedan. Douds, however, had opted for a full sized Chevy, parked right behind the Toyota, partially blocking the way. Sam swore. Without touching it, he looked in the passenger side window of the big vehicle. The keys were not in it.

"Get in," he ordered Margaret as he went back to the Toyota.

Backing into Douds' rental car, he stepped on the gas. It didn't budge. He cut the wheel sharply and pulled forward, then back again and forward once more and jockeyed his car around. Then he rammed it into the space between the Chevy and the thick growth along the drive, knocking down brush, scraping fenders and doors against fenders and doors. Then they were free.

No more than two miles down the road they saw a black and white police car headed in the opposite direction, moving fast. And then a second one not too far behind. Neither seemed to have paid them any attention and neither slowed down. Good, Sam thought as he watched in the rear view mirror. Thus far they had managed to get safely away from Los Rocos. There was a Pemex gas station coming up on the opposite side of the highway. He slowed slightly but at the last moment saw another black and white parked at the far end, the cop outside, leaning against the front smoking a cigarette and watching the road.

"Oh, shit," Sam mumbled as he rolled on past. For whatever reason the cop seemed to have noticed the car. The scrapes and white paint clear along the side, the gringo behind the wheel. Or maybe the caretaker-whatever had seen the car after all. Corbin speeded up as he watched the mirror. They were a good half mile ahead before the police car pulled out. Then there was a bend in the road and just beyond it a Mercado. Sam swung in and pulled around to the side, out of sight from the road.

Within seconds the police car appeared and went on past like the cop was in a hurry. Sam waited until he was well out of sight then pulled back out onto the pavement, continuing in the same direction. He took out the paper he had gotten from Douds, looked at it and handed it to Margaret.

"Do you recognize either one of those?" he demanded.

"They're phone numbers."

"No," she said without looking.

"Look at them, dammit."

"Okay, Maybe one of them."

"And the other one?"

"I don't know."

Then she looked out the window in time to see the big roadside sign for Las Hadas coming up. Sam drove on past without slowing down.

"What are you doing?" she asked in a worried voice.

"Going on by, dammit It's too risky."

"What about the airport?"

"Probably just as bad," Sam said. "Maybe worse. Now get your cell phone out and tell me your number."

She shrugged and told him as he dialed the number on the phone he had taken from Douds. It almost shocked him to hear hers ring.

"Pick it up," he said and when she opened it he asked if she could hear him. She nodded. "Good," he said.

"But that doesn't mean anything. They're right together."

"Doesn't matter. They still have to go through a cell tower. That means we can make calls."

"To whom?"

"What charter service would Douds have used?"

"Probably Ted Marmon up in the valley. Van Nuys."

"Does he know who you are?"

"He'd better. We've used him enough."

"Good. Let's see if we can get lucky," Sam said as he punched in the second number on the slip of paper.

"Marmon here," an American voice answered.

"Mr. Marmon. My name is Sam Corbin. I believe you know Margaret Ryan. I'm going to put her on. Here," he said to her. "Tell him that Douds has been indisposed and we will be his passengers for the return trip."

She took he phone and did as she was told. Then she listened and handed it back.

"He has a problem, too," she said.

"What's going on?" Sam asked him.

"The local police were here looking for Mr. Douds and the

man with him while I was sacked out in the plane. They said they had been informed that they were carrying illegal firearms into the country. I told them that it was without my knowledge or permission. They told me they could still impound my plane but so far had not decided to do that at the request of the informant."

"Did they say who made the call?"

"Someone from the FBI in Los Angeles."

"Well. That's interesting. What about you? Are you free to leave?"

"Only with permission. They left someone behind."

"Damn. Where's your guard and where are you with respect to the runway?

"The guard went into the terminal about an hour ago and I'm in a space about a hundred yards from the east end of the south runway. That's about a thousand feet from the terminal."

"Have you refueled yet?"

"I'm ready to go."

"Any chance we could get on board without being seen?"

"Not if the guard's awake. I think that's the main reason he's here. To intercept my passengers. I'm right out in the open. Nothing around me at all."

"Call the tower. Tell them you can't wait any longer and are leaving your passengers behind because you don't want to be involved. I'll hang on."

"Well. That was interesting," Marmon said when he finally came back on. "They said I could go after they had inspected the plane to see that no one else was on board. But what good is that? Why don't you just come out here, identify yourselves and go through channels? Or did you lose your passports?"

"That's not the problem. Douds did something seriously stupid and if we don't leave quickly, we may get dragged into it."

"What about them?"

"They're okay. But Douds created a huge problem for everybody, us included."

"Hmm. There has to be another small airstrip around here but I have no idea where. Once I'm airborne I might be able to find something and give you directions."

"We don't have time for that. What's the wingspan on that

thing and how much runway do you need? We have no luggage."

"Come on. If I did that I'd never be able to bring this crate back down here again."

"I think Miss Ryan would be more than willing to compensate you for the inconvenience."

"Well, shit. I don't know. Forty seven feet and five or six hundred feet, absolute minimum."

"Shouldn't be a problem," Sam said as he gave Marmon some explicit instructions. "I'll let you know when we hear your engines and I'll start waving. Dip your wings the first time over so we know you see us, then turn and come right in. There is little or no wind and traffic is really light."

"Get out here," Sam told Margaret a ways farther down the highway. "And take my jacket. Stay by the side of the road and wait. As soon as it's right and he's coming in, I'll sound the horn and pull across the road to block this end. At the same time you get out in the middle and wave everyone to a stop. He'll be landing in your direction so be ready. As soon as he's turned around, get the hell in. And don't get any ideas. I hope to be there by then."

"Okay. I hear you," Sam told Marmon as he stood beside the car watching the sky. "You're still a ways out but coming in the right direction..... I can see you now. Better lose some altitude. Road looks pretty clear. Just ahead now," Sam said as he walked part way out onto the blacktop and started waving his arms.

"Got you," Marmon hollered over the sound of the engines as he dropped in barely off the deck, waggled his wings, did a sharp pull up and started back around.

Sam waited until the turn was almost complete, jumped in the car and pulled out across the road, blocking it best as he could. Then he started running down the ditch, keeping his head low so as not to be clipped by a wing. Behind him he could hear the engines being throttled back. He glanced over his shoulder. The plane was no more than ten feet off the deck, settling in when the driver of a pickup truck, boom box on so loud Sam could hear it above the plane engine noise, laid on his horn and made his way around the end of Sam's rental car. The aircraft cleared the roof of the truck by inches and shocked the driver so badly he swerved into the ditch and rolled the truck over on its side. Sam kept running.

"Damn, that was close," Marmon said after they had barely cleared the rental car in the middle of the road during takeoff and had gained enough altitude to feel safe. "I wouldn't want to try that again."

"Sorry about that," Sam said from where he seat directly behind Marmon with Margaret beside him, "but we didn't have much choice. Hope it doesn't create a serious problem for you."

"You never know. Down here it could go either way. An international incident, or, hopefully because the people are so leery of the cops, no one will report us landing on the road. Not even dim bulb in the ditch. And the first couple of guys who come along will steal your car."

"That's why I left the keys in it."

Marmon shrugged and banked left.

"I'm going to get out over the water and skim along the cliffs away from the radar until we get past Puerto Vallarta. That's about a hundred and fifty miles. Once we make that there's a lot more air traffic going towards the states." Then he came about to a north westerly heading and the plane roared on, just a few wingspans away from the cliffs.

"There's a cooler back there if you could hand me a coke. Then help yourself. There's some snacks in that aluminum case too."

Sam handed him his soda, gave Margaret one, took one for himself and checked the snack container.

"Too bad that restaurant was closed," he said to her as he handed her a bag of chips and what looked to be a fast food burrito. "This might have turned out a lot differently."

Margaret took the food but didn't respond. Instead she asked Marmon if she could come up and sit in the copilot seat but Sam gripped her arm and shook his head no.

"Never mind," she told Marmon. "Maybe later."

"Okay," he said. "Whenever you want," and he was quiet. Then he put on his earphone headset and began scanning the radio for anything related to their unusual departure.

Sam did his best to stay awake. He didn't want Margaret conspiring with Marmon or Marmon on the radio for anything other than flight necessity but after the tension and excitement earlier, the drone of the engines was getting to him. Finally, however, Marmon called back to them and told them that they could relax. They had just crossed the border.

"What time is it?" Sam asked above the engine noise.

"Almost one a m. We should be on the ground in little over an hour," Marmon stated as he flipped a switch on the control panel. "Transponder," he said. "Just so they know we're out here. We're almost right on time with the flight plan I filed this morning." Then he put his earphone headset back on.

Sam leaned back in his seat and took another glance at Margaret. Unless it had been during those few moments when he was leaning forward talking to Marmon, Margaret had never looked at him once during the whole trip. Several times she had shut her eyes but the look on her face had never changed. Rigid, determined and angry. And as he studied it now, it was still the same. But what was going on inside her head, that was the big question. And what exactly was this fucked up woman all about, he wondered again in his ongoing attempt to understand his adversary. On one level he had understood her completely and had used it to his advantage but on a deeper level, what was it all about? What was behind her need for power, what had driven her to do the things that she had done? Not that it mattered any longer on a bigger level. That part was almost over. Nor was he looking for something that might in any way excuse her behavior. To hell with that. He despised her and hated her but at the same time there was another side of his brain that would have liked to be able to see what had taken her down the devious path she had chosen to walk. But in all the time he had known her, been with her, followed her around and listened to her phone calls, nothing came to him that would in any way explain it. Not even the one small secret he had found out that he bet even Rudy or Douds didn't know. And while one side of him would have liked to have dug deeper into her and made her tell him, the other side said, forget it, it was over. That was the side that won the battle. After everything that had happened so far he didn't think he even cared anymore and with that he looked past her, out the window on the right. They were still about a mile off the coast, the ribbon of lights along the shore line growing denser and brighter by the minute and extending much further inland as they headed north.

Forty minutes later they were in the flight corridor over L.A. International, headed towards Van Nuys when Corbin slid forward in his seat and tapped Marmon on the shoulder. Marmon pulled off his headset and Sam asked if he could put them down at Santa Monica instead of Van Nuys."

Marmon considered it. "As long as it's not on the freeway," he said jokingly. "But the tower will be closed this time of night. You'll be stranded there. I could probably reach my partner on the radio and have him call a cab for you."

"How about my cell phone? Will that work from up here?"

"Well, maybe. Don't see why not. Never tried it before."

They stood in the darkness watching the strobe light on the underside of Marmon's plane disappear into the distance. There was a thin sliver of moon in the western sky but only the very brightest of the stars were visible in the city sky glow that surrounded them. Margaret now seemed subdued and thus far neither had spoken. The air was chilly and she began to shiver.

"Goddammit," she said, suddenly coming alive. "Where the hell is the limo? You did call a limo, right? And not a damned cab, Jesus, I'm freezing."

"Stop complaining," he told her. Then he slid out of his jacket and put it over her shoulders. But it was the wrong thing to do. Somehow it gave her the courage to keep talking. But what did she want? All the cold hearted bitch wanted to know was who had made made the call to Mexico telling the authorities that Douds was carrying a weapon.

"Some one who turned out to be a friend in disguise. Works in the federal building over on Wilshire in Westwood."

Contemplating the implications of that one shut her up for a while and several more minutes of silence went by. She knew very well what government agency had their offices in that building. Corbin working with the FBI? How could that be? Corbin had blown up Vince Sands house. He was a criminal.

Wasn't he? Looking back, who else could have done it but him.

Finally Margaret swore.

"God damn you. Why the hell couldn't you have just been Joe Carroll?" she blasted at him but he didn't answer and that made her even angrier.

"So... Is this it?" she almost yelled at him. "Can't you at least tell me what the hell this was all about? And why? Christ. Am I going to have to spend the rest of my life looking over my shoulder, living in fear? I'd rather that you shot me and left me out here to die, you bastard."

"I left the gun in Mexico, remember? Which is a good thing because what with all the choice names you're calling me, I just might. What are you so damned angry about now?"

"I'm angry because I didn't listen to myself. Because I let you get two steps ahead of me and because I let you play me and because, god dammit. Because I let myself fall in love with the son-of-a-bitch who was trying to destroy me. Because that is just so god damned fucking stupid. Jesus," she stormed.

It was the last words spoken between the two of them until they reached Santa Monica in the limo. By then it was almost five in the morning. The sun would soon be up. There was already a hint of false dawn, enough to see by. Sam directed the driver down Ocean Boulevard to the Santa Monica pier and had him take them down the incline to the parking area where he could turn around. When the car stopped, he got out. Then he looked back in at her and motioned for her to follow. After he thanked and paid the driver and sent him on his way he started walking out over the thick planks towards the distant end. Confused, she stood there for a second, then caught up to him thinking that none of this made any sense. What was he going to do? Throw her off the end into the water? Sure as hell, he was capable of it.

He didn't have a gun, however, so it seemed like she could have turned around and walked back up the pier to the street. But did she? She couldn't. Not any longer. Did he know that it was impossible for her to leave? Is that why he kept on walking? Frightened but fascinated, she had to know how it all played out. Even if she did end up in the ocean.

254

When they came to the end Sam leaned his elbows on the heavy wooden railing and looked out over the sweep of the bay, up the coastline and then straight out to sea. They were completely alone, something so rare in a place surrounded by millions of people. But not for long. Soon the sunlight would be streaking through the tall buildings of the city behind them and strangers would be invading their space. Margaret turned her back to the view and leaned against the railing next to Sam, leaving a large gap between them, staring at him, studying his face looking for clues as to her destiny.

"It seems impossible that you could have you created all this hell and disruption just by yourself. Or did you?"

"What difference does it make?"

"A lot. I need to know."

"Okay. With the exception of a brief association with that poor cop, Vanalden, you screwed over and had killed, the answer is yes. I did it alone. So, if at any time you had had the good sense to take me for a parting ride in your limo before I blew it up, it would have been all over. And with one minor exception, you would have been home free."

"What was that?"

Sam turned to face her. "I still have tape recordings I gleaned from some of your major players that would have ended up in the hands of the cops if something had happened to me. Along with some really choice stuff I picked up from your own cell phone," he said, staring directly at her.

"But... my cell phone? That's not possible, is it? Oh my god."

"Indeed, dear lady. Even if you had killed me you would have been in a very difficult situation."

Dumbfounded as to the immensity of what he had just told her, she was speechless and could only stare back at him. Finally, incongruous as it might have sounded under the circumstances, all she could think of to say was, "Yeah. But it was good while it lasted. Damned good. No man ever got to me the way you did in a long, long time."

"Cut the crap, Margaret. That is not going to work. All I see behind you is a trail of dead ex boyfriends."

"You don't know what you're talking about."

"No, I don't know the whole story because I caught up to

you in the middle of it. And I don't want to know it all. I'm horrified enough."

"Yeah, I'll bet. After what you've done. We would have made a great pair. You're a criminal too."

"Maybe. But you're the one who got herself in trouble," Sam said, now able to see her face clearly in the increasing light. There was nothing beautiful about her anymore. He shivered too, glad the sun was coming up. "And unfortunately, I don't think your trouble is going to go away," he added.

She let the thought of that sink in. "So how did you find me to begin with?" she asked, needing to know the answer to that question also.

"I admit at first I didn't think it possible. For a long time I thought you were just a front for someone else but seems I underestimated you."

"And then I let you start fucking me. What a tragedy."

"The only tragedy is that you hadn't stayed in Las Vegas. Or where the hell ever your last stop was before coming to LA."

"You really hate me, don't you? And it was never that the sex was so good between us. Not for you. It was because you were just so damned angry. Why you always fucked me with such a vengeance, just like I accused you of. But how you even managed to do that, I don't know. You were married. You...."

"Loved her? Yes. Beyond question. Beyond everything you'll ever understand. But love and sex? They are two different things. Sometimes they go together, sometimes they don't. Having sex with you violated nothing. But forget that. None of your business. Just finish your story. I would really like to know what was driving you. Your big plan."

She looked at him. "It's not important. And why do you care?"

"Another piece to the puzzle. Are you ashamed of it?"

"Should I be? Hell no. I showed that bunch of chauvinistic, arrogant god damn bullies. Me, a woman, running a major organization like that. I loved making all those tough bastards kiss my ass. And if it hadn't been for you....."

"Damn right. Blame it on me. Is that the best you can do?"

"I, I....." she said but could go no further and momentarily turned her back to him. Then, back facing him she asked if he was recording this conversation too.

"No, my vendetta is almost over. This is the end of the line. And don't count on it, but this is where the truth may set you free."

"Yeah, and what the hell is that supposed to mean?"

"I knew beyond a reasonable doubt that Sid and Louis were the ones who put the firebomb through my bedroom window and I know that Vince Sands gave them the order to do that. And that score is settled. But they all worked for someone else. Rudy Stark at the time. At first it seemed like a dumb ass mistake on the part of those two thugs until I managed to get into Vince's basement and bug his office. It was not a mistake. Vince verified that it was the house he had been told to hit. But either way it was totally out of character for Rudy. Then Rudy disappeared from his boat with you on board and I discovered some things about my neighbor, Victor Trent."

By now Margaret had again turned her face away and would not look at him, but he kept talking anyway.

"He and you, best I could make out, had an involvement, even though he was married. And learning that brought something else back," Sam said and stopped for a minute.

"Did you know she.. my wife, was every bit as attractive as you are? ... But she was also up front and honest. She cared about people, she had compassion and all the other good qualities you are lacking. And that made her beautiful. And then I remembered that one day a while after the Trent's had moved in next door, she had been working in the yard. When she came in she told me that our new neighbor had come over and tried to hustle her. But when she wouldn't have it she said the slick bastard made the comment about how he was going to tell his girlfriend about the gorgeous woman he lived next to. Maybe it would make her jealous and she would pay more attention to him. So," Sam said as he took Margaret by the shoulder and pulled her around.

"Look at me, dammit Is that what this was all about? Jealousy? You were willing to blow some innocent person's house up because you were jealous. My God, Margaret. You killed my wife. But just as bad, you killed my unborn child. And I know you can relate to that because I've followed you down to the hospital and watched you looking in the nursery window more than once. So whatever that was all about I know you can relate to that part of it on some level. I don't know what happened to your baby but I know what happened to mine. What kind of monster are you?" he almost yelled at her. Then he continued.

"But guess what? The ultimate irony. A pure, unexpected fluke. I wasn't there when it happened like I normally would have been. A flat tire on the way home late at night and no spare so I had to wait for a service truck or I would have been dead too and you would have gotten away with it. Now isn't that something?"

She looked at him, suddenly realizing the horrible immensity of it all and how she had been doomed right from the start. Holy Christ! She said to herself and almost collapsed from the weight of it. Then he started in on her all over again.

"God damn you, Margaret. Tell me the truth. Is that what it was all about? Jealousy. Come on, dammit. Answer the god damned question."

She turned away and stood there beaten and destroyed, frozen in time, staring out into the distance, unable to think or feel anymore, almost wishing he would push her over the railing into the water far below. But he didn't. Instead, he left her alone to let it sink in and went over to a wooden bench that was close by and sat down. At least ten minutes passed before she even moved. When she finally looked around he got up, came back and stood before her.

"Yes," she said at last in a desperate, almost whisper, looking down at her feet, fully expecting him to explode and tear her apart.

By now the first sun light was touching their faces but all Sam could think of was a similar morning more than a year ago. The morning when, feeling lost, he had wandered into a coffee shop on the way home from the hospital on that fateful day where he sat numbed and lost. There had been traffic on the street, while inside the waitress was rushing about serving customers concerned only with their own demands. Cell phones were ringing, people were talking, the world kept turning. And nobody in the place had any idea as to what had just happened to him. Not a one. And no one would have particularly given a damn. He bit his lip and fought the tears.

258

Then he turned back to face her.

"God damn you, Margaret Ryan," he said, his voice full of anger and pain. "I could have set fire to you in your own damned bed. I could have blown up your damned house. I could have thrown you over the cliff or I could have set you up and left you in Mexico to rot in jail,.... But I didn't, god dammit! I didn't! So, do you know what that means? Do you? God, what a silly fucking game," he said with a fury so vivid it made her cringe.

"Well, maybe you do and maybe you don't, so I'm going to tell you, either way," he said. "What it means is this. It means that maybe there is some hope in that. For me, dammit. For her sake I am not going to kill you. And for my own sake I am not even going to pursue you anymore. Unless, goddammit. Unless you retaliate. Then I will destroy the rest of your life in ways you can't even imagine. Otherwise, it's done. I'm done, finished. And to hell with you. Go your own misguided way. Do whatever you want. I hope you can live with yourself." And with one last long glance at her, he turned around and began walking away as she looked up and watched him go, unable to move or to say anything.

And as for Sam, at last it was behind him. Over and done, he realized as he began walking faster, feeling the sunlight on his face, a new day beginning. Able now to grieve and move on. But, was he free of it? Would he ever be completely free of it? The woman he loved was forever gone, the child he wished for, still unborn. A lot of people were dead, some of them because of himself. His choice and his to live with, either way. And Margaret, damn her. Trapped in her own sorrily made web and form of madness, beyond redemption, justice served in the formal sense because she would probably spend the rest of her life in prison. Where was the joy in any of it?

www.ingramcontent.com/pod-product-compliance
Lightning Source LLC
Chambersburg PA
CBHW070550130626
46556CB00001B/103